The Choices Men Make

Dwayne S. Joseph

Black Print Publishing
291 Livingston St
Brooklyn, NY

Black Print Publishing
291 Livingston St
Brooklyn, NY 11201

Copyright © 2002 Dwayne S. Joseph

All rights reserved. No part of this book may be reproduced in any form or by any means without the prior consent of the Publisher, excepting brief quotes used in reviews.

This book is dedicated to the leading ladies in my life.
Windalisa and Tatiana.
It is for you two that I do this. You are my angels.

Acknowledgments

First, before I thank anyone, I must give thanks to the One being who made this possible for me. To God:

God I thank you for listening to me during our nightly conversations. I thank you for providing answers to my questions when you felt it was the right time. I realize every day that nothing happens before then. I thank you for helping my dream come to fruition. More than anyone, you've always known writing is what I've wanted to do. I thank you for the trials that you've put in my way. I've learned from them, grown from them, as was your intention. I thank you in advance for the obstacles that you will continue to provide. I look forward to the lessons I am to learn.

I must also thank Carl Weber. Thank you for your friendship and support. What everyone says is true: you are one of the realest, most sincere brothers I know. Thank you for helping me with my dream. Thank you for believing in me. I can only hope to achieve what you've achieved. And like everyone else, I look forward to reading all of the stories that you write.

Thank you Martha for helping make my book better. Thank you Harold for listening to me when I first came into the store.

Next, I would like to thank my wife, Wendy. You are my heart and my best friend. I love you and I am damn thankful for November 3rd. I look forward to the years of friendship and love. I look forward to raising our little girl. Te quiero chula. Nunca voy a dejarte.

To my family: Dad, my idol. We need more men like you Dad. I thank you for being the man for me to look up to all these years. Thank you for taking me around on that bike so many years ago. I am honored to call you my father.

To my mother: Mom, I am blessed to have a mother like you. This has been a wild year for us hasn't it? Mom, I thank you for letting me keep you hostage with my stories all these years. I still remember reading to you in the backyard by the pool! Thank you for being the strong, beautiful, talented woman/ photographer/ interior decorator that you are. I also thank you for being my toughest critic. You made me better, even though I whine and complain about whatever criticism you give. To my sister: Teyana (Teens), I love you and I am extremely proud of you. I admire the things you've done and love the woman that you are. To my brother: Daren, I am proud of you bro. And I am happy that you have found your passion. I know that you will be successful in your endeavors. Keep that head on straight kid, because you know Mom, Dad, Granny, Teens, Wendy and I will be there to straighten it if you can't! Granny: You are the very definition of Grandmotherdom. It's not a word but you get the point. You are my second mother, and I am thrilled that Tatiana will have you in her life.

To the rest of my family, too many to name, but thank you for all of your love and support.

To Russell and Lourdes: Thank you for accepting me into your homes and lives. I love you guys. Wendy is in good hands. Ivan and Grace: Keep growing and raising Prianna to know what a Princesa she is. Ivan, it's all about the Illuminati! Grace, you cook my food yet?

To my friends for life, Micah and Tiffany, Chris and Lisa, Gregg and Kristi, Tho, Carlos, Monte, Julian: I am lucky to have friends like you. Damn lucky. I hope you don't mind, but I've borrowed bits and pieces from all of you and incorporated them into the characters I create. I love you guys for real. Terry and David, y'all gwan mash up de yahd! Thanks for the friendship Tom Holland and Mike Howell. Charles Cumbersmart, thanks for the great help on the site.

To my first editor: Lori King. I still owe you and your husband that dinner. And congratulations on that baby! To my original group of readers: Lisa McManual, Cathy Gomez

(Congrats on the graduation), Angy Willis, Mirel Aktalay (my Genuity partner an close friend), Lourdes Trevino, Teyana Joseph, Mariana Arocho, Monte Hanes (Espire, kid), Diane Holland...all of your input helped to make my stories better. I'll be giving you the next one.

To the Nobelo's. Thank you for the love and friendship. I have not forgotten.

To all of the writers who've come before me: Thank you for paving the way and letting me know that it is possible.

To the sufferers of Trigeminal Neuralgia: I have been there. Please continue to hold on and look into the Microvascular Decompression. I've been pain-free for over a year now.

Finally, to the readers, I hope you enjoy the book as much as I enjoyed creating it. Please feel free to email me at:

Djoseph21044@yahoo.com

And check out my website at www.DwayneSJoseph.com

And lastly: Let's go New York Giants!

Roy Burges
1

"*My* boys! What uuuuuup! I didn't think you two were brave enough to show up. Are you guys sure you want to see my Titans kick that Redskins' no-game-winning ass?" I stepped to the side to let Vic and Colin step in. Behind them trailed Vic's wife Julie, and some date of Colin's that I'd never seen before. Both women had the same blasé looks that my wife Stacey gave me whenever I mentioned football.

"What's up Julie," I said, kissing her on the cheek.

"Hey Roy." She kissed me back. "Where's Stacey?"

"She's hiding in the kitchen."

"Well as much as I'd love to see the football game…" Julie said with a wink.

I smiled and looked at Colin's date. She looked no more than twenty-five, with maroon highlights in her light brown hair. I extended my hand.

"Roy Burges," I said.

She looked at my hand and cleared her throat loudly. Colin, who was taking off his coat, chuckled and said, "Oh, my bad. Roy, this is Tanecia. Tanecia, Roy."

Tanecia smiled half-heartedly, remained silent, and then shook my hand.

"Come on, Tanecia," Julie said, taking her by the hand. "Let's go help Stacey hide in the kitchen." Julie waved as both women stepped past me.

I closed the door and looked at Vic, who looked back at me and shook his head. Colin had done it again. Probably hooked up with her last night at some club or bar, bought her a couple of drinks, used a couple of mack lines, and then took her back to his place, where he would later enter her name into his book of conquests. Colin and relationships go together like fire and ice; in other words, it's just not happening. Somewhere within his warped mind is the belief that women are good for only casual, consensual sex. Marriage and commitment are out of the question. As long as I'd known him, I'd never seen him come close to having any type of meaningful relationship. *I'm a committed bachelor for life,* he always said.

I gave my boys a pound as we walked into the living room.

"So what's up, fellas? You ready to see your boys lose, or what?" Being a Titans fan from Tennessee, I was enjoying the dismal season the Redskins were having; while the Titans enjoyed a 4-1 record, the Redskins were stuck at 0-5.

Vic sat down in the sofa and shook his head.

"Man, there will be no loss for us today. This is our week."

"Vic, why do you refuse to accept the truth?" I looked at him and shook my head. "The Redskins suck. What in the hell makes you think the outcome of today's game is going to be any different from the last five?" I sucked my teeth and looked over at Colin. "So what's up, Colin? You and this unfortunate fool over here in cahoots? You think the Redskins are pulling this one out, too?"

Colin raised an eyebrow and looked at his boy.

"Vic," he said as he sat in my inflatable chair with the Titans logo on it. "You my dog and all, and the Redskins are my team, but I can't go with you on this one. The Titans are gonna kick our sorry asses all over Sunday."

"Ha, ha," I laughed, sitting in my beanbag. "At least someone has some sense."

Vic mumbled and pounded on his chest. He was wearing his Daryl Green jersey.

"I'm tellin' you two fools, this is our day. I bet sixty bucks on this game. You know when I bet money we win."

"Kid," Colin said, "You could have just given that sixty to me. I would have shown a freak a good time with that."

We laughed and then got serious as the game began. We had our game faces on. This and pool on Wednesday nights was our weekly ritual. During the football season, we always got together at each other's places on Sundays to watch the game. This week had been my turn to play the host, which wasn't a hard thing to do, considering all I needed was to buy a case of Heineken and a couple bags of chips. Julie, Stacey, and whatever date Colin decided to bring, if anyone, usually did just what they were doing as the game was on—sat in the kitchen and gossiped.

After the first quarter, the Titans had a fourteen-point lead; by halftime, the lead had extended to twenty-one. I looked at my two depressed friends and shook my head.

"Damn, it's quiet in here," I said with a smile.

"Whatever." Vic stared at the television screen.

I laughed and looked to the kitchen, where the women had hibernated, then looked back at Colin.

"So what's up with this Tanecia, man? She somebody? Is it possible that you may have found someone worthy?"

"Roy, please." Colin's eyes widened. "The only thing she's worthy of is a star beside her name. I hooked up with her at 1223 in DC last night. She was all over me. Dog, I smacked that ass 'nuff times on the dance floor. She had it just poised for me to do it. Yo, I knew when she let me do that, I wasn't going home alone."

"Colin man, why are you always hooking up with some freak? Don't you want anything real?" Vic asked.

"Real? You better get real. Sheeeit. Just 'cause you're married now, don't mean I need to be gettin' tied down. You guys know me. You know I'm not about no commitment. All I want is a freak at night, and to be left alone in the morning."

"That'll get tired, man," I said.

"For who?" Colin asked. "Surely you don't mean for me. That will never happen. You guys like that marriage shit. Not me. I couldn't handle that. Waking up next to the same woman day after day. Eating the same pie day after day. Hearing the nagging day after day. Nah...you fools can have that drama. I'll keep my bachelor-hood."

I couldn't help but laugh. He hadn't changed a bit.

I remember when we met. He came in to Carmax looking to trade in his Nissan Maxima, which was in immaculate condition. When he walked in, he wasted no time; he stepped up to me before I had a chance to go into my salesman spiel.

"You helpin' anybody?"

"No," I said, glad to have finally snagged a customer. I had just moved from Tennessee with Stacey to take the job with Carmax. So my client list was pretty much non-existent. I extended my hand.

"Roy Burges. What can I do for you?"

"Colin," he said shaking my hand. "I need a new car Roy."

"Pressed for time?" I asked as he took a quick glance at his watch. It made me wonder if he was there to browse and waste my time, or there to actually drive off with something new and put money in my pocket.

"Always pressed for time, Roy."

"OK. Well are you looking for a brand new car, or something used?"

"Brand new, Roy. Always brand new. For the ladies—you know?"

I nodded. "I got you."

"Good. Let's find a ride I can do some mackin' in."

"Well are you looking for anything in particular?"

Colin thought for a second and then said, "I want something black and smooth, with all the necessary accessories. I want a carbon copy of me." He laughed out loud and then said, "Just kiddin', dog."

I laughed and shook my head. I could tell that he had no problem with his self-esteem.

"OK, well tell me this...are you looking for a sports car, a luxury car, or an SUV?"

"Had the combo of luxury and sports in my Maxima. I want an SUV this time. Speaking of Maxima, I have it outside. I want to trade it in."

"Ok, well let's get the appraisal going for that, and then start looking at some SUV's."

When we went into the parking lot to his car, I couldn't help but whistle.

"You want to trade this in?" I asked in disbelief. The Maxima was loaded. Tinted windows, twenty-inch chrome rims, and a spoiler on the back. The inside was just as clean, with shining leather interior, and a carpet so spotless it looked like no one ever set foot on it. I looked at my reflection in the gleaming waxed black paint and said, "This thing is bad. You really want to trade this in?"

Colin laughed. "Man, I've had this thing for two years. I need something new, dog. I can't let the ladies see me in the same car for too long. Know what I mean?"

"You always make your decisions based on women?"

"Dog, what else?"

I laughed and shook my head. "OK. If you really want to trade it in..." I filled out some paperwork and then put a yellow cone on top of the car, so that it could be identified for the appraisal. Colin and I went to the lot where the cars were. It didn't take long to find the car he wanted; it was actually the first one we looked at.

"This is it!" Colin exclaimed. He walked around the Isuzu Rodeo and rubbed his hands together as if he were plotting something. And he was.

"Dog, when the honeys see me in this...Yo, let's get that paperwork going."

"You don't want to look at anything else?"

"Roy, this is the one."

"OK. Let's get that paperwork started."

We went inside, filled out all the necessary forms, and got the trade-in value for the Maxima. As we waited for a response from the banks for financing, we sat in my office and talked about his many adventures in the Nissan.

"Dog, I'ma miss that car."

"Yeah, I bet. Maxima's are reliable."

"Damn skippy they are! I could always rely on that car to pick me up a honey. Dog, I had so many escapades and inspected so much pussy in that car, I should have changed the license plate to OBGYN."

I busted out laughing at his comment. Colin was amusing to say the least. It was nice to actually deal with a customer who not only wanted a car, but you didn't mind talking to either.

"So what do you do, Mr. OBGYN?" I asked.

"I have my own software company. Ever heard of IBIS?"

"Don't think so. What kind of software?"

"You know the system the mechanics use in your service area?"

"Not too well."

"Well that's my software. Actually, our software; I started IBIS with my brother, about three years ago. Carmax was one of our first customers."

"Damn. That's cool."

"Yeah. But we don't just do the software for mechanics. We do software for anybody that wants to keep track of their inventory, ring up sales, order supplies, keep updated records and files, anything. You tell us what you want to do, we can create software for you to do it with."

"Sounds lucrative."

"Roy, dog, you have no idea. We're blowin' up. And we're going after the big boys. We want to take on the record stores next. Do you know there is only one major software program records stores use to keep track of everything going on? One! And it's outdated. At least compared to our program it is. We're creating software that a fool could use. It's in testing right now, but once it's out...Cha ching!"

"That's good, man. Real good. Nice to see brothers doing well."

"Only way to do it, man. So what's your story? I see all of these plaques and awards you have here. You the top seller here or what?"

"Not yet," I said with a proud smile. "But I will be in time. These awards are from the dealership I worked in when I was in Tennessee. I just moved here with my wife and girls two months ago. I'm still in the process of building up my clientele here. But once I do, I figure I'll be a selling fool."

"Right, right. Tennessee, huh? I thought I heard a southern accent. So that means you're a Titans fan?"

"Definitely!"

"Sorry to hear that. You may want to get hip to the Redskins."

"No way," I said. "I'm a Titans fan for life."

"We'll see," Colin countered. "So, two months, huh? And you're married? You know anyone here?"

"Nah. Just the wife and kids."

Colin looked at a picture of Stacy and my twin girls, Sheila and Jenea. "Twins, huh? Must be a handful."

"And then some," I said proudly.

Colin nodded his head. "How old are they?"

"The one on the left, in the red top, is Sheila. She's three. Jenea, in blue, is older by three minutes."

"So what made you move here?"

"I wanted a change. Plus I'd heard good things about Maryland. I started looking at dealerships here and the salaries they offer, and I saw an opportunity to make a decent living here."

"Your wife didn't mind moving?"

"Nah. Both of us wanted the change of scenery."

"Your wife work?"

"All the time. She takes care of the home and the girls. But she says she wants to learn to design web pages."

"Looks like I may have to talk to her one day. We could always use a fresh look for our web page."

"She'd be willing when she learns it. I just hope you wouldn't mind working with an amateur."

"Everyone's an amateur at some point. Besides, we gotta support each other."

"I hear that."

"Well, that's cool. But," he said removing his wallet, "we can't have you not knowing anybody. Here's my card, dog. Give me a holla. If your wife don't mind, I'll take you out sometime. Show you what Maryland and DC have to offer."

I slid his card into my wallet. "That's cool. Just don't forget I'm married."

Colin laughed. "Roy, I promise not to corrupt you too much."

We were interrupted by the sound of the beep on my PC.

"The info's back from the banks."

"What's the damage?" Colin asked.

After settling on which financing offer he wanted to take, we crossed all T's and dotted all I's, and then I handed him the key to the Rodeo. When he got in his brand new ride, he removed a CD from his pocket and slid it in. As the Wu Tang Clan blared from the speakers, Colin yelled, "Yeah, dog! I'm pullin' a honey tonight. Yo, hit me up. We'll hang."

"Will do."

"A'ight. I'm outta here."

He drove off then, and turned the volume up even louder. I smiled. It felt good to make that sale, but more importantly, it felt good to have finally met someone.

Since moving to Laurel, Maryland, I'd had no time for getting to know anyone. Stacey and I had been too busy getting the house together and taking care of the girls. And because Stacey refused to drive, even though she had a license, my free time, when not at work, was spent being a chauffeur. I'd wanted to get Stacey a car, but years before I met her she had been involved in a head-on collision with another car. Her sister, whose picture she keeps in a locket around her neck, was a passenger while Stacey drove. She died instantly. Stacey, who got away with a broken leg and a few cuts and bruises, hasn't driven since.

I hooked up with Colin a few days after he bought the Rodeo. He cruised by my place and picked me up. Vic was with him when he came. We went to Club U in DC, where they played go-go music all night long. While Colin and Vic lurked around, running game on every fine sister that crossed their path, I stayed at the bar with a beer and soaked in the different atmosphere around me. Maryland's pace was much faster than that of Tennessee. The music, the style of dance, the clothing; they were all sharper. The women were different too. They seemed more aggressive. Even the white women were running their game on the brothers. Now that was something I definitely wasn't used to seeing. Although I personally had no real problem with it, the amount of interracial couples in the club was surprising. But even though the differences were a little intimidating, it still felt good being out, even if it felt a little awkward not being with Stacey.

Unlike most guys I know, I enjoy spending the majority of my time with my wife. We met when we were both freshmen in Tennessee State University. She was majoring in psychology. I majored in business. Taken by her small, dark eyes, broad nose, full lips, and thick frame, I hounded her for a good month before she finally agreed to go out with me. We started dating exclusively two weeks after our first date. Our courtship lasted all of six months before we finally got married. Stacey was my soul mate, and I saw no reason to delay; she felt the same. The rest, as they say, is history. We had Sheila and Jenea during our second year of marriage. Being with Stacey completed me in a way I always dreamed about. She was strong in all of my weak areas, and vice versa for me. That's why I was content to keep the bar company, and listen to the go-go music, which was one style of music that I could do without.

Since that night, Colin, Vic and I began to hang out. We'd chill and play cards some nights. Shoot some pool on Wednesdays. And of course, on Sundays, when it was the season, we watched football.

Colin and Vic had known each other since junior high school, so their bond was already strong. But as time passed, they became the brothers I never had. Our personalities all gelled to form a circle of brotherhood that no one could break. We all had each other's backs and Colin and I shared best man duties when Vic, a white boy with more soul than OJ, eventually got married to Julie.

"A'ight fellas," I said, rubbing my palms together and focusing back on the game. "Second half's about to start. How many more points will my Titans score on that ass?"

Colin laughed and shrugged his shoulders. Vic, who stared intensely at the screen, shook his head and kept a tight lip. I swallowed down my beer and turned up the volume.

ROY

2

After the Titans' lopsided, thirty-six-point victory, Colin left to take Tanecia home, while Vic and Julie stayed behind for a little while. As our wives continued to chitchat, Vic and I went to the basement and shot a game of pool. As I sank the eight ball for my third consecutive victory, I asked, "Man, you think Colin will ever change?"

Vic chalked off his pool stick and shook his head. "No way. As long as I've known him, that brother is not about settling down. It would take an extremely special freak to satisfy him."

"True, indeed. Although she was a bit standoffish, that girl Tanecia seemed to be OK. And from what I was seeing when we ate, it looks like she likes him."

"Man, all the women like Colin. That pretty boy never had a problem with the women. Shit, Tanecia can like him all she wants. It won't make a difference, because she's still just another notch in his bedpost."

"You're definitely right about that."

"I know I am. He'll probably call her tonight and tell her he had a good time, and he hopes to do it again sometime. That'll get her all worked up. Then he'll call her once during the week—probably tell her that he has to go away on business, but he'll call her when he gets back. Give it about two weeks, and he'll call again to say things have been so hectic that he's got no time to do anything. But he wants to be friends."

"Yeah," I agreed. "In between that time, he'll have met at least two other freaks. *And* Tanecia will still be sweating him. The brother is definitely a player's player."

"Yeah," Vic said, hitting a nine-eleven combination in the corner pocket. "No doubt about that."

"It feels good to not have to be in the game like that, doesn't it?" I asked, watching him miss a bank shot. "I mean, I know I am truly a lucky man to have Stacey by my side to keep me sane. And even if you don't admit it to Colin, I know you feel the same about Julie. It's a relaxed feeling, being with the woman you want to spend the rest of your life with."

Vic stayed quiet as I missed a combination, and wrinkled his brow. I knew something was up.

"Why aren't you speaking, Vic? You do feel lucky, don't you?"

Vic still remained silent, and moved to take his next shot.

"Vic? What's up, man? Why aren't you saying anything?" I asked again.

Vic put his stick down and stared at me with a sigh. In his eyes I saw the look of a troubled man.

"Aww, man. What's going on? Are you guys having problems?"

Vic looked toward the steps and then closed the door to the upstairs.

"Roy," he said, coming back and speaking in a voice just slightly above a whisper. "I don't think I can be married to Julie anymore."

It was my turn to put the stick down. "What? What do you mean can't be married?"

"Man, this stays with you and me."

"OK."

"I'm not happy."

"Not happy? What are you talking about? You and Julie just got married six months ago. You're still supposed to be on your honeymoon."

"Keep your voice down. Just hear me out."

"I'm listening," I said, leaning my two hundred-and-twenty pound frame against the pool table.

"Man, you know why I married Julie. You know I was never really in love with her."

"Yeah, but you still said 'I do.'"

"Because I felt like I had to. Man, when she told me she was pregnant, I felt like I had no choice. I told you and Colin I wasn't trying to have that baby be born out of wedlock."

"Look, you made the decision to promise until death do you part. How can you just back out now?"

"Because as much as I love Julie, I'm not head over heels in love with her."

"Who says you have to be head over heels?"

"I do. I want to feel that kind of love that you feel. But I never will with Julie."

"How do you know?"

"Roy, I've always known. I was willing to sacrifice what I wanted for the baby's sake. I was determined to be in it for the long haul. But when she miscarried, I knew that I couldn't go on."

"So because she lost the baby, you feel like you have an out now? Vic, Julie loves you. She would do anything for you. How could you not love her like that?"

"Roy, listen. I know how Julie feels for me. But no matter how hard I try, I just don't feel the same about her."

"And you don't think that you can get to that point?"

"No, I don't. Honestly, man. And I've never told you and Colin this, but the real reason I'm not happy with Julie is because I love black women."

I stared at Vic for a quiet second and then doubled over, laughing.

"Man, it's not funny," Vic said, bothered by my humor at his expense. "I'm serious. You know how I feel about black women. How I've always felt."

"Look, I know you love the sisters. And I'll admit, you were the last person I expected to date a white woman. But Julie is a good, attractive, loving, woman. You can't deny that. So even though I was surprised that you ended up with her, it wasn't hard to see why. Now having said all of that, you can't really be serious about leaving her because you want a sister." I stared at Vic seriously, looking for a sign that my logic had gotten through to him.

"I can't do it, man," he sighed.

"Come on, Vic. I mean, forget color... Do you know how hard it is to find all of the qualities Julie has in one woman? Shit, I love black women too, but don't you think you're being a little ridiculous?"

"Roy, have you forgotten that I was adopted by a black woman when I was two? Or that I grew up in Southeast DC? Man, I've lived around black women all my life. I never even thought of dating a white woman until I met Julie. And I just kind of fell into that. You know I never wanted marriage. But she got pregnant. I was trying to do the right thing. But as each day goes by, I just don't feel like I fit with her. She is a beautiful person, but she doesn't have the energy of a black woman that I need. She doesn't have the attitude."

"Attitude? You want attitude? Vic, are you hearing what you're saying?"

"I've been hearing it loud and clear. Man, I love the fire that black women have. I love their no-nonsense attitude. Julie does love me, and would do anything for me, but that's a problem for me."

"A problem. Vic, are you high? How could a woman loving you and doing anything for you be a problem?"

"Man, let me show you something." He walked up the stairs and opened the door. "Julie!" he said loudly.

"Yeah, babe?" Julie answered from the kitchen.

"Hey, can you bring a beer down here for me and Roy?" Vic came back down the stairs and stared at me without saying a word. Thirty seconds later, Julie came down the steps with two beers in hand. Vic kissed her on the cheek.

"Thanks, babe," he said. When she disappeared upstairs and closed the door behind her, Vic gave me a beer, downed some of his, and kept his eyes locked on mine.

I took a sip and shrugged my shoulders. "And that's a problem for you?"

"Man, you ask Stacey to bring you a beer."

I sucked my teeth. "Shit. That ain't happening."

"Exactly. That's my point. I want that. I want that you-have-two-feet-get-it-your-damn-self type response. I would kill for that. Julie does anything I want. There's no challenge. I need that challenge."

I shook my head. I couldn't believe he was saying what he was saying. If I were into white women, Julie would have been the type of woman that I would have wanted to be with.

"Man, Julie has a great personality. She is intelligent. She is damn attractive. Come on. Don't tell me you can't find a way to be head over heels for that."

Vic sat down on a stool by my miniature bar and said, "I can't, man. I can't do it anymore. Black women are my weakness. When I see a fine sister I just get tingles, man."

"Damn Vic," was all I could say. I took a seat beside him. "I don't know what to say."

"Man, my skin is white, but you know me. What Colin is always saying is true. I *am* black on the inside. I love everything and anything about the black culture. It's all I know, man."

"I understand what you're saying, Vic, but when people look at you, they only see one thing. "

"I know that."

"Damn, man. So what, you just don't think you can be with Julie like that? I mean, have you really thought about everything you're saying? What you're willing to give up?"

"Roy, I was thinking about it when I said I do."

"So what are you going to do?"

"I don't know yet, man. That's why I'm telling you this. I need some advice. Some real advice."

I drummed my fingers on the counter and exhaled. I didn't know what to say. On one level, I understood his desire to have the fire and attitude of a black woman. Because God knows I had that in Stacey, and that's one of the things I loved most about her. I could never have Stacey do what Julie did with that beer. Stacey would never go for that. Honestly, it was a nice feeling to know that I could never walk all over my wife like that.

But like everything, there's always a negative side. And Stacey's black-woman-hear-me-roar attitude could work my last nerve sometimes. Always complaining about something, always hollering about this or that. Shit, I wish she would be passive sometimes. But then, like Vic, I know I wouldn't be happy.

"Man, I don't know what to tell you. This is something you are really going to have to sit and think about. I mean, you pledged your life to Julie. That's not easily overlooked."

"I know. And I've been thinking about it. But the more I do, the more I realize I will never truly be content. I've been holding this inside for a long time. I just can't anymore."

I continued to drum my fingers. Neither one of us said a word until Julie called his name to ask if he was ready to leave. Stacey would never have asked. She would have just told me she was ready.

Before going upstairs, I put out my hand. "Man, I don't know if you fully realize what you're saying, but I got your back either way."

Vic looked at me with sad eyes. "Thanks man. I needed to hear that."

Vic Reed
3

As Julie and I drove home, I couldn't help but think about my conversation with Roy. I hadn't planned on talking about my desire to leave Julie. But when he started talking about how happy we should have been to be married, I couldn't help but open up to him. Besides, I needed someone to talk to, someone that I could rely on to give me some sound advice. And knowing that Colin would have only given all of the wrong advice, Roy was that perfect someone. As long as I've known him, he was always levelheaded about things. And he had a knack of making you look at things from another perspective. That was what I needed. I needed to hear all of the positive things about Julie to realize that my staying in the relationship wouldn't be fair to her. She deserved unconditional love because that's what she was willing to give. After my talk with Roy, I knew that I had to leave.

I looked at my wife, who slept peacefully with her head leaning against the window. Damn, she was a beautiful and loving woman. If I wanted to, I could be married to her until one of us passed away. She was the type of woman that my adoptive mother would have loved for me to marry. She was always saying, 'Make sure you marry a girl that's gonna treat you right, Victor. Don't marry some tramp that ain't about nothin', ain't got nothin' to offer.'

Well Ma, although you passed before I married, Julie is definitely about something. She's college educated, with a bachelor's degree in Business. She's a licensed and successful real-estate agent. She knows how to cook and can't stand a dirty house. Someday she'll make a perfect mother. She's all that you would have wanted for me, Ma.

But she's not the one I want for myself.

I sighed as Julie stirred in her sleep. *Morning Dance* by Spyro Gyra played from the radio. I lowered the volume slightly; I didn't want to wake her. I just wanted to be alone with my thoughts. I had come to a crossroads in my life, and I had finally decided which way I wanted to turn. I should have felt bad about my decision, but instead I felt just the opposite. I felt like a weight had been lifted from my shoulders. A weight that had been applied the day Julie had announced to me that she was pregnant.

When we initially met, I had no real intention of us becoming a couple. My desire for black women was just too strong to really consider anything serious with Julie. I may have the blond hair and blue eyes, but the sisters always knew I was down. Not having matured yet, I was really only interested in a physical relationship with Julie. I am a man, after all, and I would be lying if I had said that her long blond hair that went down to the middle of her back, mesmerizing eyes and svelte figure didn't catch my attention. To my surprise, what started out as a couple of casual dates turned into a seven month "friendship." Never in a million years would I have expected that we would have started seriously dating and soon after that she would get pregnant.

I remember the day she told me. I had actually been preparing myself to end things with her, because the desire to be with a black woman had been getting to me. Julie was a hell of a woman on both the inside and out, but I just couldn't deny the fact that as special as she was, I couldn't go on with her. But before I could drop my bomb, she dropped hers.

"Vic, I'm pregnant."

I looked at her. "What?"

"I'm pregnant Vic. I'm two months late with my period."

"How can you be so sure?"

"I took a pregnancy test, and went to the doctor. Both results were the same."

"But you're on the pill! You *are* on the pill, aren't you?"

"Of course I am! How could you ask me that?"

"How could you get pregnant?" I yelled. I was pissed. Here I was getting ready to end the relationship and she comes with this shit.

"It's not like I tried to, Vic. You wanted to stop wearing a condom, remember?"

"Because you were on the pill!"

"And I was! And why are you yelling at me?"

"I'm not yelling!" I screamed.

Tears started flooding from her eyes. "Why are you mad at me, Vic? Don't you love me? Why aren't you happy about this?"

Damn, I hate to see a woman cry. That's like my kryptonite. I stepped to Julie and took her in my arms. Her tears cascaded down her cheeks and soaked my shoulder.

"Don't cry, Julie," I said, forcing myself to speak softly. "Don't cry, OK?"

"Vic...I...I love you," she whimpered. "I don't...I don't want to lose you. I didn't mean for this to happen. I'll do whatever you want."

Do whatever I want?

"Do you want me to have an abortion?"

Aww, Damn!

Why did she have to go and ask me that? I held on tightly to her and bit down on my bottom lip. I knew how she felt about abortions. For her to ask me if I wanted her to have one was like handing me a rope to hang myself with. I was in a no-win situation. If I were to say yes, I would be an insensitive bastard. If I were to say no, then she would be happy and I would be miserable as hell. I wasn't ready to be a father. But I didn't like the idea of being a baby-killer either.

"No Julie," I said with a sigh. "I don't want you to do that. We'll figure something out."

"I love you, Vic."

I didn't say what I know she wanted to hear. I just held in her my arms.

Vic
4

For weeks, I stressed over Julie and her pregnancy. And to make matters worse, while I wanted to keep the whole situation a secret until I figured out what to do, Julie made it a point to tell her entire family and most of her friends. Things got ridiculous after that. I couldn't go a day without someone bringing up the "M" word. That's all I would hear. Marriage, marriage, marriage. It frustrated the hell out of me. I started having nightmares about it. I'd be in the middle of a courtyard, with a ball and chain wrapped around my ankles, while beautiful model-type sisters strolled around, prancing in their thong-tha-thong-tha-thongs, whistling at me. They all wanted me, and I damn sure wanted them. Although I tried, I couldn't move. But I was persistent; I tugged at the chain relentlessly, determined to break it and be set free. And just as the chain started to give way, a loud wailing noise would split the air. As if on cue, all of the women would stand beside each other in a tight military line. And then stepping into the scene with a screaming baby in her arms would be Julie. She'd have this evil grin on her face, reminiscent of the Joker's, and then she'd say: "You could have said yes to the abortion. I gave you an out. Now you're mine for life."

I'd always wake up in a cold sweat after that. I just couldn't get away from the nightmare. Finally, I broke down and told Colin and Roy about Julie's pregnancy and about the decision I'd made. We were playing pool at the Havana Club.

"Fellas," I said above the loud salsa blaring from the speakers. "Julie's pregnant."

Roy and Colin froze in their tracks.

"What?" Colin asked first. "She's pregnant?"

"Are you serious, man?" Roy questioned next.

I frowned. "Yeah, I'm serious. And I'm gonna marry her."

Colin put his stick down and said, "What do you mean marry her? You love her like that?"

I shrugged my shoulders and didn't answer for a second. Then finally I said, "I don't know, man."

Shaking his head, Colin said, "Well if you don't know, how in the hell can you be talking about marrying her?"

"As much as I hate to admit it, Colin is right. You can't marry her if you don't love her," Roy said.

"Damn right, I'm right. Shit, just take her to get an abortion."

"Colin." Roy looked at him with a sneer. "Shut up."

"What?" Colin said, shrugging his shoulders. "He don't want a baby. He don't know if he loves Julie. Why *shouldn't* he consider an abortion?"

Roy slammed his hand on the pool table. "Man, that's the problem with you fools nowadays. Get a girl pregnant and immediately brothers want to start talking abortion. Brothers don't want to step up and assume responsibility for their screw-ups."

"Why should he marry her and keep that kid if he ain't going to be happy?" Colin countered.

"Colin, I agree with you about him getting married, but I can't agree with you on the abortion. I mean Stacey and I didn't plan on having Sheila and Jenea, but we assumed responsibility, and haven't regretted it for one second."

"Yeah, but you guys had unconditional love. He don't know what he has."

"Which is why he shouldn't marry her. But he can take care of the kid."

"He don't want that kind of a headache, man," Colin insisted. "He can't have that kid. Plain and simple."

As Colin and Roy went back and forth about me as if I weren't there, I drank my beer in silence. Neither one of them knew how I really felt about being with Julie. I'd wanted to talk to Roy about my feelings, but I just never found the right time. And I knew I couldn't talk to Colin about it, because he would have just told me to keep Julie as my number one and have some fun on the side. I didn't want to do that. I was past the player stage in my life. Besides, Julie had done nothing wrong. She didn't deserve to be disrespected like that. And now that she was pregnant, I didn't see how I could abandon her.

"Listen fellas," I said, tired of being invisible. "Both of you have made some valid points. Colin, you're right...I don't want the headache of fatherhood, but having the kid is not my decision to make. Even if I did have say in it, abortion wouldn't be an option, because Julie is against that. Honestly, I don't really like the idea of killing my own child, either."

"If you do it now then you're not really killing anything," Colin said.

"You're wrong," Roy said angrily. I could tell that as a proud father, the talk of abortion disturbed him. "He would be killing something. As insignificant as it may seem to you, he would be killing a child. A child that could grow and change the world."

Colin sucked his teeth. He wasn't trying to hear any of what Roy had to say.

"Colin," I said. "Roy's right, man. I can't do the abortion thing. I morally could not do it."

"Thank you," Roy said.

I continued. "But as far as marriage goes...I know both of you are right about that. I shouldn't do it. But I have to. For the kid's sake. I don't want this kid being born out of wedlock. I went through life without knowing my real parents. And although I never went without love in my life, not knowing them was still a tough thing for me. I won't subject my child to the same thing."

"But Vic," Colin said. "You don't have to marry the girl to be a parent."

"He's right about that, man," Roy added.

"I hear what you guys are saying, but I still have to do it. I want my kid to have both parents always there, so that every day they will know they are loved and will never be alone. I don't want them having to split their time between homes. That's kind of like being an orphan, because there still is no real, permanent home. I won't allow that to happen. Now do me a favor and raise your beers and give your boy a toast. You two are going to be sharing best man honors."

As the recollection of that memory faded away, I pulled the car into the driveway of our home. Julie stirred and then opened her eyes.

"Mmm...we're home already?"

"Yeah," I said softly. "We're home."

"I was dreaming. I had no idea I was so tired. Let's hurry inside so I can snuggle against you."

"Shit!"

"What is it?"

"I almost forgot that I have to go over a spreadsheet for work. I have a meeting tomorrow that I need to be ready for."

"Now? Honey, it's almost twelve o'clock."

"I know," I sighed, avoiding her stare. "But I really need to get this done. I put it off all weekend. I won't be too long. I promise."

Julie looked at me with a pout. I could see the disappointment in her eyes.

As she walked upstairs, I lowered my head and exhaled. As much as I wished I could, I couldn't change the way I felt. My head was never completely into the relationship, and I knew that wasn't going to change. I moved out the next day.

Colin Ray
5

"Yeah, I know I haven't called. But I've been meaning to. Things have just been pretty hectic for me lately. No, I'm not lying, Tanecia! My boy split with his wife. He's been staying with me. I been dealing with his drama for the past two weeks. Damn, why you gonna get all loud and ignorant and shit? Yeah, I had a good time with you. I'm for real. I was gonna call you. Damn, can't we just be friends? Whatever." I hung up the phone and cursed out loud.

"What was that all about?" Vic looked up from his laptop

I glowered at him. "Man, you are just fuckin' my whole shit up. Tanecia just called me a dog, man."

"You for real? *You* got called a dog?" Vic could barely hold back his laugh.

I wasn't amused. "Vic, that shit ain't funny! I have never, ever been called that. As many freaks as I've been with. Man, you are just throwin' a wrench in my shit. Ever since you showed up at my spot, I have had absolutely no ass. None! Zilch! Zip! Nada! Do you know how horny I am right now, dog? It's not like you would even help me out, and come and chill and meet some females. All you wanna do is sit and mope. Man, what the hell for? You're the one who wanted to be out of your shit."

Vic's laugh subsided and very sincerely he said, "Colin, man, I'm sorry. I know I put you in a bad way.

I appreciate you letting me crash here. But for real, man, you go out and do your thing."

"Do my thing? Do my thing? Where? What? You think I'm gonna bring some ass here to let you hear me tap it? 'Bruh, please. My shows are for me and my cam only. No peeking or eavesdropping allowed."

"So go by them."

"Dog, it doesn't work that way. I do my shit here."

I picked up my book filled with phone numbers and grabbed a pen. "I can't believe I'm about to scribble a name from the book of fame." I furiously dragged a line through Tanecia's name and then threw the book on my leather sofa. I was not happy. I'd always been good to go with the women. I had been mackin' ever since I was in high school and showed my science teacher what chemistry was really all about.

Mrs. Raymond—I would never forget her. She was fine as fine could get. She had every male in the school feenin' for her—teachers and students alike. She would come to school dressed in form-fitting skirts and blouses with just enough buttons undone to reveal some cleavage. She was the original Halle Berry, only with braids and more ass. I had special "tutoring" sessions with her during my entire ninth grade year. By the time the year was up, after not having done a single homework assignment, I passed with an A-plus average. I thought I was going to have summer sessions too, but her husband, who happened to be my algebra teacher, decided to spring a surprise vacation on her. He took her to the Florida Keys for a couple of months of R & R. When the next school year began, everyone but myself had been surprised when the police came to arrest her for having sex with a student. One of the faculty members caught her giving a senior a blow job in the bathroom.

After Mrs. Raymond, my luck didn't end, and my skills only improved. The fact that I was good looking, with curly hair, bedroom eyes (so I've been told), and a killer smile always helped to make the game easy for me. I went from being a player amongst players to being the coach amongst coaches, schooling fools on the rules of the game. By the time I hit my senior year, I'd already slept with most of the cheerleading squad, the field hockey team, and even a select few from the girls' basketball team. I was a legend by the time I graduated. And everyone loved me. If there was one thing my good-for-nothing father taught me, it was to always leave the woman smiling, and never make her feel like she didn't matter. And that's what I did. That's why my book was so full that I needed to buy a new one.

"Twenty-nine years, man," I said, grabbing the remote for the TV. "Twenty-nine years and I have never had to lose a number."

Vic closed his laptop. "Colin, I said I was sorry, man."

I sucked my teeth and turned on the TV. I didn't say a word, and instead focused on the television. An old episode of Sanford and Son was on, helping to take the conversation with Tanecia off my mind. But as angry as I was about being called a dog, I was still glad to have Vic there.

We first met in junior high. We were in the same homeroom. We were complete opposites then. Vic had been a short, skinny nerd of a white boy, who had no friends and no life. I don't know why I befriended him, as popular as I was. Maybe I felt sorry for him because he always wore hand-me-down clothes and lived in the projects, and had people picking on him about being adopted by a black woman who liked to beat his ass in broad daylight. Or maybe I just wanted to be a nice guy. Either way, I'm glad that I did, because we hit it off and became inseparable friends who backed each other through thick and thin.

We went everywhere together, just hanging. As he helped me get my grades and priorities about school straight, I helped him develop his style. Growing up around black people in the projects, I never had to struggle too much to get him to be down, because he was down like a brother. And as he got older and gained some muscle and confidence from the gym, he became a player like me. Together, we hit on every fine sister we could, leading the train at some of the most scandalous parties.

Vic was a Doberman to my Pit Bull. And he didn't really calm down until he met Julie, which surprised the hell out of me, because I knew that he loved blackberry queens. That's why it didn't surprise me much when he told me why he left her. But I had to be honest—I had come to like Julie. And the more I saw them together, the more I thought she was good for him, even if she wasn't a sister. She had all the qualities any man would want in a woman—intelligence, beauty, and a great personality. But not enough for him, obviously.

"Man, you sure you want to end your marriage?" I asked while Fred Sanford held his chest and told his deceased wife, Elizabeth, he was coming to meet her. "I mean, I know you weren't into the marriage thing in the beginning, but it seemed like it grew on you. I thought you were happy."

Vic leaned back on the sofa and kept his eyes glued to the television.

"I'm sure. I've been thinking about this for a long time. I'm just not myself with Julie. I only stuck around so long because she needed the support after the miscarriage. She was in a bad way then. I couldn't leave her like that, you know?"

"And you can leave now?" I tried to get him to look me in the eye, but he wasn't having it.

"I have no choice. My eyes keep wandering, and the temptation just keeps getting worse."

"Temptation's always going to be there, man. And it's always worse after you say 'I do'."

"Yeah, I know. But it's hard to deal with it when you see its fine ass every day at work."

I looked at him from the corner of my eye. Then I shut off the TV.

"Hey!" Vic said. "You know I like Sanford and Son."

"Bunk that. What's up with this fine-assed temptation you talkin' about? Don't hold out on a brother now that you've opened the can of worms."

Vic smiled and cracked his knuckles. "Maaan, there is this female at work—Latrice Meadows. Colin, she could make shit look good, she's that fine."

I shook my head. "You mean to tell me that you decided to leave Julie for her? Are you trippin'?"

"I didn't leave Julie for her. She was just the straw that broke the camel's back."

"What's so special about her, besides making shit look good?"

"Man, she just came to Intel a few months ago. She's a project engineer working the WorldCom account."

"Spare me the work details. I didn't ask about her resume."

"A'ight man. Anyway, she has an ass that won't quit, thick, shapely legs, breasts I want to nurse on until my stomach bursts, and best of all, she has the sweetest personality of any female I've ever known. We take breaks and lunches together sometimes, and just talk. And when we're working, we send each other instant messages. She's real cool man. And, as if you couldn't tell from the name, she's a sister."

"That's all well and good man, but she doesn't sound that much different from Julie."

"She is way different from Julie, man. I mean, she has this whole attitude about her. It's like she could be a sweet angel one minute, and an angel with an attitude the next. She definitely has fire to her. Fire that I am just feeling every time I see her."

"So what, you gonna start dating her now?"

"Nah, man. We're just friends right now. I get looks here and there from her, but I'm still not sure if she has a thing for me."

"What does her body language say?"

"Can't tell yet. She's not an open book."

"Well, all I can say is, if you want it like you say you do, then you better make a playa move. Don't hesitate so that another dude can claim the prize before you do. That's always been my way of thinking. "

"I have to do it slowly, man. I like her. I want to do it the right way. Besides, I have to move carefully because of this shit with Julie."

I nodded and turned the TV back on. I still couldn't believe he was for real about getting divorced. If I were him, I wouldn't make that move. I'd stay with Julie and keep women on the side for the rainy days. But not everyone can be a true, bonafide player like me.

"Yo, have you spoken to Julie much these past couple weeks?" I'd been busy with work, and I hadn't talked much since the night he came over.

"No. The way she screamed at me before I left, I figured it'd be better to let things cool off for a while."

"You sure she's not ready to talk now?"

"I doubt it. Besides, I don't want to face her right now. I don't want to see any more tears, because that shit is tearing me up."

"Is it?" I asked honestly.

Vic looked at me with a tight brow. "What do you mean by that?"

"Look, Vic, I'ma keep it straight with you. I hear what you're saying about not wanting to see Julie in any more tears, but I gotta be honest with you. It's almost hard to believe when you're sitting there talking about tryin' to get with some other female."

"Man, I don't like the fact that she's hurting. Believe me, if I could have done this any other way, I would have. And it really isn't so much that it's about Latrice. Like I said, she was just the straw. Colin, man, I've been unhappy for a while. Yeah, Julie is special. And yeah, I feel bad that she has to hurt. But I had to be happy. It was my turn."

"I feel you on that. I really do. And I'm not gonna front. It was big of you to do that, because if I were in your shoes, Julie would still be around and I would have the other chick, too. But sooner or later, you're gonna have to face her again. And when you do, make sure you try to smooth things out with her, because she's a good person. Besides, it's better to get shit straight before all of the legal shit really starts. Try to make it a clean divorce."

"I hear you," Vic said.

He turned his attention back to the TV, which was now showing a rerun of the Cosby Show. I could tell that he didn't want to talk anymore, and neither did I, for that matter. Talking about stress and drama was something I liked to avoid. I'd seen enough of it with my Mom and Dad to last me a lifetime. All of the arguments I had to listen to, all of the cursing and screaming—I swore growing up I wouldn't go through what they went through. And they weren't even married! That's why I dedicated my life to bachelorhood and big pimpin'. No hassles, no worries—no responsibility to anyone but myself. That's the way I liked it.

Julie Reed
6

"*I* hate him!" I screamed, as another wave of tears fell from my eyes. "How could he do this to me? After all I've done for him. After everything that I've gone through...how could he be so damn selfish and insensitive? He's not in love with me? After all of the love I have shown him...He's not in love with me? Does that make sense?" I slammed my fist into the armrest of Stacey's sofa and squeezed my eyes tightly in the hopes that the tears would stop falling. They didn't. "No it doesn't," I sobbed.

Stacey put her thick arm around me and let my head lay against her shoulder. Stroking my hair, she agreed, "No it doesn't, girl."

"I loved him unconditionally," I whispered.

Stacey said, "I know you did."

I raised my head. "A divorce, Stacey. He wants a fucking divorce!" I stared at Stacey, who kept a tight lip and shrugged her shoulders. "For the past month, I have been sulking in my empty house, just trying to figure out why he's doing this. Why he wants to end what we have. And do you know what I've come to realize?" I stood up. Tears continued to fall, although I was getting angrier. I blew my nose into an already-soaked tissue. "He doesn't want to be with me because I'm white!"

Stacey looked at me.

"Julie! Do you realize what you just said?"

I looked at her and curled my lips and crossed my arms.

"I know exactly what I said."

"Julie, Vic is white. How could he not want you because you're white? Honestly, let's be serious."

"Stacey, I am being serious. You know how Vic grew up. You see how he is. Stacey, Vic is more black than he is white. White is just his skin color. He loves black women. Plain and simple."

"Julie, will you stop talking nonsense? Vic married you. Not a black woman."

"And I'm sure he regrets every minute of it."

Stacey lifted my chin with her finger and looked at me through serious eyes.

"Girl, listen. You need to stop this crazy talk, OK? Yes, Vic may have some nigga in him, but the last thing you need to do is to make yourself believe that he left you for a black woman. I mean really, the world don't work that way. Besides, when it comes to the whole black-white issue, it usually works the other way around. Black men are the ones crazy for the white meat."

Stacey smiled, and from the look in her eyes, I could tell she was hoping I would crack one too. But I just couldn't, because in my heart, I knew that what I was saying was true. I could never ignore the fact that whenever we were out together and an attractive black female came around, his attention always seemed to drift in her direction. I tried to deny my feelings, though. I figured he was a man, and that's what men do. But I noticed that it was only the black women he paid attention to. That's why I stopped taking my pills. I wanted Vic to be my man.

He is dangerously handsome, with eyes so blue they sparkle, and a smile warm enough to make your temperature rise by a few degrees. From the first moment I laid my eyes on him I was breathless. He stood out like no man I had ever met before had. I found his pretty looks and bad-boy style intoxicating. I was determined not to let him get away.

I was a little worried at first, when I told him about the pregnancy. I didn't know how he was going to take it. But as more time passed, I began to worry less. And after our wedding, I was sure that I had nothing to worry about.

When I had my miscarriage, I was heartbroken. I was looking forward to being a mother and I was anxious to begin a family with Vic. The way he took care of me and stayed by my side through that ordeal only made my love for him stronger. So it was a real slap in the face when he told me he didn't want to be married anymore; I realized then that I had been wrong about everything.

I had been at home on the computer the night Vic told me. I was putting together a proposal for a house that I was going to be showing to a newlywed couple the next day. Vic had come in from work and went straight to the bedroom without saying a word to me. When I finished with my proposal, I shut off the PC and went into the bedroom to greet my man. I didn't know what to think when I saw him packing a suitcase.

"Babe, what are you doing? Why are you packing?"

He didn't answer right away, and didn't turn around.

"Earth to Vic...Is something wrong? Why the silent treatment? You didn't even say hi when you came in. Did you have a bad day at work?" He kept silent and continued to pack. I was starting to get worried. "Vic, honey...what's wrong? Are you mad at me for something?"

Ignoring me, he continued to pack, going from one drawer to the next. Finally, after another couple of seconds, he turned around and looked at me. In his eyes, I saw a darkness I had never seen.

"Julie, I can't do this anymore," he said flatly. Then he moved to his dresser and started packing away his boxers and t-shirts.

"Can't do what anymore?" I asked, watching him closely. He didn't respond fast enough for me, so I asked again. "Vic, what are you talking about?"

Without looking at me, he said, "Julie, I'm moving out. And I want a divorce."

My heartbeat paused when he said that, and everything around me seemed to move in slow motion. I was very suddenly no longer in my world called reality.

"What do you mean, divorce? Is this some kind of joke? Because it's not a very funny one."

"No joke," he said, finally turning to face me. "I don't want to be married anymore."

I got the chills and my legs suddenly felt weak. I sat down on the edge of the bed and lowered my head.

"Don't want to be married? What the hell are you talking about? What the hell are you trying to say?"

"I'm saying that I am not happy. I can't do this anymore. I love you, Julie, but I'm not in love with you. I'm sorry. But that's the way I feel." He turned back around and resumed packing.

I didn't respond for a few minutes. I sat quietly and tried to absorb everything he had just told me. I looked up at him, hoping to see him smiling. I only saw his back, and another suitcase being filled. I shook my head and bit down on my lip, which had started to quiver.

"Sorry? Vic, what do you mean not in love with me? You married me. You exchanged vows with me! Not in love with me? Please tell me this is a sick, cruel joke you're playing. Please? This can't be happening. You can't mean what you just said. Vic? Vic! Please tell me the truth." I looked at him through pleading eyes, which were welling with tears. He turned back around to face me; I could tell by the wrinkle in his forehead that he was very serious. But I didn't want to believe it. I stood up and approached him slowly, grabbing him by the arm.

"Vic...I love you. You love me too. Remember?"

He pulled away from me slowly and zipped up both suitcases.

"I'm sorry, Julie. I don't want to hurt you, but I can't go on with us anymore. Please forgive me. I'll be back for the rest of my things later. Good-bye."

Without another word, he walked past me, bags in hand, and headed toward the front door. I stood painfully still, not wanting to accept what was actually happening. I was still waiting for him to turn around and tell me it was all a lie. But when he opened the door, I knew that wasn't going to happen.

"Good-bye? What the hell do you mean good-bye? You son of a bitch! Why are you doing this? Is there someone else? Is that why you want to leave? Talk to me, you asshole! You married me."

Without turning around, he said, "I know, Julie. I'll have my lawyer contact you."

"Lawyer? Doesn't our marriage mean anything to you?" I stared at his back and held my breath. When he answered me, my spirit deflated.

"No," he said curtly. As he walked through the door, my tears fell in torrents down my cheeks.

"You son of a bitch! You fucking son of a bitch! I hate you! I hate you! I hate you!"

"When he left, Stacey," I continued my story. "I cried and blamed myself for everything. I even blamed it on the miscarriage."

"Julie, that wasn't your fault, and you know it."

"I know, but I just couldn't understand why he would want to leave. Then I realized that it had never really been about love for him."

"What do you mean?"

"I mean he has always had a thing for black women. Whenever we were out, I'd see his eyes wandering."

"All men do that."

"Yeah, but he never looked at white women."

"Come on, Julie."

"No, it's true, Stacey. But it wasn't just the stares. Whenever we went out and we were around black women, he always treated me differently. He was colder to me, less sensitive. There were times when I just felt like he was completely uncomfortable with me by his side."

"I don't know, Julie. The idea of him being uncomfortable is a little far-fetched. Maybe if he were black I could see it."

"Stacey, he practically is. I'm telling you, that's what it is. He couldn't deal with my color."

"Julie, I don't know. I just find that hard to believe."

"Oh, believe it, Stacey. I've known it for a long time, but I tried to ignore what I saw. I tried to lie to myself and think our relationship would last. It's the only thing that makes sense to me."

"I know you may not want to hear this, but isn't it possible that he just fell out of love with you? It happens. I've been through it."

"I know it happens. But not in this case. I'm not wrong about this."

I sat down on the sofa and thought about the things I had said. I knew I was right. Even though I tried to deny it, for as long as I'd been with Vic, I'd always felt like the runner-up in a beauty contest. I was just now admitting it to myself.

Stacey Burges
7

"I saw Julie today," I said, handing Roy his plate of food. I took my own food out and sat down across from my husband. I had already fed Sheila and Jenea and gotten them off to bed. Roy took a bite of the baked chicken I made, and then took a sip of his beer. I had been waiting all day to have a moment with just the two of us. Julie's visit had been on my mind all day.

"Really?" he asked letting out a small burp. "What did she want?"

"To talk. She's pretty torn up over what's going on with her and Vic. I have to admit I'm pretty shocked myself. I never thought they would be going through anything like this. Julie was in tears practically the whole time." I swallowed a mouthful of food and drank some of my juice. I had outdone myself with the chicken. It was good.

"Yeah, I can imagine," Vic said, inhaling the food. If there was one thing I could always count on, it was Roy and his hearty appetite.

"She's taking Vic's decision to end their marriage really hard. She's got this crazy notion that the reason he wants out is because she's white. Can you believe that? I tried to convince her that there had to be another reason, but she was pretty adamant about her feelings. Julie's my girl and all, but that is crazy. Wouldn't you agree?"

Roy swallowed the last of his chicken and gulped down the rest of his beer. Looking at me, he said very quietly, "She's right."

"Excuse me?"

"Vic told me about what he was going to do a couple of weeks ago. And he told me why."

"Wait a minute...you mean to tell me that you knew he was going to leave her, and you didn't say a word to me? And what do you mean, she's right? Are you saying he really wants out because she's white?"

"That's what I'm saying. And I didn't say anything, because I know you and Julie are close, and I figured it was best to keep quiet about it. I didn't want to be in the middle of anything."

"So what, you don't think I can keep quiet about something like that? You trying to say I have a big mouth?" I looked at my husband, crossed my arms and curled my lips. I couldn't believe he knew and hadn't confided in me.

"Stacey, what would you have done if I would have told you Vic didn't want to be with Julie anymore?"

"I would have told Julie."

"Exactly. So to answer your question, yes, you do have a big mouth."

"How could you expect me not to say anything, Roy? Julie is my friend. You think I like seeing her go through this? I mean, this is ridiculous. Her heart is broken because he wants a black woman? What kind of bullshit is that? And if that's the case, then his ass should have realized that before he ever married her. This is the stupidest thing. Vic is as white as Julie is!"

"Baby, I know."

"So why did he ask her to marry him?"

"He felt he had no choice."

"No choice?"

"He was planning on ending their relationship, but the night he was going to tell her, she told him she was pregnant. He felt like he couldn't end it then."

"Why? That doesn't make sense. What, he didn't think she could handle it without him?"

"No, that's not it. And it does make sense. Remember that a black woman raised Vic. He never knew his mother or father. He swore to himself that he wouldn't let his child grow up like that."

"OK. But why propose?"

"He didn't want the child to have to be split between two homes. He was trying to do the right thing. But he wasn't happy. He loved her, but he was never in love with her."

"So I bet he was relieved when she had the miscarriage, huh? Just like a man."

"No. Actually, he was looking forward to being a father. When it happened, he was hurt over it. And, believe it or not, he was worried about Julie, which is why he didn't leave right away. But now that time has passed, he's come to a point where he just can't live a lie anymore."

I slammed my hand down on the table.

"That is pure BS. I'm sorry that your white boy has a thing for black women, but the fact remains, he said 'I do.' You can't just change your mind and say 'I don't!' That is so cowardly."

"Look, don't yell at me about it. I didn't tell him to leave her. I even tried to talk some sense into him. I told him how great Julie is, and how lucky he was to have her, but his mind was made up a long time ago.

He said he wants the fire and attitude a black woman has."

"Fire and attitude? What does he want, a ghetto bitch?"

Roy shrugged his shoulders. "I don't know. All I know is he's not happy."

"So because she takes care of him and doesn't give him attitude, he's not happy? Does he realize how ridiculously stupid that sounds? I can't believe this."

I stood up and grabbed Roy's empty plate, and my own, which was still filled with food. I had lost my appetite. Julie is a beautiful, intelligent, kind human being. I liked her from the first moment I met her. She didn't deserve any of what Vic was doing to her. I continued venting.

"All because of her skin color? Is Vic really that naïve? Julie is special. She doesn't have one mean or ignorant bone in her body. Is that not good enough for him? I mean, does he really think he will find greater happiness with a black woman? Does he not realize that we can be bitches when we want to be, too?"

"Stacey, yelling at me is not going to do you, or Julie, any good. I hear what you're saying. But his mind is made up."

"Well then change his mind! Julie is too beautiful a person for him to do this to her. Shit, you men walk around and complain about not being able to find a good woman, and then when you do, you either dog her out like that egotistical too-damned-high-on-himself Colin, or you say she's not good enough, like that fool Vic. Y'all make me sick!"

"Stacey, again, you're yelling at the wrong person. I know I have a good thing. You don't see me complaining."

"And you better not, either. I swear if you even try to be like Colin, or that idiot Vic, I will squeeze your balls until your eyes bulge."

Roy laughed, not realizing how serious I was. I definitely had the fire and attitude, and I never made empty threats. I walked out of the kitchen and went into the living room. I was fuming, and I knew I was taking it out on the wrong person. But I couldn't help it; he was there. I popped the *Waiting to Exhale* DVD in, and forwarded to the scene where Angela Basset burned her cheating husband's clothing in his car. As the scene played, I thought, *Julie should have done that to Vic's ass.*

Roy walked into the living room when the fire was ablaze. When he saw what I was watching, he made an immediate beeline for the bedroom. He knew to leave me alone at that moment. I watched the scene two more times, and then turned off the TV.

When I walked into the room, Roy was in bed watching ESPN. I looked at him and said, "Julie is my friend, and will always be my friend. She will be coming over here. I don't want Vic here anymore."

Roy looked at me with surprise. I didn't care. And I was serious.

"Look, if Vic wants to be an asshole, then let him be one. But Julie is my girl. I don't want Vic's immature ass over here."

"Hold up, Stacey. I understand Julie is your girl, but Vic is my boy. Their problems are their problems, not mine. I suggest you adopt the same philosophy."

"So what, you're choosing his side over mine?"

"Baby, it's not about sides. They are our friends. Because they're going through something, that doesn't mean that our friendships have to change. Now, I didn't tell you I didn't want Julie here—"

"—Because you know she didn't do anything!" I yelled louder than I intended.

"Will you keep your voice down? You're going to wake the girls. Look, there is no real right and wrong here. You can't fault Vic because he is not in love with Julie. He has every right to feel that way."

"Well his sorry ass should have never married her. He's only doing her more harm. And I don't care Roy; I don't want him here. He is not welcomed in this house."

"In which house? You said 'this house'. But you're obviously not talking about *our* house."

"Hell yes, I meant here. I don't want to see him."

"Well then, you can leave when he comes over. Vic is my boy, like Julie is your girl. That's not going to change. And my friendship with him won't change."

"Roy, I swear I don't want him here." I stared hard at my husband. I couldn't believe he was taking the stance he was. I couldn't believe he was choosing sides like that.

"I pay the bills here just like you do, Stacey. As a matter of fact, I pay the majority of the bills here. So I don't care about what you want or don't want. Vic is coming over, and that's final."

"Oh no, you didn't. You didn't just go there with me and the bills, did you? I don't see your ass taking care of our little girls every single hour of every single day. I don't see you cooking and cleaning and running this household. Don't you even try to cheapen my worth to this house."

"Baby, that's not what I meant—"

"Don't you baby me, Roy. I said I don't want Vic here, and *that* is final."

I stormed out of the room before he could say another word, and before our argument got any worse. Cursing the whole way there, I went to the living room, turned on the TV, and this time I watched the entire movie. I was angrier than before. Vic's decision had brought to surface some deeply buried feelings.

Vic
8

I finally worked up the nerve to ask Latrice out on a date. I had been debating my decision for the past few weeks. I remember when I first saw her. It was in the break room, and I was getting my morning coffee and toasting a bagel when she walked in. I was like a cartoon character, whose tongue had fallen out and rolled open like a red carpet; she was that fine. She had a thick but well-proportioned hourglass figure, with thick, shapely legs, that she didn't attempt to hide with the black mini-skirt she was wearing. To go with the skirt, she wore a light blue, V-neck blouse, and even though it wasn't the tightest of tight, her breasts could still be seen swelling beneath the fabric. She was all woman. I tried my best to be discreet as I watched the sashay of her ample behind while she moved to the refrigerator and put her lunch bag inside. I was focusing on her so hard that had she not alerted me, I could have set the building on fire.

"Your toast is burning," she said with a slight smile.

I turned toward the toaster and saw the smoke. "Oh shit!" I moved to it and popped the bread, which had burned and was flaking.

With a laugh, Latrice said, "I guess you should have been keeping your eyes on that toast." Without saying another word, she left the break room, leaving me alone with my mess and my embarrassment. Since that day, I did what I could to find out about her.

Through some slick investigation, thanks in large part to my friend Al, from the mailroom, who can get info better than the CIA, I found out Latrice had just recently started with Intel's Project Engineering group. Al also informed me that she worked out at the gym religiously, had her own condo, no kids, and more importantly, no man. But of course, one major problem still remained—I was married. So for a while, I had to be content with making small talk with her whenever I could. We'd say hi and have small conversations about the job—nothing too heavy.

We eventually started trading e-mails back and forth, talking via the instant messenger whenever we weren't too busy. When our schedules permitted, we'd meet for lunch. Latrice was cool and down to earth. She also had a regal attitude about her, like she knew she was the shit. That was definitely drawing me in. The more we talked, the more I wanted to get to know her. And because of my growing desire for her, I had to make the decision to finally end the marriage with Julie.

But it wasn't really just Latrice who had led me to that decision. The fact of the matter was that if it hadn't been Latrice who had come into the picture, it would have been someone else eventually, because I wasn't satisfied at home.

Telling Julie wasn't an easy thing for me to do, but it was necessary. For so long, I had been living my life for her, trying to make her happy because she was pregnant. Then when she lost the baby, I spent my time trying to cheer her up. But enough was enough. I wanted to live my life and be happy for me. That's why I did what I did, and that's why I finally asked Latrice out.

The workday had ended, and I was tying up some loose ends before leaving. I also waited because I didn't want anyone else around when I stepped to Latrice. I was nervous, and I wasn't sure how she was going to respond to my advance. I locked my office up and went down to the other end of the building where she was sitting in her office in front of her PC.

"Hey you," I said knocking on the door.

Latrice looked up and smiled. Damn her smile was intoxicating.

"Hey Vic! What's up? I'm surprised you're still here."

"Yeah," I said, taking a seat. "I had some things to take care of. I have another all day meeting."

"Don't you just love those?" Latrice asked sarcastically.

"Oh, yeah. About as much as I love migraines, which I always seem to get when I walk out of those."

Latrice laughed then looked at her watch. "Damn!" she said.

"What's up?"

"I forgot, I was supposed to meet my girl Emily at the gym at seven-thirty tonight. She couldn't go at our normal time, so we had to go late."

"You go every night?"

"Like clockwork."

"That's cool. I go at least four days a week."

"What gym do you go to?"

"I go to Supreme Sports Club. You?"

"Emily and I go to Bally's over in Ellicott City."

"I've been there a few times. It's cool. Has some nice looking women."

"Just like a man. I thought you went to work out."

"I do," I said with an innocent smile. "My eyes are burned out after each set."

"Mmm hmm…I bet."

Latrice started to shut down her PC. My heart started beating heavily; this would be the first time I had asked anyone out since I started dating Julie. I hoped the rust wouldn't show.

"Hey Latrice, there was something I wanted to ask you."

Locking her drawers, she said, "What's up?"

"Well, you know how we've been taking lunch breaks sometimes, and chatting on IM or e-mail?"

"Yeah. It's been fun. You're one of the few people I can stand here at Intel. Consider yourself lucky."

Smiling, I said, "Oh, I do. And it has been fun. Which is why I was wondering if you'd consider hanging outside of the office one night? Maybe just chill and take in a movie or some dinner."

Latrice stopped what she was doing and looked at me. I felt my throat get dry. The look on her face was hard to read, and I couldn't help but wonder if I had crossed the boundary lines of the friendship we had established. But then shit, I had to do that to keep from falling into the doomed just-a-friend pit. I didn't pull my eyes away; I wanted her to know I was serious. An uncomfortable fifteen seconds passed before she said anything.

"Vic, aren't you married?" she asked with an edgy tone I had never heard her use before—at least not with me.

"Technically, yes. But we're getting a divorce."

"Don't tell me you're divorcing your wife to ask me out," she asked, the tone in her voice lightening just a little.

"No, no. Our relationship was over long before you and I met."

"Uh huh. Vic, why you wanna take me out?"

"You're cool, Latrice. I'd like to be able to completely kick back and relax with you away from the stiffs here. I mean, if you're not comfortable with it, that's OK. I'd understand. I'm not trying to upset you." I watched her and held my breath. I couldn't figure out how she was taking the invite. She stood up, slipped into her coat, and grabbed her laptop case. Following her cue, I stepped out of her office.

As she locked her door, she said, "A divorce, huh? Let me think about it and get back to you." Without saying good-bye, she walked away, leaving me there to wonder what her answer would be.

Latrice
9

"I have a problem, girl," I said, approaching my forty-fifth minute on the Stairmaster.

"What's up?" Emily, who was on her thirtieth minute, huffed.

"Girl, you remember me telling you about my friend at work? The one I take lunch breaks with sometimes."

"The white guy with the cute smile and the pretty eyes?"

"Yeah." I wiped beads of sweat from my forehead and increased the speed of motion. "That's him."

"What about him?"

"Girl, you would not believe what happened before I came here. Girl, *I* can't believe what happened."

Emily looked at me. Sweat fell from her chin.

"What?"

I got off the Stairmaster and said, "We need to talk, girl. Let's go get our things and get out of here."

As we got our bags from the locker room, I told her all about Vic's invitation.

"Are you for real? He asked you out?"

"What do you mean, he asked me out? You think I'm not fine enough to be asked out? Why would I make that up?"

Emily shook her head and laughed. "You know I didn't mean it like that, so don't even trip. I'm just surprised, that's all. Didn't you say that he was married?"

"Yeah, but he says he's getting a divorce."

"I see. But he's white."

"Girl, he is blacker than some of the darkest brothers at my job."

"But he's still white," Emily said.

"So are you."

"We're not talking about me, though, 'Trice. We're talking about you. And if I recall correctly, I remember hearing you say more than once that you do the right thing by not doing the white thing. Am I wrong?"

I shook my head and sucked my teeth. "Yeah I said that." And I had meant it. White men with black women had always been taboo for me—even more so than a black man and a white woman. Plus, white men were so hypocritical when it came to their attraction for black women. Unlike the brothers, who had no qualms about flaunting the "prize" on their arm, white men always kept their feelings for a sister on the down low. Oh, they had no problem hitting the ass behind closed doors, but when show time came, it was like all of a sudden black women weren't good enough to be with.

"So, what did you tell him when he asked? I hope you weren't too hard on him. From the way you talk about him, he seems like a nice guy."

"Yeah, Vic is nice. Real nice."

"You going to be able to keep your friendship with him? I mean, does he seem like he could handle the rejection?"

I didn't answer her as we walked to our cars. She noticed my reluctance to answer.

"'Trice? You're not answering me. You did say no, didn't you?"

I avoided her stare as I reached in my purse to grab my car keys.

"'Trice!" Emily pressed.

"OK, OK. Damn! No. I didn't turn him down. And no, I didn't say yes. I told him I would get back to him."

"You what? Oh no! Don't tell me you've got jungle fever." Emily clapped her hands and started laughing.

I shook my head. "Em', stop trippin'. All I said was that I'd get back to him. And let's not go there, Miss Fever-Queen."

"Hey, at least I admit it. So you're serious about getting back to him?"

I shrugged my shoulders. "Girl, I don't know."

"Latrice and a white man. Who would have thought it?"

"I didn't say yes yet! Besides, I already told you he's more black than OJ."

"OJ's black?"

"Sheeeit. Don't get me started on that fool. Anyway...like I was saying... Vic has a lot of soul. I mean at work, he plays the game well, but when it's the two of us trippin', he lets his true self, out."

"Which is?"

"Let me put it this way... he was raised by a black woman in the projects in DC."

"Really? A black woman?"

"He was adopted."

"Oh. So now back to my original question, which you never really answered. You serious about getting back to him?"

"I told you I didn't know."

"If you don't know, that means you're giving it some thought. And if you're giving it some thought, that means that you have the fever for the flavor. So don't even try to deny that." Emily raised an eyebrow and straightened her lips. Damn.

"OK," I finally admitted. "Yeah, I may be feeling him a little."

"I knew it!" Emily screamed.

"Girl, keep your voice down."

"Latrice is feeling the white boy. Latrice is feeling the white boy..."

"Em'..." I shot her a look.

"OK, OK...white-black-boy. So, Miss I'll-never-date-a-white-man-because-he-just-don't-do-anything-for-me. What is it about him that you like?"

"Girl, I don't know. There's just something about him. He's so down to earth and cool. I can actually trip with him. I mean his skin may be white, but he's so damned real. Maybe that's why the skin color doesn't bother me too much. I don't know."

"And his being married? What's up with that?"

"I told you, he says he's getting a divorce."

"He still wearing the ring?"

"No. I checked for that."

"Still doesn't mean he couldn't be lying about that. You know how men are. You know how Jeff was. A dog if there ever was one."

"Yeah I know," I said softly. The mention of Jeff, Emily's former boss and an all-around dog, took my thoughts to my best friend, Danita Evans. She used to mess around with Jeff, who was also her boss. She lost her man Stephen, who I still spoke to every now and then, over Jeff's triflin' ass. Danita died in a car accident two years ago; the same night Stephen got married to another woman. Her death hit me hard. Danita was like my sister, only closer. We were on the outs for a while because I couldn't support what she had going on with Jeff. Plus, I liked Stephen. He didn't deserve what Danita had been doing. But after he left and moved on with his life, Danita swallowed her pride and apologized to me for what she did, and our friendship continued as if it had never stopped.

The night that Danita died, everything changed. I was in a state of depression for months. I couldn't sleep or eat, which was a tremendous thing, as much as I enjoyed food. To make matters worse, my relationship with my then boyfriend, Bernard, began to suffer. It wasn't really his fault. All he wanted was a little love from me, but I found it difficult to give. As much as I loved him and wanted to be with him, Danita's death wouldn't allow me to be happy. As I sank deeper and deeper into my pit, Bernard started to drift away from me. And because I never tried to reel him in, he drifted into the arms of another woman. That was another bitter pill for me to swallow.

Over time, and not by my choice, I began to lose all of the weight I had amassed over the years. One rainy day, I caught my reflection in the mirror as I stepped out of the shower, and I had to admit, I looked good. I had lost so much weight I almost didn't recognize myself. That same day, I called Emily, who has become my best friend, and told her I wanted to join the gym, and I wanted a partner. We joined together, and since then I've lost more than one hundred pounds, and have become a health-nut. Instead of McDonalds and Kentucky Fried, I started eating nothing but salads and low-fat, low-carb foods.

I became a serious calorie-counter. And I was glad I did. As I lost weight, my self-esteem improved; my stamina increased, which was a plus in the bedroom, and the extremely fine men who used to ignore me, started taking second glances. Of course, I'd always had men salivating over my ghetto booty, which I still have, but as the weight disappeared, they drooled over the whole package, and not just a slice.

With every day that passed, I became happier and more intent on becoming a new person. Eventually I made the switch from E-Systems Communications, to Intel, Inc. Through a hook-up from a former manager of mine, I got a position as a project engineer. It was during my first week there that I met Vic. I can't lie. When I first met him I thought he was attractive—even for a white guy. He had a smile that was too pretty, innocent eyes, and a physique that told me he wasn't a slouch. I had seen him in passing a few times, but he never really noticed me. Not until he burned his toast checking me out in the break room. I walked in to put my lunch in the refrigerator while he was there getting his breakfast together. I could feel his eyes on me as I went about my business, and I made sure to take my time doing it; since dropping the weight, I made it a point to enjoy admiration men had for me.

Unfortunately, I had to break the spell when I saw the smoke coming from the toaster. As Vic blushed and went to take care of his food, I caught the wedding band on his finger. After that, whatever thoughts may have been creeping into my mind quickly went away. I wasn't trying to get caught up like Danita; I had too much respect for myself to become a trick on the side. Besides—he was white.

But that didn't stop me from becoming friends with him. We'd stop and have small talk in the hallway sometimes. We'd pass by each other's offices, just to say hi. Eventually, we spoke back and forth over e-mail and the instant messenger. The more we talked and got to know each other, the more I started to feel him. He caught me by surprise when he asked me out. Never one to talk about his personal life, I had no idea that he and his wife were having problems. But when he told me about getting a divorce, and I saw that his ring wasn't on his finger, I shocked myself by saying I would think about it.

"Girl, I don't think he'd lie. I know men will be men and boys will be boys, but Vic's different. And as amazing as this sounds coming from me, the color don't mean a thing."

Emily leaned against her Chrysler Sebring and stared at me with an open mouth. Then she put on a fake crying act.

"My girl is growing up!" she said with a laugh.

"Oh whatever," I said, rolling my eyes at her. "I'm already grown. I'm just willing to expand my horizons this one time. Maybe."

"One time, huh? Well you know girl, once you go white—"

I put my hand up and cut her off immediately.

"Don't you even go there."

Emily's face turned beet-red from laughing.

"So you're really going to consider it, huh?" she asked, composing herself.

"Maybe. I mean, I have to think of the consequences. You know I have my rep to keep up. I'm not trying to damage that. Plus, there's that whole inter-office, interracial relationship thing to think about."

"Relationship? Damn, all the man asked for was a date."

"You know how I think ahead. But anyway, I also have to make sure that he is for real about the divorce. Because I am not trying to get caught up in no drama. I don't want to have to come out my face and kick some ass."

"True. So when are you going to answer him?"

"Don't know. I'll let him wait while I analyze everything. Then I'll tell him my answer."

"OK, girl," Emily said getting into her car. "Just make sure you let me know."

"You know I will."

Emily smiled, and as she drove off, she started singing again.

"You've got jungle fever..."

I smiled and shook my head. "You're one to talk girl. You ain't ever felt anything but the fever." As I drove home, I thought about when I would tell Vic yes.

Vic
10

"Fellas, Latrice said yes," I declared, as I claimed my first victory for the night. We were at Havana Club for our weekly Wednesday night pool session. We'd been doing that since Colin first suggested it three years ago. After that first night, we'd been hooked, coming to play pool, enjoy the salsa music, check out the women, and have an occasional cigar, something the wives never knew about.

"Yes to what?" Roy asked, racking the balls. It was his turn for a beating.

"Do you always forget what we talk about, man?" Colin asked, sipping on a beer and checking out a fine Latin sister shaking her bon-bon on the dance floor. "Latrice is the honey from his job he been sweatin'. He's been talking our ears off about her."

"Oh, yeah," Roy said. "My bad."

"You getting forgetful in your old age, dog?" Colin asked, smiling.

"Man, I got two kids and a wife. Vic's love life is the last thing on my mind." Turning my attention back to me, Roy said, "So you finally worked up the nerve, huh?"

I didn't answer him right away. I was concentrating on my break to begin our game. Pool was something I enjoyed playing. I'd been doing it since I was a teenager. When things were hectic outside in the projects, and I knew better than to be a knucklehead, I'd escape to some of the pool halls, where the owners were kind enough to let me in to chill with the big boys. I learned the art of pool by getting my behind beaten. Soon enough, I started doing the ass whooping. After breaking the rack, sinking the nine and three balls, I said, "Yeah man. I figured the time was right."

"She knows you're getting divorced, right?" Roy asked.

"Yeah, I told her."

"Speaking of which," Colin said, "What's up with that, anyway?"

"Man, it's rougher than I thought it would be."

"Julie still not speaking to you?" Colin asked.

"Yup."

"Be glad she's not," Roy said. "She's been by my place a couple of times, and I hear her and Julie talking."

"Yeah, what's she saying?"

"Man, you don't even want to know."

"Damn," Vic said softly.

"Yeah, damn is right. Man, when she and Stacey get together...Well, I'll just put it like this—sometimes I'm afraid for my life. They give me looks like they want to do something evil. Let me just warn you ahead of time. When you come over on Sunday to watch the game, be ready for a very, very cold reception."

Colin pulled his gaze away from the dance floor. Looking at Roy he said, "Damn dog, your wife is hatin' like that?"

"Oh, she's past hate, man. Vic is in the infamous coward-ass-man category."

"Damn," Colin laughed. "When Stacey puts you in that category, there ain't no comin' out."

I sank another ball and took a sip of my Coors.

"I expected that to happen fellas. Stacey and Julie are tight. I knew Julie would be talking to her, and I knew Stacey would have anger toward me. That's what women do. I can't blame Julie or Stacey for being mad. But shit, it's better that I bailed out than to mess around."

"I beg to differ," Colin said.

"Colin," Roy said, finally preparing to take a shot after I narrowly missed sinking the eight ball; I had left all of his balls on the table. "Your opinion doesn't count."

"Yeah," I added. "Man, even if you had the finest honey in the world, you would still play her."

"Hey, y'all know I can't stand a one-course meal. I gotta have appetizers and deserts."

"Yeah, OK," Roy said.

Roy missed his next shot, and I went on to claim my second victory off a nice bank shot. As Colin racked for his beating, I looked at Roy.

"So Stacey is really feeling bitter, huh? What all did you tell her?"

"Nothing that she didn't already hear from Julie. I tried to explain why you couldn't go on, and how it was better that you were honest than to be like Colin."

"He's not that lucky," Colin interjected.

"What did she say?" I asked, ignoring him.

"Man, she nearly bit my head off. She couldn't understand how you could not want Julie because of her color."

"It's more than that, and you know it."

"I know. And I tried to tell her that, but it didn't make a difference. She thinks you're a coward. Plain and simple."

"Man, I'm doing the right thing."

"Never in a woman's eyes," Colin said. "We can never do the right thing. That's why I avoid the shackles."

"Oh, and get this," Roy said, downing his beer. "Stacey doesn't want you coming to the house."

Colin looked at me. "Dayum! She's hatin' on your ass for real." He all but fell over laughing.

"Don't worry, though," Roy said. "She can chew me out and scream all she wants. It's my house, too."

I shook my head. "Damn man, I can't believe she's giving you grief like that over this."

Colin answered for him. "Of course she is! That's what women do. You two probably argue at least three nights a week over Vic and Julie, don't you?"

"Man, try four. She's pissed because I still hang out with you, and won't agree to let you come over. She's gone to some extreme level, and I don't understand why."

"Women!" Colin declared. "When one of them cries over a man, no matter what he did or didn't do, they form some kind of man-hating alliance, where the objective is to give hell to every other male they can. Damn. Maybe I can afford to miss the game this week."

I shook my head. "Damn, man. I'm sorry you have to feel the effects of this."

"Man, it's cool. I can deal with my wife."

"Oh yeah," Colin said, preparing to take a shot, "Just wait until she stops givin' up the ass. You know that's gonna happen next, right?"

"No way," Roy said.

Colin sank a six-nine combination, and said, "Give it about another week, and you'll be in the same category with Vic. Shit, you might even be sleeping on the couch."

"Never in my house, man. Besides, Stacey wouldn't do that."

"Vic," Colin looked at me. "I have fifty bucks that says his ass is on the couch after Sunday."

I looked at Roy and sighed. "I'm not gonna bet on that one."

"Yeah, because you know I'm right." Colin sank another combo and then went on to kick my behind, royally. By that time, my head was out of the game.

After we played another two games, and after Colin collected a waitress's number, we all went our separate ways. I had finally gotten a new condo two weeks ago, and was settled in. Sitting on my couch, I thought about the changes in my life. I really did care for Julie, and I never intended on hurting her. Some nights, the regret for letting things between us go as far as they did hit me hard. I'd come across so many women who'd been done wrong or who'd had their hearts broken; I never thought I would actually be one of those men that they cried and complained about. I actually took some pride in the fact that I had never let a relationship end in a negative way. To this day, I'm still cool with every woman I've messed with. Julie is my first heartbreak, and hopefully my last, because knowing that I caused her tears to fall feels terrible. That's why I neglected her calls and avoided talking to her. I just couldn't deal with the guilt I felt. And even though I knew that my leaving had been the right decision, I still couldn't help but feel like I was in the wrong. I mean, let's face it, Julie may not have been perfect, but she did her best to show me nothing but love. And like Roy said, there was no denying her worth. So even if I'd tried not to, how could I not feel guilty for hurting her? But as bad as I felt, I couldn't deny the fact that I was happier. I didn't feel the same type of pressure that I felt before. I was free to be myself and not have to put on an act for anybody. *Life*, I sighed. It was never easy. I just hoped things with Latrice went smoothly.

I was in my office getting ready to go when she said yes. It had been a little over a week and a half since I'd first asked her out. During that time, I noticed how she had distanced herself from me. Our e-mail and IM exchanges decreased, and we'd only had lunch together twice. Although I was dying to know her answer, I never asked her what her decision was, because I didn't want to make her think I was pressed. Besides, I figured if she didn't want to go out with me, I at least wanted us to remain friends. But with each day that passed, I was losing more and more hope about even that possibility. So when she came by and said, "So when and what time are you pickin' me up?" I was surprised.

I looked at her for a long couple of seconds. "What was that?" I finally asked.

She put her hands on her hips and tilted her head to the side. Her feline eyes slit just a fraction.

"I know you didn't forget about asking me out."

I smiled on the outside and screamed Hallelujah on the inside. "Oh," I said, keeping my cool. "That's right. I did ask you out—about a year ago."

"Oh, you got jokes," she quipped, stepping into the office and closing the door.

"Every now and then," I answered.

"Well OK, Mr. Funny Man, when and what time?"

"Does that mean your answer is yes?"

"You know, I can leave now." She turned toward the door.

Quickly, I said, "Seven-thirty on Friday. Denzel's movie starts at ten. I figured we could do dinner before then."

"Oh, how you know I wanna see a movie?"

"I heard you talking about it, for my benefit, with your friend on the phone."

Latrice smiled an innocent smile. "Did I do that?" she asked in a high-pitched Steve Urkel-like whine.

I laughed and shook my head. "So now you've got the jokes."

"Oh, I have 'nuff jokes."

"So seven-thirty on Friday is cool?"

"Yeah. But before we set this in stone, I need to ask you something."

"Shoot."

"Why'd you ask me out?"

"Why?"

"Did I stutter? And don't answer my question with a question."

I nodded slowly. "Because I wanted to hang out with you outside of work," I said honestly. I left out that she was fine and I wanted to get to know her on a more intimate level.

"I've never dated a white guy before," she said, staring at me seriously. "Not once. I've never even come close."

"I guess I'm lucky."

"Mmm hmm. I'm not really attracted to white men. They usually don't stimulate me."

"And I do?" I said, enjoying her candor.

"Let's just say you're not as dull as the rest of them."

"Let's just."

"So tell me, do you like all women, or does my skin color fascinate you?"

"First of all, I love all women. And second, if you're asking me if I asked you out because I was curious, the answer is no. You wouldn't be the first black woman I've ever gone out with."

"I see. And you just want to hang out outside of work, huh?"

"That's right. But let me ask you something. Why did you say yes?"

Latrice licked her lips and passed her hand through her braided hair. "Did you want me to say no?"

I shook my head. "You know the answer to that, and don't answer my question with a question."

"Humph," she said with another smile.

"Was it my color that you were curious about?"

"No." She stepped toward me. "Like I said, you're not as dull as the rest of them. And you're kind of cute."

"Kind of?"

"Kind of."

I laughed. "Well, you're kind of cute, too."

Latrice sucked her teeth. "Please. I know you like what you see."

Neither one of us could hold back our laughter. Latrice removed a card from her purse and handed it to me.

"My cell number is on there. Call me for directions." She turned around and opened the door.

"Just for directions?" I asked.

Latrice looked at me over her shoulder and said, "You have the number." Conversation over, she walked out, leaving me alone with the cleaning crew. Since getting her number, we'd spoken every night. And like high school sweethearts, we talked until the early hours of the morning, which we only regretted when we had to wake up for work the next day. Latrice and I clicked better than I even thought we would. Friday wasn't coming fast enough for me.

Latrice
11

When my doorbell rang, I had to force my hands to stop shaking. I was that nervous. Not so much about being on a date, which I hadn't been on in a while, but more the fact that I was going out with Vic—a white man. If my mother knew what I was doing, she'd scream murder. I'm sure Danita was watching me from above, just shaking her head and frowning with disapproval. I know I would have been the same way if the shoe were on the other foot.

Being attracted to Vic was something I never would have imagined happening. But as the saying goes—never say never. And what I said to Vic was true; he wasn't like the others. His upbringing had a lot to do with that. He grew up just like I did—one parent, poor, and determined. That's what set him apart from most of the white men that I knew. It didn't hurt that his adoptive mother was a black woman, and that he had an appreciation for black culture.

I put my hand on the doorknob and took a deep breath. *Alright girl, you said yes. You can do this. His skin color don't mean a thing.* I exhaled and opened the door. With a Brad Pitt-like smile, Vic held out a bouquet of red roses and said, "Hey Latrice."

I took the roses and inhaled their sweet fragrance. "Hey yourself."

I watched Vic's eyes as he admired my outfit. I knew I was looking good. I had on a black skirt short enough to show off my legs, which I was extremely proud of, a red v-neck top, to accentuate the right amount of my ample cleavage, and a string of pearls Danita bought me once. I wore a pair of black pumps on my feet. I hid my smile as he smiled.

"You look good, Latrice."

"Good, huh?" I stepped to the side for him to come in. When he walked past me, I took a moment to check out what he had on; black pants with a baby-blue button down shirt, covered by a black blazer. On his feet he wore a pair of black leather shoes. His outfit was simple and manly, and he looked damn sexy in it. "You look good, too," I said.

He thanked me and then commented on my place. "Whew, Latrice. You have a nice set-up. Is that a Kebo Kante?" He walked over to where my cherry entertainment center sat with my thirty-six inch TV set, and looked at the framed photograph on the wall, titled *Legs*. It was nothing more than a photo of a woman's shapely legs extended into the air and crossed at the ankles. I was impressed that he knew who had taken the photograph.

"I'm impressed. Not many people know about him."

"You mean not many *White* people?"

"No, I mean not many people. *But*, if you *want* to go there, then yes, not many White people either."

"I have a couple of his prints. Photography was always a passion of my mother's. She used to have a Polaroid that she took everywhere she went. I mean, she would snap photos of anything—fire hydrants, kids playing, birds on a fence. I get my love of photography from her. I first ran into Kebo Kante's work when I was in California for a business meeting with my other company. I went to the Oakland Museum and was mesmerized when I saw his work."

"His work is very expressive. He says a lot with the lens."

"Yes, he does. I'm a big fan of his photomontage on wood. I have his book on it."

"I have that one on my coffee table. I have two more of his photographs. One in my bedroom, and the other in the bathroom."

"Why did you pick this one?"

"I used to be very heavy until a couple of years ago."

Vic's eyes widened. "It's true," I suppressed a proud smile. "I was a very healthy girl."

"And what happened? Not that I'm complaining."

"My best friend, who was like my sister, passed away. I was so depressed I just couldn't eat, couldn't sleep—could barely function. One day, I got a really good look at myself in the mirror and saw for the first time how much I'd taken off. That day I decided to join the gym. The rest is history. So that particular photo is symbolic to me in the sense that never in a million years would I have thought that I would look the way I do today."

"Well, if my opinion matters, your legs are the ones that should be framed."

I smiled and batted my eyelashes "Flattery will get you everywhere."

Vic gave another Brad Pitt smile, and then moved to my CD collection. "You like a lot of music, I see."

"Music is what helps me wind down after a long day."

"Speaking of long," he said, turning toward me. "You ready for a long night?"

An hour later, we were sitting in the Rusty Scupper having dinner. Swallowing a sip of my lemonade, I said, "This place is nice. I've never been here. My girl, Danita, the one who passed away, came here. She told me all about how fancy it was." I looked through the glass to the ocean below us. I was definitely feeling the romantic mood created by the candlelight and piano music. We talked for a while, mostly about work and all of the changes going on with the company, until our food came. After we finished eating, we ordered cheesecake slices.

"I'm going to have to work double time to get these calories off."

"You won't have to work that hard. You hardly ate."

"I should have ordered the catfish instead of the steak, but I was just craving some red meat."

"It's not always a bad thing to give in to cravings every now and then."

"Mmm hmm," I said, getting the message.

We looked at each other for a hot second. Finally, Vic said, "Latrice, why don't you have a man?"

"What do you mean by that?"

"I mean, why isn't someone as attractive as yourself attached? What are the men doing wrong?"

I'm glad my skin is the color of dark chocolate, or else he would have seen me blush. "I was involved with someone, up until about a year ago."

"If you don't mind me asking, what happened?"

I shrugged my shoulders. "It just wasn't the right time, and we weren't the right people."

"I know exactly what you mean," Vic said.

"But things always have a way of working out. I mean, let's face it, had he and I not broken up, you and I wouldn't be here tonight."

Vic smiled. "We better toast to our good fortune then."

We smiled and held each other's gaze for a few seconds; there was some definite chemistry going on.

"Just out of curiosity, have you heard from him since?" Vic asked.

I shook my head. "No. He's with someone else now."

"Good for him."

I couldn't help but smile. "It's nice to see you care...about his feelings."

"Hey, he's a fellow male."

"Part of the male brotherhood, huh?"

"Exactly."

"So anyway, since you asked me the personal 4-1-1... What's up with you and your wife? Why the divorce?"

Vic cleared his throat. "It wasn't working out."

"What wasn't working out? You got married...it's not always going to work out."

"I wasn't happy."

"Oh, that's different then. Why weren't you happy?"

"Honestly, I initially married her because she was pregnant. I wanted to do right by the baby. I didn't want it growing up being split between two homes."

"And what? You changed your mind?"

"No. She miscarried."

I said quietly, "I'm sorry to hear that."

"Yeah. It was hard when it happened."

I sighed. "I got pregnant by my ex after my girl died. But with the stress, I lost it. That wasn't an easy thing to deal with. I know your wife must've taken it hard."

"Yeah, she did. But I made sure to be there, to help her through it."

"And you're still not happy?"

"Nope."

"And what will it take to make you happy?"

"An exceptional woman."

"I see. Have anyone in mind?"

"Just might."

"I see. So she could be exceptional, huh?"

"I'm sure she could be."

"Could?"

"I'm sure she would be."

"Mmm hmm. And why did you ask me out again?"

Vic laughed, and I followed suit. I was enjoying our flirtation. We went back and forth, dancing around what we both knew we wanted. After paying for the check and leaving a generous tip, we left and went back to my place, where words were no longer needed. On the way there, I wondered if I could actually go through with being intimate with Vic. I couldn't help but wonder if he would be able to get me going like so many brothers had. I was nervous, but curious. My apprehension quickly disappeared when he placed his lips on mine. From that moment, it was on. I caressed the tongue he offered, and gave mine readily. Before we could reach the bedroom, our clothes were off and scattered in a trail on the floor. When we finally reached the bed, we were already sweating and breathing heavily. I don't know about him, but it had been a while for me. As he slid inside of me, all concerns about a white man's size and length flew out the window. While Vic worked some magic I had rarely experienced with even the finest of brothers, I let myself go and enjoyed the ride. I didn't stop riding until we both reached our destination.

Colin
12

There are a few things of mine no one should ever mess with: my family, my friends, my job, my possessions, and definitely not my groove. Messing with my groove is like a cardinal sin, punishable only by death. So when I was getting my groove on with Tanecia, who I had scribbled back into my book of fame, and my doorbell rang, I was ready to go to jail. I tried to ignore the bell at first, but then the knocking started. When my phone went off and I saw who was calling, I was through. I turned my ringer off and ignored the knocking, which went on for another couple of minutes. After it stopped, I threw my all into Tanecia until I released. When she finally went home, after showering in my damn bathroom, I changed the sheets then picked up the phone and hit speed dial one.

"Vic, are you crazy?" I yelled when he answered. "Don't you understand that when someone doesn't answer the door or the phone, they must be busy? What the hell were you thinkin', dog?"

"My bad," Vic said. "I figured you were sleeping."

"Sleeping? Hell no, I wasn't sleeping! Dog, I had Tanecia in here. She was riding me like a champ. Man, you nearly screwed that up for me—again."

"Tanecia was there? The one who called you a dog? Damn, how'd you swing that?"

"Dog, you forget...I am Colin Ray. Ain't a woman that can resist me. And believe me, I settled that dog shit quick. I laid some lines on her and it was over. She's back in the book. Now, again, what did you want? I need to catch some Z's."

"Maaan! Colin, man!"

"What?"

"Man, I was with Latrice tonight."

"I know, fool. You told me and Roy you were going out with her."

"No, man. I mean I was *with* her."

"Oh. For real? You hit it?"

"Twice." Vic laughed out loud. I couldn't help but smile.

"Twice? Damn, it was that good?"

"Better. You think you were being ridden like a champ? Man..."

I couldn't hold back my laughter. I was happy that he had finally gotten some.

"Man, that's good that you got some ass, because you were one wound up fool these past couple of weeks. I bet you let all that stress out, huh?"

"Hell yeah, man. I was like a volcano."

"Right, right." I yawned. "So is that what you wanted, dog? 'Cause I can't front... I'm a worn-out nigga right about now. I need my beauty rest."

"Yeah, that's all man. We're hooking up again tomorrow night."

I yawned and rubbed my eyes.

"That's good," I said. I could barely keep my eyes open. It was time for me to dream. "Yo, before I fall asleep on you, I'ma be out. I'll holla at you tomorrow."

"A'ight man. Tomorrow then."

"Peace." I hung up the phone and got under the covers. I was asleep before the sheep count reached ten.

Latrice
13

"*Girl,* I have to skip the gym tonight."

"Skip the gym?" Emily asked. "You never skip the gym. You OK? Is something wrong?"

"Girl, I am better than OK. Vic is taking me to an exhibit at the museum tonight."

"You're going out with him again? Damn, you guys have been at it for about four months now. Don't you two get tired of one another? I mean you see him at work, too."

I sucked my teeth and applied my lipstick. I was excited for the date tonight. Kebo Kante was having a special showing of his work at the museum in DC. Vic found out about it through a friend of his. Getting tickets last minute the way he did, I figured he had to have gotten them illegally, but I didn't ask. All that mattered was that he got them, and he wanted to take me. Being with Vic made my day. I loved the spirited conversations we had. More importantly, I loved the fact that he could hold his own against my attitude and stubbornness. It was nice to be around a man who wasn't intimidated by me. Four months wasn't nearly long enough.

"Girl, I don't get tired of him at all. Besides, since we started talking we don't see each other at work like that anymore. We figured it'd be better that way, so no one is all in our business."

"Good move. I know all about nosy people and the rumors they like to spread. I deal with that twenty-four seven at the office."

"Oh, I know you do."

"So you think he could be the one?"

"I don't know about the one—yet. But Em', Vic is caring, intelligent, sensitive, and fun to be with."

"And his being white doesn't bother you?"

"Girl, he has rhythm." I laughed out loud and then did one last double take in the mirror. I was looking good. I had on a long, black dress that snuggled against my curves, and earlier that day I'd had my braids re-done.

"Seriously though, the color issue is dead. He's just a good man."

"Well, I still haven't met him."

"Girl, I know. You will, though. Soon."

"I'm not pressed. Just want to check him out. Anyway, I'm glad you like him, and I'm glad that race isn't an issue," Emily said. She sighed then. I turned off the bathroom light and walked into the living room. I felt bad. Emily had broken up with her man just a week before I first went out with Vic. I knew she was lonely, and hearing about my good fortune wasn't exactly her idea of fun.

"Hey, girl, why don't we skip the gym tomorrow and go on a shopping spree during the day?"

"Sure, we can do that. What about tomorrow night? You doing anything?"

I hesitated before I answered. "Yeah… I'm going out with Vic tomorrow night."

Emily sighed. "Oh…OK."

There was silence for a few seconds, and then I said, “Hey, instead of waiting, why don’t you join us tomorrow night?”

“What, and be the third wheel? I don’t think so.”

“No, girl. Vic has a friend, Colin, who I heard would be interested in meeting you.”

Emily’s voice picked up when she asked, “He cute?”

“You know I wouldn’t set you up with no dog. Besides, Vic calls him a pretty boy.”

“Pretty boy? You know I like my men a little rough around the edges.”

“Girl, you going or not? Let me know. Vic is gonna be here soon.”

Emily huffed, but I could tell she was excited. “Yeah, I’ll go. As long as Vic’s friend is down.”

“Oh he is, girl.”

As I hung up the phone, I shook my head. From what I’d heard about Colin, he seemed like a cool guy. Vic said they were boys since junior high school. I hoped Vic could convince him to go out on a blind date. When Vic rang my bell, I decided not to beat around the bush.

“I told my girl Emily that she could come out with us tomorrow night. I hope you don’t mind.”

Vic looked at me and smiled. I loved his pretty boy smile. “It’s cool. Gives me a chance to meet her. I feel like I know her, as much as you talk about her.”

“Emily is cool. You and her are a lot alike. A lot.”

“Cool. I hope she doesn’t mind being the third wheel,” Vic said, slipping my coat around my shoulders. It was October and chilly.

Without looking at him, I said, "Oh, she's not going to be the third wheel."

"Oh, she's not? She has a date?"

"Yeah."

"That's cool. Leaves me free to put all my attention on you. Is her date a nice guy? I know you said she just recently broke up with her man."

I closed and locked my front door and without looking at him said, "He sounds nice. At least from the way you describe him."

Vic stopped walking when I said that. I continued on to the car. From behind me, I heard Vic say, "The way I describe him? What do you mean by that?" He hurried up to me and touched my shoulder. "Latrice... what did you mean, from the way I describe him?"

My shoulders slumped. "I told her that your friend Colin wanted to take her out."

Vic stared at me and raised an eyebrow. "You what?"

"Vic, she asked me what I was doing, and when I said we were going out, she sounded so down. I couldn't leave her hanging, so I told her your friend wanted to take her out. I'm sorry, boo. It just sort of slipped out."

"Slipped out? I'd say it slipped out. Latrice, as much as I care about you, there is no way I'm going to set your girl up with Colin."

"Why?" I asked, resting my hands on my hips. "What? You think I'll set your boy up with some fugly-ass chick?"

"No, Latrice. I know you wouldn't. It's just that...well...you wouldn't understand."

"Well, then help me understand." I got in his Eclipse. I was getting angry. Emily was my girl, and I wanted to help her out. I would have expected Vic to go along with that without a problem. When he got in I said, "What? You think Emily isn't good enough for your friend?"

"Latrice, I'm not worried about her being good enough. That's the least of my worries."

"So what is it, then?"

"Latrice, Colin is my boy, but he is a player's player. He is interested in only one thing from a woman. It wouldn't be right of me to set her up with Colin. Besides, he would never go for a blind date. Colin is way too stuck on himself to go there like that."

"Look, Emily is a big girl, and can handle herself. I'm sure she's dealt with men like Colin before. All I want is for her to get out of the house and enjoy herself. He doesn't have to take her out again."

"I'm telling you, Colin would never go for it."

"You saying that he wouldn't be willing to do one small favor for his boy?"

"No, I'm not saying that."

"Well, good. It's settled then. We'll go out for a bite to eat, and then go dancing. Your boy can dance, can't he?"

Vic grumbled and then started the ignition. I dropped the last bomb on him.

"Oh, by the way, Emily is white. But she's like you. She has soul. Anyway, I'm sure her skin color won't be a problem for Colin."

Vic looked at me and shook his head. With a smile, I turned on his radio. I know he wanted to protest even more, but I wasn't trying to hear it. I had to get Emily out the house. As Janet Jackson sang about how it didn't really matter, I nodded my head. It didn't really matter to me one way or the other how his friend felt. All I knew was he better show up for the date. Vic drove the car and didn't say a word until we got to the museum. The rest of the date went as smooth as silk. That night, we capped it off with another bout of headboard-banging sex. In the morning, as he was leaving, I reminded him to talk to his friend.

Vic
14

"Somebody slap Vic and wake him up! Man, you have got to be trippin'!"

I lowered my head and mumbled, "No, man. I'm not tripping."

"Roy, please tell this boy he better go out and find some lonely fool that has no plans and no life, because the one thing I don't do are blind dates."

Roy looked at me shrugged his shoulders. "You knew he'd say that," he said. I gave him a cross look, thanking him for his input and then looked back to Colin.

"Colin man, just do this one favor for me. I don't always come to you like this. It's only for a couple of hours."

"Vic, save your begging for somebody else. There is no way in hell I am going out on some blind date."

"Colin, come on... Don't act like I've never done shit before for you. Just do this for me, man. Believe me, it wasn't my idea. Please. Latrice already told her friend you wanted to take her out." Colin stared at me. I cracked my knuckles. I knew what his reaction was going to be. I knew it the moment Latrice let me know that Colin saying no wasn't an option. I had as much chance getting him to agree to go as Mike Tyson had winning a humanitarian of the year award. My only hope was that somehow he would do what he always said he would, and have my back. I looked at Roy and without words, asked for some help. Roy looked at me and put his palms in the air. I gave him another thanks-for-nothing look.

"Vic, you better tell your girl to tell her friend she was mistaken. Because you are shit out of luck asking me to go."

Colin swallowed the rest of his hot dog and picked up his bags; he was ready to go. We were in the mall checking out some females and buying a few things in the process.

I looked again to Roy, who was swallowing the last of his chilidog. Finally, he cleared his throat and said, "Colin, can't you do him this one favor? He would do it for you. You know that."

I nodded my head emphatically. Roy continued on. "All he's asking for is one night, man. Help him out."

Colin looked over at Roy. "Nigga, did you drink from the same well that fool was drinkin' from? You really expect me to go on some blind date, and set my self up to be sittin' next to some ugly chick?"

I said quickly, "Yo, Latrice said that her friend is cute."

"Of course she did! What? You think she's gonna admit that her friend could probably run neck and neck with a pit-bull? Man, she's setting her friend up on a blind date. What do you think that means?"

"She wouldn't say her friend was cute if she wasn't. Come on, Colin. Remember when I had your back when that girl you met at DC Live tried to go off on you? Who was there to back up your lies? Who was there when you set up two dates on the same night and forgot about them? Man, just do this one thing for me."

Colin seethed. "Why you gonna bring up old shit? Man, at least I didn't ask you to go out with some chick you ain't never seen before. I wouldn't do that to you, dog. Friends don't do that to each other."

Roy cleared his throat again. "Colin," he said, "I hear where you're coming from, but I have to say, man, friends would help their friends when they're in a bind."

"Man, go and buy another chilidog," Colin said, walking away. I looked at Roy and frowned. Then my eyes widened; he knew what I was thinking.

Very quickly, he said, "Hey, I might be having problems, but I'm still married. Don't even think about it."

Damn. How was I going to tell Latrice that Colin wouldn't go? I sighed.

Roy came up to me and patted me on the shoulder. "Who knows, maybe having a third wheel won't be so bad."

I groaned and then, from a few steps ahead of us, Colin stopped walking. He didn't turn around as he said, "I'll be by your place at seven. But Vic, I swear you are gonna owe me big time for this."

I went up to my boy and extended my hands. "Thanks, man. I knew you wouldn't leave me hanging."

He took my hand and gave me a pound. "No, you *hoped* and *prayed* I wouldn't leave you hanging."

"Yeah, that too."

We laughed, and then Roy said, "See Vic, you were wrong. He just might have a decent bone in his body."

"Yeah, OK big boy," Colin said. "You may want to lay off the chilidogs from now on, or else Stacey is going to kick your ass out."

"'Bruh, please. With each day that goes by, she falls more and more in love with my love-belly." Roy laughed, and so did I.

But I had to admit, "Roy, you are putting on some weight there."

"Fellas... I have a wife, two little girls, and a mortgage. I think I'm entitled. Besides, your asses aren't the ones I'm lying next to at night. So as long as my wife approves, I have nothing to worry about."

The three of us laughed and chilled in the mall for another half-hour. Then we left to prepare for the evening ahead. Roy went to rent a couple of movies for his family, Colin went to make a few backup calls for after the blind date, and I went home to chill and get ready. I still hadn't told Colin about Emily's skin color. That was not going to be pretty.

Colin
15

The only reason I agreed to go out with Vic was because he was my boy. Besides, what Roy said was true—Vic would have done it for me. But I still wasn't happy about it, because I had planned on calling Tanecia again, which would have been a real first for me, since I had just had her in my bed earlier in the week. She wasn't the smartest cookie on the planet, but she damn sure knew how to work the middle. Besides, I was horny as hell. Vic asking me to go on the blind date quickly killed that, though. I knew I was going to say yes the minute he asked me. I couldn't leave him hanging. Besides, he really seemed to be into this Latrice chick, who none of us had seen yet, and I was curious to know just how fine she was. Vic always did have good taste in women. Julie was fine, so I didn't really have any doubts that Latrice would be, too.

Shit, although I never considered dating a white female, knowing what I know now about Julie, if I could go back in time, I may have been tempted to make a play at her. Maybe. She was still white. Now, if she were a sister? No doubt I would have scooped her up without hesitation. I'm not saying I would have married her, but I would have definitely put triple stars beside her name in my book. By no means am I racist. I just love black women. It would take a lot for me to go out with a white female, no matter how bad she was.

Speaking of taking a lot, there was no way I was going to let Vic forget about my sacrifice to go on the blind date. That's something I have never done, never planned on doing, and couldn't believe I was about to do now. I'd heard too many horror stories of guys who'd heard the sweet voice over the phone and seen a beast in public. I would never let Vic live it down if his girl's friend was Medusa reincarnated. The sad thing was, all Vic could tell me was that he heard she was cute! Cute? Puppies, kittens, little kids—these are cute things. A cute woman, in my book, is nothing more than an ugly woman with a nice personality. And while a nice personality is cool, it does nothing for me in the sack. That's why I had my backup plan worked out. Instead of calling Tanecia, I called another hottie and told her I wanted to hook up later that night. I met her at the grocery store a while back. She's a fine and intelligent caramel sister, with a good job, no man, no kids, ass for weeks, and, to top it off, she's a freeeeak. She had me curling *my* toes from the sexual trip we took. The only female who comes close is Tanecia. If I weren't so unwilling to commit, maybe I'd take the time to try and find one woman to satisfy me sexually and mentally. But commitment and I go together like oil and water—we're just not compatible.

I've never been able to commit when it comes to women. That and my looks are the only traits I get from my father. He was a non-committing fool if there ever was one. That's why he and my mother never made it to the altar. Other than those similarities, we are complete opposites. Even though he's getting better in his old age, my father still has a teenager's mentality. He wouldn't recognize responsibility if it smacked him hard on the back of his bald dome. I don't remember the last time he held a steady job or had any kind of meaningful relationship with anybody other than the ho's he deals with. And I say ho's, because some of the chicks he's had, I've had.

My father's in his fifties, but looks like he's in his thirties. He doesn't know about the ladies we've shared, and they've never said a word to him. I think they like having been with the father and son. Like I said—ho's. My dad and I don't speak too often. Actually, we only speak when he calls to borrow some money. He lives in a beat-up two-bedroom apartment in DC with some crack-head looking chick named Mo. I lend him the money only because he's my Pops. Other than that, I don't deal with him. I can't say the same about my younger brother and business partner, Mike. He cut our father off from the moment he was old enough to realize what type of man he didn't want to be. He and my father haven't spoken in years. When the time comes, I doubt Mike will even visit his grave.

So, just like I play the Good Samaritan to my old man, I'm doing the same for Vic.

"I swear man, if she's ugly... you won't live this down," I said as he climbed into my Lincoln Navigator. I had just gotten the new ride a couple of weeks back, so I chose to drive. Besides, if by some slim chance Latrice's friend were in fact cute, I would at least be representing myself properly.

"She'll be all right, man. Latrice wouldn't do me like that."

"Yeah—exactly. But what would she do to me?"

"It'll be cool, man. Her friend goes with her to the gym."

"To maintain a fine figure? Or to find a figure?"

"Man. Just chill. The night's gonna be OK."

"Yeah, we'll see. So what do you have planned anyway, Romeo? And I assume you're payin', right? 'Cause I didn't bring my wallet." Vic gave me a you've-got-to-be-kidding look.

"You for real?"

"What do you mean, am I for real?" I struggled to keep from smiling. "I'm doing you a favor. You thought I was going to spend my money on someone I don't know? The real question is, are you for real?"

Vic mumbled something under his breath.

"What was that?" I asked.

Quietly, Vic said, "I got you. I just need to stop at the ATM."

I could tell by the reddening of his cheeks that he was frustrated. I couldn't hold it back any longer. I busted out laughing.

"Just kiddin', dog. Ha! I had your ass worried. Although, I should make your ass pay."

Vic smiled. "Nah."

"Yeah, OK. So anyway, what's the plan?"

"We're gonna meet them at Angelo and Maxie's Steakhouse for dinner, and then head to Zanzibar."

"Damn, man! Angelo and Maxie's? That place is not cheap. I'm not trying to spend a grip for some female I don't know."

"The food there is good, man."

"You are definitely going to owe me for this."

"Yeah, yeah. And you won't forget either."

"Damn right I won't forget."

We laughed and then got quiet. I had the volume turned up on the radio. We were both grooving to the Ja Rule and Jennifer Lopez collaboration. When the song finished, I lowered the radio.

"You know something?" I said, cruising down 295. "I don't even know this chick's name."

"Oh, my bad. I completely forgot. It's Emily."

"Emily. Funny name for a sister. Whatever. Just as long as she's not ugly." Vic was quiet for the rest of the ride, until we got to the restaurant. Since the ladies hadn't arrived yet, we decided to chill outside for a few. The night air was crisp, but bearable. I did zip my jacket up though, while Vic had his draped over his arm.

"This is about the only time I could really accuse you of being white," I said.

Vic looked at me. "What do you mean?"

"Man, I swear, it could be fifty below, and white people would still be out in shorts and t-shirts."

Vic laughed. "It's not cold, man."

"No, but it's chilly enough for a jacket. Why did you bring yours if you weren't gonna wear it?"

"Just in case I do get cold."

"That's my point... You won't get cold. Y'all never get cold. I mean, is it the lack of pigmentation that keeps y'all warm?"

Vic and I laughed, and then laughed even harder as a white couple walked by, hand in hand. They both had on shorts and sandals, but were shivering. I looked at Vic, who shrugged his shoulders.

We stood outside for another twenty minutes; the ladies still hadn't showed. I was ready to leave.

"Man, are you sure they're coming?"

"They're women. They'll be here."

I exhaled. I could never stand a woman that took forever to get ready. I turned around and looked down F Street, and saw two women strolling in our direction. One was a fine sister, with a body that made me go, "Mmm mmm." The other was a white female, with an equally fine body and cornrows.

"I'll tell you what," I said, rubbing my palms together. "If your chick and her friend don't get here soon, I may have to scoop up that fine sister coming this way."

Vic turned around. "That's them."

I looked down F Street again. "Who's them?"

"Latrice and Emily."

I stared at the two women. Keeping my eye on them, I said, "Vic... one of those females is white." When he didn't say anything, I turned and faced him. "Vic. One of those females is white," I said again.

Vic cleared his throat and looked down.

"Aww, man! I can't believe this shit! How are you gonna do me like this, man? I'm supposed to be your boy. Man, you know I don't date white females."

In a low voice, Vic said, "Man, I know. I'm sorry I didn't tell you. But I knew you wouldn't have come if you knew."

"Damn right I wouldn't have come. Damn!"

"It's only one night, man."

"Vic, I don't date white females. Not even attractive ones."

"Man, it's just dinner."

"Yeah, and then you're talkin' about Zanzibar afterwards. 'Bruh, have you lost your mind? As many females, no, sisters, as I know, what you think is going to happen when I stroll in the club with a white girl on my arm? Man! Are you tryin' to take me out of the game?"

"Colin man, I'm sorry."

"Oh, you're sorry a'ight," I started. But I was interrupted before I could say another word.

"Baby!" Latrice said, walking up to Vic and kissing him. "Sorry we're so late. But you know we had to make sure we looked good."

Keeping his eyes on me, Vic said, "It's cool. We haven't been here too long." Then he looked at her and said, "It was worth the wait anyway. You are looking damn good."

Latrice smiled and said, "Don't I know it." Then she turned toward me and extended her hand.

"We've never met, but as much as Vic talks about his boys, I feel like I know you already. Latrice Meadows."

I shook her hand and forced a smile. "Colin Ray. Nice to finally meet the woman who's been drivin' my boy insane." I looked at Vic with a deadpan glare.

Latrice smiled and said, "Nice to meet you too." Then she took her friend's arm and pulled her forward.

"Excuse me for being rude. Everyone, this is Emily. Emily, this fine man on the left is Vic, who you already know all about. And this brother, as you heard, is Colin."

Emily smiled at Vic, and said, "To repeat the sentiments of your friend, it's nice to finally meet the one who's been driving my girl insane." Everyone laughed, except for me. Then Emily turned to me and extended her hand.

"Nice to meet you, Colin."

It seemed as though time stood still while I contemplated my move. Being the creative side, the right side of my brain was telling me to jet, hook up with Denise, and do something truly artistic.

Unfortunately, the analytical side was reasoning with me. I couldn't leave my friend hanging like that—although he had done that to me by not telling me about Emily.

I took her hand in mine and said, "Likewise, Emily." When I let go, I gave another cross look at Vic, and then said, "Why don't we go inside." *Because I don't want anyone to recognize me*, I wanted to add. But I kept that thought to myself, and thought about my backup plan later on. But believe it or not, it never happened.

Latrice
16

"*You* what?" I said, sitting up in the bed. Vic was snuggling next to me, and I quickly remembered to keep my voice down. But it was hard to do, especially after what Emily just told me. "What did you just say, girl?"

"I said I just slept with Colin. He just left my place."

I got out of the bed and went into the living room, where I wouldn't have to worry about being quiet. Sitting on my sofa, I said, "Girl, why did you do that? I told you what a dog he was."

"Latrice, I appreciate you looking out for me, but seriously, I'm a big girl."

"Oh, you're big, huh? Big enough to sleep with a dog like Colin, right?"

"That's right, Latrice. I am that big."

I sucked my teeth. I was mad. Colin was a nice guy, but I could tell he was the type of brother who liked to hit and run. He was fine, there was no doubt about that, and successful, but like Vic said, he was a player; that made him ugly in my book. I was disappointed in Emily.

"Damn Em' I know you were horny, but why'd you go out like that? You only met him once. And that was last week. Speaking of which, how the hell did you hook up with him, anyway? I don't remember you two exchanging numbers, and I know he didn't ask Vic for it, because Vic didn't ask me."

"We exchanged numbers the night we all went out. We've been speaking since then."

"When? I don't remember seeing that. And what do you mean speaking?"

"We traded numbers while you and Vic were getting your freak on at Zanzibar. And I mean speaking as in on the phone—every day since Saturday."

I stood up and went to the window. I looked out to the quiet neighborhood before me. I'm sure if I opened my window, my voice, along with the crickets, would be the only sound that could be heard. I couldn't believe they had been talking and she hadn't said anything.

"Why are you now telling me this?"

"Didn't want to say anything until I knew it was real."

"Real? Girl, how many different females' numbers you think he has?"

"Latrice, I don't care about them. Why are you giving me such a hard time over this? I thought you would be happy that I'm happy. You're the one who's always saying I need to go out and find a man to release some stress with. I finally do that, and now you're tripping."

"Em'" I turned away from the window. "I said find a man. Not a dog. Girl, I just think you're better than the tricks Colin has probably hooked up with. I don't want you to be another notch on the bedpost for him."

"Latrice, I love you, but I am really capable of taking care of myself. Besides, how do you know I'm not more than another notch? How do you know he doesn't like me like that? We talk throughout the day... we talk until the late hours of the night. How do you know something couldn't be happening with us?"

"Please, Em'," I said, sitting back on the couch. "Don't even go there. Men like Colin are not capable of being in any kind of a relationship past a sexual one. Now, if you want to be in that kind of a relationship, you go right ahead. But don't even try to think it could lead to anything more than that."

"Latrice, you may not want to believe this, but I think Colin really likes me. We've shared some deep things this week."

"Please. Like he doesn't have some of those things rehearsed for other women."

"Stop being so negative!" Emily said harshly. It actually made me stop moving and stare at my phone. Emily continued before I could go off on her for defending a dog. "Do you know that he wasn't happy when he first saw me?"

"Why?"

"Because I'm white."

"White? Vic is white."

"He's never dated a white woman before."

"How do you know? I find that hard to believe."

"Because he told me so."

"Don't be so naïve, Emily. For real. You know how brothers do nowadays."

"I'm not naive. What he said was true."

"So, if he doesn't like going out with white women, why'd he come?"

"Because your man never told him I was white. He said if Vic had told him, he never would have agreed to come. Which, by the way, means you were lying to me when you said he wanted to go out with me."

I huffed into the receiver. I had been busted. "Sorry, girl. I just wanted you out of the house."

"I forgive you. I wouldn't have met Colin if it weren't for your lie, anyway."

"You can't like him like that, Em'. You don't want to like a man like him."

"Latrice..." Emily said, warning me.

"OK, OK. Not another negative comment." *Out loud*, I thought. I still wasn't happy about it. And I would be sure to let Vic know about it.

"Do you know he had another date lined up for later that evening?"

"I told you girl, men like that—"

"He'd never done a blind date before Latrice," Emily snapped, cutting me off. "He had another date lined up in case I was ugly. I would have done the same thing. Either that or pretended to be sick."

"Oh, I've done that before."

"See. So why are you getting on him?"

I didn't say anything, because she had me there.

"He's been really honest with me Latrice. That's what I like about him. He doesn't beat around the bush. And he's not fake. He knows I know about his player's card. And he doesn't try to hide that."

"So why you wanna waste your time..."

"Latrice..."

"I mean, are you sure you want to get involved with Colin?"

"Girl, I'm not sure of what exactly I want right now. But I do know this... I'm comfortable talking to Colin. We have great conversations. And I have to be honest... he is no joke in bed. He earned his degree."

"Girl," I said smiling. "You know you gonna have to give me those details."

"I will. Later. I'm tired right now. And if I plan on going to work tomorrow, I better get some sleep. I just wanted to call and tell you what happened, before Colin told Vic."

"Give me a taste, girl," I pleaded. "You know how I am."

Emily laughed like I hadn't heard her laugh in a while. "All right. But this is all I'm giving you for now."

"Until later," I said.

"Yeah, until later. Anyway, I am not exaggerating when I say that the brother is skilled with the tongue. See you tomorrow, Latrice."

Before I could beg for more, Emily hung up the phone. As I stood up, Vic called my name. I walked into the bedroom, and stared at my sexy man, who was propped up on his elbows.

"You were on the phone?" he said, looking at the time.

"Yeah. Emily called me. You were knocked out and didn't hear it ring." I put the phone back in the base, climbed into bed and straddled him. I could feel him start to grow almost instantly. I liked that I had that effect on him.

"Is there a problem?" he asked, taking one of my breasts in his hand. I moaned; I loved the way he caressed me.

"There better not be," I said softly.

"What do you mean?" he said, taking me into his mouth.

"I mean Colin better not be trying to dog my girl. They've been talking. And she just had sex with him."

Vic stopped his sucking and squeezing and looked at me.

"What did you say?"

"I said your boy, who doesn't like white girls, has been talking to Emily, and just sexed her around the town."

Vic opened his mouth to speak, but I put my index finger on his lips. "We'll talk about that later," I whispered. His throbbing had me wet. I moved from on top of him, and removed my shirt and underwear. Lying back on the bed, I opened my legs and exposed all of my flesh to him. Following the calling of my finger, he removed his pants and eased his way in between my thighs. We kissed as his sex rubbed up against mine. Never removing his mouth from mine, he attempted to guide himself into my sweetness. But before he could, I stopped him and shook my head. I pointed to my cavern as he looked at me.

"Those lips want a kiss too."

He nodded and then made his way down. When we were both satisfied, we lay in each other's arms. I'm sure Colin was good, but Vic was a master in his own right.

Colin
17

As soon as Vic opened his door, I knew he knew. Damn. And then, when I walked in and saw Roy staring at me, I knew he knew, too. Double damn. I walked in, took my leather coat off and threw it on the couch beside me as I sat down. Nobody said a word. The TV was on and set to FOX for the game. I grabbed a beer, opened it, and took a long sip. Roy and Vic continued to stare at me; the move was mine to make.

I stared at the TV; John Madden and Pat Summerall were giving the pre-game hype for the Redskins-Cowboys second match-up for the year. I tried to focus on the screen and ignore the attention I was getting. But I knew there was no way to do that.

"OK," I said as a commercial came on. "Yeah, I hooked up with Emily last night."

"Man!" Vic said turning off the TV. "How the hell did that happen, Mr. I-don't-date-white-females?"

"Yeah," Roy added. "How the hell did it happen? Because from what Vic was telling me, you were ready to go to blows when you saw her."

I looked at my boys and shook my head. "Man, will you turn the TV back on."

"Forget the game," Vic said. "The Cowboys are going to kick ass again, anyway. The game is the least important thing right now."

"When did you find out?" I asked.

"She called Latrice at 3:00 this morning."

Damn. She told her girl that quick. I sighed. Hooking up with Emily was the last thing I would have ever expected happening, especially after I saw her. I wanted to snap on Vic for real. It's not that I have anything against white women; it's just that I was always brought up to respect and cherish black women. From my mother, to my grandmother, black women were always the queens. And I was supposed to be the proud and strong king. I may hold top seat in playerville, but I always ran my game on the sisters. I never strayed—until that night. I don't know how it happened, but somehow I ended up having one of the best times I'd had in a long time. Maybe the fact that Emily was down for a white female had something to do with my digging her. I don't know. All I know is as the night went on, Emily's race became unimportant to me. I was feeling her on a level I had never felt. Emily was cool, and I couldn't front, she had a fine body and ass that most white women just don't have. I was also feeling the cornrows in her hair. But more than her body, or her light blue eyes, which seemed to sparkle, or the rows, I was really feeling her mindset. She was intelligent and had some positive and insightful thoughts on a number of topics ranging from race and religion, to the worth of women in society, and amazingly enough, the plight of the black dating experience in the 2000's—especially for women.

We were chilling by the bar at Zanzibar, while Latrice and Vic were out on the dance floor. Although I enjoyed the conversation at the restaurant, I was reluctant to go out on the dance floor with her. And even though I watched her shaking her hips smoothly to a Missy Elliott groove, I still wasn't willing to see if she could hold her own on the floor. I also didn't want anyone who knew me to see me with her like that. That was like death for a brother, because when black women saw a brother with a white female, he could forget about being respected. So I was content to just chill and talk to her while I had a beer and Emily had a Long Island Iced Tea. We were joking about a skinny brother dancing with a woman who could probably have eaten him and had seconds, when out of the blue Emily said, "Colin, I know you don't want to dance with me because I'm white. So if you see a good looking black woman, you can go ahead and make your player move."

I looked at her. "What makes you think that?"

"Oh please. You think I didn't see how uncomfortable you were earlier when you first saw me? I'm not blind, you know. Nor am I stupid. But it's all good."

I couldn't hold back my smile. She had seen right through me; I was impressed. "Is it?" I asked.

"Yeah it is. Because I understand how hard it is for black men to legitimately talk to women of another race."

"Oh, do you?" I turned and faced her. "And how do you understand that?"

"Oh, come on. It's common knowledge that black women can't stand when a black man talks to a woman outside of their race. They catch immediate attitudes when they see that. And when that happens, it's all over for the brother. Because no matter how sweet or sensitive or positive he may be, he is nothing but a sell out in the eyes of the sisters. That's not fair to the man."

I sipped on my Heineken and stroked my goatee. "I see," I said, intrigued by her understanding.

"But can you blame them for being upset about it? I mean, if you ask the sisters where all the good black men are, they'll tell you they're with white women. The majority of them feel that way. So can you really blame them when they give attitude?"

Emily shook her head. I liked the way her cornrows dangled behind her neck. "Unh-uh. I don't blame them at all. I sympathize with them, actually."

"Sympathize? How is that?"

"Look at me Colin. It's obvious that I'm no average, run-of-the-mill white girl. I grew up in the projects in New York. Really, I'm no different from Latrice, which is why we get along so well."

"OK. But you still haven't told me how you sympathize with black women."

"I understand their frustration, because whenever Latrice and I go out, I'm always the one the brothers stare at first."

"And that frustrates you?"

"Yeah, it does. See, I know that I'm not ugly, but I also know that I'm not as attractive as Latrice. The only reason brothers give me play is because of my skin color. That's frustrating to me because, one, I don't want to be admired for my skin color, and two, I don't like to see a beautiful woman like Latrice get picked second because of my skin color. So I sympathize with black woman and their annoyance over brothers who pass them up."

I drank some more of my beer. I didn't say a word for a little while as I thought about what she'd said. She had definitely impressed me. A few minutes later, Latrice and Vic came over for a break.

"Girl, I need to use the bathroom," Latrice said, taking Emily's arm. "Come on. We'll be back."

When they left, Vic looked at me. Beads of sweat were trickling down his forehead. This was our first moment alone all night.

"So, you gettin' your groove on, huh?" I asked, handing him a napkin. He took it and wiped his face.

"Yeah, man. We always get it on like that. Latrice can shake that ass for sure."

"I bet she can," I said.

"So what's up, man? What do you think of her?"

"Oh, she's cool, dog. Real cool. I'll be honest; I was shocked she was as fine as she was. It's not that I thought you would end up with an ugly chick. It's just that, despite her color, Julie was high on my scale of measurement for females. I didn't think you were going to come as close to surpassing her as you have. You and Latrice seem to fit pretty well, too. She has the right amount of attitude to match your personality. I'm happy for you, dog. You have my approval."

Vic shook his head. "That's cool, man. But that's not who I was talking about. I meant Emily."

"Emily?"

"Yeah."

I sipped on my beer and shrugged my shoulders. After all of the hollering I did about not being into white women, I decided not to tell him that I was intrigued.

"She's a'ight. Nothin' special. Typical, you know."

"So you're not gonna dance with her?"

"Hell no! Dog, are you crazy? You know I can't be out there like that."

"OK, man. Just thought it would be better than standing to the side watching me and Latrice."

"Man, I'm not watchin' y'all. I been checkin' honeys out all night."

Just then, Latrice and Emily came back. Latrice smiled and took Vic's arm.

"You ready?"

"Whenever you are."

Without saying good-bye, they disappeared back out on the floor.

"They're good together, aren't they?" Emily asked. I was actually glad that she was back.

"Yeah. They're cool." We stood silently, just watching people get down and listening to the jams that were being played. I wanted to dance. I just couldn't bring myself to do it. But a couple of songs later, I did something that shocked me all the way home. I turned to Emily and said, "So, are we going to exchange numbers?"

Emily looked at me, and said with a smile, "And what would we be exchanging numbers for?"

"To continue our discussion."

"Oh, I see. In that case, do you have a pen?"

I reached in my pocket and removed my cell phone. "I'll put it in here."

Emily took her phone out and said, "I'll put yours in here."

I took her number down, and for the rest of the night we just chilled and talked. My backup plan never came to fruition that night. Instead, I went home and did something I hadn't done in a long while—went to sleep alone on a Saturday night.

Emily and I spoke frequently after that. If she wasn't calling me, I was calling her. Our conversations were always long and spirited. Hooking up with her at her place had been planned and initially was going to stay a secret. At first, I didn't want anyone to know, because I wasn't quite sure I was in the right frame of mind. I didn't actually plan on sleeping with her, but I had gone to her place prepared with a new box of condoms. I went by her because I didn't want anyone to see her by my place. We rented a movie and ordered pizza and wings. We talked for a while, and then while the movie played, we explored each other. After our night together, I told her I didn't care if anyone knew.

"Yeah, a'ight man, it happened."

"Well I'll be damned!" Roy exclaimed, jumping up and laughing. "Colin went over to the other side."

"Shut up, man. I didn't go over to any side. I'm still me."

"How many times have you guys spoken?" Vic asked, elbowing Roy.

I looked at them. "Why you wanna know?"

"What? You can't say?" Vic asked with a smile.

"Yeah, Colin. What's up with that?" Roy instigated.

I took a sip of beer and said, "Fools, we're missing the game."

"So answer the question," Vic insisted.

I exhaled, stood up and hit the switch on the TV.

"I talked to her all week," I said as I sat down. As they dapped each other and laughed, I stared at the screen. The Redskins were actually winning, but I didn't really care. I was thinking about Emily, and the magic she worked with her hips.

Roy
18

"I saw Julie today," Stacey said as she brushed Jenea's hair. Sheila was watching TV, waiting her turn. I was at the table going over a few bills.

"Oh yeah, how's she doing?" I asked, unhappily writing out a check for the gas and electric bill. Winter months were when I really hated paying bills.

"She's been seeing somebody. Jenea, will you keep still? I'm almost finished."

"Sorry Mommy," Jenea said. I made a funny face at my daughter, making her giggle.

"Good for her," I said to Stacey. "Whoever he is, he's a lucky man. Julie's a good catch."

"Too bad your boy didn't know that."

I didn't comment on her last statement, because I didn't want to get into another argument with her. We'd been doing a lot of arguing lately. And as Colin had predicted, the sex had stopped and I'd spent some occasional nights on the couch.

"Speaking of your boy," Stacey said, "Is he still dating that Latrine girl?"

I looked at her disapprovingly from the corner of my eye. "It's Latrice, and yeah, he's still dating her."

"Humph. She must be special," Stacy said with attitude.

"She's pretty cool."

"So was Julie."

I put my pen down and looked at my wife. She was just finishing with Jenea's braids. She had an angry scowl on her face. I shook my head and said, "We're having a get together this Saturday night."

Stacey looked at me. "What do you mean, 'we're having a get together?' "

"I mean I invited Vic, Latrice, Colin, and his new friend Emily over to watch the Tyson fight."

"And when were you planning on telling me this?"

"I'm telling you now."

"How do you know I didn't have anything planned for Saturday, Roy? I mean, this is a marriage. You could have discussed this with me."

I rose from the table and went to the kitchen to get a glass of water. When I came back I said, "Stacey, I'm not about to get into another argument with you, OK?"

"Then treat me like your equal and discuss things with me before you make plans."

"Stacey, what is your problem? It's never been a big deal for the fellas to come over before. Why are you snapping? Please don't tell me it has anything to do with Vic coming here."

Looking at the girls, Stacey said, "Girls, go to your room, please. Sheila, I'll do your hair in a couple of minutes." Too used to the sounds of our arguing, Jenea and Sheila quickly disappeared. When I heard the doors slam shut, I massaged my temples. I could feel the headache coming on as Stacey got up and approached me.

"First of all," she said, strangling the comb she was using, "I don't appreciate you coming off at me like that in front of the girls. Second of all, I wasn't snapping. All I said was I would appreciate it if you talked to me first before inviting your friends over here. And yes, it has everything to do with Vic being here."

I watched her as she held the comb like she wanted to hit me with it. "Listen Stacey," I said, forcing my voice to stay calm, "I'm tired of going through this with you. What went on between Vic and Julie was none of our business. It's ridiculous that you can't continue to be his friend just because he no longer had feelings for Julie. You act as though he fell out of love with you. I am through going back and forth with you. I can't even mention Vic's name without you catching an attitude. That has to stop, because I don't have time for it." I stared at my wife very seriously. I was nearing the end of my rope. I was tired of the arguing. Stacey glared at me and curled her lips. I could tell things were going to get worse.

"Ridiculous!" she screamed. "What's ridiculous is that you can even defend him after what he did to Julie. He broke her heart. For what? Some black pussy? And what do you mean, don't have time for it? I know you're not talking to me like that!"

"Stacey, keep your damn voice down. Now, you know he didn't leave Julie for that. He didn't love her. What would you have rather he do? Cheat on her? He didn't love Julie. Can't you understand that?"

"He should have never married her, then."

"We've gone through this already, Stacey. You know why he did."

"Oh yeah, he wanted to do the right thing. Please. Didn't love her? Did he even try? While he was so busy wanting black women... Did he even try to love Julie?"

"How can you try something when it's not in your heart?"

"Now that is a ridiculous thing to say," Stacey said, slamming the comb down on the table. "And I'll tell you what else is ridiculous...You thinking that Vic is going to be able to come in here with his new woman, just putting her all in my face."

"In *your* face? Are you listening to yourself? Do you know how ridiculous that sounds? His coming over here has nothing to do with you. He is in love with Latrice. They are my friends. They are coming over to watch the fight, not ridicule you. You really need to get over this shit, Stacey. I mean, why are you so angry about it? Damn, you act like he killed her. You said yourself that Julie found someone new. If she's moving on, why can't you?"

"What Vic did is disgusting, Roy. He bought her a ring, he married her, and he cared for her when she lost the baby...made her feel like she was loved. Then he just dropped her like yesterday's news. I have no respect for that. It was cowardly and cruel. And I don't want him here!"

I stood up and held on to the back of my chair. I was definitely at the end of my rope now. I took a couple of deep breaths. I looked toward the direction of our daughters' bedroom doors. I didn't like for them to hear or see us argue like this.

"Listen, Stacey, because this will be the only time I say this. I am the man of this house. I pay the majority of the bills here. If I want my friends to come over, then there is not a damn thing you can say or do about it. Are we clear?"

Stacey scowled at me and stepped toward me. In a low, guttural voice she said, "Oh, I hear you. Now you hear me. If you let Vic into this house, the girls and I will leave it. Are we clear?"

Before I could say anything, Stacey turned around, grabbed the comb from the table, and stormed to the girl's bedroom. When I heard the door slam shut, I went to the bathroom and grabbed the Tylenol from the medicine cabinet. After that, I grabbed my coat and left. I needed to cool down and think. I couldn't believe she had taken it to the extreme she had. I couldn't believe she had threatened to leave and take the girls with her.

"There is no way in hell that's happening," I whispered as I turned my cell phone on. I called Colin as I got into my car. I needed some advice.

Stacey
19

When Roy left, I did Sheila's hair and sat alone in darkness for a long while as I contemplated what I should do. I was pissed and hurt. I couldn't believe Roy stormed out the way he did. More importantly, I couldn't believe he had gone off on me. Never in all of our years together had he spoken to me that way. And I wasn't about to stand for it. Why couldn't he just understand where I was coming from? I couldn't imagine Roy doing to me what Vic did. I felt Julie's pain, without having to go through what she did. The more I thought about it, the angrier I became. The way I looked at it, when a person said 'I do,' they just did. And anyone that wasn't willing to should never have made the vow. Vic should have never used the word. And his argument about trying to do the right thing didn't fly with me. The right thing was to take care of his responsibility, without stringing Julie along and allowing her to hand him her heart to break. That is what irked me. No one could ever convince me that what Vic did wasn't cowardly, and it made him less of a man in my eyes. Of all people, I'd expect my husband to understand that. But no, instead he chose to side with Vic. Fine. If that's the way he wanted to do it. I grabbed the phone and dialed Julie's number.

"Hey, girl," I said when Julie answered

"Hey, Stacey! I haven't spoken to you all week. How are you?"

"I'm good. The girls continue to drive me up the wall, and Roy is still Roy."

"And you love him for that."

I cracked a knuckle. "Mmm hmm. So anyway, what's going on with you? Are you still talking to what's-his-name?"

"Who, Derrick? Oh, yes! I'm still talking to him. We've gone out several times."

"Sounds like you like him," I said with a smile. I was happy to hear the excitement in her voice. It was a nice change, not hearing her depressed frame of mind.

"He's nice, Stacey. Really nice. And attentive. But, as you know, I'm not trying to go anywhere too soon. I'll be keeping my guard up for a while."

"Don't keep it up so high that you miss something worth keeping," I said.

"I know. But I have to keep it up like this."

"Does he know about Vic?"

"No. Nothing's serious enough for him to know."

"OK. I understand." I said, grabbing the remote and turning the TV on.

"I think he would be down with it. He's very understanding and easy to talk to."

"Sounds like he could be a real man," I said. I flipped through the channels, not really looking for anything in particular.

Julie laughed. "Yes, he certainly is that."

I paused with my channel surfing and said, "You didn't!"

Julie laughed. I could tell she had a big smile on her face.

"What happened to keeping your guard up?"

"I got weak one night, and it fell."

"Any regrets?"

"At first I had some. Vic was the last man I had been intimate with."

"Too bad," I cut in.

"After it happened with Derrick, I felt terrible. Like I'd cheated or something."

"Cheated?"

"I still love Vic, even if he doesn't love me. Getting over him is not an easy thing for me. And even though our relationship no longer exists, I still feel tied to him in some ways."

"Well, you better untie yourself quick."

"I know. Which is why I realized that what happened with Derrick wasn't a bad thing. It was actually good for me. It helped get rid of some pent-up stress."

"I bet it did, girl."

Julie laughed again. "You are crazy!"

"Not yet," I said, thinking about Roy and our argument. "But I'm getting there."

"Huh?"

"Oh nothing, girl. Just babbling over here. So anyway, I'm glad you're OK with what happened."

"Yeah. I am. It's a slow process, but I'm getting over Vic. Sleeping with Derrick was a necessary step in that process. But like I said, I am keeping that wall up."

"Well, good for you." I went back to flipping through the channels and then stopped on an infomercial for a knife set. It reminded me of why I had called her. "Hey listen, what are you doing this coming Saturday night?"

"Saturday night? I'm not doing anything special. I'll probably be with Derrick again. Why?"

"Oh, we're having a get together to watch the Mike Tyson fight. Why don't you and Derrick come over?"

"A get together? That would be nice. It'd be nice to see Roy and the girls, and even Colin, with his conceited-self."

"Oh, he is definitely that."

We laughed together, and then Julie said in a darker tone, "I assume Vic is going to be there."

"Yeah, with his friend."

There was a long moment of silence. I could only imagine what was going on, on Julie's end.

"His friend?" she finally said. "I see."

I could hear the sadness in her voice. It had been a bad idea.

"Hey listen girl, why don't we forget I ever mentioned Saturday? Why don't we just have a little girls' night out of our own?"

"We could do that some other time. Derrick and I are coming on Saturday."

"You are? You sure you're OK with Vic being here?"

"Vic threw us away, and I've got to move on."

"Good. I look forward to seeing you, and seeing Derrick, who you only tell me about in bits and pieces. I don't even know what he looks like. Is he ugly, girl? Please tell me you didn't find yourself an ugly man." Julie laughed out loud. I started laughing, too. "I'm serious, girl," I said.

"No, he's not ugly. I just haven't told you much about him because I want to be sure it's going somewhere. But don't worry, you'll be both surprised and pleased when you do meet him."

"Surprised and pleased, huh?"

"Yup."

"No hints?"

"Not a one."

I turned the TV off and stood up. It was nearing twelve-thirty and Roy had been gone for close to two hours now.

"OK, girl. I better get my beauty sleep."

"OK. Kiss the girls for me. And say hi to Roy. Tell him I may be coming to Carmax to see him soon."

"OK. Will do. Take care, and I'll talk to you during the week to make sure you haven't changed your mind."

"Oh, I won't change it. Actually, I'm a little curious about what Vic's friend looks like."

"Don't be."

"Have you met her?"

"I will this Saturday."

"OK. Then we can judge her together."

"Sounds like a plan," I said, looking out the window. Where the hell was Roy?

"OK, bye for now, Stacey."

"Talk to you soon." I hung up the phone and smiled. I was glad Julie was willing to come over. I peeked out through the window again, and when a car sped by the house, I sighed. Roy and I had never fought like this before. I couldn't stand what was happening between us. I know inviting Julie over was only adding fuel to the fire. Roy was not going to be happy. But then I wasn't happy either. That's why I chose my side. I looked at the clock and then called Roy's cell phone. He didn't answer, and I didn't leave a message.

Colin
20

Emily and I were on some other level of intense ecstasy when my cell phone went off, so there was no way in hell I was about to answer it. We were conducting round two, with the help of Barry White and candle wax. We had already capped round one off with strawberry massage oil and whipped cream. This was the fourth time we had hooked up. I never expected it to go past the first. I actually tried to convince myself that sleeping with Emily had been only a moment of weakness on my part. I even tried to make up for the slippage by hooking up with a couple of the finest sisters I had in my book of fame, the ones with stars beside their names. But despite the fun, I couldn't deny it; I couldn't get Emily out of my head.

Everything about her was captivating me. Being with her was cool, because I was able to keep it real. Although she was white, I soon came to realize that she was more down than any female I'd ever met, black or white. To top it off, she could match me freak for freak in the bedroom. Which is what was going on when my cell went off. That's why I ignored it. But when the knocking started on my front door fifteen minutes later, I couldn't help but get frustrated. And when that happened, my focus got all screwed up. I looked at Emily as she rode me. Damn, she was looking fine. I shook my head.

"Go and get rid of them," she said with a smile.

"Oh, I'll do more than get rid of them," I said, slipping into my boxers. "Vic is about to catch a beat down." I hurried to the door and opened it. I was surprised to see that instead of Vic, it was Roy. From the look on his face, I could tell it wasn't a social visit.

"Roy? What are you doing here?"

He sighed. "Man, I need to talk. I have some issues."

I took a peek behind me toward the bedroom, where Emily was waiting in all her naked splendor. I looked back at him. Damn, he really looked like he needed to talk. But I was just beginning to hit my stride.

"Yo dog, can this wait until tomorrow? I'm kind of in the middle of something."

Without waiting for an answer, he stormed past me into my living room.

"She said she'd take the damn girls, man!" he yelled. "Can you believe that shit?"

I bowed my head, closed the door and turned around. I was as limp as a soggy noodle. It was obvious that I wasn't going to get rid of him that easily.

"Roy, what the hell are you talkin' about? You're not makin' any sense."

Pacing and burning a hole in my rug, he said, "Stacey threatened to take the girls man."

"What? What do you mean threatened? Since when have you guys been having problems like that?"

Roy continued pacing, and spoke with his hands in full swing. "Man, she's been tripping over Vic."

"Still? Are you for real?"

"Colin, she can't get over Vic leaving Julie."

I looked at him and before I could say anything, he said, "I know. I know. It doesn't make sense. I told her that. But she's not trying to hear that."

"Oh well," I said, looking back to the room. "That's her hang up." I looked back at Roy, who did what I hoped he wouldn't. He sat down on my couch. "Now how did you go from Vic to her taking the girls?"

"Man, you know how I told you guys about coming over by me to watch the Tyson fight this Saturday?"

"Yeah."

"Well, when I told her that Vic was coming, and that he was going to bring Latrice, she lost it. She went off and said she didn't want him in the house, and if he came, then she'd leave with the girls!"

I stared down at him and crossed my arms. "Come on, dog. She said that for real?"

"As real as a heart attack."

"Man, she can't be serious about that. She can't be trippin' like that. Not Stacey."

Roy looked up at me. "She can, and is," he said solemnly.

"Damn." I sat down beside him.

"So what do I do, man? I don't want to lose my girls, or Stacey."

I sucked my teeth and lay back on the couch. Scratching my stomach, I said, "Roy, listen. I'ma be real up front with you on this one. I know you love Stacey and your girls, but let's keep it real. If Stacey were to actually do you like that, she would be completely in the wrong. She knows she can't get away with that. She's just talkin' shit, like most women do. Stop stressin' over it. If she wants to be mad, let her be mad. But I'm tellin' you, she's talkin' shit."

"How do you know?"

"Because she loves you. And she knows how tight we all are. In the end, when it comes down to it, she'll be by your side." I gave him dap and then stood up. Roy was my boy, but it was time for him to go. "Yo, dog, go home to your wife and kids. Don't sweat this."

Standing up, he said, "Thanks, man. And I'm sorry for barging in here like this. She just had me freaked when she went off."

"It's cool," I said, opening the front door. "I'll call you tomorrow, to see how things went."

"Cool, man. And I'm sorry for interrupting."

I nodded and closed the door. When I walked back into the room, Emily was under the covers, pretending to be asleep. I could tell it was fake, because I saw her eyes open a fraction.

"That's why I'm never getting married. I don't want that hassle," I said as I climbed under the covers and slid next to her.

Emily opened her eyes and turned toward me. "So most women talk shit, huh?"

I kissed her on the lips. "Nope. Not most. All women do."

She gave me a hard punch on my shoulder. "I've got your shit talking right here."

I laughed and then grabbed the blanket, pulling it above our heads.

"Talk all the shit you want, girl."

Latrice
21

I had just come in from the gym when my phone rang. I threw my gym bag down and grabbed the receiver. I was expecting it to be Vic, but when I looked at the caller ID, I saw it was not who I expected at all. I thought about not answering the call, but knowing how persistent he could be, I hit the TALK button.

"Hello Bernard," I said.

"Latrice," Bernard said on the other end. "It's been a while. How have you been?"

"I've been good," I said, wanting desperately to get off of the phone, as old memories started to resurface. Memories that I didn't want to remember. "And you?"

"Not bad."

"I'm surprised you called."

"I just wanted to say hi. Maybe talk for a couple."

"Bernard, I don't mean to be rude, but I just got in, and I'm tired."

"Just for a few minutes, LaLa," he called me by the pet name he had given me long ago. "That's all I'm asking for."

I sighed. "Bernard, we can't do this. Besides, I don't think your wife would approve of us talking."

"Wife? When did I get married?"

"I heard through the grapevine you married Lynette this past summer."

"Well, you heard wrong. Your grapevine has it all backwards. We actually broke up."

"Sorry to hear that. What happened?" I cursed myself silently for asking that last question.

"I'm still in love with someone else."

I took a deep breath and exhaled slowly. As much as I didn't want to admit it to myself, Bernard still had a hold on me. And hearing his sexy, deep voice was not the thing I needed to hear; nor was his last comment.

"She must be a hell of a woman, to make you end your relationship," I said.

"Oh, she's a hell of a woman, alright."

I cleared my throat and stared at myself in the mirror. *Don't fall back girl*, I told myself.

"What was that?" Bernard asked.

I shook my head. I didn't realize I had spoken out loud.

"Nothing." I needed to get off the phone. "Bernard, I have to go. I have plans this evening."

"Plans? With who?"

"A friend."

"A friend? Is this a male or female friend?"

I sighed. "Bernard, does it really matter?"

"Yes, it does."

"Why?"

There was silence for a long second, which gave me enough time to think about Bernard and how wonderful he was to me when we were together. He gave me all the love and respect I needed to be happy forever. He pampered me in all the right ways, at all the right times. He gave himself unconditionally. When we initially met, he was married, but unhappy. His wife was a money-hungry, selfish bitch. From the first moment I saw them together, I thought he was too good for her triflin' ass. It took a while before we developed into anything. I was reluctant because he was married, and I didn't want to disrespect that union. So we started doing lunch, then dinner, and eventually breakfast. By the time that started to happen, it was obvious to the both of us that we were falling in love. That's why he finally made the decision to leave his wife. And I wasn't complaining. When his divorce finally went through, we already had plans established for our wedding. But then Danita died, and that changed everything.

Bernard was there for me, just like he had always been, but her death had been too hard for me. I sank into an insurmountable pool of depression, and as time went on I found it more and more difficult to give anything to anyone. That's why Bernard ended up in the arms of Lynette Cooper. She was a co-worker of his who had been eyeing him since day one. As I pushed Bernard away, she was readily there to accept him into the web she was spinning. Eventually, Bernard couldn't get out, and he walked out of my life. I knew I was losing a good thing by letting him go without a fight. But I couldn't do it. I needed the time away to find the will to be happy again.

Now that I had, the last thing I needed was for the man who I had never completely gotten over to come back into my life and tell me that he was once again free.

"What do you want, Bernard?"

"LaLa, I'm not going to beat around the bush with you."

"Good. Because I don't have much time."

"LaLa, I love you. I want us back."

"Bernard, you walked away from our relationship."

"LaLa, you pushed me away. You know that. I tried to be there for you in every way possible."

I didn't respond. He was right. He continued.

"I never wanted us to be apart. I never wanted to be with anyone else."

"You had a funny way of showing that, as fast as you ended up in Lynette's arms."

"That didn't happen overnight, Latrice."

"Well, it happened."

"You let it."

Damn. He was right again. I sighed and massaged my temples.

"Bernard, we shouldn't be talking about this." I sat on my bed and closed my eyes.

"Why?"

"Because we've both moved on."

"Have we?"

I lay back and stared up at the ceiling. "Bernard, I'm involved with someone OK."

The volume in his voice dropped as he said, "I see. Is it real?"

"As real as it can be."

"But is it as real as what we had?"

I slammed my hand down on the mattress. I didn't need this.

"Why did you call Bernard?"

"Because I got tired of denying the truth."

"Which is?"

"That I am and always have been in love with you, and I feel we belong together."

I felt a tear snake away from the corner of my eye. *Why now*, I wondered. I looked over at my clock. Vic was probably on his way over. Damn.

"Vic, I mean...Bernard, I have to go." I silently cursed myself for that slip.

"Vic? Is that who my competition is?"

"This is not a game, Bernard."

"Is Vic the man you're seeing?"

"Bernard, I have to go."

Before I could disconnect the call, I heard Bernard say, "I'm going to get you back, Latrice. I'm still in love with you. And I know you feel the same."

I hit the OFF button and let the phone fall from my hand. I continued to stare at a spot on the ceiling as tears fell from my eyes. He still loved me. I loved Vic. Bernard still loved me. Did I still love him?

Vic
22

I took a deep breath before I rang Roy's doorbell. He had called me during the week and told me all about his argument with Stacey and the fact that she was still harboring ill feelings toward me. I expected that, and was prepared to deal with any attitude she was going to give to Latrice, who I'd warned ahead of time. What I didn't expect was to hear how she'd threatened to leave with the girls if I came over. That surprised me, because I could never imagine Stacey being that ugly.

Once he told me about his wife's threat, I decided that I wasn't going to go; I didn't want to cause him any unnecessary drama. But Roy was adamant about me coming over.

"Vic, listen. I want to see you and Latrice here, having a good time Saturday night."

"I just don't want to cause you any headache, Roy. Latrice and I can chill at my place and watch the fight from there."

"That's not an option, Vic. I want to see you and Latrice here, primed and ready to see Mike administer an ass-whooping of epic, round-one proportions."

"You sure, man? Believe me, it's no problem for me to chill at my place."

"Vic, it would be a problem for me. You're my boy. Stacey's going to have to accept that what went on with you and Julie is really none of her business."

"And what about her threat?"

"I'll deal with my wife. You just make sure you're here in time to see the preliminary fights. You know those will last longer than the main event."

"True. OK man, as long as you're sure, we'll be there."

"Cool. See you Saturday."

"Later."

I turned to Latrice. "You ready?"

She smiled and said, "No, the question is, are *you* ready. I don't have a problem with this woman, and if she's smart, she won't have a problem with me."

"Well, just in case she does, we're not sticking around. I'm not trying to bring you in on any mess."

"Ring that bell, Vic. I can hold my own against a nasty attitude. Won't be the first time, and it won't be the last."

I gave her a deep kiss and then rang the bell. As we waited, I couldn't help but wonder about what lay on the other side of the door. The last thing I expected to see when the door opened was a smiling Stacey.

"Vic!" she said. "How are you? Come on in."

I'm sure Stacey could read the confusion in my eyes as I stared back at her. I didn't actually speak or move until Latrice gave me a light tap in the middle of my back.

"Hey, what's up Stacey?" I said. "Nice to see you. It's been awhile."

"Yes it has," Stacey answered. Looking at Latrice, she said, "This must be the new woman I've heard so much about." She extended her hand. "I'm Stacey. Roy's wife."

Latrice took Stacey's hand and smiled. "Latrice," she said. "Nice to meet you. I've heard so much about you."

"All good things, I hope."

Latrice laughed. "Definitely interesting," she said.

Stacey stepped to the side. "Well, come on in. It's freezing."

"Where are the girls?" I asked, disappointed they hadn't come running up to me.

"Oh, they spent the night at their friend's house and left us grown-ups alone and unsupervised for the night."

"Right, right."

Closing the door, Stacey said, "Vic, you know where to put the coats. Latrice, if you don' t mind, I could use a hand in the kitchen before the festivities start."

"No problem," Latrice said with as fake a smile as I had ever seen. I could tell she didn't like Stacey. To be honest, I don't know if I did at that particular moment, either. I took her coat and hung it up with mine, and let the ladies go their way. Then I headed to the living room, where Roy was hooking up his illegal black box to the big screen.

"What's up, man?" I said, taking a seat.

From behind the TV, Roy asked, "Hey, is the reception clear yet?"

"Not yet...wait... now it is."

"Finally," Roy said, standing up. "So what's up, man?"

"You tell me. What's up with Stacey? I expected to walk into a battlefield man. Why is she being so nice?"

Roy shrugged his shoulders. "You got me. I came home yesterday, and she apologized for the way she was acting. Said that everything would be OK tonight. I'm as surprised as you are. Where's Latrice?"

"She's in the kitchen with Stacey."

"Alone?"

"Yeah. But it's cool. 'Trice can hold her own."

"Man, I'm trying to watch a fight on TV, live and in stereo, not live and in my living room."

I laughed. "Don't worry. Unless Stacey throws the first blows, it'll be cool."

"We'll see."

Roy ran to the kitchen and then came back with four beers. He handed me two of them.

"They're both alive. For now."

I took a long swallow of the Heineken. "So when's Colin getting here? And I wonder if he's bringing Emily with him? You know they've hooked up more than once, right?"

"Yeah, I know. I think I barged in on them a couple nights back when I stopped by his place. And yeah, he's bringing her. I think they might actually become a for-real-item some time."

"Damn! The world must be coming to an end. Who would have ever thought Colin would come close to having a real relationship?"

"With a white female at that," Roy said. "Man, back in Tennessee, relationships like y'all's are a rare thing to see."

"For real?"

"Oh definitely. You just don't mix like that in the South. That was one thing I had to get used to when I first moved up here. The interracial thing is like taboo in the South."

"How do you feel about it?"

"I couldn't care less. Love doesn't love anybody. The person does. And as long as the person you're with loves you back, then that's all that matters."

I held up my beer can for a toast. "I hear that," I said, as he tapped his can to mine. Just then, the doorbell rang. Roy stood up and said, "Must be Colin." He left me to get the door; I focused on the pre-fight hype. As they showed a clip of Mike Tyson from his glory days, I heard Colin's voice.

"Wasaaaaaap!" he said, walking into the living room, sounding like the guys from the Budweiser commercials.

I answered back. "Wasaaaaaabi!"

Roy trailed behind a couple of seconds later and said, "How you doin'?" in his best Italian voice.

We all laughed. Colin said, "Yo, those commercials are the shit."

"Yeah," I said. "We need to do something like that. Blow up with a catch phrase."

"Yeah," Colin said, "How about 'Where da' ho's at?'" Colin laughed and grabbed a beer.

I smiled. "You better not let Emily hear that. Speaking of which, where is she?"

"She's in the kitchen with Latrice and Stacey. And please, I say that around her all the time."

"Sounds like you're into her," Roy said, raising the volume; the first fight was about to start.

Colin sat down in my beanbag and nodded. "I can't front… Emily is cool. She keeps it real with me, and I'm able to keep it real with her."

"Uh-oh," I said. "Is the player card slowly dissolving?"

Colin looked at me and raised an eyebrow. "Please, dog. I'm a player for life."

"We'll see," I said.

We all laughed, and then watched as the first round of the first fight began. Two junior middleweight boxers, one a Mexican, and the other a black kid from New York, were going head to head, pounding each other with all they had. By the end of the third round, the black fighter's eye was so swollen that his trainers threw in the towel.

"Damn," I said, stuffing some chips into my mouth. "Latino fighters are some fighting-ass fools."

"Yeah," Colin added, "You remember Chavez? He was like a brick. And what about Duran and his hands of stone?"

"Yeah," Roy threw in. "Even the pretty boys like De LaHoya and Trinidad are tough as nails."

When the second fight, featuring Christy Martin, was set to begin, the ladies came into the living room. Emily flopped down with Colin, and Stacey sat on Roy's lap. I looked at Latrice as she came to sit down beside me. She gave me an everything's-OK look. I squeezed her hand and then out of the corner of my eye I caught what seemed to be a glare coming from Stacey. But it was hard to be sure, because when I turned to face her she gave me a smile. I smiled back and then focused on the fight. While Christy Martin pummeled her opponent, the doorbell rang. Roy looked at his watch; it was past eleven.

"You expecting company?" he asked Stacey.

Stacey didn't say a word as she got up and left the room.

I looked at Roy and said, "What's up?"

"No idea," he said. He got up and left also.

"Christy is no joke," Colin said.

Latrice and Emily both sucked their teeth; they were not feeling the female boxers. As round two began, I heard a voice I hadn't expected or wanted to hear. Apparently, so did Colin, because he looked at me and then shook his head. A few seconds later, Roy trudged into the living room. It was obvious from the look on his face, that he was not happy. He didn't say a word as he sat down. I clenched and unclenched my fist several times in a row. I looked from him to Colin. We all had the same look. I took a deep breath. I couldn't believe what was about to happen. Latrice noticed my agitation and looked at me.

"What's wrong?" she asked.

I wanted to answer her, but I couldn't. Instead, I shook my head and let my breath out slowly.

"Vic," Latrice said again. "What's wrong?"

I finally opened my mouth to speak, but before I could get a word out, Stacey's voice pierced the air.

"Everyone...look who dropped by."

Latrice
23

When Stacey announced Julie's appearance, the first thought that came to my mind, and almost slipped from my lips, was that Stacey was a true bitch. I couldn't believe what was happening. And from the evil look on Vic's face, neither could he. I looked at Emily, who's mouth, just like Colin's, was o-shaped. Emily knew all about Julie, because I'd told her all of the things Vic had told me about them being together. I gave Stacey my nastiest glare and she stared directly back at me. I was hot, ready to go ghetto on her ass, take out the Vaseline and remove my earrings.

Vic had warned me about how angry Stacey was about him dumping Julie. And after sitting with her in the kitchen, I realized her nice act had been nothing but a front. We sat and chitchatted, while Vic and Roy were in the living room, doing what guys did. We talked about things only women could love—clothes. I had on a pair of midnight-blue jeans from the Limited, and a white turtleneck. On my feet, I had on my black calf-high leather boots. She had on a pair of jeans also, with a light blue V-neck top that was just a little too tight for her top-heavy frame.

"Latrice, girl, I love those boots you have on. They are the bomb."

"Thanks, girl. I got them on sale at Nordstroms. Eighty bucks—can you believe it?"

"Eighty? That's a steal. They still have them?"

"Unh-uh. I got the last pair."

"Figures."

We talked some more about shopping, and then Stacey got personal and started talking to me about her and Roy. I knew that hearing about how they met and how long they'd been together was all part of Stacey's setup. Eventually, she decided to show her face, and asked about me and Vic.

"So how did you and Vic meet?"

"Oh, we work together."

"Oh, do you?" she said. "You work together. Imagine that."

I was sure she knew, because from what Vic told me, Roy shared everything with her, and I knew Roy knew the details about us. But I pretended to be ignorant.

"Well we work in different departments. We were friends for a while, and then we eventually got together."

"I see," she said.

She was about to delve for more information when the doorbell rang. I was glad when Roy and Emily appeared in the kitchen.

"Hey, girl," I said to Emily. "I was wondering when you would get here."

"What's up Latrice," Emily said. "Yeah, we had some things to take care of before we left his place." Emily looked at me and winked. I shook my head. Roy looked at Stacey and said, "Baby, this is Emily. Emily, this is my wife Stacey."

Taking Emily's hand, Stacey said, "It's nice to finally meet the woman who's managing to keep a leash around Colin's neck."

Emily laughed and said, "I'm trying."

"I didn't realize you two knew each other," Stacey said, looking at me.

I nodded. "Yeah. Emily is my girl."

"Wow," Stacey said with another wide smile, "Imagine that! You two are best friends dating best friends." We all laughed, but I could hear the hidden message. I knew what her game was, and what type of sister she was. I just never expected her to play the hand that she did.

No one said a word as Julie smiled and stood beside her date—a tall, and I must admit, good-looking brother. I gave Stacey a cross look and she looked back at me with a smirk of her own. She was enjoying every minute of silence that hovered in the room. I took a deep breath and held it. I was getting hot with anger. My claws were on the verge of being detracted for some serious work.

Emily, knowing how I can get, was quick to try and diffuse my bomb.

"Latrice," she said softly, touching my arm. I looked at her and didn't say a word. "I need to get something from the car. Can you help me with it?"

We walked out without saying a word to anybody.

Roy
24

How I didn't go off when I saw Julie walking through my door was amazing to me. But how I managed to keep from going ballistic when Stacey looked at me and smiled, was even more incredible. I was so mad and so shocked that I couldn't say anything. I just nodded to Julie and her date, and then went into the living room. And while everyone tried to figure out what the hell was going on, I breathed, stared at the television, and pondered about the best way to handle the situation.

My first thought was to kick Julie out of my house. I couldn't believe she had shown up like that. Worse yet, I couldn't believe Stacey had invited her over. Now I understood why she had been so damned nice. As I sat and thought about what was going on, I glanced at Vic from the corner of my eye. He looked like he was about to hurt somebody. I can only imagine what Latrice was feeling. I saw the disgust in her eyes when she and Emily walked outside. Damn. Never in a million years would I have thought Stacey capable of doing something as devious as what she did. Not my wife. Never. That's why I grabbed her arm and took her upstairs. I wanted an explanation.

Latrice
25

"*No,* those bitches didn't go there!" I yelled as we stepped outside. *I* didn't care who heard me. I raised my voice a notch higher. "Are they crazy? They just don't know, Emily. I am not afraid to kick a bitch's ass. Ooooh girl..."

Emily stood safely to the side while I paced back and forth, clenching and unclenching my hands.

"I wasn't raised in no damn suburbs, Em.' I will go ghetto. Oh no... Did you see the look on Stacey's face? Standing there with her simple ass. And Julie...like her shit don't stink. Emily, don't let me go to jail tonight."

Emily exhaled and shook her head. "I don't know, Latrice. I'm about to go to jail myself. That was some foul shit they just pulled."

"Girl..." I said. I exhaled and shook anger from my fingertips. I paced again and breathed deeply in and out several times. I had to get myself together. I didn't want Vic see me in all my glory. Besides, that's exactly what Stacey and Julie wanted. They wanted my ignorant side to come out. I stopped walking and faced Emily, who looked at me with concern in her eyes.

"I can't give them the satisfaction, Em,'" I said, lowering my voice. "I can't let those bitches make me come out my face."

"I can," Emily said.

I shook my head and furiously passed my tongue back and forth over my teeth. "We can't go there, girl. You don't want Colin to see that, and I don't want Vic to see that."

"Colin wouldn't care."

"Well, I don't want Vic seeing that."

"So what are you going to do, then? Poor Vic. He was just sitting there, not saying a word. I can imagine how he's feeling."

"Poor Vic is fuming right now," I said. "I could feel the heat coming from him. He's about to blow. Girl, if that happens... Come on. Let's get inside."

"But Latrice, what are you going to do?"

I passed my hand through my braids and closed my eyes and counted to ten. When I finished, I turned to Emily.

"Come on, girl. I'm going to finish the game Stacey and Julie started."

Colin
26

I don't know how Vic managed to keep his cool, because I know I damn sure wouldn't have been able to keep mine. I was almost ready to snap when I heard Julie's voice. I can only imagine what Vic was thinking. And then there was Latrice. I'm glad Emily had sense enough to get Latrice outside before she went off. But Vic... His time clock was about to expire.

Stacey shocked the hell out of me. I always knew women were capable of devious shit, but I never put her in the same category. She was always different, like she wasn't a woman. Even when she started tripping early on about Vic and Julie, I still kept her out of the bitches-and-ho's category I lumped most women into. But after this, her picture was entered into the database, with bold captioning reading *Number One Bitch.*

I was glad when Roy pulled her upstairs, because I didn't want to see her. But having her out of the immediate picture didn't help much, because Julie was still there, with as smug a look as I'd ever seen on her. She was definitely enjoying the tension, which had gotten so thick it could be cut with a knife.

For the first time in forever, I didn't know what to do, hence the reason for my silence. But the more I watched Vic's cheeks redden and his eyes get smaller, I knew I had to get him out of there. I decided to follow Emily's lead.

"Yo dog." I looked at Vic. "Can you help me get some more beers and chips?" Instead of waiting for an answer, I grabbed his arm and led the way.

Latrice
27

Emily and I walked in just in time to see Colin and Vic go to the kitchen. That was good, because it left me free to play my game without having to worry about Vic interfering. I gave an indignant look to Julie as I stepped back into the living room. She glared back at me. Oh, it was on, and I would be damned if I was going to lose. I stepped up to her and extended my hand. She took it with a forced smile, which was obviously for her date's benefit. By the confused look on his face, I could see that he was clueless about what was going on.

"Hi," I said, applying a slight amount of pressure. "I'm Latrice." I smiled and kept my eyes locked on hers. My grip remained tight. Although she refused to look away, I could tell she was getting nervous. Silly bitch had no idea who she was dealing with.

With a half-smile, Julie said, "Hello Latrice."

We both knew the deal, as our eyes remained locked on one another. I put on a straight smile and averted my attention to her date. I finally let go of Julie's hand and extended mine to him.

"And you are?"

"Derrick," he said. As we shook hands, banging could be heard coming from upstairs. I looked at Derrick and smiled. *Poor guy*, I thought.

"Nice to meet you. I'm Latrice, and this is Emily."

Derrick nodded to Emily, who stood two steps to my left. Her eyes were locked on Julie.

"Well, since everyone else has disappeared, why don't we sit down and enjoy the fights like we came to do?"

I stepped to the side and let Julie and Derrick walk by to take a seat on the couch. My heart was beating heavily. I had to pat myself on the back. I was putting on a good act, because all I really wanted to do was slap Julie. I sat down on the arm of the sofa.

"So...Julie and Dirk," I said, as another preliminary bout started, "you two make a nice couple."

Derrick laughed and said quickly, "It's Derrick."

"Oh, I'm sorry," I said, pretending to have genuinely gotten his name wrong. "I'm terrible with names. Please forgive me."

He smiled. "Happens all the time."

From a beanbag to the side, Emily snickered.

"So," I said, fixing my eyes on Julie, "how long have you guys been dating?"

Derrick opened his mouth to answer, but before he could, Julie cut in.

"Oh, we're not really dating. We're just friends." I kept my fake smile plastered on Derrick as he looked at Julie from the corner of his eye. The status of their "friendship" was obviously news to him.

"Oh, that's nice," I said. "At least you don't have to deal with the hassle of a relationship. That can be a pain sometimes. You know how men can be," I said, tapping Julie's leg a little harder than I needed to. She started to open her mouth, but as Derrick chuckled, she changed her mind. I laughed with him. I was having a good old time. "No offense to you, Darren."

He smiled back. "None taken. And it's Derrick."

I put my hand to my mouth. "I'm sorry. I'll get it. I promise."

From the beanbag, Emily snickered again.

"Is something wrong?" Julie snapped, looking at her.

Emily snapped her head back and gave Julie an I-know-you-didn't look.

Before Emily could answer, I said, "She's laughing because being in a relationship with Colin, she knows exactly how men can be sometimes. I must say, being with Vic, I too know. Although, I wouldn't trade my relationship with him for anything." I smiled at Julie when I said that.

Derrick gave me my next round of ammunition. "How long have you and Vic been together?"

I beamed at him. "You know, I don't remember. Sometimes it almost seems like forever. I can't even remember who I was with before him. And he never mentions his ex's name. I guess we were so made for each other that the length of time is insignificant."

Derrick, the innocent bystander that he was, nodded his head like he understood exactly where I was coming from. I know Julie did, because she stared fiercely at me through slit eyes. I smiled at her. We had all come to see the main event. But this night, Mike Tyson would have to take a back seat.

Roy
28

"*What* the hell has gotten into you, Stacey? What kind of games are you playing?" My wife looked at me with beady eyes.

"I told you I didn't want Vic in this house," she said vehemently.

I slammed my palm down on our dressing table, causing one of our wedding pictures to fall.

"Damn it! We have been through this. Whatever problems he and Julie had, are their problems. Do you understand that? Theirs! Not yours or mine."

"I don't care if it is their problem. I still don't want him here. Having Colin here, who disrespects women the way he does, is bad enough. But what Vic did was pathetic!"

"Damn, Stacey! He didn't love Julie. What the hell is so wrong with that? You know what? Forget it... I don't want to hear your answer. Just tell me why you called Julie. I can't believe you were that dirty."

"Dirty? How is inviting my friend over dirty?"

"Don't play games, Stacey. You knew Vic was going to be here. You knew what you were setting up. Did Julie know he was going to be here?"

I glared at her until she said, "Yes."

"Damn. Then she's just as much of a bitch as you are!"

Stacey looked at me, with bug eyes and an open mouth. "I can't believe you just called me a bitch!"

"Believe it!" I yelled. "Because only a bitch would disrespect her husband the way you just did downstairs."

"Disrespect? Don't you even go there. You better be the last one talking about disrespect. Even after I asked you, you didn't find it necessary to respect me and keep Vic out of this house."

Slamming my hand down again, I yelled, "Vic is my friend!"

"And Julie is mine!"

Stacey and I stared at each other. If she were a man... I shook my head to get rid of that thought. I turned away from her and intertwined my hands above my head. With my back to her, I said, "I can't believe you did this. I can't believe you actually did this. I would never have expected such a low act from you. You're not the woman I married. The woman I married wouldn't do something so...so..."

"The man I married, would never have chosen his friends over his wife."

I opened my mouth to reply back, but changed my mind. It would have been pointless. Instead, in a raspy voice, I said, "I want Julie and her date out of here, Stacey. I want them both gone before I go back downstairs."

"Julie is not going anywhere. She is my friend, and I live here, too."

"Let's not play any more games, Stacey. Just get Julie out of here."

"Or what?"

I exhaled and turned to face her. "Goddamn it! I'm tired of this bullshit! I said I want Julie and that motherfucker out of here! Now, I'm giving you the opportunity to get them out before things get uglier than they already are. I suggest you do that."

"Fuck you, Roy!"

I paused and glared at her. "Fuck me? No, how about fuck you! And while you're fucking yourself, you can get the hell out of the house, too."

"You can't kick me out. I live here!"

"Fine, then I'll leave. I've had it with this petty shit!" I moved past her and opened the door.

Before I walked away, she screamed, "Go to hell, Roy!"

I kept my back to her as I said, "I'm leaving hell right now." I slammed the door then, and left my house without saying a word to anyone.

Colin
29

Vic and I looked at each other as we heard the front door slam.

"What the hell is Stacey's problem?" Vic said through clenched teeth. "Doesn't she care that she's putting her marriage in jeopardy? Is she that pressed?"

I sighed, moved to the refrigerator and grabbed two beers. As the door was closing, I thought about grabbing one for Derrick. But then I just let it close. Two tears in a bucket. I twisted the bottle tops off and handed one to Vic, whose hands were noticeably shaking. I shook my head and took a much-needed sip.

"You alright, man?" I asked, feeling like that was the dumbest question.

Vic put his elbows on the kitchen counter and massaged his temples. Damn, I felt bad for him.

"If Roy weren't my boy..." he started.

I finished. "Yeah, that kept me from cursing Stacey's ass out, too."

Vic slammed his fist on the counter. "I can't believe Julie and Stacey pulled this stunt. I just can't believe it. I mean, who the fuck do they think they are? Stacey, with her fucking smile, just loving the drama. And Julie, standing there beside that motherfucker like there aren't any problems. Did you see him? Where the hell did she find him? And since when did she date black men?"

I stood beside him and shrugged my shoulders.

"She walked in here like she was the shit, Colin."

"I know, man. I was there."

Vic took an angry swallow of beer and slammed the bottle onto the counter. He was definitely ticking and ready to explode. I could tell by the vein pulsating in his neck. He needed to get away from the drama; hell, we all did.

"Dog, I don't know what is gong through Stacey's head, but for real, the best thing for us to do right now would be to leave."

Vic looked at me. "Who the fuck is that guy?"

"Come on, man," I said, downing my beer. "Why are you trippin' over him? He don't mean shit."

"Man, I just want to know who the hell he is."

"Why? You're with Latrice. What do you care who he is? He's nobody. Shit, I feel bad for the brother. You could tell by the look on his face that he has no clue what Julie got him into."

"I wonder where the hell she met him," Vic whispered.

I shook my head. "Forget about him already. Don't start gettin' all jealous and shit. You let her go. Now, we need to go."

"Man, I need to talk to Julie first. I need to clear this shit up." As he started to make a move to leave the kitchen, I grabbed his arm.

"Yo dog, let's grab the ladies and go." I looked at him hard to make sure he knew I wasn't going to take no for an answer.

He shook his head. "I just need to get some shit off my chest first, man."

I closed my fingers tighter around his arm. "No, you don't. The only thing you need to do is grab

Latrice before she goes ballistic, and walk out of the door. Vic, I don't care if you never take my advice again, but you're taking it this time." I tightened my grip and locked eyes with his. "Roy will settle shit with Stacey."

"But Julie..."

"To hell with Julie. You don't need any more drama, man. Let's go."

Reluctantly, Vic nodded and pulled away from me. He went to the sink and turned on the faucet, splashed cold water over his face and on his head. He did this a few times, then turned the faucet off and grabbed a kitchen towel.

"If Roy weren't my boy..." Vic said again.

"Man, let's give Roy the privacy he needs, and the four of us can go somewhere and try to make something out of this disaster."

"Only because Latrice is here will I take your advice. I don't want her to see me get ignorant."

I put out my hand for some dap. He touched his fist with mine and then we left the kitchen. As we stepped into the living room, Latrice and Emily turned to face us. Emily gave me a look. I nodded to let her know everything was under control. But I could still hear Vic's clock ticking. I made a motion with my head, signifying that it was time to leave, and Emily came and stood beside me. I watched in nervous silence as Latrice, who hadn't risen, bent down toward Julie's ear. I couldn't help but wonder if she was going to bite it like Tyson did to Holyfield. That would have been some ugly shit. Mercifully, all she did was whisper something. My eyes were focused on Julie the whole time; I could tell from her reaction that she didn't like whatever it was that was said. Then Latrice smiled at Derrick.

"It was a pleasure meeting you...Derrick."

I breathed a sigh of relief when she got up without another word and came to stand beside Vic. Nothing else needed to be said. We all left. As I closed the door, I could hear Derrick ask, "What happened?"

When we got to our cars, we all turned to Latrice. We all asked the same question with our eyes.

"What?" Latrice asked.

"What did you tell her?" Vic asked.

"Tell who?" Latrice answered with a smile.

"Come on, 'Trice," Emily said.

Finally I spoke out. "Don't leave us hangin'. I saw Julie's reaction. Whatever it was that you said, she didn't like it."

Latrice laughed and turned to Vic. "You know, only because I have respect for you did I not kick that bitch's ass. And I made sure to tell her that. But I'm letting you know now, the next time she or Stacey pull some shit like this..."

Before she could finish, a voice spoke out from behind us.

"There won't be a next time." We all turned around as Roy stepped out of the shadows.

"My nigga," I said, moving toward him. "I thought you were gone."

"Nah," Roy said solemnly. "I just had to get out of the house to clear my head." He turned to Vic and Latrice.

"Guys, I am sorry about what went down. Believe me, I had no idea that was going to happen. Vic, you know I wouldn't set you up like that."

Vic nodded his head. "It's cool, man. No need to apologize. I know this wasn't your doing. I just can't believe Stacey showed her face like that. I mean, I know she's your wife..."

Roy shrugged his shoulders. It was obvious that he was still highly upset. "I feel the same way," he said.

We were all quiet then. It was depressing. The night was supposed to have been chill, and instead, here we all were, bummed out. It had to change.

Addressing every one, I said, "Yo, it's a Saturday night, and it's still early. Why let it go to waste? Why don't we all head to Jillian's, have a couple of drinks, play some pool, and catch the highlights of the fight on one of the big screens."

Emily squeezed my hand. "That's a good idea."

"Yeah," Latrice said. "I could use a Bloody Mary right about now. Vic?"

Vic nodded. He was still visibly shaken after seeing Julie and her date. No matter how happy he was with Latrice, seeing Derrick was still a subtle blow to his ego. Shit, seeing any man with your ex was a blow.

I looked at Roy; he too had gone through a rough night. Julie and Stacey had really shown some ugly sides.

"You down, dog?"

Roy turned and looked back toward his house. He stared silently for a few seconds before he answered in a defeated tone.

"Yeah, I'm down."

We all left then, and had a better night than we anticipated. We drank, laughed, watched highlights of Iron Mike landing a knock out blow, and then went home. I stayed at Emily's place, and gave Roy my house keys. He wanted to be alone, and so did Emily and I.

Julie
30

Up until I saw Vic, I had been doing ok. While it wasn't easy, I'd finally gotten to a point where I accepted life without him. But when I saw him with Latrice, my restructured heart shattered all over again and the pain resurfaced. I knew that he would be there with her, and I thought I was going to be able to get through the evening without letting anything bother me. But that wasn't possible. I may have found a way to keep my composure and appear fine on the outside for everyone's benefit, but on the inside I was an emotional wreck. The moment I saw Vic, I regretted my decision to be there. I went from moving forward to moving backward as I longed to be in his arms again. Even though Derrick was there with me, if Vic had been alone, I probably would have tried to talk to him and convince him that leaving me had been a mistake. But he wasn't alone.

When Latrice whispered her threat in my ear before she walked away, the only thing that kept me from snapping back with a warning of my own had been Vic's eyes locked on mine. I'd never seen him look so angry and volatile. As slim as my chances of winning him back were, I knew that saying anything to Latrice, at that point, would have definitely hammered the final nail into the coffin. A coffin that I prayed was still open, despite Vic's venomous glare. So after that night, I decided to make one last effort to try and change his mind.

I went to his job instead of trying to call. I wanted to talk to him face to face and make him understand that we belonged together. I only wanted to talk. I never meant for things to get out of hand.

"What do you want, Julie?" Vic asked as he approached me. He'd had me waiting in the lobby for fifteen minutes after the guard at the front called and told him I was downstairs. I didn't care about the wait. I had a purpose.

"Hello to you too, Vic. I came to talk."

Vic frowned and folded his arms across his chest. "I don't have time, Julie. I'm busy."

I stepped to him and put my hand on his arm. In a soft voice, I said, "Please, Vic? Just give me a few minutes."

Vic glared at me at me, and for a second I didn't think he'd give in

"Ten minutes," he finally said. I couldn't help but smile.

We walked outside and sat at an empty picnic table. Actually, I sat. He stood, obviously letting me know he had no intention of getting comfortable.

"Vic..."

"What you did was childish," he said, cutting me off.

"What are you talking about?" I asked, innocently.

"Don't play games, Julie. You and Stacey knew I'd be there with Latrice. That's the only reason why you and your *friend* showed up." He glared down at me. Feigning ignorance was not going to work.

"I miss you, Vic," I said, honestly. "You're right, I did know you were going to be there with Latrice.

Yes, that's why I came. I just wanted to see you. And I wanted to see who you replaced me with."

"Julie, I didn't replace you with anybody. I ended our marriage because I wasn't happy."

As hard as I tried to fight them, tears began falling from my eyes.

"Vic, I love you."

"Julie, don't..."

"Don't what?" I shouted. "Don't tell you how much you mean to me? And how happy I wanted to make you? Don't tell you that I've never loved any man the way I loved you? And that I never want to love that way again?"

"Keep your voice down, Julie," Vic said, looking around at several employees who'd been out smoking. I didn't care about the audience, though. My tears were falling and my anger and frustration were rising. I slammed my hand down on the table.

"You fucking hurt me, Vic! I did nothing to deserve the shit you've put me through. The shit you're *still* putting me through. Why are you doing this to me? Can you tell me that, please? You said that you loved me. Is this how you treat someone you love?"

Vic's face reddened with embarrassment as a few female co-workers sucked their teeth and shook their heads in disapproval. He'd always hated to have anyone in his business, but I didn't give a shit. They could have pulled up a chair and taken notes for all I cared. I'd been holding my pain inside for so long that I quickly forgot all about wanting to talk.

"I hope your little romance with your bitch blows up in your face, Vic. I hope you get to experience the pain I'm feeling."

"Julie, goddamn! Why can't you just understand that I did this to avoid hurting you in a worse way? Yes, I loved you, but I wasn't in love with you. I wasn't happy. You deserve to be with someone who wants to make you happy. Someone who wants to be your everything. I'm sorry, but I'm not that guy."

I twisted my mouth. "Well, thank you for being such a stand up guy," I spat sarcastically.

Vic shook his head and frowned, only making me angrier.

"Doesn't it matter to you that you've put me through this? Are you that damn cold?"

"Look Julie, I'm sorry that you're hurting. Whether you want to believe this or not, I don't take pleasure in your pain. Leaving was just something that I had to do."

Had to do?

I stood up, not caring about the people who stood around to enjoy the show. I walked over to Vic, who was obviously uncomfortable with the attention.

"Go to hell, Vic!" I screamed, slapping him hard across the face. "You and that bitch!" I slapped him again, harder this time, and then stormed away.

But I wasn't finished.

With my hopes all but dead and buried, I wanted revenge of some kind. Revenge for the betrayal and abandonment Vic had heaped on me. Seething in my car, I drove around the company's parking lot until I found Vic's car.

I shut off the engine, pulled my keys from the ignition, and approached his Eclipse. I didn't care who saw me as I scratched a message across the trunk, doors, and hood.

"Sorry, Vic," I said out loud. "It was just something I had to do."

Vic
31

Angry wouldn't have been the right word to describe how I felt when I saw what Julie had done to my car. Pissed off wouldn't have even worked. I needed seven words. Seven words to explain what I was feeling inside as I stood with my hands balled up, while my fellow co-workers walked to their cars, some snickering and others gasping.

I was about to go to jail.

I walked around my car and growled at the messages left and the four tires that were slashed. I slammed my fist down on the hood. "Goddamn," I whispered.

Just then Roy and Colin pulled up. I'd called them to come and pick me up.

"Oh shit," Colin said, barely stifling a laugh.

"Damn, man," Roy said.

They walked around the car, surveying the damage.

"You are a fucking asshole... I hate you...Go to hell, you pathetic dog." Colin looked at me after he finished his oral presentation. "Damn, man, I didn't think Julie was capable of some shit like this."

"Neither did I," Roy added.

I slammed my hand on the hood again. "She's not going to get away with this shit," I said. I looked at Colin. "Man, take me over to her house."

"For what?" he asked.

"Man, if she thinks she can fuck up my car and embarrass me at my job like this and get away with it, then..."

"Then what?" Colin asked, cutting me off. "What you gonna do, dog? Beat her ass?"

I kicked my flat tire. "Maybe."

"Shut up, Vic," Colin said. "You know you ain't kickin' no woman's ass. So stop talkin' shit. Dog, she fucked up your shit. That's what women do when they're angry and hurting."

Roy shook his head. "He's right, man. At least you can get the car repaired."

"So what? You guys saying that I'm just supposed to let this go? Let her get away with this?"

Colin put his arm around my shoulder. "Dog, that's exactly what I'm sayin'. Chalk this one up to experience. She got this round. But you got Latrice and your happiness. Leave it at that, throw in the towel and go home with your black eye. Besides, you really don't want to roll to her house and leave your shit here. You've had enough people drive by to inspect the damage. Just call a tow truck and have them come and pick it up. Take it directly to the body shop."

I looked at Colin and then Roy, who nodded in agreement. Then I looked at my car.

"Doesn't she understand that I would have hurt her more if I'd stayed with her?" I asked.

"No, dog," Colin answered. "She's a woman scorned. And she loved your ass. Like I said, throw in the towel and go home. Now call the tow truck. I'm gettin' tired of seeing all these people drive by."

I sighed as I grabbed my cell phone and called AAA. I don't know how I did it, but I managed to not call Julie. I got my car back two weeks later.

ROY
32

"Daddy!"

I smiled as my little girls climbed into the car and hugged and kissed me. "Hey, you two! How are my little angels doing?"

"We're fine!" they said in unison.

"Are we going to McDonalds?" Jenea asked.

"Yeah, can we Daddy? Please?"

I looked at my twin daughters with a very serious face and said, "Are you two crazy? McDonalds? You want me to take you there and pass up on the broccoli and lima beans?"

"Yes!" they yelled as they buckled their seat belt.

"Lima beans are yucky!" Sheila said, making a scrunched up face.

Jenea followed with her own, "Ewww!"

I laughed and pulled away from the curb. I didn't even wave at Stacey as she stood by the front door. We had been separated for four months. The breakup of our marriage happened just a couple of days after the fiasco at the house. After the heated argument we had, I decided to stay by Colin for two nights. I needed that time to cool off and gather my thoughts. I wanted to make sure that when I did go back home to deal with Stacey, I would be in the right frame of mind. I didn't want another confrontation like the one we'd had. Stacey may have disrespected me, but I had crossed the line when I called her a bitch. I had never called her out of her name like that, and I was regretful for doing so. When I finally did go back home, I had every intention of apologizing for that and trying to get us back on track. The last thing I expected was to end up walking back out of the house with the realization that my marriage wasn't going to last.

"So what? Did you forget you had a family?"

I had just walked through the front door, and it had taken me a good five minutes just to do that. I looked at Stacey and sighed. She had become so ugly in such a short amount of time.

"Hello to you, too," I said, closing the door behind me.

"Don't give me a hello. You stormed out of here and embarrassed the hell out of me in front of Julie and Derrick."

"You embarrassed me in front of my friends," I said, struggling to keep my voice down. I knew the girls were sleeping. Although I had called them during my time away, I had missed them like crazy.

"I don't care about your friends," Stacey hissed.

I stared hard at her. Her eyes, normally soft and sparkling, were void of any expression except malice. Her lips, normally kissable, were curled into a snarl.

"Well that's good, because I don't give a shit about your friends either, Stacey." I inhaled and exhaled after I said that because I knew a dark cloud was about to form in our living room. Accompanying the clouds would be a few bolts of lightning. I didn't expect the tornado that followed.

"Go to hell, Roy!"

"I am standing right in it," I yelled, no longer able to keep my cool.

"Then leave!"

"Leave? I did that already. But you know what... I pay the bills here. If anyone should leave, it should be you."

"Oh, no. You are not kicking me and the girls out like that."

"Who the hell said anything about the girls? They have no problem with my friends. That's your hang-up."

"Hang-up?" She crossed her arms defiantly.

I crossed mine also. "That's right... hang-up. You're destroying our marriage over other people's problems. That is sad."

"Destroying? All I asked was that you respect me and not have him come around. You know how I felt about what he did."

"Why? Why, Stacey? What the hell was so bad about it? He was a man about what he did. He should be commended for that. It was better than cheating."

"Commended? For what? Finding a way out?"

"How can you look at it as a way out? If he didn't love her, why should he waste their time? But if you want to look at it as finding a way out, you go right ahead. At least he found a way out for both of them. Because if he had stayed, they would've both been unhappy."

"Unhappy, my ass. Julie is unhappy now that he found his way out."

"She didn't look so unhappy when she was conspiring with you."

"Conspiring? Julie is my friend. I invited her over."

"Without telling me."

"What? I need your permission? I am a woman. Not your child!"

"I'm not calling you a child, Stacey. You should have discussed it with me first, and you know that. I gave you that much respect when I told you Vic was coming."

"No, you disrespected me by not honoring my wishes!"

I turned away from Stacey and kicked the side of the couch. She was getting me worked up in a way I hadn't been in a long time. How could she talk about disrespect after what she did?

With my back to her, I said, "How could you do what you did, Stacey? I mean, cut the bullshit. How could you have been so conniving? I'm your husband. I love, provide, and take care of you and the girls. Even if you were mad... how could you do what you did to me?"

"I didn't want Vic here! Don't you understand that?"

I turned around. "No! That's my point. I don't understand. Do you love me? Because if you love me, you have a hell of a way of showing it." I watched Stacey and clenched my jaws. She stood staring at me with cold eyes. Eyes that I had never seen before. "How do you do that to someone you love?" I asked again.

Stacey stood before me, not moving or saying a word. I closed my eyes and tilted my head back. When I finally brought my head down and opened my eyes again, I saw something I hadn't seen in a long time.

"Why are you crying?" After that question, what had initially started out as a few teardrops quickly turned into a flood.

"What's wrong, Stacey?" I moved toward her. I hated to see her cry; I hated that our argument had escalated to the level it had. I tried to put my arms around her, but when I did, she put up her hands.

"Stay away from me, Roy," she said through her tears.

I was shocked. "Stay away from you? You act like I was going to do something to you. I'm your husband. Stacey, I don't want us to argue like this, and I don't want you to cry. I love you. I want us to find a way to work this problem out." I moved toward her again, and this time she stepped back and stared at me. Her eyes were red and swollen from her tears.

"Let's do this together, baby," I said pleading with my own eyes.

"We can't." She shook her head.

"What do you mean, we can't? We can do anything together." I watched her as more tears fell from her eyes. I stood confused about the pain I could see she was in, but couldn't quite understand.

"Stacey? Please talk to me." I wanted to reach out and wrap her in my arms and somehow make her understand that together we could overcome any obstacle. But as she stood silent and unmoving, I found myself doubting that.

Finally, after seconds of tense, silence crept by, Stacey, her bottom lip quivering, said, "I don't know if I can, Roy."

"What do you mean?" I watched her with confused eyes. "Tell me what the problem is."

Crying uncontrollably now, Stacey said, "I don't know if I can do this anymore."

"I don't want to argue anymore, either," I said.

"No, Roy. I mean, I...I...don't know if I can do *us* anymore."

"What? What are you saying?" My voice was barely a whisper as I studied her.

Staring back at me with a serious gaze, Stacey said, "I'm... I'm not sure of my feelings anymore, Roy. I need space and time to think about things."

Space and time? "Space and time?" I asked. "Where the hell is this coming from?"

"Look Roy," she said as she looked away. "I just don't know what I want anymore, OK? I need time. Can't you understand that?"

"No, I can't!" I yelled. "This just doesn't make sense to me."

"Roy, I'm only trying to do the right thing, like Vic. I should be commended for this," she asked sarcastically.

I kicked a hole in the wall when she said that. "Commended? This is bullshit, Stacey. Straight up bullshit!"

Without responding, Stacey ran past me and went upstairs. Left me standing alone in the living room. She needed time? I tried to figure out what happened between us. Where did we go wrong? What had I done? But the more I thought about it, the more frustrated I became.

I went up to talk to her, but she kept the bedroom door locked and wouldn't let me in. I left then, and went back by Colin. I didn't talk when he opened his door. Thankfully, he didn't press me. I just needed to think. I fell asleep on his couch somewhere in-between my thoughts. The next evening, I went back home, and instead of seeing Stacey or my little girls, a note met me—she had gone to her mother's back in Tennessee. When I called, her mother, a woman who had become a second mother to me, answered the phone.

"Hello Mrs. Bolton." I waited for her to answer. I expected a chilly reception, because she and Stacey were like best friends and I figured Stacey had only said negative things about me.

"Hello, Roy," she said.

"How are you doing? It's been a while," I said.

"I'm doing just fine," she responded. "How are you holding up?"

I sighed. "I've been better," I answered honestly.

"Roy, I want you to remember that when times are at their roughest, those are the times when you must keep the faith."

A tear fell from my eye when she said that. "I have to be honest, Mrs. Bolton, I don't have much faith right now."

"Roy, I don't know what is going through my daughter's head. I really don't. I've tried to talk to her, but for whatever reason, she won't open up to me. I know this is hard, but please try to hold on. Give her time. She'll come around."

I sighed again and massaged the back of my neck. "I'll try," I said. "Is she around? I'd like to speak to her."

There was a moment of silence before Mrs. Bolton said, "I'm sorry, Roy, but she doesn't want to talk to you. I wish I could make her, but you know how she is."

I bit down on my lip. “OK, Mrs. Bolton. Just tell her I called.”

“I will.”

“How are the girls?”

“They’re fine. They’re both sleeping right now. They know you two are having problems, so when you speak to them, be honest and answer their questions truthfully. Don’t sugarcoat anything for them.”

“I won’t,” I said, exhaling. “Can you tell them I miss them?”

“I will. And Roy, they miss you, too. And so do I. Please remember that no matter what happens between you two, you will always be my son-in-law. You’ve done right by my daughter. I know that, and I am thankful.”

“Thank you, Mrs. Bolton. I would be proud to continue to call you my mother-in-law.”

I hung up the phone and cried. I missed my family; I missed my old life. Nothing was the same anymore, and it was painful. I didn’t hear from Stacey for the next week, until she came home—without the girls. I didn’t mind, because I didn’t want them around to see what was happening between their parents. Stacey and I screamed, cursed, and broke things; we did everything but become violent with one another. When everything was all said and done, I left the house again, only this time I had no intention of going back. Stacey and I officially separated six weeks later. The judge granted me alternating weekends with Jenea and Sheila—something I wasn’t happy with, but would accept for the time being, at least until it was time to file for divorce. When that time came, I was going to fight for full custody. I wanted the girls with me.

The time wasn't coming fast enough for me, though. It all but came to a standstill during the holiday season. That was rough for me and the girls. For the first time, we didn't have our traditional family Christmas. Instead of doing it as a unit, they spent the first half of the day opening their presents with Stacey, and the other half with me. To see the forced smiles on their faces was incredibly painful. They didn't enjoy Christmas like they normally did, and that made me even angrier inside, because they were suffering and it wasn't their fault.

Christmas day had been a long and stressful one, but it eventually went by. For New Years, I let them stay with Stacey. Four months had now passed as I guided my Volvo wagon down Route 1, with the girls sitting in the back.

"OK, OK," I said playing their favorite, CD—*NSYNC*. "McDonalds it is."

"Yay!" my girls cried out in unison.

I smiled on the outside, and cried on the inside. I knew that they were hurting over what was happening, but they were intelligent and were actually dealing with it better than I ever would have expected. I just wish I never had to answer questions like, "When are you coming home, daddy?" Or, "When are you and Mommy going to stop fighting?"

I drove the car with those questions repeating in my head. I hated having to tell them the truth.

"Mommy and I aren't getting back together."

Stacey
33

As Roy drove off with the girls, I closed the door and sighed. Even though I couldn't blame him for feeling the way he felt, it was still hurtful to see how much animosity he had toward me. He was so unlike the person that he used to be. He had become cold and bitter. Of course, I expected that once I told him the news about not wanting to be married anymore. I wanted to tell him years ago, that I didn't love him the way he loved me, but I lost the nerve after he proposed. That day changed my life.

It was at his mother's house, in front of his entire family on Christmas Day. We were there for dinner, since we had spent breakfast and lunch by my mother's. It was a normal celebration, filled with food and laughter, until Roy stood up and tapped his wineglass with the back of his knife. Asking for complete silence, he turned to me. I'll never forget the silence that overtook the room. And I will always remember the feel of the spotlight that only I could see. Right there in front of all of the stares and smiles, Roy got down on one knee, took my hand in his, and removed a ring box from his pocket. Everyone gasped when the box was opened, revealing a beautiful pear-shaped ring. I felt my heart drop. Just the night before, I had been with my true love—Rashad. And I promised him that after the holidays were over, I was going to leave Roy to be with him, because I *was* truly in love with him. We had been seeing each other for a little over a year. He was the man of my dreams. We'd met at a fundraiser on campus and hit it off immediately. He did for me what Roy never really did—he made my knees weak. He made my skin tingle. I never felt that with Roy. But I did care about Roy and his family, who I had become close to during the course of our relationship. And because I was so close to them, and they accepted me as one of their own, I never had the courage to end the relationship. I knew that would hurt him, and in turn, everyone else. I didn't want that. I didn't want to be the bad guy. So instead of doing what I should have done, I stayed with Roy and saw Rashad on the side.

But the longer I stayed with Roy, the deeper I fell for Rashad. He brought a calm to my spirit that Roy, as good a man as he was, never could. I had finally worked up the courage to end things when he popped the question. But with everyone's eyes focused on me, waiting for my answer, my nerve disappeared. There was no way I was going to say no with a whole audience watching me. I said yes. And while everyone cheered and Roy hugged and kissed me and promised to always love me, I died. I was in tears when I met Rashad a few days later and told him about what had happened. I figured that despite the engagement, we could continue to go on with what we had. I couldn't say no to Roy, but I wasn't willing to let Rashad go, either.

Unfortunately, Rashad didn't share the same sentiment. When I told him, he went off. He said he no longer wanted to have anything to do with me. In tears and on my knees, I begged him to give us a chance.

"Please, Rashad! I need you."

"If you need me, Stacey, then go tell Roy no."

"It's not that easy, Rashad. His family...they were all there. I can't...Please, baby. We can do this."

"No. We can't, Stacey. I don't want to be the nigga on the side anymore. I'm through with that shit. Point blank, you either leave Roy so we can do this, or we're done."

"Rashad...Please don't make me choose like this. Please!"

"If the choice is that hard for you, Stacey, then you're not strong enough to be the woman that I want in my life. Good-bye."

Rashad left me on the floor in tears. What he said had been the truth—I wasn't strong enough. That's why I stayed with Roy, got married, had Jenea and Sheila, and pretended to be in love—all because I wasn't strong enough to admit that I wasn't.

I never thought that my marriage with Roy was going to fall apart. Although I was unhappy, I was determined to see it through until the end. I promised till death do us part, and I was sticking to that. But when Vic left Julie, everything changed for me. Old feelings that I had locked away came back to the surface. I became bitter and angry. I was so jealous at Vic for not having children, being able to make his decision and ultimately have the type of life he wanted. That's why I didn't want him around. I couldn't bear to look at him and see the happiness emanating from him. I invited Julie over to watch the fight because I wanted Vic to be as miserable as I was. I didn't want him to be there with his true love, having a good time. Yeah it was spiteful, but for me it was necessary.

I never really thought that Roy and I would fall apart as a result of it. Though in the back of my mind,

I know I wanted that. I just didn't think I was going to get that lucky. If I could have done it a different way to avoid having Jenea and Sheila get hurt in the process, I would have. My little angels are everything to me. They may not have been planned, but their time was due, and God had brought them to me. I just hope that as time goes on, they can come to terms with the breakup of their home.

I sighed again as I sat down on the sofa and stared at nothing in particular. As I sat there, I realized for the first time in a long time, I was finally free.

Latrice
34

I heard the phone ringing while I was struggling to unlock the door with the bags of groceries in my hand. When I finally got it unlocked, I rushed in and grabbed the phone, hit the talk button.

"Hello?"

"Hey LaLa."

Damn. I should have checked the caller ID.

I wasted no time. "Bernard, I told you I'm seeing somebody."

Bernard huffed. "So what? Does that mean I can't call you to talk?"

I put my groceries on the counter and looked at the clock. It was seven o'clock. Vic was working late and wouldn't be home for at least another hour. Since we were always together we'd decided that it would make more sense to pay one monthly rent. Besides, the way our relationship was progressing, we would be discussing marriage at some point, which was something we both wanted. Vic was the milk and I was the coffee; together we made one hell of a blend.

The only problem was Bernard.

Since the first time he'd called me months ago, he hadn't stopped calling. He'd call me at home whenever Vic wasn't home. I don't know how, but he always knew when it was safe to call. He'd even started to call me at work, which pissed me off because I hadn't given him my number. As hard as I tried to be a bitch, Bernard knew how to use his too-sexy voice to spit his game—game that could always make me tingle—and keep me on the phone longer than I wanted to be on. No matter how hard I tried to not let Bernard get to me, he was doing exactly that. I found myself thinking about him when I didn't want to, hearing his voice when I was supposed to be hearing something else, seeing him when my eyes were closed. Even though I denied it, Bernard knew that he still had a hold on me.

"Look, Bernard, you know you don't just wanna talk. So don't play, OK? I told you, I am involved..."

"With Vic. The white boy. I know," Bernard said, cutting me off. I knew Vic's color was upsetting to him and his ego, but I didn't care.

"Yes, with Vic," I snapped. "And as you know, we live together. So I don't think he'd appreciate you calling me like this."

"LaLa, I don't care what he would or wouldn't like. I'm not concerned with him. I don't love him."

I held my breath when he said that. I didn't want to hear that word.

"Bernard, you don't love me."

"You thinking for me now, LaLa?"

Exhaling frustration, I said, "I'm not thinking for you. Just telling you the truth. And don't call me LaLa anymore."

"Why? You're my LaLa. And you haven't spoken the truth yet."

Putting the groceries away, I said, "Oh really? And what truth is that?" I shook my head knowing I was falling into the web he was weaving. I tried to pull myself out of it quickly. "And I am not yours to be calling me any other names but my full name," I snapped.

"The truth LaLa," he said defiantly, "is that no matter how much you deny it and try to ignore the feeling, you and I both know that you are still feeling me. We belong together. You knew it back then, and you know it now. White boy or no white boy."

"His name is Vic, and I don't know anything right now."

"So you're not sure about him, then?"

"I didn't say that."

"You just said you didn't know anything right now," Bernard countered.

I passed my hand through my hair furiously. "Stop twisting my words around, Bernard. You know I didn't mean it like that."

"Hey, I'm only going by what I heard."

I strangled the phone. I wanted nothing more than to hang up on his ass, but for some reason I couldn't bring myself to do it. Had what he said been true? Was I still feeling him? No, no, no!

"Bernard, I got to go. My man is coming home soon, and I need to get dinner together."

"Oh, it's like that? He's got you all domesticated and shit?"

I slammed my hand down on the counter top. Bernard was starting to irk me. "No it's not like that! We cook for each other. Just like good couples do. And I don't need to explain shit to you."

"Then why are you?" Bernard asked matter-of-factly. I could tell that he was smiling on the other end of the phone.

"Bernard, don't call me again, OK? Just lose my number—here and at work."

"On one condition."

I broke two eggs as I was removing them from the carton to put away. "No conditions, Bernard."

"Then I can't lose your number."

Damn.

"What, Bernard? What the hell is your condition? What do I have to do to get you to lose my number and forget you ever knew me?" Damn, he had me worked up. I broke another egg, on purpose this time.

"Meet me for lunch tomorrow, LaLa. That's all."

"I can't do that. I've told you that before—all of the other times you asked me."

"LaLa, you've been dodging me for the past three months now. Why? I'm just asking for lunch. People do it every day."

"I'm with Vic, Bernard."

"All I'm asking for is a meeting between two old friends. What's the harm in that? Unless... nah it can't be that."

"Unless what?" I asked, regretting it instantly, knowing that I'd fallen right back into the web.

"Unless you're worried that our lunch date could lead to something more? But then, you're with Vic. That wouldn't be possible."

"Damn right it wouldn't be."

"So lunch, then? Say, at 1:00?"

I sighed. "And if I have lunch with you, you'll lose my numbers, right?"

"I'll lose them as soon as you say 1:00 is on."

"OK, Bernard. I'll entertain you. 1:00 is on."

"Cool. Meet me at Tomato Palace by the lake. Oh and LaLa... just so you know. You entertain me every night in my thoughts."

I hung up the phone without saying a word. My heart was beating heavily and I was warm. "You should have said no, girl," I whispered to myself.

That night, as much as I didn't want to, I dreamt about Bernard. We were making love on a bed of white roses, while the moon, in all of its splendor, glowed and illuminated our bodies. I could feel the rhythm of his body as if the music had never stopped playing. I could feel my own body sway to the groove. The dream ended in a climactic barrage of moaning and gasping; so loud that I couldn't believe Vic hadn't heard. But then, it had only been a dream.

When the clock struck one the next day, I walked into Tomato Palace with the dream replaying in my mind. I stopped just inside the entrance and shook my head. I didn't need or want those kinds of thoughts. I walked into the main dining area and saw Bernard sitting in a booth against the wall. The Tomato Palace had been one of our favorite spots to dine in when we were together. As I walked to the booth, I thought to myself that I should have insisted on a different place.

I sat down without saying a word. Bernard smiled.

"Mmm mmm. I know you said you lost all of your weight, but I didn't expect you to look the way you do now. I mean, you always looked good to me, but you definitely have worked hard. You look good, LaLa. I'm glad you finally agreed to meet me." He tried to take my hand, but I quickly let him know I wasn't having that.

"Unh-uh. Just remember the deal," I said seriously.

Bernard smiled. "They're lost. Only problem is, I forgot that I memorized them in the process."

I looked at him and curled my lips, but didn't say anything. Damn, he looked good. Better than when I last saw him before our break up. He'd put on weight—the good kind. His arms and chest were bigger, his face rounder. His weight-gain looked good on his 6'4" frame. His hair was low and faded, and his eyes were still sleepy and sexy. And he was looking damn fine in the Hugo Boss suit he had on. I made sure not to compliment him.

"I don't have long. I have a meeting to go to," I said.

"Well then, I guess we better order."

The waiter came by a few seconds later and we ordered our lunch. While we waited for the food, we madc small talk about our jobs and our lives. Bernard told me about having opened up his own auto body repair shop in Laurel, and about his plans to open another in the next coming months. I congratulated him, and told him about my growth after Danita's death. I also made sure to mention my happiness with Vic—something that, by the look on his face, he didn't want to hear. When the food finally came, we ate in relative silence. I just wanted to eat and run and avoid his gaze, because I could feel it stabbing at me like a knife. I cursed at myself silently for letting him have any type of an effect on me.

"So tell me something," he said, swallowing the last of his meal. A slow eater by nature, I was only halfway through with my spinach salad. "What does this white boy give you that you can't have with me? Because, if I recall correctly, up until you pushed me away, we had a real love thing going on."

I looked at Bernard and shook my head. "First of all, his name is Vic. You need to start using it. Second of all, it's not about what he has. It's about the person that he is. Vic is a special man."

"He's white," Bernard cut in.

I snapped back. "His race doesn't mean shit to me. He makes me happy, and that's all that matters."

Taking my hand in his, Bernard said, "I used to make you happy, too. Or do you not remember all of that?"

Pulling my hand away, I said, "I remember. But I'm a different person now, with different expectations. Different needs. Different wants."

"And you don't want me?"

"I have what I want, Bernard."

"You didn't answer my question. Do you or do you not want me?" He looked at me intensely with his brown eyes. He was trying to reel me in with his gaze. In the past, it would have worked. I would have folded and become hypnotized and powerless to his charm. And even though I still felt a little tingle for him, it was different this time.

"I have the person I want, Bernard," I said resolutely.

Bernard bit on his bottom lip, leaned back in the booth and nodded slowly.

"You know, I can see that you've changed. I can see that you're stronger now. Danita's death, horrible as it was, turned you into an even more beautiful person. And I don't just mean looks, because to me, you were always fine. I hear what you're saying. And I know you're for real about your feelings about your white... about Vic.

"But, I will say this. Even though you are serious and your mind is made up, I can tell that you still have feelings for me. You're not as past me as you're letting on. I can see that. Even if you don't want to admit it to me, or yourself. But that's cool. I will give up on trying to take your heart back. I will respect what you have going on right now. I can be a big man and let you have your happiness. But just know, LaLa, I will always be in the shadows, just waiting until I get one more shot."

"You'll be waiting for a long time," I said.

"We'll see."

There was a long moment of silence between us as we stared at each other. During that time, the waiter came and brought our check. Bernard paid, and then we walked out of the restaurant. Outside, the sun was high in the sky, and brought pleasant warmth to the crisp February air. As I slipped my hands into my gloves, Bernard looked at me.

"Well, I guess this is it, then."

"I guess so," I replied.

"You sure there's no chance for us to do it again?"

"Bernard," I said quietly. "I've moved on. You should, too."

He took a deep breath and exhaled. "Well, do I get one last hug?"

I glared at him. He put his hands up quickly. "All I'm asking for is a hug. One for the road, that's all."

I hesitated for a second and then nodded. "One for the road."

Bernard smiled and pulled me into him. He hugged me tightly, slowly passing his hand up and down my back. I can't lie. It felt good to feel his arms around me. Too good.

"I have to go," I said, pushing away from him slowly. To my surprise, before I could separate myself from him, Bernard pressed his lips against mine. At first, I tried to resist and push him away. But when he guided his tongue to my lips, my mouth instinctively opened and welcomed it inside. I met his tongue with my own, and felt my body swoon. The kiss may have lasted for only a few short seconds, but it was deep, sensual, and intense.

When we finally parted, Bernard looked at me and said, "That's the answer I was looking for. I'll be in the shadows LaLa. Respectful, but waiting. Tell Vic he better not fuck it up." Without saying another word, Bernard turned and walked away, leaving me there with hot lips and a thumping heart. When I finally got myself calmed down, I headed to my car. Little did I know that Bernard and I weren't the only ones by the lake that day.

Julie
35

Biting down on my finger was about all I could do to keep myself from screaming when I saw Latrice kissing a man that wasn't Vic.

"That bitch!" I yelled as I drove my car down Little Patuxent Parkway. I thought back to the night she gave me her warning. "That Bitch!" I yelled, again slamming my hand down on the steering wheel. Oh, we would see whose ass got kicked now.

"Let's see how Vic reacts to finding out about your little rendezvous."

As I waited for a red light to change, I dug my cell phone from my purse and hit speed dial one. I needed advice before I made the call. I hadn't spoken to Vic since I scratched up his car and slashed his tires, and knowing how much he loved his car, I know he had to be pissed. I was surprised he hadn't called to curse me out, or worse.

I let all of my frustration out on that car. The tire slashing had been done for good measure. I wanted Vic and everyone else to know how much he hurt me. I didn't regret what I had done for a second.

Until now.

Latrice had just given me another chance. Somehow I had to find a way to tell Vic what I had seen. If I could find a way to make him listen to me, he'd have to realize that he had been wrong about leaving me. I would make him see that we belonged together.

When Stacey answered the phone, I said, "She was kissing someone else!"

"Who?" Stacey asked.

"That bitch that Vic is dating." I couldn't help but smile.

"Who? Latrice?"

"Yes. La bitch."

"What do you mean, kissing someone else? Where are you?"

"I'm on my way home right now. I took the day off today. And I mean kissing someone as in, I saw Miss Thing at the lake, giving mouth-to-mouth to some guy."

"And it wasn't Vic?"

"Unless Vic got an extremely dark tan, I'd say it wasn't him."

"Dayum, girl. You're serious? What did you do?"

Blowing the horn at an elderly driver who was doing Sunday driving on a Tuesday, I said, "Nothing. I bit down on my finger and just watched. Then I left and called you. Tell me what to do, Stacey. I can't let that bitch get away with it."

"Especially after what she said to you."

"Oh, especially after that. She thinks she got the last laugh? Not after this, she didn't. I'll be laughing all the way back into Vic's arms."

"Yeah, but what about the whole car incident? You know he's got to be pissed about that."

"I know, I know. That's why I'm calling you. Help me figure out the best way to call and tell him. Stacey, I want my man back."

"Julie..."

"Don't say it, Stacey," I said, pulling into my townhouse complex. "I know what you're going to say."

"Yeah, because I keep saying it. You should let Vic go. I hate to be so blunt, but he doesn't want you."

I shook my head. No matter how true it seemed and no matter what he'd said to me, I couldn't allow myself to believe that.

"He only thinks he doesn't want me, Stacey. But I know different. I can't believe that his feelings have completely gone away like that. No matter how hard he tries to act like they have, I can't believe it. He was confused, that's all. And you can be sure Latrice did whatever she could to keep him confused. Think about it. They met at work. Do you honestly think she wasn't trying to put the moves on him when she first met him? She was probably screwing with his head from day one. That's why Vic changed his mind about us. Not because he fell out of love with me. She just got to him."

"Julie. I hear what you're saying, but..."

"Stacey, I love you, and I appreciate your friendship, but I don't want to hear any buts. I just know Vic isn't over me. That's all that matters. I'll show you, him and everyone else. Now, I called you to ask for advice on how to tell him. Are you going to give me that advice or not?"

Stacey didn't say anything for a few seconds, and I started to worry that maybe I had been too crude. But it couldn't be helped. The last thing I wanted to hear was that Vic was not in love with me anymore. I had been hearing that for too long, and at one point I almost believed it myself. But that night at Roy and Stacey's, I overheard him and Colin in the kitchen. He was worried about who Derrick was. If he were over me, he would never have cared about who I was with.

I shut off my engine and sat still for a few seconds. I pictured Latrice kissing her mystery man. I wanted to paint that very picture for Vic.

"So are you going to help me, Stacey?"

Stacey started to say something, but then she sighed. "Okay, girl. If you really want to do this."

I smiled the biggest smile I had in a long time. And I had no one but Latrice to thank for it. Without leaving my car, Stacey and I figured out a way to break the news to Vic. Hopefully, he'd give me a chance.

Vic
36

I sat across from Julie and stared at her. We were at the Macaroni Grill restaurant. It was packed with diners, endless conversation filtering through the air. So no one seemed to notice or care that we weren't speaking.

I had arrived twenty minutes late. I didn't really want to be there. After all the bullshit she'd pulled lately, she was lucky I didn't go off on her when she called me at work and asked to meet for lunch. But after her performance with my car, I already had enough people at work in my business. The last thing I needed was for anyone to hear me losing my cool on the phone with her. So I agreed to meet her.

While we were on the phone, she'd tried to apologize. Said she had a lot of explaining to do. But I couldn't have cared less about her apology. I only agreed to the lunch meeting because I had something to make clear, once and for all.

So there I sat, while the ice melted in my glass, everyone around us having a good time. I watched Julie with cold eyes. I wanted her to see how I angry I was. By the way she played with her napkin and kept her eyes focused everywhere else but on me, I could tell that she knew. After the waiter came around and took my to-go order, I took a sip of water and cleared my throat.

"Julie, I really don't care about what you have to say to me, OK? I only agreed to meet you because I want to make one thing clear to you."

Before I could say anything else, Julie put up her hand.

"Vic, before you go on, let me apologize again for the scene I caused at your job, and what I did to your car. It was wrong of me to do that."

I clenched my jaws. I was trying to avoid talking about that, because just the thought of that day made my blood boil. Julie stared at me, waiting for me to respond. I took a deep breath and tried to calm down.

"Julie, that shit you did cost me close to two-thousand dollars to fix. Add that to the embarrassment I felt at work, and you'll understand when I say I don't want to hear any of your damn apologies." I shivered from the chill in my own voice.

Julie looked at me and exhaled. "Why did you agree to come then, Vic?" she asked, tightening her lips.

"Look, I just want to make one thing clear to you, Julie. I'm not in love with you."

"Vic..." she started to say. But I wasn't finished. I cut her off.

"I've told you already, Julie. I'm sorry you're hurting. Like I've said, I don't take pleasure in it. But we both deserve to be happy. And that wouldn't have happened if I had stayed with you. Now please, don't call me anymore. Just stay the hell away from me, and my car." I stood up to leave. I had said what I needed to say. I wanted to go before I lost my cool.

"Are you in love with her, Vic?" Julie asked, before I could step away. I looked at her.

"Yes," I answered, honestly.

"And do you think she's in love with you?"

"What?"

"Do you think she's in love with you?" Julie asked again, with a smirk. I could feel the eyes of some of the diners focused on us. I gave one gentleman a look that let him know what business he should have been minding. He did, right away.

I looked down at Julie, who watched me, waiting for an answer.

"Yes," I said. I turned my back to leave.

"Then, if she's in love with you, why was she kissing another man?" Julie said loud enough for me and everyone else to hear.

I turned around and asked in a heated whisper, "What did you say?"

"Ask your bitch who the black man was that she was kissing yesterday afternoon by the lake."

I stared at her. She returned my glare with her own.

"What the fuck did you say?"

"That bitch who you say you are in love with, the one who you say is in love with you, was busy taking in another man's saliva yesterday in front of Tomato Palace. I saw it with my own eyes, Vic. Make sure she knows that."

Unable to keep my voice down, and not really caring, I sat down.

"Aren't you tired of the fucking games, Julie?" I snapped. "Haven't you done enough shit already? Haven't you caused enough damage? Do you take pleasure in being a bitch?"

"Just ask her, Vic," Julie said with cool confidence. "And when you find out, let me know. Maybe then we can work on us."

Without another word, she stood up from the table and walked past me, out of the restaurant. I sat silent while everyone's eyes were focused solely on me. I felt like I was E.F. Hutton and everyone was ready to listen to what I had to say. But I didn't say a word. I just sat unmoving, digesting what Julie had told me. Had she been serious? Was she playing another one of her games? Could Latrice really have done what Julie said she did? I exhaled; there was only one way to find out. Leaving my food on the table, I walked out of the restaurant and hit speed dial two on my cell phone. When Latrice's voice mail clicked on, I left a simple message.

"I'm not coming back to work. We'll talk when I see you tonight."

Latrice
37

From the moment I listened to the voice mail message Vic left for me, I knew something was wrong. He didn't go back to work, and he said we would talk later tonight. Nothing more, nothing less. I tried to call him, to find out what he wanted to talk about, or at least to get some type of heads up, but he never answered his cell. And when I tried the house, I got the same results. I didn't even bother to go to the gym, because I couldn't focus.

He wanted to talk. The tone in his voice had been so cold, void of any kind of emotion. What could have been on his mind? Our relationship had been as strong as ever, and was getting stronger with each passing day. So it couldn't have anything to do with us. Something must have happened. Well, if that were the case, I would make sure to cheer him up the best way I could. That's why I stopped at Victoria's Secret on the way home. Vic was my man, and my man sounded like he needed to be cheered up. I figured a sexy new outfit would be just the thing to lift his spirits.

I stepped through the front door, ready and willing to do all of the cheering he could take. I had the fire-red, crotchless panties, garter, and open-nipple bra set on underneath my business suit. As horny as I was, and as turned on as I planned to make him, I figured our talk would last all of five minutes.

"Hey, baby," I said, putting down my laptop case and walking into the living room. Vic, who didn't say a word to me, sat stone still in his favorite chair with a beer bottle in his hand. He stared past me. The TV was off and the stereo wasn't on. I walked over to him and gave him a kiss on the lips. His mouth never moved. I looked down at him; he continued to stare at nothing in particular.

"So what's up, baby? I got your message about not going back to work. You said you wanted to talk. Did something happen at work today? Because if that's the case, I have just the thing to replace that sour look with a big smile." I straddled his legs and kissed him on the forehead. To my surprise, Vic never moved, nor did I feel him get aroused.

"Vic, what's wrong?"

Finally waking from his trance, Vic took a swallow of his beer and then, without warning, stood, causing me to almost fall.

"What the hell?" I said. His demeanor was starting to get to me. "What is your problem?"

Vic put down the bottle on a side table and turned toward me. His blue eyes were the blackest I'd ever seen.

"Where did you go for lunch yesterday?" he asked quietly.

My heart started beating heavily as I studied his eyes. He focused on me and waited for an answer.

"Lunch?" I said, buying time. Did he know about Bernard? How? "I went out with a couple of girlfriends."

"A couple of girlfriends, huh? Who?"

"Just a couple of girls from the office. They work in one of the other buildings, so you wouldn't know them."

"Where did you guys go?" he asked, his eyes never blinking.

"We just went out for a quick bite to eat. What's with all of these questions?" I could feel myself getting hot, and not in the way I liked.

Vic ignored my question and asked another one of his own. "So, you didn't go to Tomato Palace for lunch, then?"

Shit. He knew.

"What's up with these questions?" I asked again.

"Just answer my question!" he yelled, his voice rising in a way I had never heard.

I tried to keep my composure, although I was worried.

"No you didn't just yell at me like that. You know better than to talk to me that way, Vic. You know I don't play."

"Then tell me the fucking truth, Latrice!" he yelled. He turned and grabbed his beer bottle and finished it off. "You know what, don't say anything, because I already know."

"What are you talking about?" I asked in a whisper of a voice.

"I have a friend who works at Tomato Palace. Remember Shantal, one of the waitresses there? She saw you. She was just walking in from the back and saw you leaving with some guy. A guy who wasn't me."

I exhaled. I had been busted. Damn.

"So what, she decided to call you up and tell you? Yes, I was there, OK? Is that what you want to hear?"

"I want the truth, Latrice. That's all. The goddamned truth."

"Vic, I don't know what all she told you, but it's not even close to being as bad as you think it is."

Vic gave a half-smile, sat down in the chair, rested his elbows on his knees and intertwined his fingers.

"Actually Latrice, Shantal didn't tell me much at all. She just said that you were there. She's not the one who saw you lip-locked with whoever the fuck you were with. The sad and embarrassing truth is that it was Julie who saw that shit. And believe me, she didn't hesitate to give me the details."

I bit down on my lip and shook my head. "Vic, believe me, whatever that bitch said, it wasn't true. You know how she feels about me."

"Oh, so you weren't kissing anybody?"

Damn. I sat down and passed my hands through my hair. I could feel my skin tingling and my hands shaking. Julie. That bitch was going to get it. I took a deep breath and tried to hold myself together. Damn Julie. Damn Bernard.

"So which is it, Latrice? Were you, or were you not kissing somebody? And who the fuck was he, anyway?"

I sighed. I knew that I had to tell the truth. I just hoped he would believe me.

"Yes," I started in a weak voice. "I kissed him. But it's not what you think."

"Who was he?"

Shit. I knew the minute I mentioned Bernard's name, Vic was going to fly off the handle.

"It was Bernard."

Within seconds, Vic was standing erect and his voice boomed.

"Bernard! Your ex! What the fuck? Latrice, tell me this is some kind of fucking joke."

I stood up and approached him, but he backed away from me.

"Vic, it's not what you think. For real. Let me explain."

"Explain? What the fuck could you possibly explain to me? You met your ex for lunch, and then you had your tongue down his throat. What more is there to say?"

"Vic, *he* kissed *me*! It's not what you think!"

"So what? You felt you had to kiss him back? I don't believe this shit! And you even had the nerve to try and lie to me about this shit! Just tell me one thing, Latrice. How long has this been going on? Damn!"

Vic turned around and swatted the empty beer bottle off the table, causing it to fly against the wall and shatter into pieces. Not since the night at Roy's had I seen him so angry. I took a cautious step backwards.

"Vic, I'm sorry about lying to you, OK? But please... believe me when I say it wasn't as bad as Julie may have made it seem."

Turning to face me, Vic said, "Latrice, you kissed him. Isn't that bad enough?"

"Please baby. I told you, he kissed me. And it didn't last. I pushed him away. He knows where I stand."

"He obviously didn't care about where you stood when his lips were locked on yours. How the hell did you hook up with him, anyway? And you never answered... how long has this been going on?"

"Vic, first of all, nothing is going on. He's been calling me for the past couple of months, trying to hook up with me. I kept turning him down."

"And what happened this time?"

"This time I agreed to meet him for lunch, only if he agreed to leave me alone. Vic, I love you and he knows that. That is the truth. The kiss meant nothing. I promise you that."

Vic stared at me and breathed heavily. I tried to plead with him with my eyes.

"Nothing is going on with me and Bernard. I just wanted him to leave me alone."

"So what, you couldn't tell me about it?"

"I handled it the best way I could."

"The best way, huh? What a way. You meet him for lunch, chitchat for a few, and then exchange a good-bye kiss. To make matters worse, of all people, Julie had to see that shit. God damn!" He turned away from me and placed his hands on top of his head. Keeping his back to me, he said, "I got to get the fuck out of here."

Before I could respond, he turned, stormed past me and left, leaving me there, pissed and scared. Julie was going to get hers—that was for sure. But had I lost Vic?

Colin
38

For the first time in my life, I was really in love. I don't know how it happened, and I sure as hell didn't plan on it happening. But it did. I was in love. With Emily. Somehow, she managed to get a hold of my heart and claim it as hers. And I had absolutely no problem with that. My player's card had been thrown away, and I was cool with that. I didn't want to be in the game any longer. Emily was my better half. Better still, she was my friend. I had never had a friend like Emily before. I could talk to her about anything, and that's what I loved about her. Add to that the fact that she was fine and could work enough magic in the bedroom to keep me under her spell, and her race became a non-existent factor.

That's why I bought the engagement ring. I had found my ONE. I knew that with Emily, we could work through any and all problems. The nice thing was I didn't foresee too many problems ahead in our future together. We'd have our arguments of course, but I knew we would never have issues like Roy and Stacey, or Latrice and Vic.

Speaking of which, I couldn't believe what had happened between Vic and Latrice. When Vic came by the other night and told me about Latrice and her ex, and the fact that Julie had seen the whole thing, I wasn't entirely surprised. After everything Stacey and Julie had done, it wasn't hard to believe that Latrice could do some shit, too. Women.

Once again, Vic was camping out at my spot. Damn, who said that my place was going to be a boarding house for fools in love? But I didn't really mind. I'm there for my boys whenever they need me. Besides, I was always with Emily. We'd started talking about getting a place together. We both wanted a house. We'd dabbled with the subject of marriage, but I always acted like I wasn't ready for it. Emily was cool with that. She was willing to be patient and not put the pressure on me. That's why I knew she'd be blown away when I popped the question.

I had it all planned out. I was going to take her back to where we first met at Angelo and Maxie's Steakhouse, treat her to anything she wanted on the menu, and then take her to Zanzibar, where I wouldn't dance with her that first time. This time I would make sure we got our groove on. Then, when the DJ switched up the music and threw on *Ribbons in the Sky*, by Stevie Wonder, I would get down on one knee and propose to her. I had it all hooked up—my boy is the DJ there, and I'd already gone over the plan with him. I wanted to propose at Zanzibar because I wanted Emily to see how serious I was about her. She always knew about my apprehensions because of her color, so I figure if I did it like that, then she would understand that I didn't give two shits about anyone's feelings but hers. Yeah. I was ready. I just hoped Latrice and Vic could get their shit settled.

Vic told me everything that Latrice had told him, and although it was a messed up thing to do, I know from experience how it could have happened. I knew that Latrice really did love Vic, and so did Emily. She spoke to Latrice and got the low-down from her. Latrice wouldn't lie to her girl. We told Vic about how meaningless the kiss actually was. But as a man, knowing that your woman was kissing another man can be a bitter pill to swallow.

He'd get over it eventually. I can't front though, Latrice definitely should have told him about the phone calls so that Vic could have put to rest anything Bernard was trying to do. But she didn't, and now Vic was upset, and Latrice was sad. But I knew they would get past it. Those two loved each other, and it would take something more serious than a moment of weakness to break them apart.

Just like Emily and I.

That's why I was humming to myself as I drove home. I was happy. The feeling I had inside made me realize how much of a fool my father had been. And how much of a fool I had been for ever following in his footsteps. I wouldn't do to Emily what my father had done to my mother. I was walking down that aisle.

Latrice
39

I was so hurt when Vic walked out and didn't come home for a few days. *I* couldn't even go to work; I was that depressed. I actually thought I was going to lose him. My fear only lessened a little when he finally came home. But even then things were still shaky, because he wouldn't speak to me much. Eventually though, we did speak, and found a way to work out our problems over my mistake with Bernard. Thankfully, Emily and Colin both helped him to understand that my mistake was just that, and nothing more. Our issue may have been resolved, but there was still something I needed to take care of.

I knew what Julie's game was the minute Vic told me she was the one who gave him the information. She wanted him back. And I wasn't having that. I also wasn't about to let her get away with what she tried to do. That's why I found out where she lived. And that's why I was ringing on her doorbell. She was going to get hers. I felt like Jill Scott in her video for *Gettin' in the Way*. I had my earrings off and my hands ready.

When Julie opened the door, the first and only thing I could say was, "Bitch, I warned you that night!"

Julie screamed out and tried to shut the door, but I wasn't having it. She had crossed the line, and I wasn't leaving until she knew that I never made empty threats. She had brought the ugly out in me. It wasn't going back in until my flesh touched hers.

I put my foot in-between the doorway to keep it from closing, and then pushed my way inside. Julie screamed again and backed into her living room.

"Get out of my house, you bitch!" Julie screamed.

I laughed. "No *you* didn't just call *me* a bitch. Did you really think your plan was going to work? Did you really think that you were going to get Vic back?" I rushed at her, but had to stop to avoid a lamp she threw at me.

"You don't love Vic!" she screamed.

"How are you gonna tell me who I love?" I asked as I watched her pick up another lamp. "You're the one who doesn't love him. If you did, you would never have tried that shit at Roy's house, and you certainly wouldn't have scratched up his car."

"He deserves better than you!"

"And what, you think you're better? Bitch, please. The only thing you proved by running to Vic with what you saw and didn't understand, was that you are a vindictive and jealous bitch, who can't get over the fact that she is not loved."

"Vic does love me. You just brainwashed him and made him think he loves you."

"So I'm a hypnotist now."

Julie threw another lamp at me, missing me by a mile. I could only laugh.

"That's real smart, Julie. Break your shit up."

"Get out of my house, or I'll call the police."

I watched her and huffed. "Oh you would do that. So you can dish out your shit, but you can't take it, huh?"

As Julie scrambled around her couch to reach for something else to throw, I charged at her, grabbed her by her arm and spun her around. Without hesitating, I gave her one hell of a smack. It stung my palm. Julie cried out, but to my surprise, she retaliated with a smack of her own. And it actually hurt.

"Oh no you didn't."

I grabbed her hair and dragged her to the ground while she swiped at me. We wrestled there, exchanging slaps and scratches. It had been a while since I'd been in a catfight, but I hadn't forgotten how to kick a bitch's ass. I savored every smack I gave her, until finally, after a couple more hits, I got up and stood over her. As she cried quietly, I touched my cheek, which she'd scratched. I sucked on the blood coming from my lip, which she'd split. Even though I'd gotten the best of her, she'd surprised me with her toughness.

"Hear me good, Julie. You had your chance with Vic, and you lost out. Stay the hell away from my man. Oh, and before you get any ideas about running to him about what just happened, let me just tell you—he knew I was coming over here. And he also knew better than to try and stop me. That's how much he loves you, Julie."

I turned around and walked away, went back home to my man. Julie didn't bother us again.

Colin
40

It was my wedding day, and I couldn't have been any happier. The night I proposed to Emily went exactly the way I'd planned it, with a little extra surprise thrown in. We went to the restaurant and ate up a storm. Well, Emily ate, a lot more than usual I have to say, while I just picked at my food. I was nervous. That was the last thing I thought I was going to be. We ate and talked for a while, and after Emily got another order of chicken strips to go, we went to Zanzibar.

We danced like we'd never danced. It wasn't our first time dancing together, but it felt different for me. I was dancing with my lady, and didn't care about the nasty glares the sisters were giving me. I know Emily didn't care, because she was too busy shaking that ass.

After I gave my cue to the DJ, he slowed things down. I held Emily close as the slow jams were played. Then, when my song came on, I dropped down to one knee. A spotlight was placed on us, and everybody in the club got quiet. I looked up at Emily, who had tears snaking from her eyes. While Stevie sang, I spoke.

"Emily, you know what kind of man I am, and you know it takes a special woman for me to do something like this. Well, you are that special woman. And I want everyone here and everywhere else to know that." I removed the ring box from my pocket and opened it. Everyone, including the sisters, gasped at the two-carat ring I offered. Emily's bottom lip quivered as I held her hand and continued.

"Em', it was here when you first called me out and kept it real. I want to do the same now. I want to keep it real with you. Will you marry me?"

Emily screamed out and pulled me up to her with strength I didn't know she had. She kissed me furiously

"Yes! Yes! Yes!"

Applause erupted around the club. Even the sisters were clapping. When the spotlight went off, the DJ replayed the song for us. We danced and held each other tightly, while the floor slowly filled with other couples. Like I said, the night went exactly as I had planned. But as Emily and I danced, I got a surprise I hadn't been expecting.

"I'm pregnant," she whispered in my ear.

I looked at her and said, "As in a baby?"

Emily smiled. "As in Mommy and Daddy."

"As in a family," I whispered, kissing her deeply.

So as Emily and I took our first dance together as husband and wife now, I could only smile. I was happy and content. My wife rested her head on my shoulder, and I looked over at my best men, who were sitting by the wedding party's table, smiling at me and shaking their heads.

I had waited a couple of days before I told them about my proposal. It was our weekly pool night at the Havana Club.

"Dogs, I have somethin' to tell y'all. You guys may want to sit down." They both looked at me with worry in their eyes. I laughed and said, "It's not that serious."

Racking up the balls for the next game, Roy said, "What's up, man?"

"Yeah," Vic added. "What's with wanting us to sit down?"

I looked at my boys and smiled. I was about to blow them away.

"I proposed to Emily last weekend." They looked at me with open-mouthed stares. I shrugged my shoulders. "We didn't say anything yet, because I wanted to tell you guys this way. She's tellin' Latrice tonight."

Neither Roy nor Vic said anything for a couple seconds; to top it off, neither one of them moved.

Finally, I said, "So? Y'all gonna congratulate a brother, or what?"

They both moved at last, and then Roy spoke.

"You for real?"

I nodded my head and smiled. "As real as Halle is fine."

Vic stepped toward me. "You mean, you *proposed*, proposed, as in, no more playa-playa?"

"Oh, I'll always be a playa," I said. "But just with one woman now. Fellas, I'm ready to settle down. Emily is the one for me."

In unison, they both said, "Dayum."

Then I hit them again.

"One more thing. I'm going to be a father. Em' told me after I proposed."

Again in unison: "Dayum!"

Vic gave me a pound and said, "Congratulations, man. You sure you're ready for this?"

"Yeah," Roy added, giving me a pound of his own. "Marriage and kids are a big deal, man."

"Dogs, I am ready and excited."

"I can't believe the playa of the year is heading to the altar," Vic said.

"Believe it," I beamed.

When the waitress came around, we ordered three glasses of champagne and toasted to my happiness. We toasted to that again as they made their speeches during the beginning of the reception.

I had to have both of them as the best man, because they were my best men. They were my brothers for life. I gave a subtle nod to both of them, and then put all of my attention back on my wife.

Roy
41

When the judge brought the gavel down, passing sentencing, I forced myself to remain composed. Despite Stacey's attempts to get full custody, the judge, a disgruntled looking white woman with iron-gray hair, had awarded me partial custody of Jenea and Sheila. Stacey, who had moved back home to Tennessee would have the girls during the school year, while I had them all to myself in the summer months. I wanted to walk up to the judge, kiss her wrinkled cheeks, and give her petite frame a tight squeeze, but I knew better. Instead, I sat quiet until the judge exited the chambers. Then I thanked my attorney, a short black man, whose name ironically enough, was Johnni Cockran, and then gathered my jacket to leave. But before I did, I walked over to where Stacey was still sitting, speechless and unmoving; her attorney had already left.

I tried to keep back my smile, but it was damn hard to do. Stacey had done so much wrong that I felt the judge's decision had been more than fair. If it had been up to me, Stacey wouldn't be seeing my little girls at all. I still harbored ill feelings for the things she had done. It didn't make matters any better when I found out she had been cheating on me prior to us even getting married. Her mother revealed that secret. She told me all about how she saw Stacey sneaking off with him after I had dropped her off one day. When I asked her how come she never told, she said, "Because she's my daughter."

"And why are you telling me this now?"

"Because you are my son-in-law. Always will be."

I didn't say anything else, and neither did Mrs. Bolton. She loved her daughter, but she was disappointed in her. I was glad that I would still be able to call her family.

I looked at Stacey. She kept her eyes focused on the judge's empty chair. I know she didn't expect the verdict to have gone that way. Especially after trying to paint an ugly picture of me in court. She and her lawyer tried to make it seem as though I were a bad father with wild ways and unscrupulous friends; the judge obviously saw through their BS.

"Stacey," I said quietly, "I hope we'll be able to raise our girls with as little conflict as possible."

Stacey didn't respond. I continued.

"The judge made her decision. I hope you plan on respecting that."

Again Stacey said nothing, but she did turn her gaze up at me.

"I only want what's best for the girls," I said.

Stacey stood up and continued to stare at me as though I were the devil incarnate. Finally, she gathered her purse and jacket and said, "I'll be by to pick the girls up in a couple of months." Then she walked past me and out of the courtroom without another word.

I let my smile bloom when the doors closed behind her. Then I turned and faced Keisha Wilkins. She and I had been seeing each other for the past six months. She had strong feelings for me, and I knew they were genuine. She smiled and approached me.

"Congratulations," she whispered as she kissed me softly. I kissed her back and held her close.

Keisha and I met when she had come to purchase a car. The attraction had been immediate for both of us. By the end of her shopping excursion, she drove off in a brand new Toyota Camry and left her phone number. We started dating soon after that, and when my little girls finally met her and gave me their thumbs up for approval, I felt like God had answered my prayers. Keisha would never replace Stacey, something I wouldn't allow to happen anyway, but Jenea and Sheila respected her and loved her a great deal. I was proud of the way my girls handled the turmoil and stress, and adapted to the new situation. Throughout the entire ordeal, my girls showed me how mature they were. They knew and understood that their Mommy and Daddy weren't happy together, and our happiness was all they wanted. Unselfishly, they pushed for me to be with Keisha.

I took Keisha's hand and squeezed it gently. "Let's go pick up the girls."

Vic
42

Roy had his new love, Keisha, and had won partial custody of his daughters. Colin had Emily and a baby on the way. I had Latrice, who I would be proposing to as soon as I found the perfect ring. Life, however ugly it could seem sometimes, had turned out to be damn good. Latrice and I were stuck with each other, and neither one of us had a problem with that. We were both happy. Latrice's announcement to me one night over dinner only made things better.

"Vic, I'm pregnant."

I stared at her for a long, quiet minute after she said that. But only for a minute. This time, the news was just what I wanted to hear.

"We having a boy or a girl?" I asked.

"We won't be able to find out for a couple more months. But I don't want to know. I want to be surprised. Are you OK with the news?" She looked at me through semi-worried eyes; she knew all about Julie and the miscarriage.

I smiled, stood up and approached her. I took her hands in my own. As she stood tall, I placed my hand on her flat belly and imagined feeling the first kick in a couple of months.

"We need to hurry and get this one out of there."

"Why is that?" she asked.

I smiled and kissed her nose. "Because then we can get started on the next one."

"Oh, is that right?" she asked, slitting her eyes playfully.

I smiled. "You know it."

We both laughed and held each other in a tight embrace. As I held her, I could never imagine letting her go. Colin and Roy were my best men for the second and final time, when Latrice and I said our I-do's, before our first son was born. We had two more boys after that. This time, I had no doubts.

END

The following is a sample chapter of Dwayne S. Joseph's up coming novel, *YOU, ME AND HE.*

YOU ME AND HE will be available IN January 2003

PROLOGUE

1/1/01—11:00pm

Diary,

Today marked a new chapter in my so-called life. I saw Jeff today—for a few minutes. We couldn't stay together too long because Stephen's parents were having a New Year's get-together. I met Jeff at the office — told Stephen I had an errand to run so that I could get away. Like I said, today marked a new chapter for me. I took a step in a direction that I had seen coming and tried to avoid, yet didn't really want to. Jeff and I made a commitment to each other today, and sealed it with a kiss. It was our first one. A sweet one. No tongue, because I wasn't willing to go there yet, although the next time I might have to get my love groove on. We held hands and stared at each other in silence afterwards. We didn't need any words. We had both taken a step, and there was no going back. When we said good-bye, we shared a hug. Also our first. I felt so safe in his arms; something I hadn't felt in so long. I don't know if I love Jeff yet. I'm still not sure about that. I just want to take everything slowly. See if this could ever develop into something. Which is going to be hard because we're both involved. I know he loves his wife and three kids. And I know that I love Stephen. I'm just not sure if I'm in love with Stephen. Does that make sense? Stephen means the world to me. Always will. He's stood by me like no other man in my life has. I will forever be grateful to him for that. But lately, I've just been so confused about what I want out of my life. Stephen wants to get married someday. He wants kids. I want those things too — just not now. At least not until I'm sure about who I love. Which is where my dilemma comes in. I started working for Jeff only two months ago, but already I feel a connection with him. He makes me feel special without even trying. And I know he feels the same, because I can see it in his hazel eyes when he looks at me. I make him feel special too. Could he love me? I don't know. That's the scary part because I can feel myself falling for him more and more as each day passes. The more time we spend together, the hotter this flame inside of me gets. I'm burning for him. Is he for me? And then there's Stephen. I honestly do love him. He is gentle, kind, sensitive, and a strong black man. The kind of man that we sisters complain we can never find. I'm lucky to have him in my life. I wish this weren't so damn hard. Sometimes I wish I had never taken that job as Jeff's secretary. At least then I wouldn't be so confused inside, because we would have never met. But then I wouldn't want that either. I want him in my life. I want to be in his life. What am I going to do?

Danita Evans

1

I'm in love with two men.

I didn't plan on it happening; it just did. Like they say, life is unpredictable. It's just one big canvas, and the paint keeps getting applied to it from the day you're born, till the day you die. I thought my canvas was pretty much complete. Especially after Stephen came along. Stephen is my man. My boo. My black knight. We've been together for over three years. Three years filled with the usual highs and lows that come with any relationship. I met him through my best friend, Latrice. Frustrated over my pickiness with men, Latrice was determined to get me hooked up. She'd been trying hard for over a year by setting me up with one shameful brother after another. And no matter how much I insisted that I was just fine, doing bad all by myself, she never gave up. It was like she made it her personal mission to find me a man. Anyway, as much as I'd accommodated her before, I swore I would never do it again, so I don't know why I gave in to her when she brought up Stephen's name.

"Girl, let me hook you up with this guy from my job, Stephen Maxwell. Girl, he is fine."

I gave her a cross look. "Latrice, please don't start this again. I have gone out on one too many of your dates, OK? I'm not about to do that again."

"Girl, they weren't all bad."

I sucked my teeth. "Please, Latrice. Some of your "fine" men were so ugly, I had to go to church and beg for forgiveness."

"Girl, what about Leonard? He wasn't that bad."

"'Trice, you know you was wrong for hookin' me up with that fool."

"What? Leonard was a nice guy. Plus, he makes money. Brother has a Jag, girl. What more you want?"

"A brother who won't scare me in the morning."

"You know what your problem is?"

I looked at Latrice with curled lips. "No. What's my problem?"

"Your problem is that you're too damned picky for your own good."

"Oh really? So you're sayin' I need to just settle for any old brother out there with money and a fancy car? Get a little bling-bling in my life, right?"

Latrice held up her hand to show off a diamond-studded bracelet her man had given her. "Ain't nothin' wrong with a little bling-bling, girlfriend."

"You stupid," I said, laughing.

Latrice smiled and said, "I speak only the truth, girl. But for real, you need to stop being so picky for a change and try talking to some real brothers. Stop waiting for your knight in shining armor, 'cause they just don't exist. You feel me?"

"'Trice, let me tell you. Money ain't a thing. I don't care what a man makes, as long as his head and heart is right."

"Well, Leonard was a nice guy."

"Child, please. Leonard may have been nice, but one thing my Mama always said to me was, 'Don't bring me no ugly grandbabies.' She wouldn't let me near the house with him by my side, girl."

"I didn't say marry him, Danita. I just said go out with him."

"Unh-uh." I shook my head.

Latrice sucked her teeth and flipped her platinum braids behind her ear. “Danita, for real, you need to quit looking for Mr. Right and make a move. You ain’t getting any younger, and you know your biological clock ain’t gonna tick that long. You need to settle and find a man soon.”

“’Trice, I’m only twenty-five. I have plenty of time.”

“Danita, all I’m saying is if you keep waiting, you’re going to end up having a child that’ll call you Grandma.”

“Latrice, you are such a bitch.”

“I know. And you love me for it.” Latrice laughed, a high-pitched whine that could almost make my ears bleed. “For real, girl, just give Stephen a try. I promise I won’t try to fix you up anymore. I promise you, he’s no Leonard. Shit, girl. Stephen will turn you inside out with his looks alone.”

“So if he’s so fine, how come you ain’t up on him?”

“Child, you know I’m seeing Bernard.”

“That never stopped your ass before.”

“Girl, I’m feelin’ Bernard.”

“Uh huh. You know I don’t believe you. If he’s as fine as you say, I can’t believe you ain’t trying to get with him. What’s the deal?” I looked at Latrice with hard eyes. She knew I knew her better than her own mother.

We’ve known each other for over ten years. We met in a step aerobics class at the gym. I had just moved from New York to Columbia, Maryland because of a job transfer. Latrice was born and raised in Baltimore, but moved to the suburbs of Columbia to get away from the craziness in the city. We were both huffing and puffing our way through the class when she looked at me and out of the blue said,

"You want to skip this torture and get some ice cream?"

Our friendship took off from there. Latrice Meadows is a big sister with a ghetto booty and wide hips. I'm the complete opposite. I'm petite with hips and a smaller, rounder ghetto booty.

Latrice has no shame in her game. She tells it like it is; that's what I like about her. We're alike in a lot of our ways, except when it comes to men. Latrice and I are complete opposites in that respect. She'll take any brother that pays some attention to her. All he has to do is stare at her for more than a minute, and she's ready to think he could be the one. She may not say it, but personally, I think she's that way because she's a big girl, and she doesn't think anyone legitimate would give her the time of day.

I wish she would think higher of herself, because she's one of the realest sisters I know. Her parents are from Guyana, so she has that whole exotic-look thing going on. She's got dark-chocolate skin, feline-shaped brown eyes that she covers with light-green contacts, and a round face with high cheekbones. Her best feature, her smile, could brighten the darkest room. She truly is a beautiful sister. She just happens to be a plus-sized woman. I've talked to her about raising the bar when she chooses her men. I don't agree with just settling, and I don't want her to, either. I want my dark knight.

"So what's up, girl? Spill it. What's wrong with him?"

"Nothing."

"'Trice..."

"OK, OK. Geesh. It's not that something's necessarily wrong with him. I just heard that he likes his women caramel and thin."

"Oh, he's one of those types."

"Naw, girl. He's cool. For real. I know him. He's a real brother. Only likes sisters. He just likes 'em light, that's all."

"And thin."

"That too. Just go out with him, girl. You'll like him."

"You said that about Leonard, too."

"Was I wrong? He was nice, right?"

"How could you even set me up with that ugly-ass? I'm supposed to be your girl."

"So he wasn't the prettiest brother on the planet..."

"Far from it," I said with a snort.

"You know, you ain't right."

"Right as rain."

"So you'll go?" Latrice asked, staring at me with pleading eyes. I knew she wasn't going to give up.

I huffed. As much as I didn't want to give in, it had been a while since I'd been out. I sucked my teeth. "Yeah, I'll go. If it'll get your big ass off my back."

"Ask the brothers about my ass."

We finished off our Haagen Dazs ice cream, which we have every Tuesday during lunch, then grabbed our purses to head back to our jobs. I was a manager for the Limited in the mall. Like Stephen, Latrice is also a project manager at E-Systems.

Before leaving for her car, Latrice said, "Oh, Stephen will be by your house at seven-thirty tonight to pick you up. Try to be ready, because he is never late. And wear that leopard skirt you have. Give him something to drool over."

I looked at her and shook my head. "You know you wrong."

"Wrong as the way OJ treats his people," Latrice laughed and walked away.

That night, I took her advice and wore my leopard skirt and white sleeveless top; I figured if I was going to go through with the date, I'd better make damn sure I looked the part. I sprayed on some of my White Diamonds perfume as an added bonus.

When Stephen rang my bell at exactly seven-thirty, I paused with my hand on the doorknob and whispered, "Girl, if he ain't fine..." Then I opened the door.

I have to admit that Latrice was on point when she described his looks. He was a fine, dark-skinned brother with light-brown bedroom eyes, soft lips, and a button nose so cute—it was too cute. I couldn't complain at all. I took a quick minute to check out his lean frame. He wore a form-fitting black cotton top, with black slacks. On his feet he wore what looked like a pair of Kenneth Cole shoes, and dangling from his neck was a simple silver cross. Nothing too gaudy—I liked that. I also liked the size of his arms and chest. I could tell that he worked out.

From the rise of his eyebrows and his struggle to keep his eyes from going up and down on me, it was obvious that he approved of my outfit. I knew he would, though. I may be tiny, with B-cup-sized breasts, but from my experience, most brothers had little problem with that, or my derriere. He extended his hand.

"Hello, Danita."

I took his hand. He had cold fingers. Good, at least I wasn't the only one who was nervous.

"Hello, Stephen."

"Ready to go?"

"Let me grab my purse."

We went to the Rusty Scupper by the Harbor in Baltimore and sat by the window, ate seafood, and talked for hours while an old, white man played love songs on the piano. Stephen fascinated me from the moment he opened his mouth. Not only was he fine, with a set of eyelashes to die for, but he was intelligent, too. And there wasn't a speck of ghetto in him, which was a plus in my book. I was tired of the ghettofied brothers I'd talked to lately.

We spoke about our likes; he loved football, I couldn't stand it. And our dislikes; he couldn't stand shopping, while that was a passion for me. We even took it to another level and talked about the philosophy of living in the now, something we both agreed on. As we talked and became more comfortable around each other, I decided to test the waters and see where his head was.

"I hear you don't date dark-skinned sisters. What's up with that?" I looked at him with my best accusatory, black-woman glare and waited eagerly for his response.

He shook his head. "It's not that I don't like dark sisters. I've dated a few blackberry queens. It's just that I've dated more light-skinned women than anything. It's not a conscious thing. I don't see color. If a woman is beautiful, she's beautiful no matter what shade or race."

"I see." *That was a good answer.*

"I'm just being honest with you."

"Honesty is always good."

"True. Lying just causes stress."

We talked more until the restaurant closed. After that, we took a silent stroll by the harbor, enjoying the warm night and each other's company. When he took me home, we exchanged numbers and made plans for another date.

When I walked inside my apartment, I heard my answering machine beeping. I knew who it was. Without checking the messages, I grabbed the phone and called Latrice.

"I want details, girl—juicy ones," she said as soon as she picked up the phone.

I laughed. "'Trice, shouldn't you be sleeping?"

"If you thought that, you wouldn't have called me. Now tell me what I want to hear."

I shook my head and squirmed out of my skirt, staring at my ass and hips in the mirror. "Girl, I'm gonna have to give you your props. He ain't no Leonard, that's for damn sure."

"See, I told you. He's fine, ain't he? Made your heart jump when you saw him."

I couldn't lie. "Brother has it going on, girl. He's sexy as sin, and intelligent. I don't see how he can't be taken already."

"He could be now, if you want him. Now, what did you two do? My eyes are gettin' heavy. Tell me before I fall asleep. Where did you two go that kept you out until two-thirty?"

"Well, *Mama*, he took me to the Rusty Scupper for dinner."

"That place ain't cheap, girl."

"I know. And it was romantic. We had a nice view of the water and talked over candlelight for hours. After that, we just walked the harbor and talked some more. Then he brought me home."

"And?"

"And what?"

"Danita, it's two-thirty on a Monday night. The clubs aren't open, and restaurants close after eleven. Don't tell me all you did was walk and talk. Why are you holdin' out on a sister? Come on, girl, you know what I want to know."

"What do you want to know, 'Trice?" I smiled and suppressed a laugh. I knew what she wanted to hear.

"Danita, stop playin' with me! It's too late for that. Now tell me—do his under-the-cover skills complement his looks?"

"I don't know, 'Trice. I didn't sleep with him."

"Didn't sleep with him?"

"That's what I said. All we did was talk. We were gettin' to know each other. What more did you expect?"

She sucked her teeth. "I shouldn't expect more from you, as slow as you move. A man that fine shouldn't have to wait to get a taste. You need to start takin' advantage of the opportunities as they come."

"Sorry girl, but some of us just don't do give up the booty on the first date. Besides, the opportunity will come again."

"Oh, will it now?"

"Yes. We exchanged numbers, and we're going out next weekend."

To my surprise, we got together a lot sooner than that; he called me after work the next day and invited me to the movies. We went and laughed our behinds off as the *Kings of Comedy* told their jokes on the big screen. We stopped for Sno-cones afterwards, then went back to my place, where we sat outside and gazed at the stars and talked some more.

Stephen never went home that night.

When he tried, we shared a hug. That hug led to a kiss, which led to a little tongue. The next thing I knew, we were in my bed, rearranging my sheets. It had been a while since I had felt a man deep inside of me, and with his thickness and length, I felt just that. He worked me up, down, backwards and forwards. I took him sideways and in diagonal loops. We made love three times that night. Neither one of us could get enough. We licked, sucked, pulled, nibbled, rode, orgasmed, and sweated our way to lovemaking that you only read about in books or see in the movies.

I didn't give all the details, but I did call Latrice the next day and let her know that I wasn't as slow as she thought I was.

"Girl, his skills in between the sheets are unmatched."

"You didn't!"

"Three times, girl."

"Dayum! You heifer. It was that good?"

"'Trice, he took me downtown, uptown, and around town."

"Dayum, girl. I need to call Bernard now. Got me all worked up."

"You better not open your big mouth and say anything to Stephen at work."

"My lips are sealed."

"They better be. I don't want him having the wrong impression of me."

I saw Stephen almost every day after that. Spent as much time together as we could, getting to know the ins and outs of each other. He told me about his family—both parents, alive and kicking, and one brother, younger by six years, only taller. I told him about mine: one parent, my Mama. Father died before

I got to know him. No brother or sister, but "I had a dog."

The more I saw of Stephen and his curly top, the more I wanted to see him. I clicked with him in a way that I had never done with any man before. He made me laugh with his sense of humor. He made me smile just by smiling himself. As each moment with him passed, I realized that he was the knight I had been waiting for.

We moved in together after dating for close to a year. Actually, I moved in with him. He made the suggestion. I guess he figured the time was right to take our relationship to another level, which was no problem for me. We both knew we were at the point where we just needed to see if there was such a thing as too much time together. A week after he suggested it, I had my things unpacked in his territory.

In the beginning, we couldn't get enough of each other. We took showers together, ate together, and woke up together — we were always doing something together. We rarely did anything apart. We even shopped for furniture and redecorated the apartment with a reflection of us, not just him. Besides, I wasn't really feeling his black contemporary flair. So we chose new, sophisticated furniture. Well, I chose—he just nodded. Before long, we had the dining room decked out with an oak dining set, the living room with a dark-cherry entertainment center and matching coffee and side tables. We replaced his boring vertical blinds with burgundy drapes, and changed the color of the bathroom from blue to a mixture of olive-green and cream. In the bedroom, we got rid of the waterbed, because it hurt my back, and bought a dark pine bed with rising columns and a matching dresser and night table. Yeah, our place was definitely starting to take on a new, more inviting, shape.

Our relationship was all that I had been wanting and more. In Stephen, I found a man who had become my best friend. He was there for me on the best and worst of days. And I, in turn, made sure to let him know he was my king, and I would always stand by his side. With every day that passed, our love blossomed. But as always, with every bright day, there's a dark night trailing behind it.

S0-CUX-495

Hello John,

I hope you'll consider this for your bookstore, online & for review.

I think it's a pretty good read.

Best,

Mike [illegible]

Within a Forest Dark

Photo by Carl Heilman II

Lake George

Within a Forest Dark

An Adirondack Tale of Love and Suspicion

A Novel

By Michael Virtanen

Lost Pond Press, Saranac Lake

To my family, for their patience

*

Published by Lost Pond Press,
40 Margaret Street, Saranac Lake, NY 12983.
www.lostpondpress.com

Copyright 2007 by Michael Virtanen

Library of Congress Control Number: 2007939708
ISBN: 978-0-9789254-2-0

This book is a work of fiction.
Resemblances to persons living or dead
are coincidental.

Cover & Frontispiece Photos by Carl Heilman II
www.carlheilman.com

Jacket Design by Susan Bibeau

Printed in Canada by Transcontinental Printing

Acknowledgments

This book began in writing workshops at the State University at Albany and the New York State Writers Institute. I'm grateful to the novelists Doug Glover and Elizabeth Wassell, the poet John Montague, and Professor Steve North for their guidance.

Also to Lost Pond Press owner Phil Brown, who risked bringing it out, after making it better, and to Saundra, my toughest critic, who inspired the best parts. And to my mother, for support beyond what I deserve, and to Doug Conklin for the same.

Several people read drafts, provided encouragement, and removed some of the many flaws: Nick Burns, Scott Wallace, Wayne Failing, Lisa Pallone, Alicia Chang, Chris Ringwald, Jeff Foley, Winnie Yu, Lawrence Van Alstyne, Doug Blackburn, Jane Gottlieb, Kris Worrell, and John Romano, with whom this whole thing started. There were other readers over a decade whose names don't immediately come to mind. Thank you. The remaining flaws are mine.

Midway upon the journey of our life
I found myself within a forest dark,
For the straightforward pathway had been lost.

Dante Alighieri, *The Divine Comedy*

I

Spring comes late to the Adirondacks. Route 9 rolls north, through fields and towns and, as you close in on Lake George, upward into the hills, past shuttered businesses and stands of black trees that look cold and vulnerable well into April, waiting for leaves. Then comes the winding climb into evergreen forests, up into the picture-postcard Old North Woods. Only sixty miles north of the Mohawk Valley and its small, grim, post-industrial cities, yet it's another land. Most people drive there on the interstate, speeding north with everybody else who's in a hurry. They gawk at the scenery, get off at their exit, and drive straight to their hotel or cabin on the water. They see only one side of the Adirondacks, the wealthy, gentrified side—tourist shops, restaurants, gleaming motorboats. I prefer to go slow, up Route 9, the old two-lane. It gives you a little more time to look around. You see abandoned 1950s motels, rickety shacks, rusty cars in backyards—the Adirondacks beneath the fine, buffed surface. There are two lands up there, and it pays to know which one you're in.

The new case is out of Lake George, on the north end beyond Bolton Landing. A claim for death benefits by a woman named Kelly. It's for $300,000 and requires collecting some statements, verifying the contents in a file. If it were a straight $100,000 term life policy, the usual kind for the usual amount, I might have done most of it by phone and fax. Even though the deceased was her live-in lover and only fifty-two. She is the beneficiary of record, and he died in the hospital, where he'd been for two days, with complications from a blood disorder. Pretty straightforward. Except for the possibility of medical negligence, which I believe in, especially when small hospitals and old country doctors are involved. If I could turn up something, somebody's malpractice carrier might be covering the death benefit. You never know, and it might be worth asking a few indirect questions. Indirection is essential up here. Don't let them see you coming.

Not that I want to be anywhere near the North Country anymore. It makes me think of Caroline, and I already have enough things on my mind.

Four years ago, I had been working in Albany for exactly one week when Cherie, the gorgeous receptionist, mentioned that she played the organ, and I said I'd like to hear her sometime, and so on that first Sunday evening I paid a visit to her father's suburban house, the one she'd grown up in, the one where her mother had lately died, the one where she still lived. The split-level ranch had a Hammond organ in the downstairs rec room. She played a few songs, and I sat on the bench next to her and asked why she didn't play the piano, which I half-joked had a little more cachet, and she said very seriously that she didn't, she played the organ. She'd always played the organ, and her mother used to, and her father and his friends liked to sing at parties when Cherie played, especially "My Way." And she looked at me as if she thought I might laugh at that. I nearly did. The rec room had a hand-knitted afghan of zigzag pale pinks and oranges and browns, draped over the back of the plaid sofa. Also, a wet bar and reprint Catholic art on the wall, Jesus and Mary with glowing halos. I felt sorry for her because it was tacky but not her fault. An unfortunate inheritance for a dutiful daughter. After she played a jazzy version of "Guantanamera," I kissed her, and she kissed me back. It was that easy.

There's a transition period when you go someplace new and possibilities open up early, and if you miss the opening then, you miss it altogether. Her father wasn't home, or expected. After she played one more song, I said I had to leave. We kissed again, and the next day I told Cherie I was still involved with my wife, who was reconsidering her decision to throw me out—now that I was out—and it wouldn't be fair to anybody to start something else, not just then.

And a few afternoons later, Caroline did call and asked me to drive up to Saratoga and take her to dinner. "I'd like to discuss things with you, if you don't mind," she said. "I miss you, you know?" I said I'd be there in a couple of hours but instead left almost immediately, got onto the Northway, and drove fast, dropping onto Broadway in about a half-hour.

Our apartment was down a side street above a storefront—through a street-side door, then up a stairway. I used my old key and went up quietly, hoping to hear her walking around, thinking maybe she'd want to make love again like we used to and then walk to the cafe a block away for dinner, which had been our habit also. I let myself into the flat, which held the faint vanilla scent of her perfume, and heard Caroline's voice from the bedroom. I was surprised, pushing open the bedroom door, to find that she had somewhat the same idea. Caroline was naked on the bed, on her knees, her blond hair hanging down her back, straddling her friend Paul. He was naked and hairy, beyond his mustache. "Oh shit!" Caroline said. "You're not supposed to be here yet."

I turned around and went out. Took the stairs two at a time and crossed the sidewalk to my car. I waited for a minute, breathing hard, wondering if my wife would come running down the stairs to stop me. But she didn't. And the longer I stayed the worse it felt. I circled the block once, trying to think about what I would say, couldn't think of anything, and drove back to Albany. You can make a Toyota subcompact go pretty fast when you're trying to get away from something as bad as that. I refused to answer the phone all weekend, refused to be civil to anybody at work on Monday.

Within the week Cherie quit talking to me unless she had to, and within the year she was contemplating marriage to the car dealer who took three months to sell her a brand-new Pontiac with flashy overpriced extras.

"Are you going to play the organ at your own wedding?" I asked Cherie once. After that, she quit talking to me at all.

As she headed toward the altar, Cherie's skirts got shorter, and she took up smoking. She and her car dealer moved in a fast crowd. She got progressively harder from the experience and seemed to stay that way.

My wife moved in with somebody down in New York City, at first she didn't say who. And the divorce went through later, uncontested. There might be more to say about Caroline, my ex-wife, but I won't go there. As for me, I haven't moved in with anyone. I'm practically a monk. But chastity among the secular is a form of passive aggression. It's another kind of rejection, the careful, pre-emptive kind.

2

Cherie walks on teal spike heels, cerulean maybe, which don't precisely match the soft, clinging fabric of her dress. She's slightly pigeon-toed, which you can't miss because by midafternoon she'll be padding around the gray wall-to-wall carpet in her nylons, in bare feet come summer. But today she's in powder-blue tights, and if you were to judge by the face of the kid who just came into the office for an appointment with me, she could be walking on water.

As soon as he opens the glass door, Cherie crosses the waiting room to file something she should have filed an hour ago. Sometimes on a slow morning I'll roll my swivel chair to the edge of the desk in the back room, prop my legs up, and lean back to watch the walk-ins. Cherie keeps things moving.

She was hired by Artie, the old owner, when this was Acme Insured. He said it was good for business to hire a good-looking woman as receptionist and bill collector. She got a half-percent of every dollar she brought in, above wages, and over time that was a bundle. Men would come in to pay their premiums in person or wait for a half-hour in the waiting room to ask Artie about raising an auto deductible or adding another hundred thousand in term life. She'd call delinquents, who paid up because they didn't want to look cheap in her eyes. Artie figured it was worth the expense and had numbers to back him up. "Don't overlook the obvious," he said.

The kid's name is Rodney Glynnis, twenty years old, and he's obviously a greaser. When he turns to watch Cherie walk to the file cabinet, the back of his neck looks like a well-oiled duck's ass in jet black, the real thing, a classic D.A. I haven't seen one of those since the sixties when I was a kid. By then it was already out of fashion. For the nineties it is perfectly retro, and way past, or far short of, common chic.

Rodney must think of himself as a wanderer over the seas of time—sort of like Ulysses. And in Cherie he has found a sea nymph waiting to whisk him to an island paradise. Most of the fools who cross this threshold are living out small-time versions of ancient myths. After all these years, all these centuries, they still tell us who we are, who we've always been.

"Hey," he says.

Cherie straightens up and looks him dead in the eye.

"What?"

Normally this is where her gaze and the edge in her voice make some middle-aged bozo start excusing himself. But Rodney Glynnis is a kid, and he doesn't seem to care. His lip goes up in defiant suggestion of a smile.

"Nothing," he says. He watches her walk back across the carpeting and around her desk. Cherie sits down and crosses her legs, the blue dress riding up her thighs, and pushes her long black hair back over one ear. She fishes in the leather pocketbook beside her chair, pulls out a Kool and a plastic butane lighter, electric blue, not quite the shade of the rest of her ensemble. The kid reaches across the desk with a classic steel Zippo, clicks it open, and lights Cherie's cigarette. It's an intimate gesture, a practiced move. She ignores it, acts as if the tobacco has spontaneously combusted, drags deep, exhales, and sets her cigarette in the circular glass ashtray on the stand behind her desk. There's a crimson lipstick ring around the filter.

Rodney reaches inside his black sportcoat, produces a pack of Marlboros, slides one out, and puts it between his lips.

"There's no smoking," Cherie says. She's not joking.

The hand with the Zippo stops halfway up to the kid's face. "Why not?"

"It's against company policy."

He leaves the cigarette in his mouth and doesn't light it. "I have an appointment," he says.

"Why don't you sit down?"

After a minute, I come out to get him. He's still standing, with the cigarette still unlit, pretending he's interested in one of the safety articles framed on the wall. Cherie wouldn't have announced him. She would have left him there cooling his heels, invited him at some point to sit down again, and forgotten him until such time as I noticed somebody was waiting.

"Rodney Glynnis? My name's Kirkland. I'm the adjuster who's got your case. Why don't you follow me back here?"

Rodney follows and drops into my visitor's chair, slouching down. He pulls the cigarette out of his mouth. "This isn't much of an office," he says. "I figured Apex for at least a twelve-story building and a lot of suits."

"You'd be about right if you went to Hartford. That's headquarters. This is a satellite. We don't even sell policies here anymore. We just handle claims. If you want to buy some more insurance, and looking at your file you'll probably need some, I can give you a toll-free number."

"Listen, chief," the kid says. "The accident wasn't my fault. That old dolly made a reckless move. I've got witnesses."

"You back-ended her, Rodney. At an intersection. You back-end somebody, you lose. It's right here in the file. The front end of your car is damaged, and the back end of her car. There's no explaining this one away. It's your fault. We pay."

"Wait a minute," Rodney says. "Whose side are you on? I've got the policy here, which I pay for. Not that old lady. I expect you to help me. Or at least give it a try."

"I am helping you Rodney. I'm telling you the truth. Most people won't."

He slouches deeper and crosses a skinny ankle over a bony knee. Jeans, silk sportcoat, white Oxford-cloth shirt, skinny black silk tie. But where he ought to have pointy shoes, the kid has black steel-toed boots that lace up. The file says he's a car detailer, but his fingernails are clean. He'll probably be handsome when his face clears up. The kid twists in his chair to see what Cherie's up to. Mostly she's reading a magazine and smoking.

"Okay, Rodney. Tell me your story."

"First you've got to understand that I drive a Dodge Dart with a slant six. They don't make those anymore. I rebuilt that machine from a rusty shit pile some peckerhead drove into the body shop and dumped. I rebored and rebuilt the engine, and if you know jack about cars you know that was a prize engine. I raised the back end and diddled the carburetor. Put wheels on it. I replaced all the rusted-out panels, some I had to go to Pennsylvania to get, and sanded off every bit of corrosion inside and out. I put soft-leather bucket seats in front—stripped out of a mangled BMW—and put in a high-end CD system. It has a precise paint job. I do not fuck with that car."

"The report said something about the air bag deploying, Rodney. If you're so careful, why do you have an air bag? They never made an old Dart with bags."

"It's a dangerous world, man." Rodney looks me in the face and points the cigarette at me. "Those old ladies will kill you. This one made a move like I have never seen. I'm on Central Avenue in the right lane, and she's in front of me, and it's icy as shit. She puts on her turn signal to go left. So she starts to go left, then she hits the brakes and goes right. Into a right-hand fucking turn. It's only because my reflexes are so good that I hit her back end and not her passenger-side door. I almost missed her altogether."

"Nice try, Rodney. Nice reflexes. But the back end's the back end."

He sits there stewing while I take one more pass through the file, which contains his previous statement, along with Mildred Desmond's, and an estimate from a body shop we use saying it will cost $1,486.09 to fix her car, including the right taillight and housing, rear bumper, and right rear panel.

"You know I could have left the scene. There was no cop, and she didn't know what the hell was going on."

"You're a citizen, Rod. And I want you to know I appreciate that."

The outer door to the agency opens, and I hear Joseph in the front room, talking softly to Cherie. She laughs, which is a sound I've heard but never actually seen her make. Joseph strolls into the back. "Well, Jack, what do we have here?"

"Hello, Joseph. This is Rodney Glynnis. He had a little mishap on Central Avenue. He was just telling me how a little old lady has made his life dangerous."

Joseph pulls the open file off my desk. "What's the story there, Rod? She back down Central Avenue and through a red light?" Joseph catches his reflection in the window glass and smoothes his suitcoat.

"Something like that."

"And you'd like her insurance company to pay for the damage to your vehicle?"

"That'd be all right."

"Well, as Apex claims examiner for this region, I can tell you that, no matter what Mr. Kirkland's told you, that's pretty unlikely." Joseph tosses the file back on the desk. "You ought to drive more carefully, son. You back-end somebody, you lose."

"That's what I said."

"That's why you're so good at what you do," Joseph says. "Of course, that's what we always say." He isn't lying. We like to do the bad cop/bad cop routine with punks and losers, with anybody making an obviously false claim, but keeping it light. We don't fight with people. But we figure a little ball-busting is an enhancement of Apex justice and client services.

Joseph saunters out into the front room, says something else that makes Cherie laugh, then heads for the small side office, the private one that used to be Artie's.

"So I guess that's your boss, huh?" Rodney Glynnis says. "And if he says I'm screwed, that's it?"

"How do you know so much about the insurance business, Rodney? You're a bright fellow."

"Tell you, chief. It's not rocket science to see that guy helps himself to whatever's on your desk and whoever you're talking to. Then he tells you the outcome of your case."

"I already knew the outcome, Rodney. And so did you. What he said didn't change anything."

"If you say so." Rodney's lip goes up in defiant disgust. "Suits like that are all the same. But what's that shit on his forehead? You know, no hair on the sides and that big curl down the middle?"

"It's called a widow's peak."

"He does that on purpose? Guy looks like a fucking cyclops."

I snort involuntarily and fail to suppress the laugh behind it.

"You know what else I don't get?" Rodney leans closer. "That chick out there seems to like him. He's her boss too, right? All right. I got it. That chick thinks with her bank account."

"It's possible, Rodney. I really don't know."

"You wouldn't, chief. You're so easy. Even if you act like a wise ass." The kid gets up to go after I stand up. He looks at my scuffed wingtips, frayed khakis, and rainforest-print necktie hanging loosely and adds, "That's why I figured you might even do the right thing by me."

"We'd probably disagree about what that means."

Rodney offers me his hand, and I shake it. He stops out by Cherie, lights a Marlboro with his big Zippo, and walks around her desk to flick an ash in her ashtray. She doesn't look up, but you can see her stiffen. Then he leans into Joseph's private office and points the cigarette at Joseph's forehead curl. "Lose the 'do, man. That cyclops thing, it isn't hip."

Rodney Glynnis goes out the front door, trailing smoke and a high, giddy cackle. I hear Joseph's chair scrape, and he comes back in. "What a loser," he says. "It couldn't be more obvious. Let's show him at fault, agree to payment; check and see if the lady might be hurt, because I've got a feeling that she might be. Let's get that over with. She was back-ended, after all. Then let's recommend we drop his coverage, or at least get him in the assigned-risk pool."

"Whatever, Joseph."

Later that day, I drive to see a house where the roof leaked when ice built up and melted. After documenting the damage, I agree to payment of reasonable estimates to tear the gutters off, put an insulating pad under new shingles from the edge of the roof to four feet up, and get the worst room painted, walls and ceiling. The water damage in the other rooms looks old, even though the owners insist it's not. Back at Apex, I find that Cherie and Joseph are gone and that Rodney Glynnis has left me a voice-mail message. "I don't mean to depress you, man," he says. "But I do need to drive."

Rodney picks up the phone on the first ring.

"Here's the deal. You don't have collision so you're on your own for damage to the Dart."

"No big thing," Rodney says. "I'm fixing it myself anyway. And by the way, do you know what you people charge somebody my age for that kind of coverage? It's a rip-off, man."

"Hold the lecture or you're going to irritate me. I told Mildred's agent that we have witnesses who'll swear that she made a hare-brained move right into your path. You can get me those statements, right?"

"Count on it, chief," Rodney says. "I'll find them somewhere."

"Probably won't need them. But get me somebody. Anyway, the agent's not too pleased, but this way it's nobody's fault. She probably won't know the difference. And this guy owes me a favor."

"Don't you mean no-fault?"

"No, Rodney. I don't mean no-fault. That's for personal injury. This is just property damage. By the way, I talked to Mildred this evening. She says her back hurts. But then she admitted her back has been bothering her for a couple years. She also says you were very rude."

"Thanks, chief. I owe you one."

"Your premiums will probably go up a little anyway, though not right away. And stay out of the office. I'm going to put this through next month when the examiner's away. He doesn't need any obvious reminders."

"You know that chick that works in your office, I think she likes you."

"Very funny, Rodney. You're going to make me change my mind."

"No, I mean it. You and her, you could really exist." He breaks into the high cackle. "Maybe not."

3

Apex Insuring is why I'm here. The company bought Artie's Acme Insured four years ago, trading on the "synergy" of similar names, took his client list and location, and made him the manager for one year with a promise of lifetime employment. It had been Artie, Cherie, and several part-time salesmen. Right away, Apex began switching renewal policies to its own lines, sent Joseph and me up as claims adjusters, ordered Artie to fire the part-timers, and by the end or the year routed most sales and account maintenance to an 800 number in Connecticut. We work out of a soulless business park on the western edge of Albany, a low-rise collection of faux-brick buildings housing accountants, insurance agents, minor trade associations, and technology salesmen.

Artie was technically our boss that first year, though he wasn't much of an examiner and any questions and big claims were handled out of the main office. Besides, Joseph and I were good. We got statements, didn't irritate valued clients too much, didn't screw up cases, discouraged the bad risks, paid documented claims. We didn't overlook the obvious. One day the old man quit, took his buy-out money to Florida, and started selling real estate.

Shortly before he left, Artie pulled me aside to say something that seemed important to him. He was doing that a lot toward the end, with both Joseph and me, dispensing the accumulated wisdom from thirty-four years in what he called the big insurance game. It was clear the old guy didn't have much pull with the company anymore, and Joseph jollied him along, but not much. I'd nod my head, half-listening until he was finished. But one observation he pulled right out of the air, apropos of nothing, and put a hand on my shoulder for emphasis. "We acquire heartbreak, and then we start passing it around," he said. "It's like a disease."

Artie didn't say how he knew that or if he'd ever had the ailment.

Cherie stayed on straight wages, but Joseph and I figured she'd socked away a quarter-million previously in commissions on collections and occasional sales. Then Joseph was giving her investment advice—stocks and mutual funds—and he said once that she actually had the quarter-million clear. It was an afternoon, and they were going someplace to celebrate. They didn't mention if their spouses would be joining them.

The evening they went out, I stopped back in the office to pick up files because I had to be on the road in the morning. The light was on in the back room, and Joseph was sitting behind his desk, across from mine, a loopy smile on his face when he looked up to see me. "Listen, pal," he said. "I need a little privacy to make some phone calls."

"Fine. How was the celebration? Did you toast your fat portfolios?"

Joseph didn't say anything, just looked at me with that smile. I looked around for the files. "I'll just be a minute."

It sounded like he giggled in reply. Joseph picked up the phone. The dial tone started buzzing. "I really need to make the call," he said. "In private."

I took the files and left. Walking out, I looked down and thought, only after the fact, that I'd seen the tips of two stiletto heels poking out below the modesty panel that covered the front of Joseph's large desk. I took a long walk through the parking lot and found Cherie's white Grand Am. A half-hour later they still hadn't come out. When I asked Joseph the next day, he said they'd had one drink and Cherie had gone home. I mentioned her car, and he said I was mistaken.

"Grand Ams are pretty common," he said.

"Not with vanity plates that say Cher1," I said.

"I don't know, pal," Joseph said. "Why don't you ask Cherie?"

I did, but she didn't bother to answer the question.

The small side office sat empty for almost three years after Artie left. We used it sometimes for private meetings with clients. Then last summer, about a month after Joseph's celebration with Cherie, and about three months after he started wearing a complete suit to the office every day, about six months after he started routing all the Hartford calls to himself, and about two years after his hairline had started to recede, a memo came down from the main office announcing that Joseph had been named the regional examiner, with adjusters in several satellite offices answering to him, including me.

"We're going to stay friends, pal," Joseph said. "Aren't we?"

Joseph and I had been in the same training class in Hartford, gone out for beers with the boys, and shared an apartment for a week, until he found his own place. I didn't see him much for a few years, when he had a job in Connecticut near the city and I was mostly up in the northern regions of New York, driving toward the rolling horizon. Then they sent us to Albany to work for Artie. For almost a year, until it was clear this would be semi-permanent and his new wife could move up with the baby, Joseph bunked with me again, three weeknights. Nice guy, no trouble, diligent worker, would buy you back a drink if you bought him one, favored high-end beers. He offered to pay rent once, and when I said no, that was the end of it. He didn't offer again. We took turns taking cases as they came in. Except Fridays. He worked a four-day week then, went home on Thursday nights, let me pick up his unavoidable Friday stuff. He covered some cases for me when my father died. His wife lived with her mother, and he saved enough that year for a down payment on a house. The fact is I was better at the job than Joseph, just a little more thorough, pursuing the last detail, getting beyond the obvious. But he was more politic, careful with anybody in a position of authority, very amiable then. Diligent worker, though. No trouble. Nice guy.

Then Joann came upstate with baby Joseph, and they found a starter home, had me out to dinner a few times, nested, had me out to dinner once the next year. Joseph got promoted the year after that.

I tried to figure out how long it had been since the last dinner and wondered for a while if it was my fault.

4

Margaret Kelly's house sits off a country road on a hill, surrounded by forest. It's a naked A-frame, recently built, in a small clearing at the end of the curved gravel driveway. Even on a leafless morning, the hemlocks screen the house from the road. The rural mailbox is neatly painted with the name of the deceased, Kind. Fifty yards up the drive, a white Land Rover, the light-duty suburban type, is parked by the house, and I pull up beside it. Nobody answers my knock. The front of the A-frame is mostly glass, a southern exposure with a lot of light and what must be a fine view from the two picture windows framing the door. It's the kind of smoked glass you can see out of, not into.

On the raised porch along the front of the house, I sit in a recently painted Adirondack chair in the morning sun and wait. For two days I phoned and got no answer. Instead of sending a letter I decided I needed a day out of the office. Footfalls sound on the gravel, a quick, steady rhythm that makes no allowance for the hill. I see her through the trees, a blur of red and black. Suddenly the head turns in my direction. It's as if she sensed my presence, her eyes freezing me in place. More wolf caught off guard than deer in the headlights, she keeps running, disappearing briefly on a path through the hemlocks, and then I hear heavy breathing as she emerges into the clearing, slows to a walk, and approaches the house.

Margaret Kelly is tall and lean, wearing a crimson T-shirt, black Spandex shorts, and white Nikes. Her russet hair hangs in a short, straight bob. The pale skin of her face and neck is blotchy red from exertion. She has high cheekbones, a long nose, and perfect teeth. Her eyes are pale blue. She mounts the stairs and holds my gaze until I have to look away.

"Who are you?"

"Jack Kirkland." I stand up and put my hand out. "Apex Insurance."

"Why are you here?" My hand just hangs there.

"I'm the claims guy. I'm the one that makes sure you get your check."

"What check?"

"The $300,000 death benefit from the policy of William Kind." I don't usually pretend to be Santa Claus.

"Let me see your card." She paces the wooden porch, catching her breath, while I fish a card out of my wallet. She takes a look, then shakes my hand. Hers is surprisingly cool.

"How far did you run?"

"Six miles," she says, unlocking the door with a key from a chain around her neck that she pulls from under her T-shirt. "I try to go every day."

Inside, the A-frame is one large room with a wide-plank wood floor. A stone fireplace in the left wall, the open kitchen beyond it, and what must be the bath behind that.

"Do you want coffee?" she asks as she sets about making some in an old steel percolator.

The bed, back on the right, is big and circular, next to a wrought-iron spiral stairway that leads to a loft with a desk, a personal computer, and a sofa. The wood stove at the center of the house, raised off the floor on a slate slab, has a low-burning fire. Club chairs squat in front of one picture window; there is a rough-hewn dining table in front of the other. A black bearskin rug, the head attached, lies in front of the cold fireplace hearth. But it's warm inside. Efficient design. Thick walls, no doubt full of insulation, very snug, and cheap to heat.

It's modern Adirondack, except for two anomalies. A black silk bomber jacket is hung over the back of a chair, a circular crimson dragon on the back, its fangs nearly touching its tail, and the word *Korea*. Someone has been to Itaewon in Seoul. I'd been in the Army for three years, one year not far from Panmunjom, near the demilitarized zone, within easy rocket and bomber range, and a jacket like that was the only good thing I had to show for it. A beautiful jacket for the price, about twenty dollars U.S. On the wall next to the fireplace is a garish painting of two grinning men, their eyes huge, skin reddish-brown, hands clutching machetes, engaged in a crazed dance that suggests they are about to pop right out of the canvas and attack the viewer. It's a likeness of an image I've seen in a magazine, of tontons macoutes, Haitian figures that are a meld of voodoo, folklore, children's nightmares, and bloody post-colonial politics. I read about them. The phrase means something like "your old uncle," but the reality was more terrifying.

They were secret police who carved up Baby "Doc" Duvalier's opponents in the night, and his father's before that.

"Haiti?"

"Yeah." Margaret Kelly looks up but doesn't say anything else.

The grotesque figures fade into the recessed shadow beside the stone hearth.

"Did William Kind build this house himself?"

Margaret Kelly smiles and adds a small laugh. "More or less. He designed it and did some work. I was his laborer."

"It's great." I examine one picture window, which is perfectly framed and plumb. "Nice work. Very painstaking."

"You have no idea." She laughs again. "It's all we did for two and a half years."

Probably not all. This is a lovers' hideaway. Fireplace, fur, circular bed. Smoked glass. No neighbors in sight. Throw in a hot tub, and it's a brochure for the Poconos. I walk to the back window to glance out, and there it is, on the wooden deck—a small, deep, circular tub, the top covered, plugged into an outlet on the house.

"Hot tub?"

"Yeah. Actually I was going to soak for a while. I do that after I run. It keeps my muscles from getting too stiff."

The coffee pot starts perking. She goes out the back door, unsnaps the cover from the tub, turns on the whirlpool jets, and comes back in. She puts out two mugs and a carton of heavy cream.

"When that's done, pour me a cup, too, okay? I like my coffee strong, but very white. I have to get into the tub before I stiffen up."

"Fine. I'll bring it out. That's the way I like my coffee, too. It's my one indulgence."

She smiles at that, then goes out and closes the door, taking a fluffy black towel with her. She sits on the bench to pull off her running shoes and socks, sets them aside, then stands and pulls off her T-shirt and spreads it over the railing of the deck, with her back to me. Her movements are deliberate, unhurried. She stands by the tub in her Spandex shorts and sports bra, the only other thing she's wearing, very still, with one hand in the water. For a long moment she looks like Sir Edward Burne-Jones's Andromeda, strong, perfectly proportioned. I imagine myself Perseus, slaying her dragons. She steps over the wall and into the tub, submerging up to her neck in the bubbling water, from which steam rises in the chilly air. She leans back and closes her eyes, her face lit by the late-morning sun, her chin just above the water.

She slides up when I come out and takes a mug. "Thanks," she says, taking a sip. "That's exactly how I like it." I try not to watch the pale skin just beneath the water. She smiles, sets the cup on the edge of the tub, and slides lower in the water. "I can't tell you how good these water jets feel," she says. "Have you ever been in a hot tub?"

"Never."

"You should try it sometime." She closes her eyes and slides a little lower. Her feet come up out of the water, pressed against the far wall of the tub. "The water jets feel great against your body."

"They're in the walls, right? Must feel good on your back."

"Yeah," she says, her eyes closing. "And there's some in the bottom. It's heavenly on sore feet."

I say nothing. "So, what can I do for you, Mr. Kirkland?" she asks.

"I have to verify some things." While explaining the case, I keep thinking that this is one of those temporary openings, wondering how to turn the conversation away from insurance, but the subject is necessary and grim. She confirms that Kind went to the hospital with what he'd said were recurring symptoms of mercury poisoning, which he developed a few years earlier while living in Haiti. He also had pneumonia, or contracted it in the hospital, and died two days after being admitted.

"Do you think they failed to treat the pneumonia correctly?"

"They gave him antibiotics the second day and put him on oxygen," Margaret says. "He died that night."

Against all rules, I walk over and take her hand, warm now from the tub. Her face looks as if it might crack. I try not to look at the rest of her. She squeezes my hand.

"Thank you for being kind," she says. "Maybe you could come back when this is over."

On the way back I dawdle awhile in Lake George village. It's empty of tourists this time of year. Most of the businesses are closed, the ice-cream shop, the T-shirt emporium, the wax museum. It's a little depressing. In summer, I sometimes hang out at a joint on the waterfront with a patio and outdoor tables. It's a cheerful place for a cold beer in a plastic cup and a cheeseburger and for watching young women in their shorts and halter tops, old guys in Hawaiian shirts, punks in their beaters, kids spilling soda and dripping ice cream, the masses making their way to Million Dollar Beach. Caroline used to like it here. She thought kitsch could approach high art if you knew what you were looking at. I guess I never could tell the difference.

5

The death certificate of William Kind was filled out by a doctor whose signature is hard to decipher. The first name starts with C, the surname with B, ending in a letter with a big loop below the line. Middle initial is T. At a handwriting seminar for adjusters several years ago, one intended to help us spot liars, the handwriting analyst said a lot of things that may or may not have been true. About the only ones I remember had to do with crossing T's: a high cross is self-assurance, even arrogance; a low cross means lack of self-confidence. And big loops below the line mean highly sexed. It turns out the mysterious doctor's full name is Charles T. Brody. He crosses his T's high, has one of the biggest loops I've ever seen, and he recalls Margaret Kelly instantly. A tall, slender, balding, middle-aged man with a cheerful disposition, Brody is the county coroner as well as head of the hospital's emergency department and walk-in clinic. And he has his own internal-medicine practice in the building across the parking lot. He seems to have no trouble fitting me in without an appointment.

"You know my title is coroner," Brody says, closing the door to his office and sitting back behind the desk. "But I really like to think of myself more as a medical examiner. For years the coroners were funeral directors. Incredible. No medical training at all. They used to sign the death certificates at the hospital and then take the bodies away for embalming and burial. We don't have a medical-examiner system, but that was the argument I made fifteen years ago to get this job, when it became an appointed position. Do you remember the television show *Quincy*? That was around then, and I convinced the burghers they were missing the boat. If there was foul play someday, they'd need a little forensic science to solve the case."

"Have you solved many that way?"

"A lot of the time the answer is in the blood work. Around here, people usually die in their cars, if they die violently, that is. Sometimes it's farm accidents. Very dangerous places. I remember old man Maclean, when he got crushed by a tractor, he was drunk as a lord. Of course he was drunk every day. But one day he slipped in the mud right under the back wheel of the tractor. He was trying to put a board under it for traction. It wasn't negligence exactly. This was the way he worked. Of course we saw him a few times. Broken leg. A shredded finger we couldn't reattach. There was an exclusion in all his policies, I guess, against operating farm equipment while intoxicated. No insurance money was paid. Mrs. Maclean never did forgive me. I'm sure I don't need to tell you about such things." Brody gives me a significant look, as if to say that he knows exactly why I'm here and that he's on my side.

"Now the case you're talking about, William Kind, I don't think there's anything like that at work there. I wasn't his doctor, but I admitted him through the emergency room. And I told his girlfriend that I'd keep an eye on him. She asked me if I would. And I did. I tracked his case." Brody gets the file from a drawer and opens it on his desk. "Let's see. He was admitted on a night when I happened to be rounding. Complaining of general fatigue, aches, stiff joints, headache, insomnia. Said he'd been mercury poisoned once upon a time, and the symptoms were back."

"Now that's the interesting thing." Brody leans forward for emphasis. "He told me it happened in Haiti. I remember that. He was the engineer on a turbine project. His landlady was sprinkling his apartment with mercury to keep the evil spirits away. Incredible. He said he was there for almost two years, then he got sick and took early retirement."

"So what do you do for that?"

"Nothing. You go someplace where there is no mercury. Hope that the symptoms diminish. Frequently they do. I think that's why he came to the Adirondacks."

"I mean, what did you do for him in the hospital?"

"Took some blood and urine specimens and admitted him."

"I'm sorry, doctor. I'm confused. If there's no treatment, why admit him?"

"Well, I thought he'd be better off with us." Brody's face creases into a frown. "Patients know what they think they have. Sometimes they're right, sometimes they're wrong. Either way it's not very scientific. Frankly, that was the problem here. I'm not an expert, but mercury is usually expelled from the body after about a year. He did have some symptoms. But we needed to verify mercury poisoning or rule it out. He might have had some other problem."

Brody turns over another piece of paper in the file. "The lab results showed he did have elevated levels of mercury. But that wasn't the problem. We had to figure out what was really wrong with him. We did."

"Pneumonia?"

"Right." Brody flips back through the file to the bottom document. "When he was admitted ... here's the sheet that the nurse filled out when he came in the ER. He said he had no trouble breathing. At all. Or any respiratory complications or history. Or cardiac history. And he said he wasn't taking anything. So we treated him for his complaint."

He flips through a few more pages. "Now the next day his nurse on the floor reports that he's having some trouble breathing, and now he's got a low-grade fever. And he tells her he had the flu almost two weeks earlier, but it went away. He never told me that, or the ER nurse. He didn't have a fever when he came in. So when his doctor makes rounds later, he orders a chest X-ray." Brody holds up the radiology report. "And he's got pneumonia. You can see it right here. Both lungs."

"Who's his doctor?"

"Elias. He's a GP. An old country doctor with an office in his house. He's not a bad doctor. His diagnosis wasn't swift, but it was accurate. He put the patient on antibiotics and oxygen that afternoon. The patient died the next morning."

"Were they the right antibiotics?"

"What do you mean?"

"William Kind died. Would he have done better with other drugs?"

"Elias followed the usual protocols. It should have been the right combination for pneumonia."

"What time did he die?"

Brody flips the last page. "After midnight."

"What time did his nurse actually find him?"

Brody flips back to a photocopied page and squints behind his bifocals. "The code was called at 1:24 a.m. They tried to resuscitate him, and he didn't respond. He was declared dead at 1:55."

"Probably they tried pretty hard."

"We do," Brody says. "There was a resident on. He's also the one who covers the ER overnight for me. He's good. Very promising. He did everything he could." Brody closes the file.

"How did Margaret Kelly take it?"

"Funny you should ask. I got called at home about two. Went in and signed the death certificate. I found her in the waiting room, and I told her." He points to the black streak near the shoulder of his lab coat, smiling a little despite himself. "That's from her mascara. It won't wash out."

I have visions of Brody providing as much solace as he possibly could. "Do you know the name of the nurse who took care of him that night?"

Instead of looking back at the file, Brody leans his head out the office door. "Hey, Shirley," he shouts, "who's that night nurse on the A wing? You know. The new one on nights. The big one."

"Beverly Wilbur."

Brody turns back to me. "Anything else?"

"Doctor Elias. How do I find him?"

"You don't. Not here. He's in Florida now. He retired."

"When?"

"Last month. He said it was his last winter in this godforsaken place." Brody laughs. "He said he was finally ready. It was someone else's turn to keep evil at bay. That's what he said. He was tired."

"Spring is an odd time to head to Florida when you're trying to get away from northern winters, isn't it?"

"Elias is an odd bird. Cranky. A lot of thunder and brimstone. Yelled at patients all the time, especially the smokers, the drinkers, the obese ones." Brody laughs uneasily. "He'd tell them what's what. For years, he wasn't getting any new patients. And after a while, the old ones were dying off."

Without hesitation, Brody agrees to give me a copy of the documents in his file on William Kind, and he has his secretary Xerox them while I wait.

6

At Apex, the closed sign is in the window and the door is locked, which is curious since it's not yet 4:30. Through the glass I can see that Cherie's not at her desk. When I slide my key into the lock and open the door, I hear noise in the back room, and she comes walking out and glares at me.

"Catch you napping?"

"That's right."

"Well, don't let me stop you. Where's Joseph?"

"He's around." Cherie sits down and lights a cigarette with a red butane lighter that doesn't quite match the crimson of her blouse. She goes back to the *Wall Street Journal*, neatly folded open to NASDAQ tables.

"I need the number of that new medical-malpractice lawyer we use. We may have something for him." Walking past her and toward the back room, despite the hostility and the smoke from her cigarette, I catch the sense something's off. But it takes a moment to register.

"What are you doing?"

"What are you talking about?" Cherie says.

Walking around to the front of her desk, so she can't ignore it, I repeat the question. "What are you doing?"

"What the hell are you talking about?" Cherie says. "Have you lost your mind?"

"Not yet. But I'm getting closer." She won't look at me now. Her hair is matted flat on the back, and her makeup is smudged, quite uncharacteristic. "A better question is what you did with your scruples."

Cherie sits, smoking and glaring. "You know, you just don't get it. It's none of your fucking business. You don't know anything about me. Who do you think you are?"

It feels like an entire argument is about to spill out of my mouth, then something about casting the first stone, then nothing.

"You're right. It's none of my business. You're supposed to be a fully formed adult, you do whatever you want." The crack about fidelity stops in my throat. "I don't care. I wouldn't do it, but that doesn't mean anything."

"You," Cherie says, "wouldn't do anything. Period."

I carry my briefcase and coat into the back room, where Joseph is emptying the contents of his desk drawers into a box, on top of a plaid picnic blanket. The sense of lovers interrupted is stronger back here. "What are you up to?"

"I'm finally moving all my stuff into the office," Joseph says, sitting back in his old swivel chair, sorting through papers, without looking up. "We may need this desk one of these days. I know you've been overworked since I became examiner."

"I'm just fine."

"Actually, I think you need some help."

"You know, Joseph, I covered two jobs frequently, even when you had the other one. So this past year hasn't been that much different."

Joseph's head snaps up, his face turning red. "That's not true."

"Do you really want to talk about what's true?" I sit down in my swivel chair, across from Joseph, like in the beginning when we would sit together back there and talk things over, when Artie was still the boss. "So why did you close the office early?"

"You know, you've always had a hard time keeping your mind on business," Joseph says. "You're always confusing it with something else. It's why they didn't even consider you for examiner. They wouldn't promote you."

He adds, "You miss the point."

"What's the point? Do you mean splendor in the grass? Or should I say splendor on the picnic blanket over the linoleum? That's business? That's the point?"

"We were cleaning out my desk."

He goes back to sorting through papers. Now his face is red, and he won't look at me. I pick up my case and coat and head for the front door. Cherie's still smoking. "Don't worry," I tell her. "I'm not going to tell anybody." I mean it, and no doubt they'll both believe it, but the moment it's out of my mouth, I feel an intuitive unease that giving up an advantage like that was a big mistake.

The phone's ringing in the apartment.

"It's me," Caroline says. "I've been thinking about you, you know?"

"Why?"

"How've you been? What have you been doing?

"I've been working a lot. Evenings and weekends. Moonlighting a little as an independent, too. I finally paid off the divorce lawyer. I think he liked me. He asked me to do a job for him. An insurance case. Not a divorce."

She doesn't react at all to the sarcastic tone, and after a pause she starts talking. "I'm running this gallery? You know, the one in SoHo? It's not exactly SoHo, but it's close. And we've got some really nice pieces. It's mostly photography, but it's good. We had a Mapplethorpe. And an original Arbus. It's small. You know, it's not a big gallery. But Paul's got me pretty much running it and taking clients out and everything. It's almost like it was mine. I mean, it's pretty much mine."

"Do you paint anymore? That's what you went to college for."

"I'm too busy. Besides, nobody liked my landscapes."

"I liked your landscapes."

"Yeah. You did. But nobody else did."

"Just because you think that professor trashed your senior show. He said your work was lyrical, for God's sake."

"That was an insult. God. But you're sweet. That's why I was thinking about you. I just kind of wondered, you know. If you still approve of me."

While she hangs there, I start thinking about Joseph and Cherie, and Margaret Kelly, and how everything has been reduced to work. "You couldn't know this, but I met someone today. It was on a case at Lake George, of all places. The man this woman was living with, he died. Which may or may not be a big deal. Do you know what the funny part is? I think her heart may or may not be broken—I can't tell that kind of thing anymore—but it's made her free. She doesn't care what I think, or what anybody thinks. She just does what she does and doesn't give a damn. Maybe she was always that way. But she doesn't have anybody to answer to. Like me."

Now Caroline doesn't say anything.

"It was funny. I was talking to her, and at one point she just took off her clothes and got in her hot tub."

"And you think that makes her free? You're an ass."

"The truth is, Caroline, I used to love you. But then it got old. Or I got old. It turned bad, and it died. Or maybe I died. Or maybe you did. Now you're a corpse."

"That's sick."

"I'm not. I'm not sick. You know what's sick? Necrophilia. Loving dead people. That's sick. Even pretending to talk to them. As if they could."

I don't know if she's still on the phone at the end, and I don't really care if she did hang up. She's in her own little hell, and far be it from me to play her Orpheus and get torn to bits. I set down the receiver but pick it up again a moment later. She's not there anymore.

7

There are mornings where you wake up weightless. For most people, it's when they're falling in love. But some mystics were like that all the time—and I don't mean simply lightheaded from fasting and contemplating eternity. The feeling this morning makes me think maybe Jesus did walk on water, maybe that wasn't just a variation on the Poseidon myth. Maybe the feeling is just the shadow of a dream, unremembered.

I arrive at the office an hour before opening, a good time to chat with John Casey, Esquire, about the case of William Kind, deceased. Casey says the failure to diagnose the pneumonia for an entire day and the apparent failure to listen to his lungs on admission could be something for him to use in talking to the hospital's malpractice carrier. "It's always better if they screwed up at least twice," he says. "Why don't you go back through everything and check on the antibiotics and oxygen—what was ordered and what was administered when. Sometimes the night nurses don't get around to it. That'd probably be enough to shake loose a settlement. That and the screwup when they admitted him. You're sure the first mention of pneumonia is a day later?"

"Yes."

"He could have developed it in the hospital," Casey says, playing devil's advocate, trying to see their argument.

"Full-blown pneumonia in both lungs? It would have taken more than a day. He was in trouble when he went in. They should have noticed it, and at least listened to his lungs."

"At least listened," he says. "Certainly. So check on the other thing and call me back. This could be a nice piece of work, Jack. Save your company three hundred grand. Minus my fee." He laughs. Casey used to be part of a big firm that represented hospital corporations and doctors' practices. When some HMOs started cutting reimbursable services to the point where care was compromised and patients were tossed out, he saw his opportunities on the other side.

"There are so many screwups these days," he says. "This one hospital is putting so-called techs, people right off the street with a few weeks' training, into jobs that used to be done by nurses. Even in the operating room. Some are quite good at what they do, but not all of them. They had this one guy handling equipment in the OR, and he wasn't keeping things sterile. That was all he had to do. Keep himself clean and hand over equipment when it was asked for. A few patients a week were developing post-surgical infections. And the nurses knew it was this guy, and they'd been complaining about him. But the administration thought they were just bitching because they were losing jobs to the techs."

"It was beautiful," Casey says. "I got one case from a family whose mother went in for routine disk surgery and almost died from the infection. I had an investigator track it back, and he came up with six more from one two-week period. I contacted those families. Seven settlements out of one case. Hospital did its own investigation, of course, to find the common link. At first the dumb bastards thought it was a sloppy neurosurgeon. They finally fired the right guy. And I think he's suing them, too. Employment discrimination. Says they failed to train him adequately." Casey emits a deep, satisfied laugh. "The cheap bastards deserved it."

"What hospital?"

"Can't tell you, sport. Trade secret. One of the conditions of the settlement. But it's a gift that keeps on giving. I'm getting checks. So get on that one, and call me back."

William Kind's emergency-room record shows his temperature, blood pressure, and heart rate, all only slightly elevated, and lists his complaints. His later charts have minimal entries by the nurse who had him the first evening and overnight, Beverly Wilbur. She's his nurse again the second evening and overnight, apparently doing double shifts, and briefly charting only a few things: unchanged vital signs, dinner served, IV antibiotics at 10:30 p.m., code called for unresponsive patient at 1:45 a.m.

The detailed charting of the day nurse and the notes by Elias show other things from William Kind's one full morning and afternoon in the hospital: elevated temperature at 7:15 a.m., normal blood pressure, no appetite for breakfast, complaint of respiratory distress and sounds of congestion at 9:15 a.m., elevated heart rate and blood pressure, X-ray taken at 11:15 a.m., pneumonia diagnosed, followed by Elias's order for antibiotics and oxygen STAT at 1:40 p.m. Oxygen started at 1:45 p.m.; IV antibiotics at 2 p.m.—to be repeated every four hours.

The math is easy. According to the chart, Kind got his second dose of medication at 10:30 p.m., more than four hours later than was ordered, and he never got the third scheduled dose, which according to the prescription should have been given hours before he died.

Casey is enthusiastic when I call him back, and he asks me to fax him copies of the records. "It figures," he says. "This may sound odd to you, but in my experience, screwups generally run in threes. Was there anything else?"

"Actually, there was another odd thing. The day nurse's entry says Kind didn't eat his lunch, that he was somewhat disoriented and agitated, and he tried to pull out his IV and remove the nasal cannula giving him oxygen. He wanted to leave the hospital. Loose wrist restraints were ordered by the doctor and applied at 3:30 p.m."

William Kind was tied to the bed.

8

The door to Apex opens at precisely 8:30 a.m., and a young woman walks in. She has thick, brown, curly hair, loosely tied back, a smart skirt and blouse under a fashionable trenchcoat, dark stockings, and low heels, somewhere between practical and the extra few inches that she needs to approach medium height. She has an angular face, with little makeup, but striking gray-green eyes and an engaging snaggletooth smile.

"Good morning," she says brightly. "I'm Ruth Benjamin."

"Welcome to Apex," I tell her. "What can we do for you this morning?"

"I have an appointment with Joseph Sweet."

"He should be here soon. Would you like to have a seat? I can hang up your coat if you like."

"No, thanks." She folds the trenchcoat over the back of a chair in the waiting area, places her black-leather briefcase and matching pocketbook across the seat, and settles in an adjacent chair. Her perfume is as faint as her makeup. She's pretty enough to interest him, but whatever else Joseph's been up to, this is a professional call. Another insurance agent, maybe. Somebody seeking to negotiate or sell something. She pulls out her datebook and a pen, and I go back to work.

Engrossed in the medical records, I barely notice Joseph's arrival. He and Ruth Benjamin go into his office for a while and then appear in the back office.

"Jack, you've met Ruth Benjamin?" Joseph says. "She's the new adjuster I was telling you about. The one we need to help you out with all the cases you've had to take on."

"You're kidding."

"Oh, no. I'm quite serious. Ruth is coming here straight out of training in Hartford. But she's very bright," Joseph says, giving her a big smile. "And very hungry and aggressive. Isn't that right?"

"I just want to do a good job and learn everything I can," she says.

"I'm sure you will. And Jack is the best teacher you could have. He's thorough and thoughtful. There is not much about insurance adjusting that he doesn't know and nothing he won't try to find out." Joseph gives me a significant look. "And I'm sure he'll try to teach you all of it. Won't you, Jack?"

"Of course, Joseph." I stand up and shake Ruth's hand, which is small but strong and manicured. "We're colleagues, aren't we?"

Joseph walks her over to his recently vacated desk. "This is yours," he says. "Later today I'll have you start to review all of Jack's current files, and then the rest of the week you can follow him. But first I want you to come back to my office. I'll fill you in on how things work around here. And you can fill me in on what's new in Hartford."

"Nice to meet you," Ruth says. Joseph doesn't look back.

"Yes, you too." I somehow didn't expect my designated replacement to be so young. And no mistake, as soon as she gets up to speed she'll be Joseph's "go-to gal," a phrase he returned with after a weeklong round of management training. "Jack, you're my go-to guy," he'd said. And I'd said, "I have to be. I'm the only one here." And she'll get an earful of that kind of twaddle, and I'll be lucky to get a return ticket to Hartford or the chronic stack of crappy cases—once she gets up to speed. If she's an idiot that will take a while. But in the present environment, there's no telling. So many incompetents around, people whose chief skill is kissing up to the boss, or creating false perceptions about the quality and volume of their work. It's difficult not to despise such people, and I lose about five minutes wondering if Ruth Benjamin is one of those.

Then I pull together the entire file on William Kind and leave with it, passing Cherie, who's coming to work about forty minutes late, which won't count against her on anybody's time sheet.

"Tell Joseph I went back to Lake George," I mutter as she walks in and I walk out. Cherie, who under her black-leather coat is wearing tight banana-yellow pants and a pale yellow blouse, with spike heels that almost match both, doesn't acknowledge me. "He's in his office with your competition. Watch out. She's very hungry, and very aggressive."

Cherie looks in at Ruth Benjamin, who's leaning forward and talking animatedly to Joseph, and frowns. "That's the new adjuster," she says.

"I knew you weren't deaf. I tell everybody. Cherie hears just fine. She's just not that good at thinking clearly."

"Asshole."

The word hangs there long enough to have meaning. Not as a casual insult but as an anatomical metaphor. What it was before it got overused.

"Just tell him I went to Lake George and I may not be back today. There are files back there she can help herself to. And if something comes up, the two of them may be able to figure it out. If not, maybe you can help. Maybe not."

Like Rodney Glynnis, I start to laugh going out the door. But unlike his, my laugh sounds forced, and harsh.

9

On the way out of town, I stop on a woodsy suburban street outside Schenectady where the houses are small and close together but well kept. Mostly Cape Cods. The woman who called lives in a one-story ranch with cedar-shingle siding painted colonial blue. An old Chevy Chevette sits in the narrow driveway. A child's tricycle on the low front porch, the door beside a picture window. The ring of the doorbell sets off fierce, high-pitched barking. The wooden door opens, and a haggard-looking young woman eyes me through the glass storm.

"Yes?" When the barking gets louder, she pushes with her foot the little yellow dog that's making the racket. "Griffin! Stop it!" The dog disappears for a moment, then appears at the picture window again, barking and snarling against the glass.

"He's a killer."

She doesn't react to the wisecrack. "What do you want?"

"I'm from the insurance company. You called about a homeowner's claim."

"Yes. Come in. Don't mind the dog. He won't bite."

"Promise?"

She doesn't promise, but the dog doesn't bite. Griffin leaps down from the back of the couch, growls, runs at me, leaps waist-high, then sniffs my leg and starts barking again. I show him my hand, he noses it, and his stub tail starts moving. I rub his nappy back.

"What is he, some kind of poodle?"

"A cockapoo."

"Yeah, okay. I see a little cocker spaniel in him. Long ears. He's pretty aggressive."

"We're going to get him neutered. My husband's opposed. But it's just too much trouble."

"It's definitely that." She doesn't find that funny either. "So you had some damage."

"It's outside. Just a minute. I'll show you." She walks down the hallway to a room that has the background sound of a television. "I'm going to step outside for a minute, Sweetie. So just watch your program. Griffin will be here with you."

She returns and slips on a winter coat from the rack by the front door. The narrow yard slopes down toward the back, with a small patio along one side, a chain-link fence enclosing the whole thing. Ten feet of concrete foundation are exposed below the back wall of cedar shingles, with four small basement windows up high. Lattice window covers made of pressure-treated wood lie broken on the ground. The windows aren't broken, and they don't open.

"Is that it? Those four windows?"

"That's all we know of."

"This was last night? What happened? Did someone try to break in?"

"I don't know." She wraps her coat tighter around herself.

"Do you have any idea who did it?"

"No," she says, and looks away.

"Why don't I take another walk around, look for anything else that's damaged, then we'll talk."

"Those lattice pieces are pretty expensive," she says. "They were custom-built."

Back inside, the dog is under the living-room sofa, barking and snarling. A little girl, about three years old, is sitting in front of the sofa, stretching her legs underneath to try to reach the dog. Each time she touches him with her foot, he gets a little crazier, and she shakes her brown curls and lets out a peal of laughter.

"Jessica, stop that!" her mother yells from the kitchen, where she has gone to get coffee. "He's going to bite you."

The little girl pulls her feet back. "Griffin, come here," she coos. The sofa has wooden legs that raise it almost a foot off the floor. The dog inches forward, and the girl stretches out her legs again, which sets off another outburst of barking and snarling. She laughs, and I do, too.

Her mother comes out with a tray with a single cup of coffee on it. "Jessica, this is the last time I'm going to tell you."

The child gets up reluctantly and goes back down the hall and into the room with the television. "Come on, Griffin," she says. But for the moment he stays hunkered down under the sofa.

"Well, I looked around, and I didn't see anything else damaged or broken. Just the lattice pieces. I'm not sure what happened. Maybe that's vandalism. Has somebody been locked out?"

"No."

"Have there been any problems in the neighborhood with burglaries or break-ins?"

"I don't think so. Not that I know of."

"And you're saying this happened last night? When did you notice the damage?"

"My husband noticed it this morning, before he left for work. But actually Griffin went wild about nine o'clock last night. I was watching TV, and he was up at this window and just started going crazy as if somebody was out there. So I turned on the outside light. I didn't see anybody. But this morning, my neighbor across the street told me she saw somebody at my front window. She thought it was my husband, but it was dark and she couldn't really see. He was at work. It's really creepy."

"Where does your husband work?"

"He moonlights as a cabdriver. I called the dispatcher, and he came right home. He ended his shift early and stayed home. Then today he went in early to get more hours. We need the money."

"Did you call the police?"

"No."

"Well, here's the problem. The total replacement cost of the wood for the lattice pieces is about twenty dollars, maybe fifty with a generous estimate. Even if you were to pay a carpenter forty dollars an hour to construct them, again being generous that's maybe another one hundred sixty dollars. And your deductible amount is five hundred dollars. I don't really think you have a claim here that we can do anything about."

"I can't believe it," she says. "What's the point of having insurance?"

"You choose the deductible amount. We don't. Look, I'm sorry you're having a problem. Why don't you call the town police? They'll take a look around, tell you if anybody else is having a similar problem, and maybe have a patrol car drive down your street at night for a few weeks. You're living in Niskayuna, a tony suburb. They don't appreciate break-ins."

"That won't take care of it. You don't understand."

"Is there something else?"

"We need the money. We can't just replace the lattice pieces. And there's no back door. We need to get one put in. The bedrooms are in the back. What if something happened. Shouldn't the insurance pay for that?" She flexes and twists her fingers.

"What would happen?"

"What if somebody broke in, or what if there was a fire."

"Why do you think there would be a fire?"

"Never mind."

"Do you suspect arson?"

"I really have nothing else to say to you. If you're not going to pay for the damage, you can just go."

"Unfortunately, now you have to talk to me. Fire's a serious thing. Even the threat of it. If you don't talk to me I'll have to review your policy and maybe we'll have to cancel it. Without an insurance policy you'll lose your mortgage. And you'll be out."

It's an exaggeration, of sorts.

"You'll cancel it anyway."

"No, I won't."

"You can't tell anybody, especially my husband, that I told you. Or the police."

"Talk to me, and we'll see."

"You can't."

The story comes out quickly, like she couldn't wait to tell somebody. Her husband is the rental manager and bookkeeper for a block of Schenectady buildings. He deals with the tenants, businesses downstairs, apartments upstairs, and collects rents for the owner. He also does the books for several small businesses—a comic-book store, a bar, a pornography shop, and a couple of others. The porn shop's the problem. The landlord owns it. He has two other porn shops in the city. He accused her husband of stealing. The shops run on cash, thousands of quarters pumped into machines by customers for the peep shows in private booths. Roger was counting the quarters by weight. The owner felt that the bags, which Roger filled and collected, were light.

"Roger says the last guy they accused of stealing—and he was a clerk—they burned his house down. Somebody called him to tell him about it. Now they're threatening him. What are we supposed to do?"

"What do they want?"

"I think they want money. Roger agreed to keep working there with a cut in pay until they sort it out. They said they'd let him know."

"Did he steal from them?"

"No. I don't know." Her fingers are in knots. "Roger says they're just trying to scare him."

Fun Haus occupies a grimy storefront on a beat-up block of three-story buildings. The door opens to a front room lined with magazines and videotapes for sale. The glass counter holds assorted sex toys and novelties; behind it is a stoop-shouldered man with gray hair, wearing a cardigan over a flannel shirt stretched over his paunch. He looks like the nasty old uncle you made it a point never to visit.

"How's business?"

"Up and down."

Neither of us laughs. His delivery is tired, indifferent.

"You want some quarters?" A long silver tube sticks up over the counter. He pushes a lever four times and catches four quarters from the bottom. "That's a dollar."

"I don't need any quarters. I'm looking for Frederick Schmitt."

He grunts noncommittally.

"I was told his office is here."

"Who told you that?"

"I'm from the insurance company."

"What do you want?"

"To talk about an insurance claim. About whether to write the check." He puts the quarters back in the top of the funnel and ignores me.

"It's to his benefit to see me." The butterflies in my stomach from coming to his place of business are gone. No doubt this geezer has a blackjack or club behind the counter, maybe a gun. But I'm feeling pretty sure I can kick his ass anyway before he can reach them.

"There's an office in back."

"Through here?"

He doesn't answer. Through the inner doorway, the warren of peepshow booths divides into four narrow hallways. Each closet door has a still photograph and description of the films shown on the small projector inside. Most are straight sex. Some are gay, some lesbian. Some doors are closed. You can hear quarters dropping. A few men are wandering the hallways, studying pictures. I walk down each corridor twice, find no office door, and walk back out.

"Where's the office?"

"It's around back."

"That's not what you said before."

He turns away from me and switches on a small black-and-white TV behind the counter to horse-racing recaps and betting odds.

I start around the block on foot and find the back of the building. Today, I'm a Templar on the old Jerusalem road, defender of maidens, protector of children, hope of frightened pilgrims. Or Quixote, a fool who might get a beating.

Wooden stairs lead to an unmarked door. They comprise the first segment of a wooden fire escape, an obvious violation of the city building code. For whatever reason, nobody's making him comply. After three loud knocks, a deep voice rumbles from the other side. "Who's there?"

"Kirkland. Apex Insurance."

"Put it in a letter."

"It's about money."

"Put it in a letter."

"It doesn't work that way."

"Come in."

The door is unlocked. Frederick Schmitt is sitting behind a gun-metal gray desk in a padded black faux-leather swivel chair. The woman described him from her husband's say-so, without ever having seen him, and there is no mistake. The blond comb-over, thick eyebrows, and meerschaum pipe. Thickset, about sixty, wearing sportcoat and slacks. One door, leading to a closet-size bathroom, is open. He looks me over.

"So what's this about money? I hope you brought a check."

"What check?"

"You're the one who came in talking about a check. So you can just write the check and leave."

"We actually might write a check. It depends a little bit on what you say."

"Did you say Apex? I don't have any insurance with Apex."

"No. But one of your employees does."

"So what does that got to do with me?"

"Mr. Schmitt, may I sit down and try to explain?"

"My name is Smith. Sonny Smith. I'm in the entertainment business. I think you got the wrong guy. Don't sit down."

"Mr. Smith, I'll be brief. I'm an insurance investigator from Apex. I got a homeowner's claim from a woman who had a prowler last night. She wants me to write her a check. She's afraid that somebody was at her windows last night and wants to burn her house down. This is a nice woman. She has a sweet little kid. Somebody scared the shit out of her."

"So why tell me this?"

"I checked, and it turns out her husband works for you."

He stares at me and says nothing.

"She needs help. Here's my dilemma. The husband doesn't know she called the insurance company. She did it because they need the money. She has no idea I'm here. What happened to her house looks like simple vandalism, but she won't call the police. I could, but I wouldn't for something as minor as that. Really, who cares? We pay claims. We just hate paying big ones. Like when a house burns down and people are hurt or killed. But these people need some help, and I'm hoping you will."

"Do what?"

"Help them."

He stares at me a long time. "You know, buddy, I don't know what the fuck you're talking about. I don't know these people. But I will tell you this. And I think you'll learn something. If you're smart enough to pay attention.

"I used to be a printer, which was a good job once upon a time. I was an apprentice, and you know in those days you could make a pretty good living at it. You could become a journeyman and travel around the whole country and get work in any city. Just show up at the newspaper and show them your union card. Good money, too. Well, one night I'm working down there in Albany, and I dumped this whole tray of type. The entire fucking newspaper was late that night. An hour late. Late to the newsstands. Late to the route drivers. Late to the paperboys. Late to people's houses. A hundred thousand newspapers. All of them late. You know what the night boss says to me? He's this Irishman, a real prick. He says, 'Sonny, you're a good man, but I'm gonna need you to do something for me. I'm gonna need you to wash my truck on Sunday before you come in. And wax it.' So guess what happened? I'll tell you what happened. Best fucking wax job that pickup truck ever had. Every Sunday for six months."

"But you didn't stay in newspapers."

"No. After that I worked for a place that printed magazines. And one thing led to another. But you see my point?"

"Not really."

"When you got somebody who's a pretty good employee, and then they make a mistake, a big fucking mistake, that's when that person becomes a very good employee. A model employee. That guy will make the extra effort. And really, that's what you want."

"I see your point."

"Do you? So don't worry, buddy. You want to write them a check, you go ahead. But I think it's a bad idea. I'm just guessing here, but I believe they'll be fine. That was just kids and vandalism, like you said. You want to write me a check, that's a good idea. Why don't you just write me a check?"

"Thanks for your time."

"Don't mention it. By the way, leave me your business card. Just in case. Maybe I'll have some business for you sometime. That way I'll be able to get in touch with you if I need to. I see what kind of guy you are. Maybe I could do something with you."

10

Margaret Kelly comes pounding up the drive almost the same time as the day before, wearing deep-purple Spandex tights and a white sleeveless T-shirt that shows the definition of her biceps. The sun is shining, and it's unseasonably warm for these hills. She's sweating and breathing hard—glistening—and still makes no allowance for the rise. The healthiest animal I've seen in a long time. She smiles as she reaches the porch. As I sit in an Adirondack chair, she paces back and forth in front of me, catching her breath. When she notices the briefcase at my feet, she turns and watches me with her pale eyes.

"I thought you were going to come back when this was over."

"It almost is. I have a few things I wanted to check. It looks like they made a few mistakes at the hospital."

Margaret leans against the porch railing. She lifts the bottom of her T-shirt to wipe the sweat from her forehead. Her abdomen is strong, flat, with a faint outline of the muscles underneath, and shiny. "I'll answer your questions. But first you have do something with me. There's a place I like to go to, and I haven't been there in a long time. That's where I was going, and now you're here."

"Where is it?"

"A short drive and a nice hike. It's an overlook that's too far for most people to go to."

This could be one of those fateful openings. Miss this, and miss it altogether. "Fine with me," I answer, trying to disguise my eagerness.

"Really?" She seems surprised. "All right. If you can make it, I'll talk to you again. But those shoes won't do. You can wear Bill's old hiking boots. They'll be large and not well broken in. He didn't use them much."

She puts on pants, a light jacket, and her own worn hiking boots. The boots she gives me, leather, size 11, are still stiff, the lug soles still clean and shiny. Dead man's boots. I lock my files in the car and get in the Land Rover. She drives south along the lake a few miles. The surface is unruffled, no wind, no motorboats. Near Silver Bay, the road veers west, away from the lake. Margaret pulls into a small parking area next to an old quarry that's filled with water. We walk a short distance farther down the road to a trailhead sign: Fifth Peak 2.6 miles.

"Is that where we're going?"

"That's where everyone goes," she says. "We're going past that. To French Point Mountain."

"French Point Mountain? Is it called that because the French do everything better?"

She grins. "That's what they say. The French. They say they do everything better. For the most part, they're right."

"You mean, like surrender? Isn't that what the French do best? Start a war, then look for somebody to surrender to?"

"For that, you can carry the pack." She hands me the small day pack. It's surprisingly heavy.

"What is this, filled with rocks?"

"Mostly water," she says. "Don't worry. It'll get lighter as we drink along the way. You'll be glad we brought it. You don't go into the woods very often, do you?"

"No, but I'll keep up with you. Or die trying."

She gives me a long, searching look. "If you can't make it, I'll collect you on the way back. But you'd better make it. You've got my water. How are the boots?"

"Not bad. "

"You must have big feet."

"And hands. I have very big hands."

She's smiling a little like she's okay with that kind of teasing, unoffended anyway. She starts up into the woods at an easy pace. The trail rises and falls modestly, crosses a wooden bridge, then turns uphill, rutted with roots, in places muddy. The forest is cool and dim under a canopy of evergreens and hardwoods budding into leaf. We pass a slender waterfall running over rocks that step down toward Northwest Bay. Farther up, the path gets steeper, cut into wide switchbacks, and climbs through a dark cluster of hemlocks. Margaret keeps a steady pace. I'm panting for oxygen, staring at her ass for inspiration, trying to fall no more than twenty yards behind. Finally, the trail flattens as we come to a junction, and she stops. It's brighter here, with fewer evergreens.

"Let's have a drink," she says. Reaching into the pack, she pulls out a plastic bottle, unscrews the lid, and takes a long pull. She hands it to me, and I gulp the water down, spilling some on my white shirt, which, like the khakis, is damp with sweat.

"That's about two miles in ninety minutes. We're not moving very fast," she says. "Don't you have to be somewhere?"

"No."

"It's a couple more miles. Let's pick it up a little."

She puts the bottle back in the pack and resumes hiking, now at a faster pace. The trail drops down, circling a crag of gray rock, winds through the hardwoods, and ascends to a rocky bluff where you can see part of the lake far below. Then down and up again, and a third time. Once, she glanced back and saw me reach onto a rock ledge to steady myself.

"Don't do that."

"What?"

"Put your hands onto the rock ledges without looking."

"Why not?"

"There are rattlesnakes up here."

"What?"

"They won't bother you. They're kind of timid, actually. Unless you threaten one."

"Did you ever see one?"

"Just one, last spring. It was in the undergrowth. It was mostly black. When I stepped too close, it started to rattle. Sort of like a buzzing sound. So watch where you put your hands. You don't want to surprise them."

"What about me?"

"Keep your eyes open." She laughs. "Who's in more danger, really? You or the snake?"

Spotting a broken branch, I pull the twigs off and use it for a walking stick, pushing it into piles of dried brown leaves, rotting logs, and small crevices, scanning the ground before every step.

On the second bluff, you can see the main lake on one side and Northwest Bay on the other. Mounting the third bluff, the path enters a stand of scrubby trees. Light pours through. The ground is covered in cool green grass. At the edge, the old trees shift and creak in the wind. Suddenly we're standing fifteen hundred feet above the long lake, with a view of ten miles in either direction. The crooked, blue-black sheet of water is bordered by steep mountains, clothed in various shades of green.

"Wow," I exclaim. "Elysian Fields."

Margaret turns, where she's been standing at the edge of the bluff. Her cheeks are wet.

"Exactly," she says.

We linger on the bluff, passing the second water bottle back and forth until it's empty. Afterward, she takes a seat in the grass. The midday sun is bright, hot.

"Okay," she says. "Let's talk. The mistakes you were talking about before. What do you mean?"

"Well, did they check his breathing when you first brought him in? I mean back in the emergency room?"

"I don't know. I don't remember." She wipes her face with the tail of her shirt. "I do remember that when I told them he had a blood disorder that nobody wanted to get too close to him. I think they thought it was AIDS or hepatitis. That's what they asked about anyway. So maybe they didn't."

"And do you remember, once they started giving him antibiotics, how often did they administer them?"

"I have no idea." Margaret seems weary of the whole business. "It was a long night. They didn't come around very often. I do remember one nurse coming in and fussing with the IV bags and cursing, like something was wrong with them. Whatever it was, she seemed to get it straightened out. And of course that day nurse got angry because Bill pulled the IV out. Then she tied his arms so he couldn't do it again."

"Why did he pull the IV out?"

"He got confused. He thought he was back in Haiti. He wanted to leave."

"Really?"

"Yeah. He'd been detained there once. And for some reason, he thought he was back there. And when they tied him down, he was convinced."

She turns away. "I really don't want to talk about this anymore."

"Okay."

"So what will you do?"

"Ask some questions at the hospital. Talk to our lawyer again."

She turns back around, looking dejected.

"Look, don't worry about it. I shouldn't tell you this right now, but here's how it's probably going to go. Apex will pay your claim, then our lawyer will shake a settlement out of the hospital's insurance carrier, one that will cover the claim plus his substantial fee."

"That's it?"

"Unless you sue. In which case the immediate life insurance benefit will be held up, and you'll be on your own for the malpractice."

"I don't think I want to sue."

"Before you decide that, you should know that it looks like malpractice. The kind that's easy to prove. There's documentation, or lack of it. The kind that's easy to get a settlement from. A much bigger settlement than $300,000. If that's what you want to do."

I stand up and take a step away. "I shouldn't be telling you this. The company doesn't want me telling you such things. It's about money. But I don't want to lie to you. Or hide anything."

"I don't want to sue. I want it to be over."

"I know a good lawyer—and a good investigator. I'm pretty good at this."

"You'd do that for me?"

"I wouldn't be leaving too much behind right now."

Margaret Kelly stands up, looks into my face, and takes a step. She wraps her arms around my neck and gives me a long, slow, gentle hug, the contours of her body pressing softly against mine. And then the promise doesn't seem reckless at all, trading the past four years of misery for this moment.

"You want to be my hero?"

"White knight."

"White knight." She repeats it. "You're something."

"Sure, a modern-day Lancelot. A hopeless romantic. A French fool."

The hike out is uneventful. No snakes. We polish off the third bottle of water at the trail junction. On the descent to the road, neither of us says much. When we reach the jeep, I peel off the dead man's boots, which have rubbed my left foot raw in two places.

"I guess my feet are bigger than I thought."

"You're a surprise," she says, turning the ignition. "There's a little more to you than I would have expected."

At the house, she doesn't say anything. I hand her the boots, start to hobble away, and then stop.

"Can I come back?"

"When?"

"Tomorrow."

"Do you think you're strong enough?" she says. "You're not moving very well."

"The fun doesn't start until somebody's limping."

"That would be you. The one limping. Don't you have work to do?"

"I'm done."

"Okay."

II

Following a dreamless sleep, I wake late. After wolfing an English muffin with coffee, I drive straight back to the hills of Lake George, not bothering to phone the office. Margaret is pacing in the driveway, cooling down from her morning run. She gives me a hug, then leads me by the hand through the A-frame and out the back.

"I got your clothes damp," she says, sliding the jacket off my shoulders. She unsnaps the cover of the hot tub and turns on the whirlpool jets. "Do you have to be anywhere?"

"No."

She pulls her shirt over her head and lays it on the rail. "Then come in with me," she says.

She sits to pull off her running shoes and socks, concentrating on the task, then stands to remove her sports bra, draping it on the rail. Next she lets her shorts fall to her feet. Margaret slides into the water, leans back, and closes her eyes. Having hoped for this moment, I caution myself not to say something stupid. And then I do.

"You look fit. It must be all that running."

Margaret opens one eye and smiles, as if at an amiable dunce. Undressing takes time, putting socks in wingtips, hanging every garment on the rail, trying not to laugh out loud.

"You look fit," she says. "And you're not limping. Are you a runner?"

"No." I slide into the tub opposite her. "I always considered running something you did to get in shape for something else."

"In shape for what?"

"Boxing."

Her eyes widen with interest. "Do you like to fight?"

"I did."

Margaret extends her leg and pushes me against the wall of the tub, pressing her foot against my solar plexus. "So you like to fight, and you don't like to run. I guess that makes you some kind of tough guy." She smiles. "I think I'm going to need that in a white knight."

I wrap my hands around the back of her knee. "Whatever you need, let me know."

She crosses the tub and kisses me hard with her mouth open. "I'll tell you what I don't need," she says. "Sorrow or sympathy. Or weakness. I've had enough of that. And I'm sick of it."

She kisses me again, deeper, and for a while it feels as if I can't breathe, suffocating beneath the pleasure of her wrath.

The wooden deck wraps around the back and side of the A-frame, with a partial view over the wooded hills of a long, blue slice of Lake George. The air is still; the forest obstructs the prevailing west wind, and Margaret hangs towels over the railing to stop any lingering breezes. For a few hours, it feels like summer. The sun heats the deck and our bodies, now stretched out on the wide planks in a tranquil drowsiness, face down. Margaret rests a hand on my arm and sweeps it down until our fingers touch lightly. She smiles vaguely, her lips pulling down in a suggestion of irony, a downward smile, contradicting itself. Her eyes open wide, very blue, not surprised but alert, watchful; they close again, and she sleeps. I study the contour of her jaw, the dark rouge of her lips, her auburn hair pulled behind a pink ear, translucent in the sunlight. The white slope of a shoulder, an outline of her triceps, hips rising smoothly beyond. I try to fix in my mind each impression, recreating them, one at a time, with the precision of an Edward Hopper painting in which reality becomes so overpowering it assumes a dreamlike quality.

The slap on the ass jolts me out of my reveries. "You're losing the day, Galahad," she says. The Earth's tilted. The springtime sun is nearing the southwestern stand of trees, and it's about to get chilly. "Let's see what it takes to make you run."

"What?"

She stands up. "Have you ever run barefoot and naked through the forest?" She looks down at me, smiling. "You have to run as fast as you can, as if your very life depended on it. It's a very old thing to do."

"You don't mean it." I rub my ass, which is still smarting from her slap.

"It's best if someone's chasing you. It doesn't take quite so much imagination."

"And what if I catch you?"

"You won't." She leans down, squeezes the back of my thigh, slaps my ass again in the same spot. "But you'll try very hard."

"Damn."

Margaret laughs, running down the deck stairs and out past the garage. I get up and follow, taking the stairs in a jump, cross the small grassy backyard, and turn the corner behind the garage to see her fleeting image disappear down a narrow track into the woods.

The path loops through the mixed woods of maples, white birch, and pine. The ground is cool and damp, covered by old leaves and needles, sometimes twigs that hurt the feet. The branches of the trees and underbrush scratch when I get too close. But hearing her ahead, I run faster and faster, feeling as though I'm pursuing a wood nymph and wondering what I'll do if I catch her. The Scandinavians say wood nymphs are as empty inside as they are beautiful outside—and pity the man who chases one into the dark forest. He never returns. When the trail enters a clearing of tall grass and saplings, I see she's only thirty yards ahead, her haunches flexing with each stride, arms pumping, breasts swaying. She sees me, lets out a laugh, and runs a little slower. But she disappears again into the forest, and by the time I reach her yard, she's sitting on the edge of the tub, one foot in the water, the other in her hand. She's examining it for cuts and slivers.

"You'll have to run faster," she says.

I walk up to the deck, breathing hard, sit opposite her, and drop my muddied, scratched legs into the tub. There's a cut along one instep that stings.

"Sorry about the blood."

Margaret shrugs.

"It's not important," she says. "Though Bill wouldn't have liked it."

"Did he ever catch you?"

She looks at me with a grimace. "He never ran, not if he could help it."

"So who chased you?"

"Demons, imps, the usual lot. Never a white knight."

"Are they faster than I am?"

"Much faster," she says. The sun has dropped, leaving us in the shade. "Let's go. It's getting chilly."

Later, with dusk approaching, she tells a story about Haiti. That she went there from Paris, with a man who owned a beachfront resort away from Port au Prince. She spoke good French, which was necessary, and he hired her as concierge. He said he liked her smile and her energy, which were almost French in style, and her Irish-American ethnicity, which would help with the the Americans. That's where the money was. The French tourists were cheap.

She doesn't say how she got to Paris, who the man was, or what her life was like before. But her voice suggests New England—Boston, maybe—and Ireland itself. A vague nasal resonance, a soft lilt. I let my mind drift along with her words, wondering about questions, not particularly wanting answers. Wanting only to lie there and listen.

She lived in a small room at the back of the resort and worked seven days a week, just mornings when it was slow. She often ate in the kitchen, where she picked up a few things about fine cuisine. She stayed for six years, through the downfall of the Duvaliers. The hotelier bribed everyone to keep them safe during the unrest. She went to Port au Prince sometimes. She learned something about the voodoo, about the spirit world, and it reminded her of the the old Druids her mother told her about. Spirits everywhere, in everything.

She didn't have many close friends and often went places with guests who wanted a guide. That's how she met William Kind, who was working on an engineering project at the big power plant, installing a new turbine. It took two and a half years. He moved into a house but still went to the resort to dine some evenings. He would ask her to dine with him. Often she would. He was well traveled, worldly, organized, and intelligent. Meticulous to a fault. He told stories about Tanzania and Indonesia and South Korea, and they often made her laugh. Even if he didn't know what it was about them that was funny.

Then his health faltered. She went with him once to his apartment in Port au Prince. Because she knew a little about voodoo, she looked for and found tiny droplets of mercury on the window sills. She questioned the landlady in French but already knew what it was about. Every time the woman cleaned, she would finish by sprinkling a little mercury at the doorway and windows. It was meant to keep evil spirits away. When Margaret told her that she had to stop, the woman began scolding her, accusing her of all sorts of things. So she told Bill, who moved out, making the landlady's fears come true—the very thing she was trying to forfend. She lost her good tenant.

Kind didn't get better right away. He moved back to the resort, which was doing poorer post-Duvaliers. The hotelier was thinking about selling for whatever he could get. Bill decided to retire. He asked Margaret to come with him. The island had no more fascination for her. They moved to the Adirondacks for the clean air and the real estate, fairly inexpensive then as long as it wasn't waterfront.

She doesn't say what happened to the hotelier, or whether she had any money of her own at the end. Or how she felt about William Kind. It never comes up, and after a while she stops talking.

12

Beverly Wilbur starts her shift at the hospital by dropping a handful of ice into a deep plastic cup and pouring in half a liter of Diet Pepsi. She snaps on a lid with a straw and sucks down most of the beverage, then opens a pack of chocolate Hostess Cupcakes, eats each one in two bites, finishes the Pepsi, then refills the cup from the remainder of the liter bottle. She has three more bottles in a plastic grocery sack behind the nurses' station. When I introduce myself, she doesn't appear too surprised to see me and says right away, "There's things you don't know." And, "I'm not going to lose my license over this."

"Nobody said you would."

"That man died, and he shouldn't have. They would have let it go, but now you're here, and they'll need to blame somebody. Have you seen the incident report?"

"What report?"

"About why he didn't get his meds on time." Still sitting behind the nurses' station, she takes another long drink of Pepsi.

"I never saw it. What does it say?"

"I'll tell you what it says. That when I checked on his drip, the tubing was kinked and nothing was going in. And the next time I checked, it was turned off."

"What?"

"His IV was clamped off. It wasn't dripping."

"When did you notice that?"

"I don't know. But I didn't do it. I turned it back on."

"You didn't turn off the drip while you straightened it out and then accidentally forget to turn it back on?"

"That's what the supervisor tried to say. It wasn't true. I wrote in the incident report what happened. I refuse to take the blame for that. I turned it back on. Ask Doctor Elias. He believed me."

"I can't reach Doctor Elias. He left town."

"I have his phone number. He said this wasn't over with yet, and I should stand my ground."

Beverly Wilbur has a copy of the incident report folded up in her purse. The report was written and signed by her, stating just what she told me about the kinked tubing—found at 7 p.m.—and the shut IV valve, found almost three hours after that. So by her account, the lack of prescribed antibiotics was not her fault. But the report does make her look suspect, like she's trying to cover up her mistakes.

Elias answers the phone after several rings. "What's your name?" he asks twice. "I guess I knew I'd be hearing from you eventually." He immediately launches into his narrative of William Kind's case, allowing for no questions or comments. Finally he says, "They were the right drugs. And they were in time. That Beverly is an excitable girl, and a little sleepy, but she's not stupid. And I saw the bent tubing myself. Now the girl who was on earlier, that nurse might have made the mistake with the tubing with all that was going on. Though she's a good nurse, too. And this fellow was big, and he was thrashing about, so we had to restrain him. He would have pulled everything out, otherwise. Also, Beverly said this man's girlfriend kept climbing up on the bed with him and cuddling him. She could have caused the problem."

"What about turning it off?"

"I don't know. But even that's academic. You see, he shouldn't have died. Even with no antibiotics and no oxygen. Despite that mercury business, even despite the pneumonia, that was a healthy specimen. He should not have died."

"But he did."

"Yes. We all go in God's time. But I'm troubled by this case."

"Is that why you left?"

"What? Don't be stupid. I'm an old man. It was time. If I were a younger man, maybe I would have rounded again in the evening and that fellow wouldn't have died. I used to do that, whenever one of my patients was in the hospital. Just to see how things were progressing."

"What else could have killed him?"

"Hell, I don't know. Brody didn't do an autopsy. That fellow had been in the hospital for more than twenty-four hours, and correctly diagnosed with pneumonia, so it wasn't necessary to him. It appeared that the cause was respiratory failure. Brody took it on its face. He blamed the pneumonia. Which is another odd thing. This man never spiked a fever. Just low-grade. And he was disoriented and couldn't talk to us. Maybe we missed something. I didn't take a culture. It might have been viral, but I don't think so. I had nothing to prescribe for that anyway. And if it was bacterial we treated that aggressively. We didn't wait for a culture. And it's prophylactic against secondary infections. What really killed him it's hard to say."

"Why don't you ask that red-haired girl what happened," Elias adds. "I'm told she was in the patient's room the whole time."

After finishing the call on the pay phone, I find Beverly Wilbur clearing a dinner tray from one of the half-dozen patients on the floor, stacking it in a cart in the hallway. She sees me coming.

"Do you remember if William Kind's girlfriend was in his room the entire night?"

"Every time I went by the room she was up on the bed. I told her once she should get off and let him sleep. One time she'd knocked the oxygen cannula off his nose."

"What did she say?"

"She hissed at me. She told me to get out and let him sleep."

"What about the last time, when you found him?"

"The last time, she was gone."

13

Instead of driving straight back to Margaret's, I drive north toward Ticonderoga, taking time to think about things, trying to sort it out. At an overlook, with the car parked, sitting on the warm hood, I look out at the lake, watch dusk settle and then darkness spread upward over the ridge. I whisper a question into the night sky. "Do I have to fall from grace?" There's only wind in the trees. And I shout the question, one that's occurred to me in the past, and feel silly. In a moment, a mumbled, mocking echo bounces back from the ridge. I get back in the car, stuck with the memory of another time I drove full of hope on the roads north, full of what passed for love.

Flying low along the ancient glacial lake, the Toyota makes good time, and I keep hoping Margaret's not asleep yet. But the lights are out in the A-frame, and it takes her a long time to answer the pounding on her door. The spotlight goes on, bathing me in its glow, before the lock turns and the door opens. She's standing in a red football jersey that hangs to her knees, gray knit socks pulled up high and the short bob hanging in her face. She's puffy and warm and smaller, and for a moment I wonder if it's the wrong woman, if somehow I've made a wrong turn and wound up at the wrong A-frame, one occupied by a frumpier woman.

"Hi," she says. "I fell asleep."

"I'm sorry. I didn't mean to wake you. I'll go."

"No. That's okay." She takes my hand and gently pulls me toward her. "I'm glad you're here." She pulls me through the doorway and with the other hand turns out the spotlight and locks the door. She shuffles through the dappled darkness, leading me past the hearth and the stove to the big round bed. Moonlight streams through the small windows, the furniture casting odd shadows among pools of light. The quilt and sheet lie in a heap, and she releases my hand and climbs under them. "I'm going to sleep for a while," she says and pats the mattress next to her. "Come lie down."

I stand there, straining to see her face in the moonlight. "What's wrong?" she murmurs, patting the bed again, more softly this time.

"Nothing."

"Then come on."

I loosely fold and lay my tie and jacket by the bed, unlace both shoes and slip them off, and look at her again.

"You don't need your clothes," she says.

I stuff socks into the shoes. The shirt and khakis get folded and set on top of the shoes. In the moonlight, where every ridge of muscle and vein casts a shadow, mine looks like the body of an overgrown middleweight in navy-blue boxer shorts. In the full-length mirror on the wall, you can't tell it's gone soft, not in this light.

"Hurry up," she says. "Before you get chilled."

Under the covers, she turns her back and spoons into the hollow from my chest down to my knees. She falls asleep with a gash of pale light across her white neck and hand. She looks vulnerable and no longer sad. I lay my arm lightly across her, palm resting on the bed in front of her flat belly, and watch, feeling alternately joyful at being there and lonely at her self-contained sleep that shuts me out.

After an hour she stirs, turns to me, and snuggles into my chest. She reaches up and tilts my face down with her hands, kisses me on the mouth, a long, quiet kiss, her lips pressing gently, moving hardly at all. A faint odor of soap overlays her own natural scent, which I recall instantly from the afternoon, a scent I could never grow tired of. The soft light traces her ear, her cheek, the line of her jaw. I kiss her back lightly, afraid of breaking the spell, waking her to the realization that I'm not the man she'd thought I was or always hoped for.

She presses harder against my lips, opening her mouth, then wraps a hand around my back and pulls herself close, slipping a leg between my thighs. There's no mistaking my desire, and she pushes me onto my back, rolling herself on top, kissing even harder, probing deeper with her tongue, squeezing me with her arms and legs. I might suffocate without uttering a word in protest. Suddenly she straightens up, pulling her jersey over her head, pulling the boxers down to my knees, and straddles me. She's fast now, and rough, and it feels like something old and violent, not making love exactly. It's frightening, exhilarating, and when she's done and lying on top of me, panting, her heart throbbing wildly, I wait for whatever she'll want to do next.

She gradually grows still, her breathing slower and faint. A line of perspiration drips down my side below her breast flattened against my ribs. A shaft of moonlight slashes across the small of her back, another across her thighs. I move a hand from her hip and lay it on her shoulder and kiss the top of her head. She stirs, slides herself up, and tries to look into my face.

"Well ... ?" she asks.

"That was great."

"Don't lie to me."

"I wouldn't."

"No? Good. Don't. I need something to believe in. So I'll believe that you won't lie to me, okay? No matter what. You have to always tell the truth. Even if you think it's ugly."

"I think you're beautiful. Like a goddess. But earlier tonight, when I first got here, you seemed more human, like anybody. But you're a goddess now. Venus probably. That was amazing."

"Was it? Are you frightened of me?"

"Terrified. And exhilarated." It was the truth. "I want you."

"What about tomorrow?"

"I'll still want you."

That seems to satisfy her. "You'd better," she says and kisses me on the mouth again, hard. "Let's go outside."

Margaret walks to the back door, naked in the moonlight, an otherworldly presence, except for the rhythmic flop of her footfalls on the hardwood. Outside, a wind from the west carries an undercurrent of warmth and a promise of spring. The moon is below the trees. To the west and north, the sky is filled with thousands of stars, and more seem to emerge as we watch.

Margaret unsnaps the cover of the hot tub, slowly, and lays it on the deck. She feels the water and flips on the jets, which make a low hum, followed by the slight splashing of flowing water. "I didn't lower the temperature from this afternoon," she says. "I was hoping you'd come back."

She climbs into the tub, stands for a moment, and submerges into the steam and hot water. She comes up with a mouthful and sprays it onto my stomach. It runs down. Margaret laughs, like we're kids and she's daring me to do the same. When I climb in, the heat is astonishing, shocking after the chill, and I have to catch my breath before sitting down. Margaret takes another mouthful of water and sprays it into my face. I do the same to her, and she leaps across the tub and grabs me by the neck and tries to pull me under, but I slip the headlock and hold her gently in a bear hug from behind. She keeps struggling, and I let her go. She moves to the other side of the tub, takes another mouthful, and sprays me again. It's a little annoying. She's still laughing.

"It's beautiful here."

"It is," she says. "I do love it."

She scans the sky and all the stars.

"There's no light pollution here," Margaret says. "Except mine. That's why I leave them off at night."

"It's the primordial sky."

"It's clear," she says.

"I could sit in wonder here a long time."

"For a long time?" she says. She stands up and turns off the jets so the only sound is the wind. She steps up onto the ladder and stares at the cascade of stars, her silhouette bluish in the pale light, gleaming.

"Maybe you're Cynthia, goddess of the moon."

She laughs. I reach to wrap her in my arms, my face at her belly. After a while, she climbs out of the tub and sits with arms and legs folded, huddled against the cold, her head bowed. She gazes up at the sky again, waiting for me to exit. Back inside, she falls asleep. I get dressed, take her hand and gently kiss it. I take the interstate home, windows open to keep me awake in the early morning. The rush of cool air mingles with a stream of erotic thoughts and images.

14

At the apartment, I shower and change for work, taking stock of lovers' marks, which might be abrasions and bruises, soft-tissue injuries in the clear light of a claims examiner's report, and unwelcome questions begin to raise themselves.

Margaret seems to expect the phone call. "Hey," she says. "I just made a fire. I was thinking about you. Why don't you come out? I'm lying here on the bearskin with a mug of coffee. Very white. The way you like it. Come on, Galahad. There's a lady in waiting."

"Galahad. Yeah. Did you ever hear about the serviens? They weren't knights exactly. They had all the weapons, the horse, some even had an attendant. They were soldiers but not nobles. The knights were nobles, mostly younger sons who didn't have any land themselves. They stirred up the Crusades. At least the first one. They had weapons but no land, and they were marauding around Europe, even around their own neighborhoods. The nobles who did have land called on the pope to liberate the Holy Land. Some Christian pilgrims had been harassed in Jerusalem, it was true, but it wasn't a big deal."

"Does this story lead somewhere?"

"Yeah, sorry. I got carried away. I like to read. History, literature, mythology. Anyway, the nobles simply needed to send their outlaw boys somewhere in search of fortune in order to keep the wealth at home intact. All kinds of carnage followed. A lot of the troublemakers died, which wasn't a bad thing. I'm sure a lot of the knights couldn't fight very well. They didn't necessarily have to. They employed serviens and, beneath them, foot soldiers. They managed to take Jerusalem in the first Crusade and kept it for almost a century. But at heart it was a corrupt venture. Pillaging all the way. And finally it failed. That went on for centuries. I don't know why, I was just thinking about it on the drive back."

"Okay, Galahad. So maybe you're more of a servien than a knight?"

"*Servien* comes from a French verb. To serve."

"That's you," Margaret says, laughing softly. "French service. Bien sur."

"It was a pleasure, you know. You are."

"Yeah," Margaret says. "So what's your point? So why don't you come over?"

"I have to work. Actually I have to finish your case."

"Aren't you done yet?" There's a slight edge, the sleepiness gone from her voice.

"Close. It was just kind of odd yesterday."

"What do you mean?" Sharper now.

"The nurse who took care of your friend, I went to see her, and she said she didn't screw up his drugs, which I expected her to say. But the doctor said he shouldn't have died anyway. That there must have been something else. And that kind of threw me. Anyway, they both said you were in the room pretty much the whole time. Was there something else?"

"What do you mean?" Her voice is cold, hard, distant.

"I don't know. What happened at the end?"

"Bill fell asleep, and I went out to the lobby to sleep so I wouldn't bother him. The next thing I knew, they were waking me up to tell me he was dead."

"Who told you?"

"Doctor Brody. I think it was about two."

"Yeah. That's what he said. He said you were pretty upset."

"What did you expect?"

"Sure. Of course. Sorry. Do you still want me to come out?"

"I don't think so," Margaret says. "You'd probably think it was some kind of corrupt Crusade."

The thing about chivalry is that it was a code invented by those with the means to abide by it. For a guy just trying to make his way, it's always been a stretch.

15

Rodney Glynnis is sitting in the reception area when I get to the office a little before 9 a.m., which is a bad sign. Cherie's already at her desk, in an ensemble of varying shades of white, and she smirks at me, another ill omen. The receptionist who in four years has never come in early. And I can see Ruth Benjamin in the back, with all my case files stacked on her desk. The adjuster who after one day is already taking over. And Joseph, in his small office with the door open, doesn't bother to look up. The boss with a grudge. Sometimes you'd need a miracle out of Beckett's bones just to get through the day uneventfully.

"Hey, chief," Rodney says. "I've been trying to reach you."

"No kidding. Why?"

"I had a little accident."

"I know, Rodney. I know about that."

"Another one." Instead of brash, he sounds sheepish. And instead of a greasy D.A., his hair is clean, parted in the middle and brushed back. "It happened yesterday. I tried to call you, but you weren't in. Then this guy's agent called your boss, I guess. He was pissed. He told me to be here at nine sharp if I ever want to drive again. And something about insurance fraud. That's bullshit, right?"

"I have no idea."

"You've got to talk to him. My old man's completely frosted already. I was in one of his cars from the dealership."

"What?"

Joseph comes out and says to Rodney, "Why don't you just cool it, pal. Jack, I want to see you in my office." Cherie's grinning like crazy. She lights a cigarette with an off-white lighter, approximately the shade of her shoes, sees Rodney reach inside his suit coat, and says, "Don't even think about it."

Joseph closes the door to his tiny office, which is about the size of a walk-in closet, sits behind his desk, and motions me into the chair in front of it.

"What the hell is that kid doing back here?" I can smell the sour coffee on Joseph's breath. From this distance, it's like medieval torture.

"I don't know. Apparently he had another accident."

"And why is he still driving?"

"Oh, yeah. I probably should have told you about it. The other rep agreed that his client, that elderly woman, may have been partly at fault."

Joseph leans forward. "I talked to him last night. He said you called in a favor and that you pressured him to get this Glynnis kid off the hook."

"Really? He said that?"

"That is in direct violation of what I told you to do." Joseph's face is bright red. "And I've written it up in a report that I'm sending to Hartford today to put in your personnel file."

"Are you kidding?"

"That's gross insubordination. Which is a firing offense. And where the hell were you yesterday? You never even called in. You're on notice as of this moment."

"Fine. You know it saved the company money. I'd like that in my personnel file, too. And I'm going to write a letter in response to your letter saying just that. Pointing out that while you're trying to spend Apex money, I'm actually saving it. I welcome the opportunity. Which is my right. Let me know who to send it to."

"And I'm putting you under my direct supervision from now on." Joseph picks up a sharpened pencil and points it at my face. "I'm dividing the cases and assigning each one."

"That's a waste of your time."

"Apparently it's not."

"Besides, I have a lot of cases I'm wrapping up."

"Not unless I say so."

"Oh, come on, Joseph."

"I'm giving Ruth this Glynnis kid's case."

"Whatever." I stand up to leave.

Joseph's voice drops a few decibels. "And by the way, I don't appreciate you calling my home and leaving a message that since you couldn't reach me at the office, you were going to call Cherie's house to see if I was there. I don't care about your stupid suspicions, but don't you dare try to share them with my wife. Who do you think you are?"

"I have no idea what you're talking about. I didn't call."

"Get out."

Ruth Benjamin smiles brightly when I get to my desk in the back room. "You know what's the most interesting thing?" she says. "Rodney Glynnis's father owns a Ford dealership. Joseph thinks he's loaded and set up his son with the body shop. Actually, I think we did them a big favor by keeping Rodney insured. I'm going to call his Dad to make sure he knows that."

"What does Joseph think?"

"He agreed. He told me to do it. Though he does think that letting Rodney off the hook in the first case really led to us having to take care of this accident from yesterday. He ran a red light. But Joseph said the big Ford dealer should know what great service Apex provides in this market. Who knows? Maybe we could bring some of their business on board eventually. That'd be a coup." Her delivery is artless, suggesting she doesn't know about Joseph's little knife in my back.

"No kidding."

"Absolutely. I'm going to call Mr. Glynnis after our meeting this morning to talk about the repairs to his showroom car. We think he'll have it fixed in his own service area. I think we are going to pay the claim if he makes one. But that could be the end of Rodney's driving for a while."

Joseph has Rodney in his little office, and through the glass you can see it's a heck of a lecture. Rodney's nodding, the sly smile gone from his face.

"What'd Rodney do this time?"

"He ran the stoplight as it was turning red and rear-ended the car in front of him. Apparently he'd taken the car from his father's dealership without asking anyone. It was a 1964 Mustang. They kept it in the showroom with the new cars. I always wondered how they got the cars out of there." Ruth starts to laugh. "Really, we're going to wait and see what the father wants us to do."

Joseph comes in. "We're ready for you now," he says. He waits at the door for Ruth to pass through, resting a hand on the small of her back. They crowd into the small office, Ruth leaning against a wall at Joseph's elbow, both talking to Rodney.

I stick my head into the front office to talk quietly to Cherie, who has been catching my eye and smirking. "Hey, did you have somebody call Joseph's house to get him in trouble? He's going to figure it out, you know. He'll know it wasn't me. It's not my style."

Cherie smirks again, picks up a piece of paper, and crosses the room to file it.

"You know, he's pretty familiar with that new girl already. She's cute."

Cherie's mouth creases. She loses the smirk. It's not something she wants to think about, but it's clearly there already. It doesn't make sense that anybody else would be trying to get Joseph in trouble, except maybe Cherie's husband. It's unlikely that anybody else even knows what the jerk has been up to.

"He's going to fire you," Cherie says. "And I hope he does."

There are only two other cases getting special handling, both files in my briefcase, and I clear the easier one, writing a $600 check to the young mother in Niskayuna who had the prowler, after calling a workman I know who'll guarantee, sight unseen, that he can put a back door on her house for less. He plans to stop there in the afternoon. The woman herself sounds a little less nervous, agrees that the money will go to paying him.

"Otherwise I'll cancel your policy," I tell her on the phone.

"You don't have to keep saying that."

"If there's any left over you can pocket that. But you'll need steps built, so I don't think it will be much. Have you had any more trouble?"

"No," she says. The lack of hesitation makes it sound likely. Maybe Frederick Schmitt was just putting a little scare into them, hoping to get his truck washed for free, so to speak, by an employee who'd screwed up royally. Maybe he wouldn't appreciate my writing them a check and giving them a backdoor in case of fire. Just possibly I'd be hearing from him, a k a Sonny Smith in the entertainment business.

About an hour later, the Glynnis kid is gone. Ruth has separated most of my files into two stacks, and she hands me those she says Joseph wants me to have. Then she starts asking questions about the others, and taking notes. Joseph comes in again.

"Do you have the Lake George file?"

"What about it?"

"Let me see it."

"Why?"

"Let me see it." He sees it open on the desk, where I've been transcribing notes from yesterday's interviews, closes it, and takes it into his office, where he's on the phone. He comes back fifteen minutes later without the file.

"I'm personally taking over the Lake George case," he says.

"No, you're not."

"You bet I am. Margaret Kelly just called me. She wants you off it. She said you offered to work on it for her independently as a medical-malpractice case."

"What?"

"Do you deny it?"

"No."

"Then get out. You're fired."

16

Joseph was right about the insubordination; it is a firing offense. A pretty good heavyweight in the late sixties and early seventies named Randy Neumann once wrote that the best job in the world was to be a sparring partner for a fighter you can beat. Pretty good pay and easy work, less than an hour a day. But you can't knock the boss on his ass. Just as a squire in a joust doesn't unhorse the knight who's his benefactor. You're there to lose. Sometimes it's enough just to know that you're better, that you could kick the boss's ass if you really felt like it. On some level, he probably knows it, too. But it doesn't translate to the office very well. Pushing paper for somebody who's not as good as you will make you crazy after a while, or shatter your confidence if you come to accept that the corporation sanctioning this arrangement knows its business.

Not quite six years earlier, Joseph Sweet handed me the best day of my life. I was working up north when he called looking for a romantic country inn where he could take Joann for the weekend. I hadn't seen him in six months, since training in Hartford. They were together again, in a small apartment in Stamford. Things weren't great between them, I gathered. I told him about the Mirror Lake Inn at Lake Placid, and he complained it was expensive, but he went for it. He asked me to meet them for breakfast at the inn on Saturday morning, ostensibly so I could suggest things for them to do. I think it was to give them a break from each other's company if they needed it. I invited Caroline, a student in an art lecture I was auditing at Skidmore, and to my surprise, she accepted.

In those same six months since Hartford, I'd rented an apartment in Saratoga, worked hard at claims, enjoyed the spring and summer driving all over the North Country, found a gym, and taken up boxing again for something to do. There was a pretty good amateur welterweight named Carmen Reid, just out of jail on a burglary conviction that he said was bogus, and he was thinking about turning pro. Within a few weeks, he and I had pretty much cleared the gym of other guys who wanted to spar, except the heavyweights, and we wound up in the ring night after night. One time he kept connecting with his jab, and the next day the area around my eye turned black and blue. I stayed away a week and then went back and got whacked in the same spot. The next day, that side of my face looked like a rainbow.

I'd taken to slouching in the back of the lecture hall, listening to the professor's critiques of various painters. I wasn't paying or supposed to be there. A slender blonde often sat in the back as well. She didn't pay any attention to me, but the day after the rainbow appeared on my face, I bumped into her while browsing the labyrinth of shelves in the Lyrical Ballad, a used-book store in the basement of a former bank. She was thumbing through a volume of Nabakov next to the old vault. I was surprised that she seemed to recognize me.

"Aren't you taking the History of Master Painters class?" she asked.

"Yes, I am," I replied.

"Don't get me wrong, but you don't look like the artistic type."

"Well, I've got the suffering part down pat."

"I can see that," she said, pointing at my black eye. "That's a beauty. You've got the entire commercial palette right there. Cyan, magenta, yellow, and black. Amazing. Listen, I want you to pose for me."

"When?"

"Now? Right away? I don't think that color's going to hold, you know?"

We drove to a small studio at Skidmore, and I sat on a stool while she took photographs at slow shutter speeds using available light, putting her box camera, an old Rollex, on a tripod. There were some canvases in a corner, and I admired them.

"My landscape period," she said. "That was sophomore year. Now I'm interested in faces. You've got a good one. Strong jaw, penetrating eyes. Almost haunted, you know?"

She wanted to know the source of my sorrow, and I said it was trouble slipping a jab. She liked that I was a boxer. She had me pose with my shirt off. She liked that I investigated accidents, occasionally deaths. They made her nervous but fascinated her. She said her father worked as a lawyer in New York, and when she was a girl she was afraid for him on the commuter train. She said her mother wanted her to marry well, and that was one of the reasons she was at Skidmore. It still had some worn-out cachet as a school for sturdy trophy brides. She was dating a guy from Williams.

"There is no way that I'm going to do that, you know?" Caroline said. "There is no way."

She wasn't going to do the thing her Scarsdale mother wanted, and she would prove it by marrying me. But at first it felt like true love. Our courtship began at the Mirror Lake Inn, a rambling collection of wooden buildings in the classic Adirondack style, white with green trim. We had breakfast in a dining room with latticed windows; from our table we could look across the lake toward the High Peaks. Spread before us were fruits, juices, muffins, omelettes, blueberry pancakes, coffee, and all the time in the world to linger.

"God," Caroline said, "this is beautiful. How romantic."

"You should see the quilts on the bed," Joann said. "Just gorgeous. And the ducks, they are so cute. They're checkered black and white. There are two in this old Adirondack painting in the room. I'd love to take it home. Do you think we can?"

"I don't think so," Joseph said. "I don't think they sell them."

"There are some places that sell wildlife art just up the road," I said. "They actually might be loons in the painting. Narrower bills."

"Thanks, pal," Joseph answered.

"Do you think we could go?" Joann said. "I'd love to get one to bring home. They are so cute."

"I like ducks, too," Caroline said. "Can we go?"

Turned out that we couldn't find a painting that suited Joann, which suited Joseph just fine. I then took them to meet Wallace LaFleur, a whitewater-rafting guide. I wanted Caroline to see that I had a friend, or at least an acquaintance, like him. He reminded me of the ancient Argonauts, the original seafarers. He'd come up out of Utica, and after a few years of taking juvenile delinquents on wilderness outings for the state, he got into guiding. With Wallace, you could raft the Hudson River Gorge in the spring, catch trout in summer, go horsepacking in the fall, stalk deer in late autumn, far from other hunters, or ski the backwoods in winter. He'd bring the gear, pack the wine, and do the cooking. He had courage, taste, and skill. He always carried out what he brought into the woods and often what others, less thoughtful, left behind. He was clear and direct about everything, embarrassed about nothing.

I couldn't afford Wallace, but I liked him. We met after one of the mass-market rafters flipped a boat in the Hudson and a girl was killed. Their guides were kids, who tried to hit waves and make the rafts buck. Wallace had come along later and gone for help. She was backboarded out but died anyway, and after finally settling a claim that was tied up for a couple years in court, Apex dropped the company as a client. They had to get insurance elsewhere. That was me. I made it happen. It wasn't their fault, but I didn't know that for a long time. Somebody died, and I chose to take it personally.

Wallace ran a B&B outside town. The guests occupied the front of the house. He lived in back, in a single room that ran the length of the building, with southern exposure and a wall that was all glass from the waist up. The narrow room felt like a ship's cabin. He had a long worktable under the windows, personal computer and papers along one side, gear he was mending on the other. He slept in a high, wide bunk. A dream catcher hung over the doorway. The space was well-ordered, reflecting a discipline that was efficient without being austere.

When I knocked, Wallace looked out. A smile split his black beard as he let us in. "Well, how are you?" he said, pumping my hand, shaking his shaggy head. He was compact, average height, with strong, thick legs. He wore jeans, hiking boots, and a long-sleeve fleece shirt. He shook everybody's hand.

"I just wanted to stop by and say hello," I said. "I know you're probably busy."

"Well, I'm glad you did. I was just starting to pack for a trip tomorrow."

Wallace pointed to the trailer out back with the inflated crimson raft and to some boxes and water-tight containers on the ground nearby.

"Going down the gorge?"

"Yup. Yup. Got a group of executives who want to do a little bonding in the wilderness." Always the ladies' man, he smiled at Caroline, who smiled back. "It's nice to have people cleanse their souls and connect with nature in a place like that."

"You might get a couple white-collar sharks, kind of like your old state clients."

"Well, you know, Jack, it's possible. But I don't think any of these guys are killers."

"What do you mean?" Joseph said.

"Well, once upon a time I was a counselor for the state Division for Youth. What we would do is take groups into the wilderness for four weeks on a behavior-modification, character-building program. Then they'd go home."

"But the last time . . ." I interjected.

"The last time, some of them tried to kill me," Wallace said. "After that, I decided I needed a different clientele."

"What happened?" Joann asked. "Didn't you carry a gun?"

"Never. The only weapon I carried was a rope. Weapons can be used against you. And mostly they were nice kids. If somebody got really bad, I'd tie him to a tree. See, there were always eight of them and two of us."

Wallace continued to chat while packing for the raft trip. He was modest and funny. Caroline was taken with him. We left after a half-hour.

We drove south and west to Big Moose Lake, site of a murder that inspired Theodore Dreiser's *An American Tragedy,* and ate lunch on the porch of the Big Moose Inn. Since I was the only one to have read Dreiser's book, I related the details of the 1906 killing. We hiked to a lookout called Billy's Bald Spot, and I pointed out the bay where Chester Gillette drowned his pregnant girlfriend. Next we drove to Old Forge and visited its celebrated hardware store, which sells everything from canoes to woolen blankets to classic novels. Afterward we went to an art gallery, which Caroline loved; it inspired her second landscape period. On the return to Lake Placid, we stopped in Long Lake for ice cream and in Newcomb to look at the upper Hudson running cold and clean. The river was quiet and tranquil, offering no hint of the treacherous rapids that await the unwary. Caroline took my hand on the walk back to the car, my old Cadillac convertible. I was thankful the car had held up for the trip.

Leaving Newcomb, we passed a small park with a magnificent view of the High Peaks, dark blue in the dusk, the summits suffused with alpenglow. Nightfall came quickly. Passing Chapel Pond, we saw a bonfire on the beach below the cliffs and heard shouts and laughter. Probably rock climbers. By the time we started the ascent through Cascade Pass, a half-moon had risen on our right. Then it appeared on our left, which puzzled Caroline.

"Hey, what happened?" she asked. "A few minutes ago the moon was on our other side."

"We're actually driving south at the moment," I explained. "The road doubled back to go between the mountains. We'll be heading north again soon enough."

This got Joseph to thinking in cosmological terms.

"What an excellent day," he said from the backseat, his arm around Joann. "You know it's the last day of summer. September twentieth. Today is the equinox."

"Isn't it always the twenty-first?" Caroline asked.

"Usually, but not always," Joseph said. He had nice manners then and almost never contradicted anyone directly. "It depends on the length of daylight because of the tilt of the Earth. Day and night are nearly the same. Tomorrow, the night will be longer than the day."

Joann was close to him, on the passenger side, her hair blowing in the wind. "At least it will be cooler in our apartment," she said. "It's a hothouse in summer."

"It should be," he said. "And soon I think I'm going to get the transfer to upstate

New York. Where at least it's cool and we can buy a house. I'm not too crazy about Connecticut. Jack, maybe you should apply. There's going to be a new office in Albany."

"That would be good," Joann said.

I agreed to look into it, and I would discover later that I was already down for the reassignment.

Joseph and Joann told us that they started dating back in high school. Neither had really dated anybody else. And right after they finished college, they got married. "Joseph was kind of a nerd," Joann teased. "I don't think he ever even asked anybody else out."

"I wasn't that much of a nerd."

"No. You were a cool guy," she said. "It's just that I was the first one to notice it."

Caroline was turned around, leaning over the seat. "Are you happy?" she asked.

"Now that we're together," Joann replied. "Living apart was terrible. That was so lonely."

"You were living with your mother," Joseph said.

"I was still lonely," she said. "I missed you."

"And I missed you, too," he said.

"Did you really?" Joann asked. "Jack, did he really miss me when you guys were in Hartford?"

"Of course he did," I said. But the truth was I couldn't remember him moping too much about it.

"If I got married, I wouldn't ever want to live apart," Caroline said. "I mean, what would be the point, you know?"

After we dropped them in Lake Placid, Caroline suggested I go to the campus art studio on Sunday so she could try to paint my eye while it still held traces of the CYMB palette. It had been a running joke all day, with all the comments it elicited from storekeepers, waiters, and the like. When I dropped her off at Skidmore, she kissed my cheek and said thanks.

There had been some burgundy in the maples that day. In another two weeks, the mountains would explode in color, but most of the leaf-peeping tourists would never see it. They'd go to Vermont instead. I wanted to take Caroline back to the Adirondacks, but the Cadillac blew a gasket. I didn't terribly mind, though. That was my best year. I don't think everybody has one of those. But they should. I doubt Joseph ever had a year like that, except maybe a long time ago, when he was too young to appreciate it, and that probably explained a lot.

The next day was warm, and Caroline painted from late morning to late afternoon. She wore faded jeans and a man's Oxfordcloth white shirt, wrinkled and soft, the top several buttons open. Her hair was tied back severely, ponytail hanging down her back, and no makeup. She talked while she painted, about her life, her family, her older sister, their rivalry, what she liked about Joseph and Joann, what she didn't like about college, including a professor and a graduate student who were hitting on her, some phonies who were doing pretentious installation art, and the winters. In midafternoon, she took her jeans off, said they were bothering her, and went on painting wearing just the long shirt and panties. It didn't seem to be intentionally sexy, though it was very. It seemed to be more about comfort, and trusting me, that she could, or was willing to try. She walked up once and kissed me full on the lips and then walked back and kept painting as if it hadn't happened. She finished three studies of me. Two were lifelike. The other I thought was surreal.

"Expressionistic," she corrected. "Don't you know Chagall?"

"Only a little."

"Then I'll have to show you." She did, one winter afternoon at the Met. We rode the train down to New York from Rensselaer.

We got married less than a year later, at the start of her senior year. She had spent the previous summer in Saratoga, working on an independent project in color analysis, and we did some sailing in a rented boat up on Lake Champlain. Caroline's family did not attend the wedding. A judge presided over a ceremony in the courtyard of the Adelphi, a fine old Saratoga hotel, after the racing season. It was charming, even though it drizzled. Caroline's dress was clinging, white, Victorian. Her hair was up, laced with baby's breath, and damp from the rain, and she made me think of Ophelia. The hotel was preparing to close for the winter, so the day had a sense of being sweetly sorrowful, somewhere at the end of things. My family couldn't get their act together, except my surfer brother who drove up from Florida. He gave the toast: "Much joy, brother and sister." And Joseph, whose wife was beginning to look a little frumpy, kissed the bride longer than he should have. I wondered if I should have said something. Caroline and I went to the Mirror Lake Inn for two nights. Afterward, we moved into a flat in downtown Saratoga, a few miles from the uptown campus. Occasionally, some of Caroline's student friends would come by, and they all appreciated the art of her affair.

Less than three months later, Joseph and I would both be working in Albany, approaching the dead of upstate winter with competitive enthusiasm. I never would have dreamed that one day he would become my boss and fire me. In my experience, every manager at Apex is slippery to the point of dishonesty. So perhaps Joseph couldn't help but fall in line.

It's been time to go for a while. But there is the lingering question about Margaret, who is expecting my call.

"So what happened?" she says.

"He fired me."

"He said he would do that, though I didn't want him to. I'm sorry." She sounds sorry.

"Why did you call Joseph?"

"I told you. I wanted it to be over." Regret gives way to complaint. "But you didn't listen to me. You wouldn't let it alone. Why did you have to do that?"

"I don't know. It's my job." The stupidity of the remark becomes apparent the moment the words form. "I'm sure that means you don't want an investigator for a malpractice case."

"I told you. I want it to be over. You know, I thought for a while that you'd call back and apologize. But you didn't."

"I got kind of tied up. I'm sorry. Can I come out just to see you then?"

"I don't think so."

"Why?

"Because you don't really want to."

"Yes, I do."

"And I don't really want you to."

She lets the silence grow into a long, awkward pause. I try to think of something to say, something to salvage this now, and it doesn't come.

"Okay?" she says.

"Yeah." I feel stunned, like I've just been slapped. I wonder if I should drive up there. Maybe, if we meet in the flesh, she'll change her mind.

17

A call to Apex, and Cherie is nearly civil for the first time in years, cheered that I was sacked. "What a jerk you are," she says.

"You're right, of course. I am a jerk. And whatever mean things I did to you, Cherie, I apologize."

"Why are you so mean?"

"I don't know. I just apologized."

"You are the most egotistical, self-centered, self-pitying bastard I have ever met. You act like you are the only person in the whole world whose marriage ever broke up. And you take it out on everybody."

"When you know what it's like, we can have this conversation. Meanwhile, I called to see if you'd have the courtesy to give me my phone messages for a few days. There are a couple of loose ends that nobody else will know what to do with. Now that you've said what you wanted to say, can you do that?"

"I'm supposed to collect your messages and put them on Joseph's desk."

"Can you get them back?"

"I didn't put them on his desk yet. There were only two. Joseph's not here. He went to Lake George."

I have a suddenly worse hollow feeling and an unreasonably jealous thought of Joseph trying to get into the hot tub. Cherie seems to share this suspicion. "He's such a shit," she says.

"Then why don't you help me?"

"Because you're an asshole."

"So what? What were the two messages?"

"Jack Casey called to see if you were still handling his malpractice case, which I guess you're not because Joseph already placed a call to him. And there was one from California, from Jennifer Kind."

"She's the dead guy's daughter. I've been trying to reach her. What's the number?"

"I do know what it's like," Cherie says, before giving me the phone number. "I've been divorced for almost two years. So don't think you're special."

"What?"

"But how could you know that? You couldn't even bother to say good morning. Asshole."

"You're kidding. I'm sorry."

"Don't talk to me."

Jennifer Kind's name had been on her father's life-insurance policy as beneficiary until two years ago. I don't know if there's any point to calling her, except that I want to be sure I'm not missing something. She says she's still a graduate student at Berkeley, that her parents divorced when she was a child, and that she seldom saw her father, who was always working in some distant part of the world. She did not find out he died until almost two weeks afterward. Her mother was notified by the engineering company that employed him and that transferred his stock holdings, which were substantial, and rights to his pension into a trust. His bank accounts were nearly empty; they'd been drawn down in the previous two years. The life-insurance policy now listed his girlfriend as beneficiary. A lawyer affiliated with the company handled everything.

"Did you ever meet her?"

"Once. After he left Haiti. He was kind of sick then, and she seemed to be taking care of him. She'd been a hotel concierge in Port au Prince, I think. She spoke fluent French. She seemed awfully young for him. She couldn't wait to get him away from me and out of California. He'd planned to stay a week, and they left after two days. I never really knew him. I was pretty disappointed by the whole thing."

She was never told that she had once been the beneficiary on the Apex policy. And she didn't seem too concerned about money. Her father had been paying her bills, and now the stock dividends were doing it.

18

An old wooden barn stands out back among the trees, where the gravel ends at the top of William Kind's driveway. The barn has a wide door and a small one, and one small back window. It looks much like it did the first time, all closed up. But there have been some changes to the property in the past twenty-four hours. It's now posted against trespassing, with signs at the bottom of the drive. And Joseph's little Miata is parked behind the Land Rover. It's nearly 4 p.m., which means he's been here for more than three hours. Cherie said he took the papers to discharge the claim. Typically, Joseph would take a long time to explain all the details and why a payment makes Apex a generous carrier. But it shouldn't take three hours. All Margaret has to do is sign and wait a few days for a check worth $300,000.

From here, Margaret's lack of inhibition looks staged, a trap to turn the heads of fools like Joseph and me. But I have no intention of leaving. I back my car out and park a hundred yards up the road, out of sight, then walk back quietly along the grass, stopping to listen to be sure there's no splashing from the hot tub out back. It's quiet, and I walk around the house, past the tub, and lacking the nerve to walk in the back door, or even peek in a window, I wander up to the barn, entering through the small door. All I want is to hear the sound of Joseph's Miata starting up; I kill time by poking around William Kind's workshop. It's very neat, with a concrete floor, recently poured, and the whitewashed walls. The private space of a meticulous man. A ten-year-old Volvo is parked inside, covered with a cloth. A worktable runs along one wall, with saws and other tools neatly arranged and hung above it. On the table is a half-finished outdoor planter, made of cedar and brass, skillfully done. On an adjacent wall are landscaping tools and two fishing rods. There are several lights and electrical outlets, but no woodstove or space heater.

His file contained a homeowner's policy and letters relating to a dispute over the replacement value of the house. By Kind's reckoning, his time was worth, at minimum, ninety dollars an hour, and he worked painstakingly, so he estimated the replacement cost of the simple A-frame at $250,000. The policy covered only $150,000. Kind had written three times complaining that this was unfair. He had a point. And he was a pain in the ass about it. His daughter said he was a difficult man. It sounded like a judgment she'd acquired elsewhere, maybe from her mother.

He was fifty-two and had retired to a love nest, with stock dividends that would have paid him well enough until his pension kicked in. All he had to do was make simple things with his tools, build fires, breathe country air, sleep with Margaret. He had it made.

His barn fills me with envy. Then my grandmother's saying comes bubbling up: "If you've got your health, you've got everything." And now Kind had gone to extremes to prove her right. He had no health at all. A vintage thermometer hangs on the wall above the center of the worktable. It's chilly in here, and gloomy; I shine my penlight to check the temperature. The thermometer's broken. The ball that once held the mercury is cracked, and the tube is empty. It's the only broken thing in the room. No trash, no nails, no odd scraps of wood lying about. Even the table saw is clean, without a speck of sawdust.

I look in the trash bin and find a small paper bag containing an empty box for liquid Tylenol. Then I hear Joseph's car start and roll down the gravel driveway. But I can't stop rooting around. I shine my penlight into the trash, and when I discover an eye-dropper, my stomach tightens. I pick it up, wondering if it contains traces of mercury. Holding the dropper above my head, squinting in the deepening gloom, I don't hear her come in.

The pitchfork hits me in the shoulder and back, the tines striking all together, a hard, sharp, wide blow that sends me sprawling forward and into the wall. My face hits the wood, bounces off, and I go down hard, falling in the narrow shadowy space between the Volvo and the wall. I roll part way under the car, in case there's another blow coming. But it's silent; then I hear her running to the door. Lying there, straining to listen, I hear after a while another car. I crawl out and move slowly to the door. It's nearly twilight, and there's a sedan in the driveway with its engine running, a spotlight blazing against the front of the barn; an amplified male voice starts yelling for me to come out. Which seems like a bad idea. The locked door at the back of the barn is difficult to locate by touch but easy to push open. With all the commotion out front, nobody notices that I've gone out the back.

After sneaking through the woods, I find the car right where I left it. I take the back roads to the hospital parking lot, where I fall asleep with the motor running and the heat on. Near midnight, I wake, go inside, and approach the nurses' station, where Beverly Wilbur sits alone with her Pepsi, a bag of Fritos, and a *People* magazine.

"What do you want now?" she says.

"I need your help."

She objects at first but then reluctantly examines and cleans the puncture wounds, two on the shoulder blade, one on a rib, another in soft tissue. "It just missed your spine," she says. "You were lucky. And I don't think it got your lungs. Close, right here. I should page a doctor, though. Or send you down to the emergency room. You might have something broken."

"I'm going to need some antibiotics."

"I can't do that. Somebody'll have to write an order."

"Nobody'll know."

"It's my license. And you're already trying to take it away from me. I shouldn't be doing any of this for you."

"Then why are you?"

"You need my help. And I'm going to need yours. Who did this to you?"

"I'm not sure."

"This was about her, wasn't it? That red-haired bitch is trouble. She plays every man she sees. You should have seen the skirt she wore the first time she came in here. It was up to here." She points to a place on her blue scrubs, high on her thigh. "Doctor Brody couldn't keep his eyes off her. And don't think she didn't know it."

"I don't know what you're talking about."

"Look at you, you're blushing," Beverly Wilbur says. "You're lying! You men are all alike."

"What else do you know?"

"I wouldn't trust her as far as I could throw her. She's probably shacking up right now with the farmer that did this to you. Am I right? Probably she was doing that before when her boyfriend was still alive. I'd heard about her before she even came in here."

"What?"

"My ex-husband's a deputy. He told me about her. Naked as a jaybird half the time up in those hills."

"So?"

"And you can just tell. You know that man, big as he was, he was afraid of her. And she didn't want me in the room with them. The way she hovered over him. At first I thought that he was afraid of me. But that wasn't it. He was trying to get out of bed because he was afraid of her."

"Were you afraid of her?"

"Are you nuts? My ex-husband's a cop. A vicious SOB. I'm not afraid of her." She's quiet for a while, taping a gauze bandage on my back, then suddenly adds, "She's the one trying to screw me, isn't she?"

I don't deny it, while the nurse cleans the blood off my face. With tweezers, she pulls two splinters from my cheek and gets an ice pack for the swelling. It's very intimate, gentle but firm. And then it's done.

"You're not just saying that to place the blame elsewhere?" I ask.

"I had a lot of doubts about this. You know, I get tired. Sometimes at night I do forget things. But not the meds. I did turn that patient's IV back on. It's not the kind of thing I forget. I always check to make sure it's working. I'm very careful with the meds. Somebody turned it off again. And the only person who could have done it was her."

19

The next day, I can hardly move. The wounds swell up, and it's a complicated task to get some topical over-the-counter antibiotic onto each one. Beverly Wilbur refused to give me any drugs. But it's peaceful, like after a tough fight, when all you have to do is hang around and heal and think. You don't have to be back in the gym for a while. Just rest. I keep the doors locked, sleep, moving from the sofa to the bed and back again, turning things over in my mind, always coming to the same questions.

I figure it this way. Margaret broke the thermometer. Or maybe it broke by accident. Maybe she didn't have a real plan then. She collected the mercury but didn't throw it out. William Kind got the flu, but he saw no harm in continuing to woodwork. Besides, he probably wanted to put that planter to use this spring. Maybe because he didn't know how cold the barn was, he stayed out there when he shouldn't have and got sicker. It became pneumonia. Margaret saw this and brought him Tylenol to mask the fever and fool him into thinking he was getting better. Then she started putting drops of mercury in his Tylenol. By the time she brought him to the hospital, he was delirious. They had to restrain him. And she stayed in the room, making sure he didn't get the antibiotics and oxygen. She made him sick and then made him sicker. But how did she know he was going to die? And why did she hate him that much?

Two nights later I'm woken by a phone call. It's Jennifer Kind, whom I had told to call if she could think of anything else about her father that might be important.

"I got to wondering after you called," she says. "I guess you called because you had some questions. Is it that you think he didn't die of natural causes? Is that why you're asking questions?"

"The coroner's report says your father had pneumonia and died in the hospital of respiratory arrest."

"Yeah, but you're asking questions. I guess the insurance company just doesn't like to pay out money so you ask questions to find a way out of it." She's stating the accusation that you hear sometimes from claimants. But she's asking, not accusing.

"It's fairly routine. If that's what you mean. Insurance companies are in business to make money. So they don't particularly like to pay claims, especially false claims. But they pay claims every day. It's what they do."

"So there's nothing different about this?"

"Your father was a relatively young man. And what I wanted was to be sure he got adequate medical care."

"Did he?"

"I'm trying to find out. Why? Do you know something else?"

"I was just checking. When your biological father dies, you want to know why."

"I don't think you have any kind of genetic health issue here."

"Okay," she says. "I was just checking. You didn't find anything peculiar in his medical history?"

"Nothing like that. Just that he'd had mercury poisoning in Haiti and had been having a recurrence of symptoms."

"Yeah. And you were asking about Margaret," Jennifer says. "You know he found her in Haiti."

"Do you think there's a connection there?"

"Like she's made of mercury? I don't think so. Was she a toxic individual? That's a good question. I did think she was way too young for him."

"What else do you know about her."

"I told you about when they came to see me at Berkeley, remember? He'd written me a letter about her before they arrived, I think so I wouldn't be shocked that she was twenty years younger. I found the letter. I'd kept it."

"What did he say?"

"He said they were moving to the Adirondacks together. That she was a linguist and spoke perfect French, and he was retiring, and they were going to take a break from things for a while. I had the feeling they were going to get married."

"But they didn't."

"No. He called me a couple months ago, and I asked him if they were. He said no. That was around the holidays."

"Why not?"

"I don't think he wanted to."

"What else did he say in the letter?"

"He said Margaret was this great linguist and she even knew Creole. And some Gaelic. That she was older than her age. Her parents were Irish. She was born in Brooklyn and grew up in Providence and for a little while in Dublin. Her mother moved back to Ireland when she was a girl. Her father raised her, and then he moved back to Ireland, and she'd been on her own for a long time. They were both dead. What else? I'm looking at the letter. She studied at the Sorbonne in Paris. Then she got the job in Haiti as a concierge, and she did that for a while before he met her. A few years. I guess that would make her what, not even thirty when he met her?"

"That sounds about right."

"Much too young for him."

"Did you tell him?"

"I didn't know him well enough. He didn't raise me. He was gone by the time I was three. He only kept in touch with birthday cards and gifts, and at Christmas. And sometimes letters. Those were mostly after I got to college, though. And child support. I don't really consider him my father. My mother's second husband, Dave, he raised me. I consider him my father, really."

"So when you met Margaret, what did you think?"

"She had this energy. It was pretty overpowering. She smiled a lot. I felt like she turned it on for me a little bit. And she turned it on for him a lot. He liked that. And she could be sharp. Of course, he could too. My mother said that was why she left him. That he was verbally abusive. Also he was gone all the time. They took me out to dinner in San Francisco, and he was driving up on Russian Hill and took a wrong turn and then almost got in an accident. We almost got hit by a trolley. In a way it was kind of funny. She really let him have it. 'What did I tell you? Why don't you listen?' Whatever. I guess most couples do that."

"Did they love each other?"

"I thought so. I don't know. They didn't stay very long. After two days, she wanted to leave. So they did. And the way she could turn it on and off. Blow so hot and then so cold. She gave me this huge hug when they left and said she'd stay in touch. But she didn't. I wondered if she was a phony."

"What is that thing they call mercury—quicksilver? Always changing." Jennifer Kind thinks about this for a moment. "Something like that," she says.

She promises to call again if she thinks of anything else and wants to know exactly how much Margaret's getting from the life insurance. Since I no longer work for Apex, I don't mind telling her.

The phone rings again the next morning. "Is this Jack Kirkland?"

"Yes."

"You don't know me. But I used to work in a bookstore in Schenectady. I heard you were looking into adult bookstores. And I thought you might want to talk to somebody who knows about it."

"Who are you?"

"I'm Mandy."

"Mandy, how'd you get my name?"

"Somebody told me. See, I know what it's like there. Because I used to work in one of Sonny Smith's stores. I don't work there anymore. But I heard you were investigating him. And I thought you'd want to know some things."

"What kind of things?"

"Like the guy who comes up to collect the quarters. And the tax case. I'll bet you didn't know about that. They make a ton of money. But it's all cash."

"What do you know about arson?"

"Oh, Jeez. I had a boyfriend who worked for them. He stole from them. I know he did. There was so much money. He said they'd never miss it. They burned his house down."

"How do you know that?"

"I just do. If you want to, we can meet and talk about it."

"Where do you want to meet?"

"I don't care. You can come to my apartment. Or I can come to yours."

"You know what, Mandy? I'll take your phone number. But I don't think so. See, I'm not really investigating them. And I don't work for that insurance company now. So I'm pretty much out of it."

She gives me her number and her address. "If you're interested," she says, "call me."

There's no one around to appreciate the irony of that call.

Two nights later, I hear footfalls on the stairs to my flat, which is unusual. The landlord, an elderly man who lives on the first floor, seldom comes up. I also hear muttering, then laughter, a high, loud cackle. I open the door to find Rodney Glynnis on the landing. His hair, without pomade, now hangs straight to his shoulders, and it's bleached blond. With him is Cherie Stoddard. You could have knocked me over with a feather.

"Hey, chief," Rodney says.

"What's this about?"

"Aren't you going to ask us in for a drink or something?" Rodney seems genuinely disappointed at the cold reception.

"I told you," Cherie says. "He's an asshole. He wouldn't do anything for anybody, except himself."

"Hello, Cherie. Nice to see you." She's wearing the shortest skirt I've ever seen her in—black leather and barely covering her butt. She's got on black-leather stiletto heels, held on by straps, black sheer nylons, a short leather jacket, also black, and a crimson blouse. Her lipstick is the same shade of crimson; the rest of her makeup is slightly dark and gothic, but within reason. "I see you finally got a color coordinator."

"Isn't that something?" Rodney says. "I had to talk to her about that. Hard to go wrong with black, though." He's wearing a black trenchcoat, black steel-toed combat boots, jeans, and a white T-shirt. He looks punk, except for the 'do. They actually look kind of good together.

"Shut up," Cherie says. "I don't take advice from children."

"She scares me," Rodney responds, smiling. "I just do what she says."

"And what's that?"

"Drive over here to see you," Rodney says, smiling now like a conspirator. "Thought we'd enjoy a cocktail and some conversation."

"It wasn't my idea," Cherie says. "I just gave him directions."

"Come in. I'll get you a drink. How old are you?"

"Twenty-one," Rodney says. "You know that's right. You've seen my file."

"Yeah. I've seen your file. By the way, when's the last time you hit something, Rod?"

"That's very funny, chief. You're a card."

Cherie walks in and sits on the sofa where I'd been lying, curls her legs up under her. It looks like she's wearing no skirt at all. "I'm twenty-one also," she says, and giggles.

"I know. I've seen your file, too."

I grab a bottle of Southern Comfort from a cupboard in the kitchen and three short glasses, put a single ice cube in each, and pour some whiskey. The truth is I'm grateful for the company. I liked this kid, which in a way is where the whole thing started.

"So what are you doing here?"

"Fact is, chief, I want to apologize," Rodney says, swirling his glass and taking a sip. "I know you got shit-canned. And I know you did me a favor. I'm grateful, and I'm contrite."

"Don't worry about it." The heat of the whiskey feels good going down. I didn't want to drink alone, thinking I wouldn't stop once I got started. "It happens."

"This isn't much of an apartment," Cherie says. "Where's all your furniture?"

"This is it. You're sitting on it."

The living room has a hardwood floor, the old sofa, one club chair, and a lamp.

"You need help." Cherie giggles again. "Now I know why you're miserable."

"Well, that's cool," Rodney says. "You know, I talked to your boss, that Joseph clown. I told him to hire you back, but he wouldn't do it. My old man got to him. I mean, if my old man told him to shit a walnut, he'd be eating an oak tree right now."

"An acorn," Cherie says.

"What?"

"He'd have to eat an oak tree if he was going to shit an acorn," I explain.

"Okay, professor," Rodney says. "It's my metaphor. If I say it's a walnut, it's a fucking walnut."

Cherie laughs out loud.

"I think you're being kind of literal," Rodney adds, and drops his cackle on top of Cherie's. He whips out the silver Zippo and a Marlboro. "Mind?"

"No."

"Light me one," Cherie says. Rodney lights her a Kool that he fishes out of her pocketbook, and she takes it and watches the Zippo while he lights it.

"He's dreaming if he thinks he's getting any piece of the old man's business—except mine, that is—but he's such a jerk he's got his nose planted right up the old man's rosebud." Rodney shakes his head. "People are so ignorant."

"So where have you two been tonight?"

"Clubbing," Rodney says. "You should see this chick. She can move."

As if on cue, Cherie asks if I have any decent CDs. I point to the boom box and small stack of jewel cases in the far corner of the living room, resting on the hardwood floor. She stands up, pulling her skirt down, walks over to the CDs, squats down, and examines the stack. She puts on an old Bob Marley disk and selects a track. "Single-disk player," she says. "That's quaint."

When "Get Up, Stand Up" begins, she cranks up the volume, closes her eyes and moves her hips, in a deep circular motion, in the middle of the room. Rodney and I sip our drinks.

"See what I mean?" Rodney says, almost shouting. "This chick can move."

Cherie smiles, hearing him.

"What kills me," Rodney says, "is that guy's such a nobody. That he could ever get a chick like this. That kills me."

"I would like to be able to say," Cherie says, "that I simply made a mistake."

"Got that right, sister," Rodney says.

"Listen, junior," Cherie says, still dancing, with no urgency. "You have a ways to go before you start judging everybody. Rich kid. Daddy's boy. It's all easy for you."

"You're easy for me," Rodney says, winking at me.

"Got that wrong, brother," Cherie says. She pushes the buttons on the CD player. Marley skips back to "No Woman, No Cry," and she's still dancing, more slowly, hearing the music. After a refill of drinks, Cherie says I don't have any music worth listening to and she wants to leave. Rodney stands, and they head to the door.

"I am sorry, man," Rodney says. He shakes my hand.

"It's okay. I needed to make a move. You were just the means."

"Good move," Rodney says. "That place you were working, it was nowhere. That's what I told her."

Cherie turns as if she wants to say something, then doesn't.

"Keep taking the fashion advice," I suggest. "It's working."

"Asshole," she says. Only now it sounds almost friendly.

20

There's an agency we use for background investigations, and although they're expensive—three hundred dollars just to pull basic data—I ordered a full report on Margaret, backdated it on company letterhead, and had it sent to my address, with the bill routed to the Apex account. Joseph will have some explaining to do. The bill comes to twenty-five hundred dollars. The report's author, a private investigator out of Boston, did some interviewing and wrote a narrative on top of the usual Social Security, motor-vehicle, passport, criminal, credit, and school records. A copy of his log shows he got hold of one of her old teachers, a friend (or at least a classmate), a landlord, and her father's former employer. The file contains photocopies of her high-school yearbook picture and her New York driver's license. He located her parents in Ireland, not deceased, and for an additional fee offered to conduct trans-Atlantic interviews. I was pretty sure I would decline. It would take about two weeks for accounting to kick this bill back to Joseph, and he'd be after me for the money. The report says:

Margaret Isolde Kelly DOB 7/8/64 Brooklyn N.Y. to John R Kelly and Susan L Kelly citizens of Ireland. Probably for purposes of obtaining US citizenship. Departed US 8/12/66 and arrived Dublin Ireland 8/13/66. John R Kelly, Susan L Kelly, Margaret I Kelly returned to United States 5/3/77. John R Kelly employment Celtic Tiger Concrete Products LTD Providence RI 6/77-10/81. John R Kelly and Susan L Kelly have no known record of other children or criminal complaints. There is no record of Susan L Kelly employment in US. She departed US 3/28/78 and arrived Dublin Ireland 3/29/78. There is no record of her return to US.

Margaret I Kelly has no known criminal complaints. She attended Our Lady of Lourdes High School 9/77-6/81. School closed 1987. Yearbooks show her with track team, cheerleaders, Latin Club, French Club. Former French teacher recalls her as hard-working student.

Records indicate college scholarship to study foreign languages. Enrolled Providence College beginning 9/81.

John R Kelly departed US 10/16/81 arrived Dublin Ireland 10/17/81.

There is no record of his return to US. Margaret I Kelly vacated their apartment 1/82. Claim for $3,600 back rent owed. Claim unresolved against both father and daughter. Margaret I Kelly departed US 5/21/82 arrived Paris France 5/22/82. College tuition remains unpaid except scholarship amount. Grades not released and barred from registering pending settlement of claim for $4,567 tuition balance. She was believed to have been living in Paris and attending classes at the Sorbonne. Margaret I Kelly departed Paris France 9/11/84 arrived Port au Prince Haiti 9/11/84. Traveled on American passport.

Margaret I Kelly departed Port au Prince Haiti 4/5/89 arrived US 4/6/89. New York drivers license 4/23/89. Residence Hague NY. She has no US criminal complaints. She has no US record of employment. She has no known US credit history. She is believed to have been employed at Lido Beachfront Hotel Haiti 9/84-4/89. She has filed no US income tax returns.

Which means she's not quite twenty-eight years old. Much too young for William Kind, deceased. And she's been on her own since seventeen, too young to be abandoned by a deadbeat dad, and without her mother since she was thirteen. The rest pretty much stacks up with what she said. Old for her years. Experienced. No known crimes. Light on money. Alone. Parents living, not dead as Jennifer Kind and maybe her father were led to believe.

After several days of convalescing, sleep becomes intermittent. It comes and goes on its own schedule, like the occasional freight trains that pass by near the end of the street. Twice in as many days I am woken up by the telephone. Both times when I pick up the receiver, I hear silence and then a click. Someone could have called the wrong number. The second time was tonight.

A steady, soft rain is falling. I sit at my desk in the spare bedroom, at the window inside the dormer, and listen to the raindrops against the roof and the new leaves on the old maples along the street. The pavement glistens with puddles and reflections from streetlights. There isn't much traffic. The street dead-ends near an old railroad siding.

Listening to the rain, lighting the desk lamp now and then to reread parts of Margaret's report, wondering whether it's possible to forgive somebody who nearly killed you, I don't hear her come up the stairs. Just soft tapping at the apartment door, as the rumble of a freight fades in the distance. It takes a few moments even to figure out what the sound is. She's on the landing, arms crossed, leaning against the door jamb, dressed in a gray T-shirt, blue jeans, and sneakers, black U.S. Keds. Her hair is damp, and the shoulders of her shirt are dark from the rain. She's shivering.

"Can I come in?" she says, without looking up.

I try to see if she's carrying a weapon, following my second impulse, which is to be afraid. But she's not. She doesn't even have a pocketbook.

"Yeah, sure." I give in to the first impulse. She smiles, but it's tentative, and she looks up. She's not wearing makeup, and more than anything she reminds me of the high-school girl whose picture is on my desk. She wipes her wet sneakers on the mat by the door and steps inside.

"I didn't think you'd let me in." Her back is to me. She looks around the flat, which is silent now, except for the soft drumming of the rain.

"Why not? Just because you tried to kill me?"

"I didn't." She turns around. "I didn't know it was you. Not right away. I was frightened. And then I realized it, and I was more frightened. That's why I called the police. In case you were badly hurt."

"Right."

"No, I mean it." She steps forward and takes my hand. "I'm glad you're all right."

She moves closer, wraps her other arm around me, and through my shirt feels the wounds in my back.

"Oh, God," she says, turning her face up, exposing her neck like a sacrifice. I kiss her mouth furiously, fueled by tension and desire. The sex is direct and passionate, selfish, and it ends on my bed in a few minutes. Margaret starts to cry. She's shaking, and I have my arms around her. I roll her over, and we make love again—longer, slower, but driven by the same impulse.

When it's finished, she says, "I want to see where I hurt you." She pushes me onto my stomach, turns on the table lamp. She examines the puncture wounds, one at a time. She softly touches each one, then runs a finger in a circle around the raised flesh. Her touch is soothing.

"They look good," she says. "Only this one looks dangerous." She retraces a finger around the wound between the ribs in the lower middle of my back. "I think your lung is right there. That could have been bad."

Margaret pushes a finger slightly into the tiny hole. Then there's a sudden, sharp shooting pain as if she's trying to jam her finger right through the wound and into my lung.

"Damn!" I try to thrash, but the pain is so great that I can't move sideways. She seems to be pushing harder, putting all her weight on it.

It's only a twin bed, which is sad for an adult, to sleep in a kid-size bed. My arms hang over the sides. But between the mattress and box spring, head high, I keep a .32-caliber Harrington & Richardson revolver. I bought it when I was in the service in northern Virginia and left it taped under the car seat that year in case some chance encounter or traffic beef went way wrong, which happened sometimes down there. It's small, snub-nosed, and badly weighted, with a hollow plastic grip. It was a favorite of petty criminals, cheap and reliable, and you didn't need a license in Virginia. A Saturday-night special. I kept it, even though it was illegal here without a license, and dangerous, especially when I was in the deepest funk after losing my wife.

I didn't forget the pistol was there while Margaret and I were making love. Despite the riveting agony of her finger in my back, I make a lunge, grab the gun, and wave it in her general direction.

"I'll blow your head off," I squeak.

She sees the gun and reaches for it with her left hand, the finger of her right still in my back. That bends her finger in such a way that she yells, and it hurts so much I let out an involuntary spasmodic cough. But it stops her, and she withdraws her fingertip. I move with a sudden lurch and put the gun right in her face. She's holding the index finger of her right hand in her left. It looks dislocated.

"Get out," I sob, holding the gun against her eye. "Get out." I'm afraid I'll faint before she leaves. Tears are flowing down my face. She grabs her clothes and sneakers with her left hand, stuffs them under her right elbow, turns the doorknob with her left hand, and goes out on the landing naked. Her white skin has large red blotches all over it. Her face is mottled and blotchy. She says nothing.

I slide to the floor in the doorway to the bedroom. "You betrayed me," she says finally, turning her head. She doesn't say anything else. I keep the gun pointed at her back and bolt the door behind her when I hear her halfway down the stairs.

21

There are some things you can see clearly only after the passage of time. It was that way with my old man. He was a super salesman when we were kids in San Diego. My brother Chuckie called it right. He was older than me and noticed things sooner. He said that back in San Diego, you'd go someplace with the old man and everybody knew him. Everybody loved him. It was a gift. He was in the business of wining and dining the company's big clients. He got to be VP sales, and we got to grow up for a while in a place where you could take surfing for gym class and sunshine for the normal state of things. The old man's annual cocktail parties—one for the clients and one the next night for friends and neighbors—were catered affairs. He seemed happy. He conducted business on the golf course and in fancy restaurants. His wife was happy, too. Julie had a housekeeper and a house that was worth having somebody to do the keeping. That was the insurance business we grew up with.

My brother had a rusty Volkswagen bus for his first vehicle, big enough to fit a couple of long boards in the back. He memorized the phone numbers to get the surf conditions at a half-dozen breaks. He had a dose of the old man's charm and used it to attract the best-looking girlfriends. He was generous to a fault and teaching me what he knew.

Then the old man made his big move, got a line on a little agency for sale in Utica—a city we never heard of—and moved us to upstate New York before we got out of high school. The economy turned south just about the same time. It was the early seventies, and he didn't see it coming. Within two years, he lost the business under a mountain of debt and dubious claims by greedy clients, went into Chapter 7, and sold the house. His social drinking became regular binge drinking. Our mother left him, and Chuckie and I bagged groceries to help pay the bills.

She moved us into the house behind the supermarket, a rental, found Bob, her boyfriend, who was also divorced, and got a job at a title-search company. Julie did pretty well after a time. For a few years, the old man hung around town in one job or another. Then one day he was gone, and he turned up clerking at a general store on Lake Champlain. I went to see him, uninvited but welcome, and he was living in the upstairs apartment with a woman half his age, buying the store in little installments from the decrepit owner, and he was all right with it, with what happened. He wasn't drinking anymore. He said he was to blame for not foreseeing the recession that killed his business. "I was so anxious to get moving, to get out on my own, that I ignored the signs."

He didn't apologize for it, either, or for all the hurt it inflicted on his wife. She'd still talk to him now and then. Chuckie didn't, however. The moment high school ended, he put his old boards in the back of a beat-up Impala and went straight down the coast. He found a job in a surf shop south of Daytona. And he stayed. Got a permanent girlfriend, got a mortgage on a tiny bungalow five blocks from the beach, had a kid, then another. For a few years he bugged me to come down and live the life in Florida, but I only visited. The last time, he was starting to go bald. "Another gift from the old man," he said. But I think his genetics were off. The old man still had his hair at the end. And I've still got mine. We share that, and blind spots.

With my own wife, I see now how much trouble our marriage was in and how quickly. Thinking about the old man's story starts to put it in perspective. You have to move forward, regardless of the consequences. In college, I read a linguistics book that said the future tense is fiction, about stuff that may never exist, and it's completely necessary. You have to be able to imagine the future to keep going in the present—despite the knowledge of past and present troubles and the certainty of how it's all going to end. The future is always better. Caroline was unhappy in Saratoga—isolated in the apartment while I was working into the evening every day, thirty miles away. Even I couldn't see any prospects besides a promotion and transfer within Apex.

Caroline soon quit talking about the future, a sure sign of deep trouble. She was asphyxiating in the present. Then she asked me to move my things out during a cold, bleak March, six months after we married, because I was angry all the time and suspicious. Controlling. I didn't like her friends and scolded her about money she couldn't spend and everything else. I'd quit boxing and didn't have anywhere to lay off all the aggression, but that was only part of it. While it now seems clear what her beef was—a new bride with little to show for it except loneliness and no prospects—I had thought at the time that I was right about everything and her dissatisfaction was the problem. Standing stubbornly in my own way.

Now I'm afraid to go out. I spend the entire day waiting to see if I'll cough up blood, but it doesn't come. Listening to my breathing to try to determine if Margaret nicked my lung, using a hand mirror to inspect the wound in the bathroom mirror. It looks like I'm not only not dying, my ribs were as strong as her finger. Manage to get some alcohol on the wound for protection, hop around and writhe for an excruciating minute. And since I don't have health insurance—Joseph canceled it right away—and don't want cops nosing around, I don't call an ambulance or the police.

Wondering how I got into this fix, this life, I can think of two things I could have done different. Gone into business for myself as a private investigator or kept boxing and turned pro. Or both. I wasn't that good at either, but I could have given it a shot. I might have survived long enough to convince my wife that she had a future with me.

But I wasn't taking risks then or putting anyone else ahead of me. When all is said and done, perhaps the only thing that counts is loyalty—another thing I'm not very good at. That was Caroline's grievance, at bottom. That I wasn't too interested in her future. And I guess it's Margaret's grievance. I turned my back on her, too. I won't do that again. Listening to the freights, I finally fall asleep with the pistol in my pocket.

22

The question of loyalty doesn't trouble Joseph too much. On Monday he calls to say they've got a lot of work. Do I want to subcontract until he gets another staff person?

"Sure, Joseph. It would probably work better that way. But my rates are going to be higher than what you're used to paying."

"You're still my go-to guy," he says. "You always have been."

"Right. And how's Ruth Benjamin working out?"

"Pretty good. You know, it takes time. But she's a comer."

"And Cherie? How's your lovely receptionist? Is she her same cheerful self?"

"Actually, Cherie quit. Last week, soon after you did. Which actually brings me to another question. How's your sofa? For old time's sake, pal, what about letting me bunk in again until I find a place."

"I didn't quit. You fired me, shithead."

"I didn't. It's just outsourcing," Joseph says, and laughs like it's our joke. "That's the trend. I did you a favor."

"I might actually let you stay, Joseph. But it's going to cost you this time."

"How much?"

"Fifty bucks a night."

"I can't pay that."

"It's about half the company per-diem rate for Albany. You'll figure it out. And also the truth. You have to tell me what's really been happening."

He doesn't want to do that either, but Joann emptied the bank accounts, cashed out the stocks and mutual funds, hired a lawyer, and canceled his credit cards before throwing him out. He doesn't have anywhere else to go, and he comes over and he starts talking. It's like the old days, when we used to speak honestly, though simple honesty is beyond him now. “You won’t testify against me in divorce court, will you?”

“You know better, Joseph.” And he probably does.

He had been spending time with Cherie. She’d found out her husband started cheating soon after their wedding. She got an annulment from the church, following a divorce from the court, but both took time. She was angry and available. “She wanted to,” Joseph says. “But I wouldn’t get involved. So I spent a little time with her to cheer her up. Not a lot. It was just for laughs.”

“She probably didn’t think so.”

“The fact is she moved back home to take care of her father. I was the only social life she had. She was grateful. We were just friends. But she wanted it to be more. And I said no.”

“You’re such a liar. What if I told you Cherie told me everything.”

“I wouldn’t believe you. She hates you. And even if she did I’ll deny it if you say anything. And cancel your contract.”

“We haven’t signed one yet.”

“We will,” Joseph says, being magnanimous. “I’ll keep you busy.”

When he began spending a little time with Ruth Benjamin, his new adjuster, and then went to see Margaret Kelly in Lake George, Cherie apparently felt slighted and called his wife to tell her point-blank that they’d been having an affair. Joann called Cherie some choice names. It took a few days for each of them to punish him, which they did separately.

“You’re such a prize. Why do they like you?”

“Because the world is full of losers, pal.” He allows for a significant pause. “And I’m not one of them.”

“So how’s Margaret Kelly?”

“I haven’t seen her since I took her the check Friday. She had me escort her to the bank. She said she was afraid you’d been trying to push her into a malpractice suit just to get out of paying the claim. Or else blame her somehow. She said she wouldn’t feel safe until it was deposited in the bank. Oh, yeah, she’d also had a prowler out in the barn.”

“Who was it?”

“She didn’t get a good look at him, and he got away. She called the cops. I don’t think they got anywhere. And I don’t think they will. I talked to the deputy. He didn’t even have Margaret’s name spelled right.”

He clearly doesn’t know it was me.

“So did you sleep with her?”

"I don't think so." Joseph's face reddens. He brought over a half-case of Irish ale. He goes into the kitchen to get one.

"There's the door," I call after him. "You can leave now."

"I didn't."

"But you tried."

Joseph comes back, taking a long pull from his glass. "I know you slept with her," he says. "She hinted at that right away. The first time she called. Boy, was she angry. I was thinking, there's a little more to Jack than I know about. She was extremely angry with you." He wags his finger at me. "You had it made there, pal. Typically, you couldn't leave well enough alone."

"Go on. And?"

"So after you bungled this case, I went to see her, to talk about it. And that's it. She was hot, as if I was to blame for your bad behavior. So I explained things. That you were unethical in this instance. I also told her I fired your sorry ass. After I explained the entire policy, and the restrictions on any later claims, I had her sign the release. She made me go all the way through it twice. Word for word. It took a few hours. And then she called the next day because she'd had the prowler, so I went out there again. And she was even more upset."

"So what'd you do?"

"I took a look around. There was nothing damaged or stolen, as far as she could tell. Except a little blood in the barn. Apparently she stuck the jerk with a pitchfork. And I talked to the sheriff. They didn't have anything. It was probably some farm boy who'd heard about the hot tub. The sheriff told me Margaret is known to be a little eccentric up there. 'She likes to get naked in the hot tub' is how he put it."

"And then?" I'm anticipating some disclosure and can't seem to wait for it.

"That's it. On Friday, I took her the check—the first thing Friday morning—and then we went to the bank. She seemed genuinely worried and wanted to deposit it right away. She wanted to draw some cash against it, with me right there. To make sure nobody was going to take it away from her. Which I understand. It's a little paranoid. But it's a pretty good check."

"And?"

"And then she wanted a drink." Joseph smiles despite himself.

"Where?"

"In the hot tub."

"And?"

"And I fell asleep. It was very innocent." Joseph's face, as revealing as he is devious, turns red. "Except did you actually see . . . never mind."

"Go ahead, Joseph. I'll keep your secrets. What's one more, anyway?"

He returns to the refrigerator for another ale. Comes back, pours it into the tall glass and drinks off half. I want to slap his face.

"Nothing happened. I'd tell you. I think she wanted to get back at you, but not that much. I can't believe anybody would prefer you. She must have been drinking." Joseph laughs and shakes his head. "We were drinking rum. I think she has a hollow leg. I fell asleep. Later when I woke up, she was just sitting there staring at me. From about three feet away. Scared the shit out of me."

"Then what happened?"

"I got up."

"Did she say anything?"

"She laughed. She didn't sound too happy, though. Actually she'd been crying. Oh, yeah, she said something really bizarre. It was about you. She said, 'Tell Jack. He believes I'm the succubus.' What the hell's a succubus?"

"It's a demon who'll suck the life out of you while you're sleeping. After she seduces you. It's what happened to our friend William Kind."

"You're joking."

"Maybe not."

When he hears my theory, Joseph starts poking holes in it. He devises an alternative theory. He says Kind probably broke the thermometer himself, accidentally, and got the mercury on his hands and in his clothes. He poisoned himself. Joseph says the guy was probably giving himself Tylenol and used the eyedropper to extract the medicine. I ask him to explain the wounds on my back.

"It was almost dark," he says. "She didn't know it was you. And she was perfectly within her rights to stick you with a pitchfork. What were you sneaking around like that for anyway?" Then he thinks about it some more. "Thank God it wasn't a real burglar. She'd probably be getting sued by now, and we'd be stuck with the claim."

"Do you think she could have smothered you while you were sleeping?"

"What, are you nuts?"

"What about a guy tied to a hospital bed?"

"I don't think so. I think you're out of your mind," Joseph says. "So what are you going to do with this crazy theory?"

"Probably nothing. She cashed the check. And there's no way that coroner's going to reopen the case and do an autopsy. I asked him."

"What did he say?"

"He said it was an interesting theory. He also asked how desperately Apex wanted to get out of paying on the life-insurance policy. Apparently the hospital's already started its own internal investigation in response to Casey's malpractice claim. Our guy didn't waste any time."

"I put him on it right away," Joseph says. "It seems pretty clear to me they screwed up."

"All you care about is getting the $300,000 back. Even if the hospital screwed up, it wasn't enough to kill the guy."

"How would you know? Because some geezer doctor told you? Who left town? Come on, pal. Or the nurse who's in danger of getting fired? Come on. Besides, $300,000 isn't that much money."

"Not to you, maybe."

"You don't kill somebody over three hundred grand," Joseph says. "That's not enough reason. Not by itself. A million bucks maybe. But she doesn't need to kill for money. Not with her looks. It doesn't add up."

"We've seen cases where people got whacked for the contents of their wallets."

"Punks and losers," Joseph says. "Margaret Kelly is neither. You're overlooking the obvious."

I tell him about the last encounter, about the finger in the back and the revolver, which was the Friday night after she'd cashed the check. "She tried to rip my lung out, Joseph. Right here in this apartment. Three days ago."

"You pulled a gun on her, champ. An unlicensed and illegal gun, I might add. And you've been trying to have her arrested for murder. Really, that's what you've been doing. And what, she's going to kill you with her finger? I don't think so."

Joseph takes a closer look at my wounds. He says that even the big one doesn't look like much and laughs at me. "She's an angry woman, pal. She was torturing you. That's normal. Look at what's happening to me! And maybe she's a little nuts. Wrapped a little tight. You know as well as I do how common that is. You're a little nuts, too, by the way. You have been ever since Caroline left you. Pretty hard to take sometimes."

Joseph wags his finger. "Let me tell you one other thing, pal. I'm going to tell you the truth, because most people won't. That's our motto with the bad risks and the tough cases, right? And you're both. You come on with that passive-aggressive, good guy, hangdog business. But the fact is you're on the make. You're always on the make. You just don't want to admit it. At least I'm honest. You don't take any risks, emotional risks, or give anything serious in return. You're not a serious guy. You'll never get anywhere that way. And women hate you for that."

That evening, as he makes his bed on my sofa, Joseph lets on that he drove up to Lake George that morning and found the A-frame was locked. The Land Rover was there, but if Margaret was, she wouldn't open the door.

"I acknowledge the possibility that Margaret didn't exactly plan this thing out. It may have been, as the Buddhists say, the pretense of accident."

Joseph scoffs. "You mean like everything is preordained?"

"No. I mean those two were who they were, and did what they did because that was the way it was going, and things came up, and they helped it along. I don't know."

"You're right, there," Joseph says. "You don't know. What really happened is you lost your new girlfriend and you lost your job. In one week. At least I'm helping you get one of them halfway back. And what do I get for it—complaints and accusations. That's gratitude."

"One last thing, Joseph. You can stay exactly one week. And you have to pay me in cash, every day, to stay, starting tomorrow. After that you have to move out."

"I have nowhere to go."

"Go back home. Beg forgiveness."

And when he has to, he does.

23

Some acts of loyalty you don't deserve credit for. They're a given. Like walking your dog on a leash and pulling it out of the way of a car. You just do it, and so what? If you didn't do it, the fabric of everything would come unraveled. You'd run out of dogs pretty fast, anyway. After my old man and my brother left, I didn't feel like I could leave my mother immediately. It just didn't come up. I worked at the grocery for a few years and worked up to cashier, took night classes at the community college in whatever interested me—Western art, literature, accounting (to prove I could do it)—and spent a lot of time hitting the heavy bags at the YMCA.

My wind was pretty good. Chuckie and I had swum for a year on the high-school team before we had to quit and work. Because we came from California and Chuckie was still into surfing, theoretically, we both got tagged with the moniker "Dude." It was intended as a funny put-down. The guys resented Charles, because girls liked him. One night, he was walking home. It was a Sunday in late winter. A car stopped, and he was knocked down from behind and then punched and kicked for a long time. He curled up to protect himself. He never saw his attacker, who only said, "Take that, you son of a bitch." He came home bruised and bloody and frightened. It was after the old man's business went belly up, leaving some clients without the insurance coverage they had paid for. The old man wondered if the attacker was really getting back at him. I didn't care who it was. I was angry and determined to learn how to fight.

Karate lessons were too expensive. I took out a library book on boxing, the old low-rent sport, and got a discount membership at the YMCA downtown. After about a year learning to jab and cross and hook, hitting the bag, and how to keep my hands up, I bought two sets of gloves and sparred with nearly anybody who was willing. I weighed about 175 and found I could handle the pumped-up power lifters, who were big and strong but slow and clumsy. After high school, I found a boxing gym where amateurs could train for free. The old ex-fighters who ran the place, Tony and Jimmy, taught me a few things. How to move your hands to block a punch. How to throw a body shot. They were genuine tough guys, these little old men, but I didn't know it. The slick middleweight who won the regional Golden Gloves taught me something else: I wasn't as good as I thought.

After Bob moved into my mother's house, I still stayed awhile. Some guys used to come into the grocery to buy their smokes and liked to call me Bag Boy Dude. I thought they'd outgrow or get tired of it, but they didn't.

One night after a workout, I ran into a former schoolmate in a local bar. He was drunk and told me what I had been waiting so long to hear. He said the guy who beat up Chuckie was his friend, a big jock who got dumped by a girl who had a thing for my brother. This guy and the jock were driving by and just happened to see Chuckie walking home. The jock jumped out and hit Chuckie in the head from behind and then beat on him. "You shouldn't blame him," his friend said. "Because that girl broke his fucking heart."

The jock was still in town and married to somebody else. He was still big, but he was going soft. I went to his house two nights later, knocked, and told him I wanted to talk to him about something.

"What do you want?"

"I want you to apologize, you fat shit, for what you did to my brother."

"Get out of here," he said. When he started to push open the storm door, like he was coming out to get me, I pulled it open and slapped his face twice, hard. He jumped back inside and slammed the door. That night, I called my brother and told him. Chuckie laughed about it. He seemed kind of pleased. The next week, I drove north to see my father and found him sober and making a life on Champlain. He said he was glad to know it wasn't his fault that Chuckie got his ass kicked. But I don't think he really remembered it.

I asked my father to help me get a job in insurance, but not selling. The old man called somebody, and eventually I got into Apex as an adjuster. Not right away, though. It took awhile. Three years in the Army first. So in Hartford, I was older than nearly all the other trainees, most fresh out of school, and befriended Joseph, who also was a little older, and already married.

We hit it off. It's not always clear who your enemies are. But false fronts take effort, and usually they'll show themselves in time. It's important to know who, finally, is on your side and who's not. Joseph is out for himself, but he is not particularly against me.

24

One morning when I go out to buy the Albany newspaper I find one of my tires slashed. Probably local punks. Then again there is a short list of people who might have it in for me. A pair of whitewater rafters who went to jail, maybe a pornographer, clearly Margaret, and one angry husband—not that he had a reason, but he thought he did. It takes me half an hour to change the tire. I spend the rest of the morning with the paper, but I'm not really interested in anything I read.

In the afternoon, the phone rings for a long time. Nothing feels good, and Joseph's at work. The ringing stops. Then it starts again as if somebody knows I'm home and not picking up. Finally, I lift the receiver but don't say anything.

"Is this Jack?"

"What."

"Jack, this is Mandy. Remember me? I called the other day."

"What do you want?"

"I'm a little worried, and I think we really need to talk." She sounds slightly breathless.

"I told you it doesn't have anything to do with me."

"I don't think you can just say that."

"Why not? What do you mean?"

But she won't explain it except in person. And after turning down her apartment and mine as meeting places, we agree on a downtown cafe in Schenectady a good distance from Smith's place.

Forty-five minutes later, Mandy slides into the booth at Ambition, a bohemian diner and bar. It's long and narrow, opening onto a cobbled pedestrian street. You can see everybody who comes and goes.

"You can't get away from me that easily," Mandy says. She unbuttons her peacoat and touches her hair, already pulled into a dark ponytail. She has a delicate face, large dark eyes, and a mouth that stays slightly open in an inadvertent smile. Some people are built that way, with facial features that incline them to expressions of happiness. If they're lucky, if they don't see too much hardship, the appearance becomes the real thing. It's a gift. Mandy is about twenty years old, maybe a little older, and it looks like her gift has unwrapped a little.

The cobalt-haired waitress comes out from behind the bar to hand us plastic-coated menus. When the waitress returns, Mandy orders green tea and a bran muffin. She's a vegetarian.

"I used to come to this place," she says. "When I was a kid we used to hang out here and drink coffee and smoke cigarettes."

"Long time ago?"

"Seems like it." Then she hears the irony in my question. "Not that long."

"So you called?"

"It's kind of a long story," she says. "Then there's something I want to show you. You look tense. You don't have to be afraid of me." She laughs like I'm being a sorry old man.

By Mandy's account, there are two groups of pornographers around town, each connected to a different guy in Pennsylvania. Those two guys used to be partners, but now they're in competition and don't like each other. But everyone's making a lot of money. Lots of cash with the peep shows. And now they're starting to sell videos for home viewing. An ex-biker drives up every Tuesday from Pennsylvania, in a Thunderbird, to collect the bags of quarters. He leaves with the cash in the trunk. The IRS staked out one of the stores a couple years ago, counted customers and quarters dropping, and filed a claim for almost a half-million dollars in unpaid taxes. The company listed as owner of the shop went into bankruptcy. The shop never closed, though. The company that was the landlord took it over. Guess who owned both companies?

"How do you know this?"

"I worked for almost a year at Fun Haus." She adds quickly, "I was the cashier. My boyfriend Royal got me in. He was working at one of the other stores. The money was really good. I was making fifteen dollars an hour. That's, what, three times minimum wage?"

"So why did you quit?"

"I didn't. But you see Royal got in some trouble. For a couple weeks Sonny thought the bags were light from his store and Royal was taking some money. He thought somehow Royal got a copy of the key that opens the coin boxes and was helping himself."

"Was he?"

"I don't know. It doesn't matter. The boss thought so. He told him he had to pay back some money. Royal refused. He said he didn't take it. And he's a big guy. I don't think he was afraid. He doesn't intimidate. But I think even he was kind of scared."

"And then?"

"They burned his house down."

"Who did?"

"We didn't know for sure. But we had a good idea. Sonny never said a word about it. That was the skeeviest part. We could have been killed. And he didn't say a word."

"Where was this? When did it happen?"

"I don't remember the exact address. I'll have to ask Royal. I think it was on McClellan Street, not too far from St. Clare's Hospital. It was two years ago. In the summer."

Mandy picks at her muffin and sips the tea.

"So what did you want to show me?"

"It's back at my apartment. One week I kept a record of all the cash that came into the shop. All the bills that were exchanged and how many quarters went out. I've got a copy of it you can have. I want you to take a look at that. Royal heard you were doing an investigation."

"I'm not. Why should I care? I was an insurance guy working on a case, and I don't work there anymore. Not since last week. As far as I know, the people who were worried about things, the people I was looking to handle a claim for, are okay. I've called them. Why don't you just call the IRS and show them your documents. I'll bet they'd be interested."

"Are you crazy? I mean, that's insane. Royal and I were working under the table. They'd come after us."

She also needs a ride home. She lives in the Stockade District, a slightly shabby but fashionable neighborhood of brownstones and brick homes, some two centuries old, near the Mohawk River. When we get there, she says I might as well see her stuff. So I follow her up the stone steps into a first-floor flat. She leaves me alone in the postage stamp of a living room. In fifteen minutes, she comes back transformed. The thin girl in jeans, bulky sweater, and peacoat is replaced by a young woman in a pale satin blouse and short skirt, her face made up.

"I have to get ready for work," she says. "It'll just take a minute."

She sits in a chair, just a few feet away, and unrolls the tights in her hand. She pulls them up one leg, then the other. It takes some time, and her blouse falls open as she bends to straighten the material on her thighs. When she glances up to see me staring at her cleavage, she smiles.

"I hate these things," she says. "They're so hard to put on."

She releases her hair from the ponytail and shakes it out. She pulls out a hairbrush and begins stroking her long, flowing curls.

"Where do you work?"

"At a club. The money's not too bad."

She doesn't say anything else; she just sits there brushing her hair. Suddenly, the front door flies open, and a large man in a black-leather coat steps in. He shuts the door hard. "What's going on here?" he demands.

He glares at me, then looks at Mandy, whose skirt is still hiked, one of her feet up on the wooden crate that serves as a coffeetable.

"Nothing's going on here, Royal," she says. "This is Jack. We got something to eat, and then he gave me a ride home."

"Oh, yeah? What is he doing here?"

"Nothing," I mutter.

"Nothing?" Royal takes two steps past Mandy and towers over me and the sofa. It's not too surprising that he'd be irritated to find another man alone with his girlfriend, but it seems like more than a coincidence that he came in just now.

"This is my home. I believe I should feel welcome and comfortable when I come into my own home," Royal says. "I'm not feeling very comfortable."

He's probably six-foot-four and stocky, built like an oak. He wears a small black mustache and a deep scowl. He looks a little like Sonny Liston, who frightened everybody except Ali and a banger out of Philadelphia named Leotis Martin, who won a nine-round war late in the old man's career. Royal shakes his head.

"You know, a brother works hard. He takes care of things. He's got a home. He's got a woman. And there's always some white guy messing with his business. I don't understand this. But I know it's wrong."

He begins squeezing and flexing his hands, which are hanging by his sides. The door suddenly looks farther away, and I just want to get through it and wonder how quickly the blackjack in my cowboy boot can be slipped out. Probably not fast enough, not with my pant-leg pulled over the boot.

"Mandy, do you want to explain this?" I ask quietly.

She doesn't say anything and sets the brush down. She takes her foot down from the crate. She's looking at Royal, not me. Her face is set in a pout, as if whatever he's thinking isn't too far off the mark, and she's just annoyed at getting caught.

"Explain this?" Royal says. He's staring down at me. "I don't think you can explain this, motherfucker. I think the only thing you can do is be sorry."

"I'm going to leave."

"You're going to leave when I tell you that you can leave. That's when you can leave."

Mandy is still watching him. She straps on a pair of open platform shoes. She stands up and pulls a cashmere overcoat out of the narrow closet by the front door.

"I'm going to work," she says. She goes out the door and pulls it closed behind her. Royal doesn't acknowledge her departure. He continues to glare at me.

"I don't know what you're thinking—"

"You're goddamned right you don't know what I'm thinking," he interrupts. He shifts his weight to fully face me. The violence appears imminent, and there's no way out. I stand up.

"Listen, I didn't do anything and wasn't sniffing around. You know that. She asked for a ride. I'll tell you one other small thing. My grandparents got to America about 1916 from Scandinavia. They kept to themselves. So whoever's been fucking the black man in America, it wasn't us."

We're only a foot apart, my forehead near his chin.

"I could bite your nose off," Royal says. He clamps his teeth for emphasis.

I start to walk around him without turning my back to him. Reaching the door, I feel for the knob. It's locked. I have to turn briefly to find the mechanism and unlock it.

"I like your style, though. You've got a nice girlfriend."

As I pull open the door, he stomps his foot. I flinch, and he laughs.

Turns out there was only one house fire two summers ago in the neighborhood where Mandy said her boyfriend lived. The fire investigator's report blamed it on faulty wiring. A couple with two kids owned and lived in the house. Either Mandy made up the story about arson or was confused about the location.

When I get home, I place a call to Frederick Schmitt, a k a Sonny Smith. He won't even admit it's him on the line, but he's disinclined to hang up.

"I met two of your employees, or ex-employees. Royal and Mandy. They're interesting. I'm guessing they're the kind of very good employees you like. The kind who made a mistake once, and now they do what they're supposed to. Anyway, that's what I'm thinking."

"I don't know what you're talking about. But I will tell you this," he says.

"There's some people who claim to be this and that. And you never know. And there's some people who will make a lot of noise. For this cause and that cause. That's very common. I hate those fucking people. But take a man who can stand up for himself, just himself. He tells you something, you can probably believe him. Usually. Anyway, he's not going to be blowing in the wind with whatever the next person thinks or what his wife tells him. And he's not going to be blowing smoke up your dress."

"So is this a good thing or a bad thing?"

"It is what it is," he says. "But it provides a certain amount of clarity."

"More every day."

"The other thing this tells you sometimes is that this is a person who doesn't listen. Who doesn't know how," Schmitt says. "So am I gonna have a problem with you?"

"I thought we were done."

"I thought so, too," he says. "Lose the phone number. Don't call me anymore."

And he hangs up.

An hour later, I'm still jittery but thinking that just maybe, by taking action, I've resolved the trouble with Sonny. Maybe the same approach would work with Margaret. I decide to go back and see.

25

It's overcast and damp, like most spring days in the Adirondacks. Margaret isn't running this morning. She comes out the front door of the A-frame barefoot in gray sweatpants and a rumpled T-shirt. Her short hair is unkempt. She walks to the edge of the porch and looks down on me. I shut off the engine and get out of the car.

"What do you want."

"I need to see you."

"Why?"

I cross the grass, go up the steps, pull her close, and kiss her mouth. She kisses me back, then pushes me away and slaps me with an open palm, followed by a backhand. It stings, and my ear is ringing. All the boxing experience in the world won't prepare you for an attack by a woman you just might love.

"I'll leave if you want me to."

"No."

"I think I figured it out, and you know what? He wasn't man enough. Neither is somebody like Joseph Sweet. But maybe I am. And if not, maybe I'll die trying. It's like that poem, you know. More than hope or money, wisdom or a drink. I need you, to love you. More than anything else."

She looks at me, her eyes hard.

"I hate you. I despise you. You're a bastard. You betrayed me. Don't ever—don't ever—hurt me like that again."

I pull her close one more time, my arms over hers so she can't hit me, my feet between hers so she can't knee my testicles. Her face is at my neck, and she bites, drawing blood when I pull away. I taste it, kissing her, bruising her lips, careful to keep my tongue away from her teeth. Her hand, trapped by my thigh, slides inward, but instead of clawing, she strokes. I carry her inside, partly to make the point that I can, and lay her on the bearskin. We make love slowly, rising and falling in sync, as natural as breathing, and it goes on wordlessly, for a long time. Later, she lies curled into me, and I see she's covered in scratches, a twig and pine needles in her matted hair.

"Demons chased you."

"Demons chased me."

She turns her back to me, snuggling close, and I'm in her again. She moves only those muscles. Steadily, rhythmically. For an even longer time. Then she convulses and lies still. We don't move for an hour.

"What I said about not needing a drink, I brought a bottle anyway. In case you did. Whiskey."

"Not Irish."

"No. Canadian."

"Good. Let's drink it."

I dress and get the bottle from the car, and she comes out on the porch with two tumblers. She's wrapped herself in the bearskin rug. We sit opposite each other in Adirondack chairs, and I break the bottle's seal and fill the glasses. A light drizzle starts. We drink without talking, as drops collect and fall from the bearskin, from Margaret's hair, and from mine. The greens and browns of the forest look richer in the wet sheen. I refill the glasses. The day turns grayer.

"You've been left before."

"Yes."

"Your mother, and then your father."

"How do you know that?"

"A background check that was done. You were just a kid, the first time."

"Did your background check tell you that he beat her? That was why she left?"

"No."

"He said it was my fault. All the bloody crying. That's what he said. Hers and mine. And good fucking riddance. For a time there she fancied that she was a witch. But she was weak against him, wasn't she?" She empties her glass again. "And did your background check tell you that the last day he beat me was the day he left?"

"No."

"That was the day I cracked him with a cast-iron skillet. Right on the head. I told him he would not hit me again. Never. And he didn't. Not after that. He fell to the floor like a sack of wheat. Right in the kitchen. Thought I'd killed him. But he got up, eventually. Took all the money and bought a ticket for Dublin the same day." She laughs. "He acted like the devil himself was after him. He was right."

"You don't let anybody hurt you."

"Not like that. No. Not anymore."

I fill the glasses a third time. I'm soaked through, starting to shiver. The rain has washed Margaret's face clean. It looks raw and glistens. She lifts her glass and looks up.

"Are you still investigating me?"

"No. It's over."

"But you got a background report."

"A few days ago. They take time. It doesn't matter."

"What else do you know about me?"

"That you went to France and Haiti. And to Catholic school."

The last part is meant to lighten the moment, but she doesn't smile.

"So why did you do it?"

"Investigate you? It was my job. I was trying to do the right thing. You know, do justice, love kindness, walk humbly. I don't know."

The rain slows and stops. Mist shrouds the trees. It seeps out of the forest and surrounds the house. We watch it approach. Sipping from the tumblers. The bottle is nearly empty.

She doesn't look at me. It's as if I'm not there. I keep trying. "When people hurt you, you pass it around. That's kind of normal. Sometimes it ends up in the right place. Sometimes it goes wrong."

"You know what evil is, don't you?" I can't seem to shut up. "It's choosing to do wrong when you know the difference. It's choosing to hurt somebody when you know you will, and you're pretty goddamned sure that it's not for their own good, or for anybody else's. I'm trying not to be that. That's all. I don't want to hurt you."

Margaret stares at me. Her gaze is flat, her face implacable. She doesn't say a word. When I ask if she wants to go inside, she shakes her head. When I ask if she wants me to leave, she nods.

26

The day Joseph leaves, he's out by 6 a.m. I shower a long time, letting the hot water run until it's gone. I drive to the grocery and the drugstore to spend a little of his cash. The sun is out, so are the birds, and everything smells fresh after days of rain. The store clerks are cheerful. It feels mindlessly good just walking around. I drive home and park in front of the house. As I'm carrying the grocery bags up the stairs, the landlord sticks his head out of his door.

"Did you break something?" he asks.

"Excuse me?"

"I heard a loud noise before. It sounded like a pop," he says. "I thought you might need me to fix something."

Mr. Tregonis is friendly enough, and a little nosy. I'm not sure what he's talking about and wonder if he heard something the other night and wants an excuse to come up and look around. He's retired and takes pretty good care of the house. I'm his only tenant. It's just him and me.

"I don't think so."

"Well, let me know if you do."

"I'll do that."

On the landing, I set the groceries down and fish for my keys. Inserting the key, I notice a looseness in the brass-plated doorknob. Also, there's a chip in the door jamb next to it. Somebody jimmied the door, probably with a screwdriver, which would be easy, and I'm kicking myself for never having got a deadbolt lock. I listen for a moment and hear only the landlord's television and distant traffic. Instead of going in, I backtrack down the stairs and knock on his door. He comes out again in his pressed slacks, flannel shirt, and slippers.

"How long ago did you hear that sound?"

"I don't know. Maybe a half-hour. A few minutes before I heard you leave."

"I see." I'd been gone almost two hours. He is a widower who's mostly alone, but he's sharp enough about things. "Did you see me leave?"

"No, but I saw a pickup truck leaving. I thought you were in it. Why? Is there something wrong?"

"Not at all. Did you hear my friend leave before?"

"A little before nine, I think it was. At least, I assumed it was him. That's about the time he leaves for work, right?"

That actually had been me. Joseph left while the old man was still asleep. I have no idea whose pickup he saw.

"Anyway, Joseph's gone. He went back home." I'd told him a little bit of Joseph's story.

"My wife never threw me out," Tregonis says. "Though she thought about it now and then." He chuckles.

"That's because you're such a good cook." I'd had fried eggplant and marinated steaks with him one night. And a few glasses of sweet wine. But I don't want to involve him in my problems.

Tregonis grins. "Yeah. We'll have to do that again," he says. He turns back into his apartment, which has the same layout as mine. "You need me to fix something, you let me know."

Once in my apartment, I check each room and closet. There's no obvious sign anybody else has been there. But my revolver is gone, and so are the two files that I had left on my desk. One contained my notes on Sonny Smith. The other contained the investigator's report on Margaret, my interview notes from the case, and an outline of my murder theory. If Margaret took the file, it will give her something to think about. If it was somebody sent by Sonny Smith, it's an entirely different problem. But no worse.

Margaret hasn't answered her phone for two days. The night before I had a vivid dream of her. She was sitting by my bed, where I lay sick and injured. "Now it's your turn," she said. She faced me, and there were no eyes in her sockets. When I awoke in a sweat, I was thinking about Chuckie, something he told me once that I spent years ignoring. "You choose your own friends," he said. "There's nobody to blame but yourself if you don't choose them better."

I go through the kitchen cupboards and the refrigerator, removing all the food, anything ingestible, and stuffing it into trash bags. Then I scrub the fridge, the cupboards, and every dish, glass, and utensil in the place. The entire flat gets vacuumed, dusted, and washed. It takes hours. I bag all the bedding and clothes for the laundry, including Joseph's sheets from the sofa. In a down pillow, pulling the case off, I feel something sharp and find a straight pin, the kind used in sewing, and I wonder how it got there, if it might be coated with poison. It's nearly nightfall by the time I'm done and the apartment feels safe.

Joseph's still at the office and answers the phone himself. He sounds happy. "A lot of work here, my friend."

"I have to talk to you. Can you come over?"

"I'm kind of busy," he says. "And my wife's expecting me home for dinner. And I'm late as it is. Why don't you come here?"

"Are you alone?"

"Yeah. Ruth went home a little while ago. So did the temp secretary, though she was barely here at all for the purposes of work. I've got to get somebody."

"I'll be there soon. Don't leave."

"I'll be here. Your girlfriend's coming by, and I have to wait for her anyway."

He hangs up without explaining.

27

In the otherwise empty parking lot are two vehicles, a red Miata with the convertible top up and a green Dodge Dart with a raised back-end and oversize rear tires. They're in different rows and far apart. The lot isn't particularly well lighted, with just a few high lamps on the sprawling perimeter, only one near the Apex office. I park farther back than the other vehicles, turn off the lights, and wait a few minutes. Nobody else comes. Judging by the cars, I expect to find Joseph inside with Rodney Glynnis. I walk to the side of Building No. 6, away from the light, and move quickly over the patch of lawn and through the door.

"Hey, chief," Rodney says when I enter the Apex office. "What are you doing here?" He's standing by the desk in a black-leather jacket, jeans, and combat boots, hair slicked back again, an unlit cigarette in his mouth. Cherie's next to him, also in a black-leather jacket and jeans. They look like escapees from a biker film. Cherie's arms are crossed; she frowns at me. Joseph's sitting at her old desk with a calculator and the company checkbook.

"It's severance-package time," Rodney says. "We're just trying to figure out how many extra zeros to put in there."

"The final paycheck," Joseph says without looking up, "has to come from payroll. This is just expenses."

"That's three hundred dollars documented," Cherie says. "There's nothing to figure out. And you promised to continue my health benefits for six months."

"How can I do that," Joseph replies, "when you're not an employee anymore?"

"You figure it out."

"What about my benefits?" I ask.

Both Cherie and Joseph glare. "You don't work here anymore," he says.

"Nice try, chief," Rodney says. "Don't get sick."

Joseph fills out the check and signs it. "There you go. You'll get your final paycheck in the mail, probably next week."

"And the insurance?" Cherie says. Her arms are still crossed.

"I'll just leave you on the policy for six months. Hopefully nobody will question it. That would be a problem."

"That would be a problem. Just so you know, I'm going to call them every week for the whole six months to make sure. Don't think about cutting it short. And I already filed for unemployment. I expect that to be uncontested."

"Sure. Go ahead," Joseph says. "And don't forget your check, Cherie. I hope this works for you."

Cherie takes the check from the desk. "That," she says, "is none of your business."

Rodney follows her out the door. "Let's get going. I think I feel an accident coming on," he says, and winks at Joseph. His high cackle follows him out into the night.

"Thank God that's done," Joseph says. He closes the checkbook. "Now I can go home." He steps into the small office for his briefcase. We hear tires squealing in the parking lot. "I can't stand that kid," Joseph says. "What the hell is she doing with him?"

"Where's Margaret?" I've been half-expecting her to pop out of the back room, pistol blazing.

"Who?"

"Margaret Kelly."

"I haven't seen her," Joseph says.

"I thought you said my girlfriend was coming?"

"I was being facetious. I meant Cherie." He smirks.

"Then you haven't seen Margaret?"

He shakes his head.

"Tell you what. I'm going to walk out with you. Somebody broke into my apartment this morning and stole my gun. And unless you took it, I think maybe she did. Or some other guys who shouldn't ever get their hands on a firearm, especially mine."

"It wasn't me," Joseph says. "But when we walk outside, don't stand too close to me. It's you she hates."

He sounds like he's only half-joking. After he locks up, we walk quickly out the entrance and hear tires screeching again, from behind another building in the office park.

"Damn kid," Joseph says. "Maybe you lost the gun."

"Not a chance. Whose car is that?"

There's a red pickup parked a few rows ahead of my car. It looks empty.

"This is where I get off," Joseph says, stopping at the Miata. "Good luck."

"Thanks. You're a pal."

He's driving off in the little sportscar before I've taken ten steps. Passing the pickup, I walk close enough to peer into the darkened windows. When I'm right there, within a few feet, a figure pops up in the front seat and looks at me. Margaret stares out through the glass.

I run to the back of the lot, trying to work my keys out of my pocket. The pickup's engine starts. I fumble at the lock, get the door open, and slam it closed, just as her headlights are bearing down. The truck screeches to a stop alongside me; its window opens, and her hand reaches out, pointing a pistol at my head. I duck, hit the ignition, drop into first, and speed away. Only then do I hear a bang. Maybe she's just trying to scare me. More likely, she's just learned how hard it is to squeeze the trigger on a double-action revolver. I turn out of the parking lot, getting up to fourth gear on the access road, make a fast turn onto the crossroad, run a red light, and turn down an entrance ramp to I-90. I don't see her following, but she must be back there somewhere. I'm going eighty-five miles an hour, zigzagging across lanes to pass cars, half hoping to attract a cop.

When bright lights fill my rearview, I know she's caught up. We're heading east over the hill toward the exits for I-787, going too fast to make the turn, and she pulls up on the left and begins to force my subcompact off the highway. Then there's a crunch, and the pickup lurches forward. I hit the brakes, slowing down enough to slide into the turning lane south. She's stuck going the other way, continuing east over the Hudson River. A car behind me hits its brakes hard, screeching, and follows me onto I-787 toward downtown Albany and its collection of office towers. Looking in my rearview, I see the dome light come on in the other car. It's Rodney. He's waving and laughing. Only it's Cherie who's driving. She looks fierce and pleased, like a Valkyrie, but bringing the living and not the dead home from the battlefield.

28

I had continued to box in the local gym after I moved to Saratoga, but I got hit in the head too many times. Everybody does, finally. One night, when I couldn't remember how I got from the sparring ring back to my apartment, I quit for fear of brain damage. It's important to know when to walk away. But some things you remember, like how to get your weight behind a big right hand, how to duck and roll and come up leaning the other way, ready to throw the counter, and what it feels like to get hit in the face.

My ex-wife Caroline's gallery lies behind a dingy narrow storefront in Manhattan. It's south of Houston Street, but farther east, not in SoHo, not a fashionable address, unless you're betting on future gentrification. It's barely wide enough to walk into. Inside are framed black-and-white photographs, an overstuffed chair, a narrow writing table with a computer, and a credit-card machine. Her friend Paul is sprawled in the chair, talking loudly on the phone about mutual funds. He looks up briefly but keeps talking. Almost a half-hour later, he ends the call and starts dialing another one.

"Are you still here?" he says. "What do you want? Caroline's not here."

"Where is she?"

"I don't know. So if you don't mind, I'm busy."

It's his attitude that starts things rolling. "Since you're here, I'd like an apology."

"What?"

"You slept with my wife, and you never apologized."

"I've got news for you, slick. She's not your wife."

"She was. And you were sleeping with her then. I'd like an apology."

Back then, he was an art student, a graduate assistant studying restoration in Williamstown and doing some teaching. But Paul came from money and planned to make a killing in the art market. Caroline said he had held a martial-arts black belt since he was a kid, one that he maintained, and I should watch out for him, this tall, rangy, adulterous patrician.

"What's that, some kind of joke? I'm real sorry I had Caroline while she was your wife. I should have waited till she threw you out. There. That's your apology. Now get out of my gallery before I call the cops."

"Some gallery."

"What would you know?"

It's a gray afternoon. The street is nearly empty, rather seedy, mostly commercial. No one asks why I'm loitering there. I'm brooding. I hadn't caught Caroline in her affair until after she had thrown me out. From what Paul said, though, they had been at it for some time before. It's almost 6:30 when he locks up.

"What do you want now?" he says.

"Penance. Or at least remorse."

I'm blocking the sidewalk. He pushes me into the building to get by, and I push him into a parked car.

"Jesus," he says, and throws a long left jab that catches me high on the forehead. "I'm going to kick your ass."

He throws a flurry of karate punches, and I duck right, roll left, and hit him with a straight left counter to the face. The big right hand comes up behind it, catches him flush on the face, and he slams against the car and sinks to the pavement in slow motion. I almost feel bad for him. I reach down to help him up, but he flails his arms, afraid he's going to get hit again.

"Do the penance," I tell him. "I'm tired. And we've all got a lot to be sorry for."

Walking to the car, parked two blocks away, I break out in laughter. Giddy, deep, exuberant laughter. I feel free, finally, of demons I had been unable to confront.

29

Within a half-hour, I'm out of the city. Before the traffic thins out on the Palisades Parkway, I take Route 9W north, along the west side of the Hudson, in the wavering dark, then cross the river again near West Point and wander down old Route 9 before getting on the Taconic Parkway. There the traffic north drops away altogether. The farmstands advertise fresh greenhouse produce and early-season cut flowers—tulips, daffodils, crocuses. Spring comes early to the lower Hudson Valley. It's green in the headlights, and the air is cool and sweet in the softly rolling hills.

At Albany, I keep driving north, into the mountains again, thinking they're not really too far out of the way, not if you're taking the slow road. I've got time, if nothing else. It may be that Margaret Kelly is a stone killer. But speaking as one who had been dead inside for years, who doesn't want that anymore, I don't feel like I'm risking too much by trying to find her again.

It's pitch black on her road. The mailbox is gone, so I miss the house and have to backtrack. I walk up the driveway. Spring has appeared here, too, with less certainty. There's a warm night breeze. I hear a barred owl hoot in the woods. There's no Land Rover, no lights on in the A-frame, and no one answers my knock. The hot tub out back is drained and covered. I enter the garage and shine my flashlight. The old Volvo is gone and the trash bin is empty, but the tools are still hanging on the walls—William Kind's tools. My blood is smeared on the floor. She's gone. It feels like she's not ever coming back.

I talked to the police after the shooting, but there wasn't much to go on—no bullet, no witnesses, no Margaret. And the detective seemed to lose interest as soon as he heard we were lovers. He tried a few times to call her, but she never answered, and then the phone was disconnected. He did want to know how she got a handgun, and I didn't tell him. But the episode put her on the record as a likely suspect should I turn up dead. I sent her a letter saying so. There's no point in keeping that kind of information to yourself. I hope they're forwarding the mail.

Rodney offered to make something up to help the case along, but I declined. And we couldn't talk about the third time in a month that his vehicle had back-ended somebody. He and Cherie were in a side lot when Joseph and I left the Apex office that night. He had been giving her a lesson in acceleration. When they saw my car speed away, pursued by the pickup, they decided to follow.

Joseph, of course, continued to doubt my interpretation of events. He refused to try to get Apex's money back, suggesting that the bang I heard was the product of a vivid imagination or just a vehicle backfiring. He said Margaret may have wanted to talk and was surprised when I took off. And why the pickup? She probably rented it to move some stuff.

It's after midnight when I get back to the apartment. There's no message from Margaret, and none from Caroline, which is disappointing. On my forehead, where her boyfriend hit me, there's a lump, and behind it a headache. Probably I should have punished him a little more. I lock the door with a new deadbolt, one that can be keyed from the outside.

In the mail is a final paycheck from the company, enough to pay the bills for a month. There's also a typewritten note from Jack Casey, saying he's sorry I've left Apex. He's getting the malpractice settlement he wanted in the case of William Kind, deceased. Nice work, he says. And if I come across any similar cases in the future, think of him. He's not offering to share any money, however.

But most interesting is the letter, postmarked Boca Raton, Florida, from Dr. Elias, written in tight script—the T's crossed high, but only average-size loops under the line.

I reviewed my files for William Kind and remembered something after your telephone call. That red-haired girl came to my office one winter back. She was with William Kind, who had contusions and a hairline fracture of two facial bones. He said he'd fallen down stairs. The injuries were consistent with what I've seen too often. I asked him if he'd been in a fight. He said no. He said he fell down unfinished steps. It was a possibility. I made a note that I thought her face may have been bruised as well. I scheduled him to come back for a follow-up visit, just so I could check up, but he didn't do that. And I lost track of it. In the hospital, I never spoke to him about it, and I never spoke to her at all. I believe she avoided me there. And I didn't connect the cases then. I don't know. I prefer not to malign the dead. They can't speak for themselves. But I'm having my receptionist send you his medical report. Perhaps it's germane. I've reconsidered his case. I remain surprised that he died. Perhaps I missed something. But some things you can't know.

Elias is suggesting that Margaret had some motivation to kill him. Perhaps William Kind had a foretaste of what he got later, a forced and untimely end. But the doctor's leaving it up to me to decide.

William Kind was a big man, but he may have been getting soft in his old age. I'd seen Margaret frightened and betrayed, and she didn't take it well. I frightened her myself and had scars on my back as a result. She made sure it cost me my job. Maybe William Kind scared her, too. Threatened her, maybe even slapped her. She wouldn't have taken that well, and she would have struck back even harder. It sounds like that's what she did. He had no intention of getting married after that. Jennifer Kind had been pretty clear on that point. Maybe Margaret suddenly decided she needed a more secure future.

And yet she was sad about his death. I've seen a fair amount of sorrow, and you can tell. You can feel it. What you can't tell is exactly who or what somebody's grieving for. Sometimes it's for themselves—the old version that's suddenly lost. I was way too good at that kind of crap myself. I file the letter in the new drawer for expired but interesting cases; perhaps I'll send Elias a note telling him that Joseph has closed the case already. I think also about the hot tub and Margaret. If I had closed the case myself, she might still be around. The threat of her is intoxicating.

There's a message on the answering machine from Joseph, who says he has a half-dozen cases for me as a contractor and to call him immediately, or sooner. But not at home. And there's one from Cherie, who says that if I'm going independent, she might be willing to consider helping to open the office. She could do the filing and collect the bills, at least for a while. Call her for a drink, she says, and maybe we can talk about it.

MICHAEL VIRTANEN is a graduate of Colgate University and the University at Albany, where he earned a master's degree in English. He is a veteran journalist whose articles on the Adirondacks and other topics have appeared in newspapers across the country as well as in the magazines *Adirondack Life* and *Adirondack Explorer*. On one assignment, he suffered frostbite on his toes while skiing through the High Peaks Wilderness, but he still relishes the Old North Woods. He enjoys hiking, paddling, and rock climbing. Michael lives with his wife, Saundra, and their ever-watchful dog, Daisy, in upstate New York.